"Brodsky's writing has claws.... They sink in with the first word and don't let go until you are finished with the book"

Darynda Jones, *New York Times* best-selling
author of *First Grave on the Right*

"A richly imaginative, multi-layered tale that stimulates the heart and the mind in equal measure"

Ian Caldwell, *New York Times* best-selling
author of *The Fifth Gospel*

WINTER OF THE GODS

"Stellar...intelligent, versatile, and esoteric...a satisfying adventure that remains true to the spirit of the original myths while granting them several millennia of weight, consequence, and even regret"

Publishers Weekly (starred review)

"Readers who enjoy detective fiction, ancient Greco-Roman myth, and a bit of romance will enjoy this series"   *Booklist*

"Cleverly examines mythology and religion while still giving readers a thrill-packed adventure"   *Bookish*

OLYMPUS BOUND

By Jordanna Max Brodsky

The Wolf in the Whale

Olympus Bound

The Immortals
Winter of the Gods
Olympus Bound

The

WOLF

in the

WHALE

JORDANNA MAX BRODSKY

www.orbitbooks.net

ORBIT

First published in Great Britain in 2019 by Orbit

13 5 7 9 10 8 6 4 2

Copyright © 2019 by Jordanna Max Brodsky
Map by Crystal Ben

The moral right of the author has been asserted.

A CIP catalogue record for this book
is available from the British Library.

ISBN 978-0-356-51260-0

Printed and bound in Great Britain by
Clays Ltd, Elcograf S.p.A.

Papers used by Orbit are from well-managed forests
and other responsible sources.

MIX
Paper from
responsible sources
FSC
www.fsc.org   FSC® C104740

Orbit
An imprint of
Little, Brown Book Group
Carmelite House
50 Victoria Embankment
London EC4Y 0DZ

An Hachette UK Company
www.hachette.co.uk

www.orbitbooks.net

For my parents, who took me into the wild

HISTORICAL NOTE

ᛉ

A thousand years ago, Norse explorers led by the children of Erik the Red left Greenland and landed on the shores of North America, in a place they called Vinland. *The Saga of the Greenlanders* and *The Saga of Erik the Red*, written two centuries later, tell us their story, detailing internal strife and hostile encounters with native people in a land rich with grapes, grain, and timber. The ruins of their settlement, in what is now Newfoundland, can still be seen.

Around the same time, Inuit hunters began their own far more successful explorations, migrating eastward from Alaska across the Arctic Sea to what is now Baffin Island in eastern Canada. While the Norse eventually abandoned their attempts at settlement, the Inuit established a society that has thrived there ever since.

In *The Saga of Erik the Red*, the Norse kidnap two boys from a family they encounter north of Vinland. The story describes the natives as a family dressed in white, living in a hole in the ground. The father, it notes, has a beard. This brief description is the only surviving written record of a possible meeting between Inuit and Norse in the New World. The rest is up to our imaginations.

BOOK ONE

SUMMONING

On the darkest day of winter, when the weakened Sun cannot even pull herself above the horizon, a man stands vigil upon the snow-covered roof of his sod home. He is the angakkuq, the shaman, and his eyes must never leave the sky as he watches for the two bright stars that herald the Sun's return. But on this night, Ataata's gaze strays. He cannot stop looking toward the square patch of light beyond the camp. Sometimes the light flickers as the women inside the iglu pass before the ice window. Ataata has never stepped inside a birthing hut, for doing so would break the strictest taboo, but neither has he ever worried before. His own wife, whose spirit now shines among the other stars above him, possessed such strength in her youth that Ataata never feared for her, but his son's widow is not the same.

Ataata looks again at the sky, nervously fingering the bear claw at his throat. A faint orange glow, like light seen through a caribou hide scraped clean, brushes the horizon—the closest the day will come to dawn. The heralding stars now hover in the eastern sky. The angakkuq watches still, waiting to see if the stars will catch the false dawn before they fade away in its light. Even once the stars rise directly above the glow, the Sun herself will not return for many more days.

Tonight, her brother, the Moon, rules the sky in her stead, looking down with a cold, unfeeling eye on the small birthing iglu and the young woman struggling inside. Once, the angakkuq could have helped his son's widow, for this is an age of magic and mystery—a powerful shaman should walk as easily through the spirit world as through the world of flesh. He should speak to the Ice Bear, seek the stars' protection, change the very course of the wind. Or ask the Moon to see a baby safely through its passage from one world to the next. Yet Ataata stands helpless on his roof. He can only watch the sky, not command it. The spirits who once guided his steps have now turned against him—against all Inuit.

Three moons earlier, on a desperate hunt to seek some game, any game, to save their families from starvation, all four of the camp's young hunters drowned. Among them Omat, Ataata's only son. The old man, as renowned for his hunting skills as for his mystical powers, watched the two cracks in the ice as they raced across the floe like summer lightning, widening so fast that the young men, as fleet as they were, could not reach the landfast ice. Ataata had never seen the ice behave like that, as if a great spirit had stepped upon the surface of a frozen pool, splitting it apart beneath his boot sole.

Ataata shouted an alarm, and Omat started running, but the firm sea ice had ruptured into a narrow, floating pan, as unsteady as an iceberg. With his pounding strides, the entire floe began to rock. The other young hunters sprinted at his heels. Ataata tried to warn them that their weight would tip the ice, but they could not hear him in their panic. The floe tilted into the water, Omat and the others scrabbling, screaming as they slid one by one into the sea. Lying on his stomach, arm outstretched, fingers grasping at air, Ataata called for his son. But the current was too fast and the water too cold. Soon the camp had lost an entire generation of hunters.

Ataata looks once more at the distant iglu. He knows that his daughter will help in the birth, but even her skills may not be enough to save his son's widow.

Inside the birthing iglu, Puja sits behind Nona, her arms clasped around the younger woman's waist, pressing on the distended dome of her womb. All through the long darkness, Nona squats on her heels, thighs spread, laboring to bring Omat's child into the world. She never gives in to the urge to lie down, to scream, to cry, for she knows any sign of weakness from her will weaken her child. Puja wipes the sweat from Nona's brow. The woman's legs shake from exhaustion.

"You must rest," Puja says.

Nona grunts a pained refusal. She was strong once, a smiling girl whose songs could bring the camp to tears of mirth or sadness, but since Omat's death, she never laughs. She has grown thinner and thinner, though Puja and Ataata give her every spare morsel of meat. Her bulging stomach protrudes grotesquely from her bony frame.

"Come, Nona, the babe won't survive if you don't lean on me. Just for a moment." Puja tries to ease her brother's wife back against her own chest.

"No!" Nona barks. "This child will carry Omat's spirit, and he must be strong like his father. Strong enough to take his place."

"Even if he's born with Omat's soul, he will never take Omat's place. You know that."

"Your father says the spirits of the dead are reborn into the living. I believe him. I must."

The older woman brushes Nona's damp hair out of her eyes. "Yes, of course. But we shouldn't think only of the past. There's the future. There's your child. Don't give up hope for yourself."

"That's why I must give this child everything I have," Nona gasps, pulling Puja's hand back to her stomach as another pain seizes her womb. "I'll never have another child—there are no other husbands, no other men."

Puja cannot argue. Here at the edge of the world, there are no other camps, no other families beyond their own near relatives. She and Nona both lost their husbands on the ice—they will never find others.

"I would've given my life to see Omat live." Nona forces out the words through a groan of pain. "And if I have to, I'll give my life now to see him live again." Her voice tapers to a low wheeze as finally, with both women pushing together, the baby's head appears. Puja releases her grip on Nona's stomach and moves between her legs.

At the moment of the child's birth, the young mother looks up through the ice window in the roof and smiles through her pain, for she can see the *heralding stars in the dawn sky and knows the Sun will soon return to warm her child.*

The floor of the snow house glistens red with blood, but Puja catches the baby in the clean fur of a white wolf before it falls to the earth. She cries out in relief, yet her shout of joy soon slips into choking grief: Nona has finally surrendered to the pain. She lies still and gray, resting now forever.

The child in Puja's arms is silent.

She rocks the baby, heedless of the blood. "Go ahead, little one. You may cry, even if your mother could not," she urges, her voice catching.

But the baby makes no sound beyond the faintest rasp of breath.

As the stars fade in the ever-lightening sky, Puja cuts the umbilical cord, chafes the child's limbs, rubs its narrow back, and swipes the fluid from its mouth. Again and again, she urges it to live. Instead, its arms and legs lie still; its lungs barely swell.

Struggling to her feet, Puja pulls her parka over her head but does not put her arms through the sleeves. She clutches the baby to her naked breast instead to shelter it from the cold as she hurries outside to find her father.

Atop the roof of his qarmaq, his sod home, Ataata still stands. He turns, smiling, when his daughter approaches, but his expression quickly falters. "The heralding stars have caught the dawn. The Sun will return—yet you bring bad tidings."

"Nona's gone." Puja's usually stoic face twists. "And the child..."

She lifts the hem of her parka so her father might see the bloody infant. The old man slides off the qarmaq's roof. He holds the child up to his face. It doesn't open its eyes. He places his ear to its tiny, gaping mouth. He sighs, although the babe does not.

"It has so little strength that it cannot breathe in its spirit." He speaks the words calmly, though misery burns his throat. He passes back the child. "It's like one of the undead. Soulless."

And so, with the hope of the entire camp dying in her arms, Puja carries the baby beyond the circle of domed huts. She scrapes a cradle in the snow and places the bloodied child in the embrace of the ice. Puja has not wept since her childhood, when her own mother died. She did not weep when her brother and her husband and the other young men drowned in the icy sea. But now, staring at the thin blue lids that hide the child's eyes, Puja feels tears course down her cheeks. The drops fall upon the child's face like rain, freezing an instant later into shards of brittle ice.

The Sun's rays appear—a single flare of pink at the horizon—before sinking away like a doused lamp. The Sun herself stays hidden. Puja speaks to the Moon instead. "Bring back this child, and I'll feed it from my breast," she vows. Her own son is near weaned. She has milk enough for Nona's.

She waits. She watches. Now the sky is the deep purple of a ripe bearberry. The Moon soars overhead in an endless circle, ice-bright and full, sweeping Puja's moonshadow across the snow. When the finger of darkness falls upon the child's motionless body, she finally stands and turns back to the camp. She has surrendered the baby to Sila, the unfeeling Air—only It will decide the child's fate.

When she emerges at the next false dawn to gather snow to melt for water, Puja expects the baby to be either frozen or gone—carried off by a fox or bear. Instead, Nona and Omat's child still breathes—and it is not alone.

A great white wolf crouches in the snow, its long muzzle searching the tiny body. Despite Puja's resolve to surrender the child, she cannot bear to watch it torn apart. She runs to scare off the beast, but it lies down instead, chin resting on its paws. Puja stops a few paces from the unlikely pair. The wolf, she sees now, has not harmed the baby, merely licked the blood from its skin, cleaning and warming the child with its hot breath.

Cautiously she kneels, her knees sinking into the snow, head bowed. She knows now that her brother, Omat, has sent the Wolf Spirit to save his child. The Wolf has breathed a piece of its soul—and Omat's—into the babe.

The animal rises and stares at Puja for a moment, challenging her with eyes like yellow stars. Then it stalks away, tail low, ears swiveling. Its walk turns to a lope, then a gallop, all four paws suspended above the ground with each leaping stride; then the Wolf disappears, white fur invisible against white snow.

Puja gathers up the child, its body warm despite the frigid morning. Its eyes are open, a luminous brown like her own. Like her brother's. She slips her arms free of her sleeves, tucks the babe beneath her parka, and guides its mouth to her breast. It sucks hungrily.

When two moons have passed and the Sun has returned her warmth to the land, Puja and Ataata stand once more upon the qarmaq's sod roof. The tears Puja once shed still lie upon the child's cheeks, turned from icy drops to tiny brown birthmarks, reminders of the sadness with which it entered the world. And yet the baby smiles as once its mother did and shows its father's strength in the grasp of its tiny fist.

Cradling the fur-wrapped baby against his chest, the old man appeals to the spirits for guidance. For the first time since the icy sea swallowed the camp's young hunters, the spirits answer his question, confirming what he and Puja already suspected: his son lives again in this child. It will take Omat's name and be taught to hunt and paddle as its father had.

"With the spirit of the Wolf in its heart," he proclaims, "this child will one day grow to be an angakkuq even more powerful than I."

His words are strong and full of hope. They must be. For Inuit alone at the edge of the world, hope is the only thing left.

Now you know the story of my birth. At least the story my family told me in my childhood. I know now that Ataata and Puja were not the only ones watching my mother labor beneath the winter sky—far from it. Other beings far more powerful than any angakkuq witnessed my birth: spirits of sky and sea, gods from the lands beyond our ken—all watched that night as the Wolf licked the blood from my cheeks. Even then, the great spirits of the world knew I was no ordinary Inuk.

They say that from the moment I took my first breath, I have lived between many worlds—between Sun and Moon, man and woman, Inuk and animal. So perhaps it's not surprising that I have seen worlds my family could never imagine.

I have seen the painted men in their bark houses, and I have slept beneath trees as tall as a whale is long.

I have spoken with the spirits and walked in their land.

I have seen men who could harness the wind, men with hair the color of flame and eyes the color of ice. And when their own great spirits set foot on my shore, striking thunder from the stars and calling monsters from the deep, I have battled with their gods of war—and wept with their gods of love.

CHAPTER ONE

𖤓

Tap. Tap. Tap.

I woke to the sound of Puja pushing the lamp wick into place with her small blackened poker. Bone striking stone, urging the light to rise in small mountain peaks of flame along the lamp's crescent edge, then tamping down the burnt moss so it wouldn't smoke.

A sound I'd heard every morning of the eight winters and eight summers of my life. Usually the tapping brought me comfort. The woman who had nursed me at her breast would never let me waken to a cold tent or a dark iglu. Yet on this morning, I pulled the caribou sleeping robes over my face and hid from the light, afraid of what the new day might hold.

"You don't need to be scared," she assured me. "Ataata will come back. Maybe even today."

But I couldn't help it. I'd been scared for a long time. Hunger does that to a child.

"Go on," she urged, tugging the robe off my face. "Kiasik is already outside. Go play with him."

I pulled on my trousers and summer parka, slung my small bag of

toys and tools over my shoulder, and crawled from the tent, looking for my older brother. He was out of sight, but the new puppies
whimpering in their pen would make good playmates, too. Puja
had warned me many times to stay away from the older dogs—a
hungry pack could rip a child apart. But the puppies merely whined
and licked my fingers, trying to sate their hunger with the salt from
my skin. I picked up the white one with the black face—Black
Mask, Ataata called her. Her ribs felt like the driftwood spars of a
tiny kayak frame.

"If I put you on the ground," I whispered against her petal-soft
ear, "would you float away on the tundra like a boat on the sea?"
I imagined myself as a great hunter, sitting atop the dog and paddling with a tiny oar. "We would have such adventures together.
I would hunt whales from your back, and you would snatch fish
with your teeth, and we would never go hungry."

"A nice dream, Little Brother." Kiasik strode through the camp
to peer over my shoulder. "But just a dream. That dog will be mitten fur by tomorrow."

I frowned. "Don't say that. She'll hear you. Ataata warned us—
animals can understand." Black Mask swiveled her ears toward me.

Hunger made Kiasik's usually bright eyes as dull as dark slate
in a dry riverbed. "If the dog is so smart, then it knows the truth
already." He was only a little older than I, but always eager to prove
himself many winters my senior in wisdom. "There's no food for
it. Didn't you notice? Its mother stopped nursing it days ago."

The dog's thin frame suddenly seemed too fragile—not like a skin
boat I might paddle, but like an eggshell I might crush. Many days
had passed since Egg Gathering Moon, yet the humiliating memory
of yellow ooze dripping down my parka still burned fresh; I'd cried
over my failure. Kiasik had pointed and laughed, but when my slow
tears turned to rough sobs, he'd helped me wash the yolk from my
clothing. I'd whimpered, sure it would never come clean.

"Baby birds like to drink tears," he warned, urgently scraping the caribou fur. "So if we don't get all the egg off, you'll wake one morning with chicks hatching from your armpits."

I gasped in dismay.

"Ia'a!" he cried, noticing a particularly thick glob at my parka's hem. "Not just your armpits, but your navel, too." He took me by the shoulders and said sternly, "You must be careful that when they start to flap their wings, they don't lift you off the ground and carry you away forever. That won't do—you and I have to be great hunters together, remember?"

For another breath, I believed him. Then I caught the flaring of his nostrils, the twitch of his lips, and knew he teased me.

Standing before the dog pen, I remembered the lesson beneath his joke: a great hunter does not cry. Even if the thought of killing such a perfect puppy made him want to weep. Very carefully I replaced the dog in the pile with her siblings. Little Black Mask buried herself in the warm press of her family, just as I snuggled between Puja and Ataata on cold winter nights. Even now, in the warmth of late summer, the wind that blew from the distant sea carried the promise of ice.

"Come, Little Brother," Kiasik said more gently. "If the elders kill her, she'll just come back as another puppy, born in a better time. By then, maybe you'll be a hunter grown, and she can pull your sled."

I knew he was right, but that didn't make it any easier. From the small pouch looped around my shoulder, I withdrew a tiny scrap of dried fish.

"Where did you get that?" he demanded, suddenly stern.

"I saved it from yesterday, when Puja gave us the last of the fish cache." I popped it into my mouth and chewed until the hard flesh melted into a gummy mass. It took all my will not to swallow it down and soothe the ache in my empty stomach. Instead, I spit it back into my palm.

"What are you—"

I slipped the soft morsel of fish between Black Mask's lips. The dog gulped it down, licked her jaws, and panted up at me in obvious anticipation.

"That's all I have, little one," I apologized.

"Did you forget the elders' teachings?" Kiasik huffed. "*An Inuk survives.* He doesn't starve himself to feed a puppy!"

The sight of a hunter approaching the camp spared me any more lectures.

"Ataata!" I called, instantly recognizing the old man even at a distance by the white stripes of bear fur decorating his parka like walrus tusks. Puja had been right. He had returned.

We ran to him, still holding out some hope that he carried meat, but his slow step told of his failure. A hunter burdened with game, no matter how heavy, would come swiftly into camp to share his bounty.

As we walked back toward our tent, Ataata, the only father I had ever known, placed a hand on my cropped hair. Although my head barely reached his chest, he spoke to me with great gravity. "Have you been practicing with your bow, Little Son?"

I smiled my assent. Over the long, dark winter, Ataata had carved a child-size bow and three matching arrows from a piece of caribou antler. Kiasik had received his own set the winter before. Now it was all Puja could do to stop us from shooting at her pot or lamp or drying hides. "Good." He patted my head. "Soon you'll see a great caribou hunt. If you watch closely, you'll learn how to use your bow."

"So you found the herd?" begged Kiasik breathlessly. We had asked the same question of each empty-handed hunting party that returned, but so far only lemmings and ptarmigan tempered our hunger. We longed for the rich brown meat of a caribou. We wouldn't survive much longer without it.

"I found them." Despite his words, Ataata did not smile.

Kiasik's face brightened. "Was the meat so heavy you had to leave it behind? Can we go and help you carry it?"

By now the women and other children had emerged from their tents to listen. Ataata addressed them all. "I found the herd, or most of it—but they were all dead. The foxes and the ravens got there first. I saw nothing but bones."

Old Ujaguk's voice rose in a mourning cry. The others in the crowd followed suit. I almost let out my own moan of dismay, but I noticed Kiasik clench his jaw against the impulse. I followed his lead. Let the women grieve. We hunters knew better.

"Enough!" Puja said sternly. "Come, Ataata, let me take off your boots." She believed firmly in the proper order of things: First Ataata must be taken care of, his damp boots hung on the drying rack so his feet wouldn't sicken. Then he could tell us his news.

As our angakkuq and finest hunter, Ataata had the largest tent in our summer camp. Even with Puja, Ataata, Kiasik, and me seated on the sleeping furs, the others could join us inside. Not until Puja had removed Ataata's boots and parka and made him comfortable on the pile of caribou robes did we finally hear his story.

"Do you remember how this winter was so mild?" he began. "Omat and Kiasik, you played with your kicking ball outside even in the Moon of Great Darkness, when usually we'd be laughing over the cup and pin game inside our qarmaq, waiting for the wind to die down."

In a childhood defined by play, I did indeed remember the recent winter. After the Sun had risen for the last time, Kiasik told me scary stories of how long and boring the dark winter would be, with us trapped in our sod-and-whalebone home under Puja's watchful eye. And yet, despite the darkness, the weather had stayed relatively mild, and by the time the Sun claimed half of every day, Kiasik and I could play outside wearing only our thin inner parkas.

"The snow began to melt early," Ataata continued. "We moved from our qarmait to tents long before the seal pups appeared on the ice. But then, do you remember the cold snap?"

We murmured our agreement. One morning, just as we were sure winter had finally ended, the cold had come raging back, freezing the ground into a solid sheet of ice. Puja had grumbled as she slipped on her way to the meat caches, and no one liked digging through the ice on the drinking pond, but for the most part, I'd enjoyed sliding on the slick ground like a wobbly seal pup. Puja chided us for ruining the soles of our boots by skating on the ice—that didn't stop Kiasik and me from racing our older cousins across the frozen ground, slipping and tumbling as we went. The ice sheet remained for nearly a moon, finally melting into muddy slush as spring arrived.

"When the days warmed, the caribou thought winter over. They moved north to eat the lichen and the moss," Ataata explained, "but when the cold returned, even their sharp hooves couldn't break through so much ice. They starved. Those few that survived couldn't fight off the wolves. I found the whole herd in a valley three days' journey inland, all their bones picked clean."

"But Ataata..." It was not my place to speak before the adults did, but my father had always indulged me. "You just said that I'd see a great caribou hunt. How?"

He smiled down at me. "When a caribou dies, its spirit is reborn somewhere else. No caribou disappears forever. They are somewhere—we just need to find them. I will speak to the Ice Bear Spirit. He will help us."

As a creature of both land and sea, the ice bear is the most powerful animal in our world, and an angakkuq with such a guide is mighty indeed.

The elders said that as a child not much older than I was, Ataata had fallen through the ice on a winter sealing journey. Lungs filling with water and limbs freezing solid, he saw a bear swimming toward him, its broad paws stretched like paddles. Rather than attack, the bear pushed Ataata toward the surface with its black nose, right into his parents' outstretched arms. He should have died—or at least lost his fingers to frostbite—but the Ice Bear Spirit protected the boy, and he survived his ordeal unscathed. Later, as a young angakkuq on his spirit journey, Ataata found a single black bear claw on the ice near the spot where he'd fallen so long before. He placed it around his neck on a sinew cord. Ever since, the Ice Bear with the missing claw had appeared to Ataata when called upon.

I found it strange to imagine my father as a young boy like me, when now he seemed as ancient as the stones beneath my boots. Gray streaked his hair like the silver rivers that braided their way across the dark tundra. His thin mustache and the wisp of beard beneath his lips were pure white, and his heavy-lidded eyes were tinged red from long winters of blinding snow and short summers of unending sun. Yet despite his aged body, Ataata still held power beyond my understanding.

The Sun, which had refused to surrender her place in the sky for most of the summer, now consented to set again, though I knew she hid just out of sight, impatient to return. Clouds brushed the sky with pastel blues and pinks, cupping us in the hollow of an iridescent mussel shell. As we gathered amid the tents to witness the summoning of the Ice Bear, the sky finally darkened to something resembling night. One by one, the stars flickered into view. The spirits had oil for their lamps in the sky, but this far from the ocean we hoarded what little seal fat we had left; we built a low fire of dwarf willow twigs and dry moss instead. I was unused to the flickering light, the erratic crackle, so different from the silent, steady glow of a lamp. In the gloaming, the fire transformed my father's lined visage, usually so familiar, into a terrifying mask of shadow and flame.

He held his black bear claw between the knuckles of his left fist. He became a bear.

I huddled close to Puja, hiding my face in her parka. Never before had I witnessed a summoning; my heart fluttered like a bird's. I much preferred that Ataata's bear claw stay hidden beneath his parka, not pointed so menacingly at me.

Puja stroked my head until I lifted my eyes. "Don't look away. He journeys as a bear, but he'll come back to us a man."

Her thin mouth tugged upward at the corners, not quite a smile. I pressed closer to her, seeking the comfort of her thickly muscled body beneath the thin hide of her summer parka. But despite the familiarity of her shape, the dancing willow fire made even Puja look strange. Tonight, the tattoos that decorated every woman's face and hands were more threatening than beautiful. The thin black lines running from mouth to chin and across her forehead made her into a wrinkled old woman. Her black hair, usually bound in two tight braids, hung loose to her shoulders, flying in soft hanks in the light breeze.

Kiasik peered at me from where he sat on Puja's other side. "If you're too scared," he warned, with that half smile that meant he was only half teasing, "you can always hide in our mother's hood."

I pushed myself away from Puja's embrace and glared at him. "I'm not scared!" I squared my shoulders, wishing I were as tall as he was.

"*Hnnnn.* Then why were you holding on to her like a little child?"

Puja calmly warned us both to be quiet or she'd send us back to the tent. As much as I feared watching the summoning, I dreaded missing it far more.

The rest of the gathered band watched us rather more indulgently, waiting patiently for us to settle down so Ataata might continue. Ipaq, Ataata's older brother, smiled at me as he readied the round hand drum. Although he handled the instrument with ease, its hoop stretched nearly as wide as his own impressive stomach. He began to sway like a coursing fish, weight shifting from left foot to right as he spun the taut caribou-skin disk by its long handle, hitting one side of the rim and then the other with his mallet. Each sharp clack of antler against antler sent a low, resonant boom through the air, the thrumming barely fading away before another took its place. The drum hummed like an insect.

The other adults nodded their heads to the rhythm. Dour Ququk, the camp's other hunter, looked even more serious than usual, his face as lined and solemn as a carven mask. Ujaguk, his wife, circled her thumbs above clasped hands, as if they were the only part of her she could allow to dance. Their grown daughter, Saartok, struck her thighs lightly, always an awkward beat behind the drumming. Ipaq's own family moved with more ease. His adopted son, my round-cheeked cousin Tapsi, bounced up and down, acting far younger than would be expected of a boy with the first black wisps of hair sprouting above his rosy lips. Ipaq's adopted daughter, Millik, and his wife, Niquvana, moved their torsos in unison, graceful as a pair of long-necked cranes.

I couldn't lose myself in the music. Not with Ataata undertaking a journey more dangerous than any hunt.

My father stalked around the circle, his bear claw still raised. Puja started the singing to help him on his way. Everyone took up the refrain, and I found some comfort in the simple chant: *"Aiiya yaya, aiiya yaya ya ya!"* Sounds of joy and lamentation, supplication and command all at once.

On all fours, my father continued hunting his imaginary prey. Like the bear's, his hind legs were longer than those in front. One leg swung forward in a shallow arc. Then another, just like the stride of the lumbering animal. Faster and faster Ataata circled the fire. His head swayed from side to side as he looked for prey. Our song intensified. Sweat ran down Ipaq's cheeks, and his gray hair lifted as the swinging drum fanned the air before him.

Finally Ataata stopped. He stood as still as a stone, his front feet together, his back tensed, staring at prey only he could see, like a bear about to attack. Suddenly the light left his eyes, his face fell, and he collapsed to the ground, trembling. His eyes rolled back in his head, and he began to shout in the secret angakkuq tongue that none of us could understand.

I leapt to my feet with a cry, but Puja held me back, warning me with a glare to be silent. Ipaq lowered his drum, and he and Ququk stole toward Ataata with lengths of walrus-hide rope in their hands. They bound my father's wrists together and then looped the rope around his ankles to fold him in half. He still shook and struggled in his trance, the ropes rubbing his wrists raw like the limbs of a fox caught in a snare.

Puja put her mouth to my ear, whispering, "They tie his body to one spot so his soul can find it when it returns from its journey." I began to protest, but she continued quickly, in tones so low I could barely hear: "We must not make a sound while Ataata is traveling, lest we pull him back too quickly, and a part of his soul is left behind in the spirit world."

I was convinced it might already be too late, that at any moment my beloved Ataata would stop shaking, open soulless eyes, and stare accusingly at me—the child who'd lost his spirit by crying out. Then I'd be banished from the camp forever, left to wander alone through the tundra with no one to feed me.

I squeezed my eyes shut and willed him to stay in the trance state as long as he had to. But the trance went on so long that soon I began to worry that he'd never find his way back to us. What if my father was gone forever? Transformed from the strong, unflappable hunter I knew into a raving, shaking man, possessed by the Ice Bear? But finally, when the willow fire had crumbled to embers and my bones ached from sitting still, he ceased his trembling.

Puja began to sing, and we all joined in, welcoming him back to this world.

As the other men hurried to untie him, Ataata sat up. I held my breath as his eyes fluttered open. Although they shone once more with his familiar spirit, his fist remained knotted around the bear claw. As he told of his journey, he pried his fingers open with his other hand. No one else seemed bothered by this paralysis, but I worried my father had grown too old for such a dangerous journey.

"The arch of sky and the mightiness of storms moved the spirit within me," he began, his voice hoarse. "I was carried away, trembling with joy. I flew out of this camp, high up, so you all looked like lemmings in the grass." Kiasik snorted a laugh—the thought of huge Uncle Ipaq as such a tiny creature was funny indeed—but one glance from Puja silenced him. "And among the stars, I met with the Ice Bear, who took my hand in his jaws and brought me back to the earth, far from here, up the river. We flew in moments, but it is far—a walk of nearly five days. There, in a deep valley, a herd of caribou awaits."

The adults and older children grinned and laughed, all tension drained. Ataata swept me into his arms and pressed his nose to my cheek. Despite our empty bellies, we would sleep well that night, confident that fresh meat lay in our future.

I didn't ask him why he'd let us go hungry for so long before summoning his helping spirit. We all knew that the spirits of the animals and ancestors were fickle and easily antagonized. Even as a child, I understood that an angakkuq risked their wrath if he sought them too often. There would come a time when I'd be forced to ignore that lesson. When, again and again, I would cry out for the great spirits above to save me. And again and again, they would ignore my pleas.

For now, I shed no tears Ataata couldn't dry, suffered no wound Puja couldn't heal, faced no monster Kiasik couldn't scare away. *They* were the great spirits of my life, and I believed they'd never abandon me.

CHAPTER TWO

We walked inland for days, our goods bundled upon our own backs and those of our dogs, our kayaks carried on the men's heads, until hunger once again slowed our steps. The puppies grew too weak to walk. All but Black Mask, whom I kept alive on mushrooms and insects and other foods even a starving Inuk disdains. Finally, just as Kiasik had foreseen, we started killing her siblings one by one, parceling out the tiny scraps of their flesh among the children and old women. My favorite puppy would be next, and I would not stand in Ataata's way when he brought his knife to her throat. For all I loved her, I loved my family more.

The Ice Bear kept his promise just in time to save me from such a choice. I must've seen the great herds before in my childhood, but this is the first one I remember. With their backs mottled white and brown from their summer molt, the caribou stretched across the valley like patches of dirty snow scattered to the horizon. More caribou than stars in the winter sky, more caribou than snowflakes in a twilit storm.

"We will survive." I whispered the words against Black Mask's hollow cheek before staking her leash beside our tents.

Our tiny band couldn't hunt the caribou by itself—Ataata said we must build stone men to help us. He led us away from the herd to a deep, fast-running stream. The children's job was to scour the bank for stones of the proper size: long, flat rocks for the shoulders, great square boulders for the legs and head. When we found a good stone, the women harnessed the dogs and dragged it to the men.

Ataata, Ipaq, and Ququk lifted the rocks into place, working carefully to keep their creations upright. Though hunger weakened us all—we'd eaten little but boiled sorrel greens and raw crowberries on our journey—the thought of fresh caribou meat kept us going.

Soon, three *inuksuit* rose around us. With only old men and one boy to hunt, these faceless giants of stone were all that stood between us and starvation.

When all was ready, Ataata gathered us together. "Tapsi, are you ready for your first hunt as a man?" he asked my cousin.

Even I could tell that the boy, usually as jovial as his adoptive father, was nervous.

Ipaq put a hand on his son's shoulder and handed him a spear. Although far shorter than a harpoon or lance, the weapon still towered over the boy. Tapsi gripped the shaft with his small fist and looked anxiously up at Ipaq, who tried valiantly to keep a smile on his round face. The boy was young to begin hunting large game—only last summer I'd noticed the first hairs sprouting at the base of his penis—and his head barely reached Ataata's shoulder. But if our family was to survive, we needed young hunters to assist the old, and Tapsi, as the eldest boy in the camp, was our best hope.

Beside me, Kiasik lifted his chin. I knew he longed to hold his own spear. I, on the other hand, held no such ambitions. Not yet, anyway. I was short for my age; I knew I'd get trampled by even the smallest caribou. Even as a child, I was more cautious than my brother.

When Ataata said that the smaller children must stay far away from the hunt, I thought Kiasik might cry from disappointment. I put a hand on his sleeve, but he shook it off and stalked toward the distant ridge. If Kiasik ever wept, I never saw it.

Tapsi's sister, Millik, a few winters older than I, ignored Kiasik's ill temper. Glad to be excused from the hunt, she wandered toward the ridge at her own pace, searching for berries among the low scrub. I knew only a little about the plants beneath my feet—gathering them was women's work. I took one look at Millik, her two long braids swinging close to the earth as she hunched over the ground, painstakingly putting each tiny berry in her sack, and made my choice. Slipping my child-size bow over one shoulder and looping my sling around the other, I scrambled up the ridge after Kiasik.

From our perch, the whole hunting ground spread beneath us. On one side of the hill, the stone inuksuit bordered the path to the river. Ququk, hampered by his aching joints, lowered himself slowly into his slim kayak. Ipaq squeezed his girth into the opening of his own boat. He had built it as a younger man, before his once-broad chest had settled as fat around his waist; we had no driftwood to build him a new one.

Ataata and Tapsi pushed the boats into the water. Fighting the strong current, the kayakers jammed their paddles between large rocks to steady themselves until the hunt began. Then Ataata and my young cousin returned to the gathered women and led the small band around the base of the ridge. The women wouldn't hunt, of course—they were strictly forbidden to even hold a man's weapon—but we'd never bring down the herd without their help.

I scuttled closer to Kiasik. He ignored me, concentrating instead on inspecting his arrows. They were far smaller than those used by a real hunter, intended for play or shooting lemmings.

"What are we going to do with these?" I pulled out one of my own arrows.

"I don't know what you're going to do," he replied. "But I'm going to kill a caribou."

I glanced back at the herd. The bulls, with their huge antlers dragging down their narrow heads, would prove difficult targets for even the strongest hunter. Even the calves had hooves as sharp as harpoon points; I'd seen the wounds they could inflict on a hungry wolf. Nonetheless, Kiasik was my elder. I would follow him anywhere. With an indrawn breath, I readied my own bow.

Ataata's band moved silently across the mossy ground, spreading out to surround a small portion of the herd. The females looked up at these new two-legged beasts and nudged their brown, spindly calves away from the strangers, but they seemed relatively unconcerned. They'd probably never seen an Inuk before—they didn't know to be afraid. The caribou, my father always said, are a proud race, overconfident in their ability to outrun the swiftest wolf. But wolves couldn't build stone men to help, nor could they fashion kayaks and spears.

With a silent signal from Ataata, Tapsi and the women began to run at the caribou, flapping their arms and shouting. The resting beasts leapt to their feet, and those already upright reared on their hind legs and plunged around the ridge, straight toward the waiting inuksuit and the kayakers.

Kiasik and I dashed to the opposite side of the ridge to watch the caribou approach the stream. The lead bulls tried to swerve away from the water, but the inuksuit stood in their way, towering creatures more threatening than any human hunter. Bugling their distress, the caribou veered back toward the water and the waiting kayakers. Ataata and Tapsi, weapons raised, ran to take their positions on large rocks at the shoreline. My father held a bow, my cousin a spear.

The caribou crashed into the stream, high-stepping with their sharp hooves until forced to swim, their escape made slow by the rushing water. Now Ququk and Ipaq pushed their kayaks into the current, maneuvering among the thrashing animals. I held my breath, worried that a hoof or antler would tear through the thin hide of the boats and the men would be pulled under by the water's strength. But, though their arms may have lacked the strength of younger men's, the two old hunters wielded their paddles as deftly as a whale uses its flukes. Ququk moved beside a young female; in one fluid motion, he secured his paddle and hefted his spear in its stead. With a swift jab through the throat, the caribou tumbled into the foaming water. Ququk's wife and daughter waded waist deep into the stream and dragged the carcass back to shore with a long driftwood pole. Soon, for every cluster of caribou that made it across, one animal floated downstream in the swiftly reddening water.

From his post on the rocks, Ataata shot arrow after arrow at the swimming animals, his body moving with the grace and speed of a hawk in flight. Puja and the other women hurried after the kills before they could drift out of reach.

Tapsi, however, stood as still as an *inuksuk* on his own small rock. Even from the distant ridge, I could see his spear shaking. Its haft was still clean, unblessed with blood. I turned to tell Kiasik.

He was gone.

I jumped to my feet, scanning the valley, the riverbank, the ridge, but saw no sign of him. Scurrying down the steep hill, I cried out to Millik, who sat halfway down the slope, more interested in her sack of berries than in the hunt in the valley before her.

"Have you seen Kiasik?" I demanded.

"No." She made no move to help me. "Omat!" she cried as I ran past. "They said not to leave the ridge!"

Just as I came within earshot of Puja and Ataata, I finally spotted my brother. He stood in the shadow of the tallest inuksuk, his narrow back pressed against the giant's stone leg. Not four arm's lengths away, a massive bull caribou faced him with antlers lowered.

Kiasik's bow was drawn, his small arrow nocked and ready. His face was calm.

"Brother!" I rushed toward him over the spongy ground. The caribou swung toward me; seeing his chance, Kiasik loosed his arrow. It hit the beast on its flank but bounced harmlessly off its thick fur.

Annoyed, the caribou turned back toward the boy. I could see its sides heaving, hear its labored breath. It pawed the ground with one large hoof and lowered its head for a killing charge.

Knowing my own toy arrows would be just as useless as Kiasik's, I unwound my sling. I snatched a round stone from the ground as I ran and slipped it into the sling's cup. Still running, I called out to the bull.

"Look at me! Look at me, caribou!"

Its huge head swung back toward me. I whirled my sling around my head and then flung it forward, putting all my weight behind the throw. The stone struck the caribou right between the eyes.

It merely waved its big antlers as if shaking a mosquito from its nose.

Then it charged me.

Dimly, I could hear Puja's screams through the roaring of blood in my ears. I don't know if I held my ground or turned to flee or merely fell to my knees in fear—I like to believe I stayed brave in the face of death, but after all, I was only a child.

I remember only Ataata standing before me, his broad shoulders blocking the bull from my sight.

With his hands outstretched before him, he spoke in the angak-kuq's tongue, flinging his words at the bull as I had flung my pebble. The caribou stopped in midcharge, reared onto its hind legs, and bugled at my father. Then it crashed back to the ground and stood quietly, listening as Ataata spoke. Finally the animal turned and trotted blithely away, chin aloft and antlers bouncing as it loped back to its herd.

Then Ataata was holding me in his arms, and Puja was running toward us, her face a twisted mask of rage and relief. Despite her sodden trousers and bloody hands, she wrenched me from my father's grasp, her fingers like talons on my shoulders. "Why did you leave the ridge?"

I remained silent, but Ataata cleared his throat and looked

pointedly at Kiasik, who'd retreated into the long shadow of the inuksuk.

"Come here!" she ordered her son. Ever proud, Kiasik walked toward us with his head held high. But I saw his bow trembling in his grasp. "Did you bring Omat down here?" Puja demanded.

"No." I answered for him. "Kiasik left me safe on the ridge."

He shot me a grateful glance. But Puja's anger only sharpened. "You know Omat always follows you!" she shouted at him. "You risked *his* life as well as your own."

My brother looked stricken.

"You're lucky Omat has more sense than you do," she went on, tucking me firmly against her hip.

Her words struck at his already bruised pride. "I was going to kill a caribou." His eyes narrowed in my direction, his gaze burning with something new. Something that sent a chill across my skin. Jealousy. "I almost had him when Omat distracted him."

"The caribou almost had *you*," said a small voice from behind me. Millik stood clutching her berry sack, her eyes downcast but her voice firm.

Ataata placed a warm hand on my head. "You were very brave, Omat, to try to help Kiasik."

"And *you* were very foolish!" Puja growled at her son.

"If Tapsi can't be a hunter, someone has to!" he shot back.

Poor Tapsi still stood on his rock amid the water, the caribou gone and his spear still clean. His head jerked toward us at the sound of his name; then he looked quickly away with burning cheeks.

"It won't be you!" Puja fumed at Kiasik. "No hunter would be so reckless."

He stood for a moment, his hurt gaze flicking from Ataata to his mother to me. Then he fled back toward the ridge. I moved to follow, but Ataata held me back.

"Let him go, Omat. He'll come back when he smells the feast, no?"

I found a smile for Ataata. Finally we'd fill our bellies and those of our dogs. Even Puja relaxed her scowl. She knew her son well; his hunger would overwhelm his pride.

—— =◆= ——

Despite the steaming mounds of dark caribou flesh, the feast that night was solemn. Tapsi sat with red eyes, avoiding the pitying glances of his mother and sister. Ipaq didn't even look toward his son, drowning his disappointment in ever-larger chunks of meat. Somber Ququk spoke quietly with Ataata, his concern clear. With Tapsi useless, the future of our band looked bleak.

Kiasik had returned, his mood little better than Tapsi's. Puja's eyes followed him like a dark cloud, her wide, feathery brows drawn low. He wouldn't look at her—or at any of us. I knew his coldness sprang more from shame than from anger. He should not have put me in danger. Should not have disobeyed his elders or blamed me for his failings. I longed to sit with him and tell him all would be well. He would be forgiven. I wanted to tell him of my fear facing the caribou, just so he could tease me for my weakness, then insist that *he* had felt no fear at all. I would know it was a lie—but it would make us both feel better. Instead, the memory of his jealous glare stood between us, draining all my joy away.

Only my father seemed truly happy. After Black Mask and I had both gulped down our portions of glistening meat, I settled myself beside him. He beamed down at me.

"Yes, Little Son?"

"Ataata, will you teach me to be an angakkuq like you? So I can speak with the caribou?" Before he could reply, I added, "Then I could protect Kiasik better. And the next time you go journeying with the Ice Bear, I could go, too. So you wouldn't be alone."

He regarded me for a moment, a faint smile raising the edges of his mustache. "Omat, Little Son, you're already a greater angakkuq than I."

I could only giggle at such nonsense. Ataata clenched a long strip of flesh between his teeth, pulled it taut, and slashed off a hunk with his knife. As he chewed, he pulled me onto his lap. The tang of meat upon his lips made me feel warm and safe. I'd never starve with Ataata to keep me fed. I tucked my head beneath his chin, resting my cheek against the soft caribou hide of his summer parka. When he spoke, it was in a whisper only I could hear.

"Do you remember what you said to the caribou before you shot him with that pebble?"

"I called his name, I think," I replied hesitantly.

"Yes. But you didn't call him *caribou*—you called him by his true name. His name in the angakkuq tongue."

"I don't know how to speak like an angakkuq!" I protested, craning my head back to look at him.

"I've never taught you, and yet you know."

"How?"

"How does the char know to swim upstream? Or the snow goose to return in the summer?" He shrugged. "Some things you aren't taught, you just know. Perhaps the Wolf Spirit teaches you in your dreams. Perhaps the caribou himself whispered his name to you as you faced him. But I think, most likely, that my son's soul guides you."

"Am *I* not your son?" I asked, wide-eyed.

"My son and my grandson, too!" he said with a laugh.

"How?"

"Look around us. You see only a few people in the camp, no? Who do you see?"

"Ququk, Ujaguk, Saartok," I listed obediently, looking at the stern old hunter, his wife, and his grown daughter. "Ipaq, of course, with Niquvana, Millik, and Tapsi. And Puja and Kiasik."

He waited patiently through my recital. "Hnnnnn. But what you don't see is that our tents are filled with the souls of many more Inuit than that. Each of us carries the spirits of our ancestors, and those spirits carry the spirits of *their* ancestors, and on and on, like the spiraled shells of the sea creatures—so small on the outside, but containing curl upon curl, tightly packed inside. Within your little body," he continued, poking me playfully, "is the soul of your father, the son of my blood. The drum we play on feast nights, that Ipaq used when I journeyed with the Ice Bear—your father Omat made that drum to help him summon the spirits and sing their tales. He was learning to be a great angakkuq when he died, and he has left his magic with you."

"But I'm not an angakkuq!" I insisted.

"You still have much to learn," he agreed. "But you already carry a power in you that I can't match. Perhaps I should take you with me to talk with the Ice Bear after all," he teased, "since *you* are why I can speak with him in the first place." He pressed my cheek again against his chest so I couldn't see his face, and stroked my hair as he continued. "Before you were born, I had lost my magic. No spirit would speak to me or do my bidding."

"What had you done?" I gasped. In order to incur such punishment, he must have disobeyed one of the *aglirutiit*, the sacred rules that defined the boundaries of our lives. I knew this much about our world.

"I still don't know which *agliruti* I broke. But the spirits wouldn't have taken my son from me, and all the other young hunters, if I hadn't done something to offend. After your father died, I would listen to the air with all my strength, but there was only silence." He blew the breath out through his teeth, close to my ear, drowning out the noise of the feasting around me until I heard only the roar of wind. I squirmed in his arms, trying to get away. He laughed and rubbed his nose against my cheek, tickling me with his mustache until I smiled.

"How did you get your magic back?"

Ataata grew somber again, brushing the cropped hair from my forehead with calloused fingertips. "When the Wolf Spirit gave you to us, he filled you with the soul of my son. And when I took you in my arms I felt my senses return. I felt the Ice Bear Spirit come to me once again and make me strong. I could listen to the

world and hear the wail and growl of ice forming and cracking far
away. I could feel the earth thunder as the caribou moved south and
see the waves swell as the seals moved north. And when the wolves
howled, I could understand their speech."

"Will I be able to do those things?"

He smiled, revealing his lower teeth, worn and yellowed,
beneath the thin line of his mustache. "Maybe you already can—
you just don't know it yet."

━━ ✦ ━━

After the night of the caribou hunt, I understood my place. To
be born already so heavy with names is something all Inuit children must bear—there are no new names, no new spirits. We come
into the world already someone's father, someone's aunt, someone's
grandmother.

Even after I understood that the man I called *Ataata*, Father,
was my grandfather by blood, he was no less a parent. To me, he
was both father and guiding spirit. I thought he could command
the stars themselves to light our way. Puja was my aunt, my sister,
and my adoptive mother, for she had nursed me side by side with
her own son, Kiasik—my cousin, my sister's son, my milk-brother.
It may seem onerous, this burden of names, but in a land without
other Inuit, the spirits of our ancestors kept us company in the
long, sunless winters.

In the legends passed down about life in other camps, hunters
from afar would come to marry widowed women and father new
children. But we were unlike any other camp. When Ataata was
just a babe, his parents and three other young couples had left their
homeland far to the west and come here, to the edge of the world.
They had thought others would follow. Instead, no other Inuit had
ever arrived.

I realize now why Ataata celebrated that night. When Kiasik
had proved himself too rash to be trusted, and Tapsi too weak, he
feared our family would starve once his generation passed away.

Then, with a single word in a secret tongue, I'd answered all his prayers.

After his death, I would lead our people. I could help them survive until, someday, the spirits would guide another band of Inuit to our lonely corner of the ice.

I became my grandfather's apprentice, in both the world we could see and the one we could not. First he taught me the angakkuq's language. From now on I would call the great spirits by their true names: Singarti the Wolf, "One Who Pierces"; Uqsuralik the Ice Bear, "The Fatty One"; Qangatauq the Raven, "One Who Hops." Then he taught me the story-songs of our people—tales of adventure, cunning, creation, and death. Always at the heart of these tales loomed the great powers that guided our world: Sanna the Sea Mother and Sila the Air, Malina the Sun Woman and Taqqiq the Moon Man. We feared and revered them in equal measure.

So, too, I learned to navigate by the shape of the snowdrifts that Sila created with Its long winter winds, and how to test the ice on Sanna's breast with the spiked end of a harpoon shaft. How to predict the weather from the color of the halo around Malina's golden face, and how to judge the seasons by Taqqiq's crescent shape. With each new moon, a new season of prey. Seal and caribou, walrus and fish, goose and ptarmigan. Always Kiasik stood at my side, testing me, teasing me, urging me on with his very presence. Together, we learned to hunt the animals.

But only I learned to speak with them.

CHAPTER THREE

$\int$

I woke out of breath, clammy and cold despite the heat beneath the sleeping furs. Kiasik, Puja, and Ataata still slept soundly beside me. Only my grandfather's gentle snoring broke the silence. Yet the dream voices still echoed in my mind.

Omat! A voice that could've been my grandfather calling to his drowning son, or my long-dead father calling to me. I didn't know which. In that first instant of awareness, the dream lay bright and clear in my mind, like a lake bottom seen through a layer of new-formed ice. The fear still tightened my chest. Though we'd been in our winter camp for several moons, in my dream I'd walked on summer tundra, bright-green moss cushioning each step. Before me, small in the distance, appeared four young men. Although I couldn't see their faces, and I'd never met them in my waking life, I recognized our four dead hunters.

I began running toward them, but the spongy moss turned to sucking marsh beneath me, shortening my steps. With each stride I sank farther, the ground giving way. Water poured in the tops of my boots; mud caught my knees, my hips, my shoulders, my neck. I lifted my chin, gasping for breath like a drowning man. In that last instant, when the ground crept between my teeth and down my throat, I saw the world as a lemming would: the intricate tangle of moss and feathered plates of lichen, the air rising in plumes of steam from the sun-warmed dirt, the insects that trundled and flitted and hopped, heedless of my agony.

The earth swallowed me.

Then the screaming began.

In the blackness of my earthen shroud, I couldn't see the hunters die, but I knew they, too, had drowned in the soft ground—just as they'd drowned in the icy sea before I was born. The screams I heard weren't theirs: they were the voices of the wives and fathers and mothers left behind.

I slipped from the sleeping furs, knowing that though only four winters had passed since I'd first spoken the caribou's true name, I could now dream like an angakkuq. Unlike Ataata in his trances, I couldn't control these visions; they left me weak and dizzy, snatching at the quickly fading images of ancestors long dead, of animal spirits, of the Sun and Moon.

I crawled from the sod-covered qarmaq and gazed at the familiar surroundings of our winter camp—Land of the Great Whale, we called it, for the shape of the mountain that rose to the west. Our domed qarmait lay in a cluster just below the whale's eye. Once there had been many homes. Now only three remained roofed with whalebone, skin, and sod. The others were little more than pits ringed with earth and stone, abandoned when we'd lost our young men.

I turned my face away from the dense fog of my own breath and pulled my hood tighter. In the reflected moonlight, the world glowed thin and blue. A dusting of snow brightened the ground between the roofs, covering the stains of emptied night pots and butchered seals. In weather like this, I'd seen Ataata break the icicles from his mustache for a midhunt drink. Kiasik had tried the same trick with the first few wispy hairs upon his lip, to the vast amusement of us all. Tapsi, who had finally managed to kill his first large game only a winter past, now sported a scraggly patch of beard at each corner of his mouth. As my cousins always reminded me, my own upper lip remained perfectly smooth. I longed for the day when Taqqiq the Moon Man would grant me a mustache.

The sky slowly lightened from black to bruise to palest purple. The color crept upward like the wavering heat of a lamp until only the topmost reaches of the sky remained black. Although Ataata had promised that the Moon of Great Darkness would end today, Malina the Sun still rested beneath the world's rim, biding her time. She moved slowly in the winter, like a woman too fat to rise from her bed. I had plenty of time left before she appeared.

I ducked back through the entrance tunnel and into the qarmaq to retrieve my spear. Ataata sat up slowly, blinking in the dimness. "What takes you outside, Little Son?"

"To check the fox traps." I was too young to hunt seal or walrus with the grown men, but that hadn't stopped me from catching all manner of smaller prey.

"Don't be too long. You don't want to miss the feast. We're all waiting to hear you sing!"

In preparation for the Sun's return, we'd raised a large *qaggiq* in the center of camp. I'd helped Kiasik and Tapsi shape the snow blocks and lift them to the men standing inside the growing walls. By the end, Ipaq had needed to stand on a tall pedestal of snow to lift the last block into the ceiling. Tonight, after the Sun had finally returned—then sunk once more—we'd gather inside the enormous iglu to celebrate with songs and stories. It would be my first performance; I'd practiced for many days.

"And don't forget your parka," Puja mumbled from beneath the sleeping furs.

I already wore two garments, a lighter *atigi* with the fur turned against my skin and an outer parka with the fur turned against the cold air. "I'm not a child, Little Sister," I insisted. She grunted to herself and rolled over, ignoring me as she usually did whenever I called her Little Sister rather than Mother or Aunt.

As I passed by Ququk's qarmaq, shouting tore through the entrance tunnel. As if chased by her parents' voices, Saartok scrambled outside.

"Where are you going?" she asked breathlessly.

I paused for a moment. I'd looked forward to a solitary walk so I could practice, using my song to scare away any ravens who hoped to feast on the contents of my traps. Never good company, Ququk's daughter looked even more downtrodden than usual. She'd seen more than twice my winters and by rights should've spent her time confiding in Puja, the only woman close to her age, rather than in a boy like me. But Puja had never been one for gossip or idle chatter.

As a girl, Saartok had been promised to my uncle Nasugruk, a great hunter despite his youth. She had worshipped him, but Nasugruk died on the ice, just like my father and all the others, leaving her without even a child to carry his name. So she spent her days tending her old parents, who in turn spent their days making her life, and each other's, as miserable as possible.

"I'm going to check my traps to see if there's something I can bring to the feast tonight." My pity finally got the best of me. "Do you want to come along?"

She wore her hair long across her forehead, but the thin wisps couldn't hide the excitement in her eyes. Together we walked out of the camp and over the low rise of hills, our boots squeaking on the new snow. Saartok was taller than I, but her stride shorter—a dainty, knees-inward gait. Her woman's parka slowed her still further. The long front flap would protect her knees when she knelt on the ground to gather plants, but it knocked against her legs while she walked. And with every stray gust of wind, her capacious hood blew straight up in the air. She struggled to hold it close around her face like a hunter wrestling a thrashing seal. When the wind died, the heavy hood lay limp against her back like an empty waterskin. When I was young and wondered why my own small hood fit tightly around my cheeks, Puja explained that women carried their babies on their backs beneath their parkas, pulling their wide hoods over the baby's head so it might stay warm and safe. She'd shared her own hood with me for the first winters of my life. But Saartok's hood would always lie limp.

I itched to walk faster, to leave the woman behind. To distract myself, I searched for subtle signs on the ground—fox scat, wolf prints, the shapes of snowdrifts—and stored these markers for use later, when I would go out with the men to hunt.

Saartok had little interest in such things. "I can't wait for Caribou Shedding Moon, when I can collect willow bark again. My father complains of headaches," she said mournfully.

I almost replied, "Of course he does, with your mother's voice in his ear for so many winters," but I held my tongue. I spotted my trap in the distance and hurried toward it.

"Go on," she offered, "I'll catch up."

Two moons earlier, I'd built a large stone cairn with holes in the top and bottom. I'd kept the trap full of meat scraps. Foxes got used to jumping down through the top hole, stealing the food, and exiting through the bottom unscathed. Then, two days ago, I'd replaced the bait and blocked the bottom hole. As I approached the trap, I could hear whining and scratching. I peered inside; sure enough, a trembling white fox stared back at me. The animal bared its teeth at me, its nose sliding up its snout in wrinkled fury and fear.

"Thank you, little fox," I said respectfully.

Saartok came up panting beside me. *"Alianait!"* she exclaimed. "It's beautiful!"

Proud of my imminent kill, I felt a surge of generosity. "If you'll skin it for me, you can have the tail."

She clapped her mittened hands and smiled. Puja would regret losing such a pretty tail for her own parka, but I couldn't resist bringing some joy to Saartok's life.

With a quick thrust of my spear through its ribs, the fox's growling ceased. I held the spear in place a moment longer; its final death spasm shivered up my blade and into my palms. I broke apart the cairn to remove the body, then carefully reassembled my trap. The fox's blood would serve as bait for the next animal to come along.

With the white carcass slung over my shoulder, we headed back to camp.

"Omat," Saartok asked tentatively, "have you dreamed lately?"

The whole camp knew of my strange nightmares—but usually they respected my status as an angakkuq's apprentice too much to speak about them.

"We all dream," I replied carefully, scanning the distance for signs of other prey.

"You know what I mean."

"They may just be dreams." I tried to feel as indifferent as I sounded, but in truth I was flattered. No one had ever come to me before with questions about the spirit world. I knew in my heart I had no right yet to speak as an angakkuq—I hadn't even met my helping spirit. But I was a proud child even then. Besides, it was a relief to share the burden of all those voices.

"Have you dreamed of Nasugruk?" Saartok asked, her voice catching. As usual, she couldn't even speak of the man she'd loved without veering toward tears.

"I dream of them all," I said carefully.

Saartok caught her breath. "He's still here?"

"No babies have been born to hold his spirit," I said. "He has only us, and so his soul stays here."

"I would've had his baby," she stammered, her eyes filling.

"He knows that," I said on impulse, clasping her hand awkwardly through my mitten. "He misses you. He calls your name sometimes. So mournful and deep that the sound carries across the ice and under the ground." I strayed from the truth. The hunters in my dreams did little more than moan and scream.

"I can't hear him," Saartok whimpered.

"But I can."

"Why didn't you tell me before?"

"I didn't want to upset you," I lied. "There's nothing you can do."

"If I had a baby, his spirit might have a home."

"Perhaps. But who'd father it?"

She aimed her next words at the ground. "There's talk that I might find a husband."

"Tapsi?"

Her cheeks reddened. My gentle cousin's hunting skills remained too poor to provide for a wife. I couldn't imagine a more unlikely pair, one always smiling and the other always weeping.

"My father doesn't want me to marry him," she confided. "I tell him there's no one else, and I'd be happy to be his wife, but he doesn't hear me. He says Tapsi will only bring home such poor caribou that we'll spend the winters hunched over against the cold, with no thick parkas to keep us warm. He'd rather I become second wife to Ipaq." She shuddered. My fat uncle had seen more summers than anyone else in our camp; his hair was thinning and white, his step no longer sure on the ice.

"Ipaq could never make a baby," I protested. "Everyone knows he hasn't lain with Niquvana since their first son died!"

"I know. It makes no sense. I think perhaps..." She clutched my hand in hers.

"Go on."

"I think perhaps he'd rather I stay in our home and be *his* second wife."

"Second wife to your own father! There's no greater agliruti! Better you should marry your brother's son, Kiasik!"

The aglirutiit guided every aspect of life and death; they were sacred rules passed down from the time before time, from angak-kuq to angakkuq, mother to daughter, father to son. Do not wear caribou hide when hunting for seals, lest you offend Sanna the Sea Mother. Do not play string games when the Sun has disappeared in winter, lest she get tangled in the threads and be unable to rise again in the spring. Do not let a woman hunt, lest she scare off the prey with her bleeding. Rules for everything: eating, hunting, playing, and, of course, sex. You must not mate with your own sibling or parent, or with the child of your parent's sibling.

"I'll speak with Ataata about this."

Saartok dropped my hand and stepped back. "No! Please! My father will be so angry!"

"Saartok," I said sternly. "This affects all of us. If Ququk breaks such a sacred agliruti, the entire camp will suffer. As it is, we'll barely make it through the winter with so few hunters and so many mouths to feed. Do you want all of us to pay for your mistakes?"

I must've spoken more harshly than I intended, for tears brightened her eyes again. "Please," she whispered. "What should I do?"

I was too young now to provide for a wife, but one day I'd be both the best hunter in the camp and the world's most powerful angakkuq. Saartok held no attraction for me with her limp hair, stooped shoulders, and the first faint tracks of age fanning from her eyes, but I had few options.

I turned to face the older woman, squaring my shoulders. "When I am old enough, I will marry you." Ataata would no doubt approve of my generous sacrifice.

To my astonishment, Saartok began to laugh. Not the gentle laughter directed at the foibles of children, but the loud, long gales directed at a fool. This woman, who so rarely even smiled, now doubled over with glee as if she were in pain.

"Omat," she finally gasped, "I couldn't marry a girl!"

CHAPTER FOUR

A girl?" I heard myself croak.

Saartok clapped a hand over her mouth, her laughter suddenly silenced. "*A'aa*, Omat. Don't you know what you are?"

"I...I am Puja's brother, her son, and her brother's son. I am Ataata's son, his grandson. I am...many things."

"You're also a girl." She laid a hand on my shoulder.

I shrugged her off violently. "What are you saying?"

"You don't have a penis, like the other boys." She spoke to me as if I were a baby, when before she'd shown the deference due a man.

"I know that," I snapped. I wasn't stupid. I peed squatting, like a woman, while the other boys stood, gleefully directing their stream in patterns across the snow. Kiasik and Tapsi teased me, certainly, about my girl's parts, but no one ever questioned my maleness. When I took my father's name, I inherited his spirit, and was raised as he had been raised. I'd always imagined my adult life would be a continuation of my childhood—I'd become a great hunter, take a wife, father children. Eventually I'd lead our camp as Ataata had done. Now I felt my whole life tumble apart like a calving glacier. My heart raced; sweat pooled in the palms of my mittens.

Ataata. I must talk to Ataata.

"Wait!" Saartok called as I began running toward camp. "Can I still have the fox tail?"

I tossed the whole animal to the ground and raced away, no longer hampered by Saartok's crawling pace. At the crest of the tallest hill, I paused for a moment with my camp spread before me, my breath coming in heaving gasps, my eyes stinging with childish tears. There, amid the snow-covered qarmait, lay my entire world. And now I no longer knew if I could claim it as my own.

Ataata emerged from our qarmaq's tunnel. I watched him stretch upward, yawning hugely. He squinted at the lightening sky, checking the pace of Malina's rise. I'd seen him do the same thing nearly every day of my life—look at the sky to gauge the weather by the shape of the clouds, the color of the light, just as he had taught me to do. Just as *all* hunters must do. Why had he bothered to teach me if I'd never hold a harpoon? I stood shaking, my fear now giving way to anger. Ataata turned toward me and raised a hand to his eyes. Something in the way my fists clenched at my sides made him start toward me. As he walked up the hill, his stride still long despite his age, I saw the concern in his furrowed brow. I almost ran from him, suddenly unwilling to face the answers to my questions. But when I turned away, my grandfather clasped my arm.

"Where are you going? What's wrong, Little Son?"

"Little Son," I spat back at him, unable now to stem the flood of tears coursing down my cheeks. "Why didn't you tell me?"

"Tell you what?"

"That I'm... that I'm a girl."

"Aii...," he sighed in dismay. He dropped my arm. His shoulders slumped. Even his mustache seemed to wilt.

"'Aii'? That's all you can say?" I shouted like a little child, but I didn't care.

"Omat," he said softly. "You have a girl's body. Didn't you realize?"

"You told me I'd be a hunter!"

"You will be. You have a girl's body, but a man's spirit."

"I don't understand." My voice teetered on the edge of a wail.

"You're still a child, Omat," he continued, his voice as calm and clear as a puddle of snowmelt. "As a child, you're no different from the other boys, and so I've treated you no differently. Only when you begin to bleed will you be a woman."

I knew what he spoke of. Every moon, Puja and Saartok spent several days isolated in a small iglu lest they scare off the animals. I'd just never paid much mind before. A woman's cycles didn't concern me.

"A woman!" I choked. "Why did you bother to train me as a man?"

"To respect the soul of your namesake. But when you bleed, many will say that you may no longer hunt, no longer live as a man. That's what my own father would have said," he admitted. "And yet I can't believe that you must change. Perhaps it's my own foolishness. My own desire to have you still as my son." He smiled gently. "I haven't trusted myself in this. I even asked great Uqsura-lik about you."

"What—what did he say?" I imagined my grandfather conversing with the Ice Bear Spirit, walking by his side like an old friend.

"He wouldn't answer me." Ataata's voice darkened. "A cloud lies over your future, Little Son. Even the spirits don't know what awaits you. So I decided long ago that I'll leave it up to you when the time comes. Perhaps you'll choose to live as a woman after all."

"Why would I choose that?" I spluttered.

He laughed. "Then you will continue as a man. You have the makings of a great hunter, even if you'll never be as tall as the other men. Some may protest. You'll have to prove yourself more useful as a hunter than as a wife or mother. But you should know that I'll always stand behind any decision you make." He lowered his brows, but the laughter didn't leave his eyes. "Did you really think I'd raise you as a man and then take all that away from you?"

"I . . . I didn't know. When Saartok said . . ."

"Saartok? Hnnnn...," he said, as if that explained everything. "She's wrapped herself in grief for too long—she hasn't been listening. But the rest of the camp understands. You are a boy. You will be a man."

His words couldn't dispel my worry. "When will this blood come?"

"It might come soon, or perhaps not for a few more winters. Or, maybe, never at all."

"Never?" I asked, my voice tight with hope.

Ataata chuckled. "It's a rare thing, but sometimes the spirits look down on a child like you, one whose body and soul do not match, and they stop the blood from coming. I've never heard of a woman growing a penis, but the legends do tell of the *uiluaqtaq*, who is neither woman nor man but something in between. A uiluaqtaq never takes a husband, but lives instead as a hunter and never bleeds, never bears children."

"Then that's what I'll be," I said firmly, wiping the tears from my cheeks. "I'll pray every day to Taqqiq the Moon to withhold his blood from me. And to the spirits of the ancestors. And to the animals, too, for good measure. They'll listen to me. The caribou listened, didn't he?"

Ataata bent to place his cheek against mine. I did not push him away. "You will always be my son, Omat. I will always be your father. No blood can change that. I have raised you to be a great angakkuq, a leader of your people. If that's what you want, then I promise you it will happen."

I didn't reply, too uncertain, too afraid, to trust my own voice. I let him lead me back to camp. One by one, my aunts and uncles and cousins crawled from their qarmait to look at the sky. Malina's rays limned the horizon with a single line of gold, bright as a lamp's curved wick. We'd seen such a display for two dawns now. I held my breath, suddenly afraid that darkness would quench the light. That Ataata had been wrong. This time, the Sun would never return.

Instead, the glowing line broadened, brightened. The men and women around me gasped, and the Sun rose farther, as if pulled upward by their indrawn breath. Color striped the sky: the dark red of old blood above the hilltops brightening to the fresh magenta of fireweed before fading into the gold of a blooming cinquefoil, the pale yellow of an ice bear's fur, and the pastel blue of a snail's shell. Finally the Sun herself rose above the horizon like the bright hump of a white whale. Ataata led us in song.

> I rise up from rest,
> Moving swiftly as the raven's wing
> I rise up to meet the day—
> My face turned from the dark of night,
> My gaze toward the dawn,
> Toward the whitening dawn.

Then, as if satisfied by her single suck of air, the Sun sank once more into the deep.

Ataata placed his arm around my shoulders, and I felt my fear finally subside. Every winter, he promised that the Sun would return after the heralding stars arrived—and he'd always been right. Now he promised I wouldn't be a woman if I didn't want to. And I believed him.

Kiasik and Millik had hastened to the qarmait to snuff out the lamps—a task for children, but one assigned to the young people of our childless camp. Every winter, I'd followed them, racing to see who might douse the flame first, then watching Puja and the other grown women relight the lamps to honor the Sun's rebirth. But today I stayed beside Ataata.

I watched Ququk shepherd his family back inside their own qarmaq. Saartok handed my discarded fox to her mother while trying to avoid her father's gaze. I'd never noticed before how the old man's face always turned toward his daughter's slim form. Now that I saw, shivers coursed over my skin.

"Do you think Saartok could marry Tapsi?" I asked Ataata.

He fingered the patch of hair beneath his lower lip, considering me carefully before replying. "Tapsi's no real hunter. Ququk wouldn't agree to it. And Saartok still pines for Nasugruk. She may have to wait until another man comes to our camp."

My grandfather often spoke of the day when others would come—a day we all hoped for, but one I was far too young and impatient to wait for. If Ataata was right—and Ataata was always right—I would one day lead our people through the worlds of earth and spirit. But I was still a youth, and that time felt impossibly far away. Why wait so long? I would start proving myself a man by helping Saartok.

And I would start tonight.

CHAPTER FIVE

ʃ

When Ataata and I returned to our own qarmaq, Puja had already relit the lamp. She sat beside it, hard at work, softening a seal hide with her teeth. She pretended she hadn't seen us earlier, but I knew she'd caught our heated discussion on the hill. She shot Ataata a searching glance, and my grandfather widened his eyes in silent acknowledgment of our conversation.

She spat out the piece of hide. "How was your walk with Saar-tok? I saw you leave together."

"I wanted to be alone."

"You're alone too much. Didn't you enjoy walking with her?"

"Saartok is just a girl," I said carelessly. "No real company for a hunter."

Ataata smiled, but Puja looked stern. "Then I won't speak to you, either, for surely a woman like me is no good company."

Usually I would've pressed my nose upon her cheek, asking for forgiveness. But I had little patience for querulous old folk when there was work to be done.

"I have to practice," I shot over my shoulder. When I lifted the sacred drum from where it hung beside the lamp, Puja opened her mouth to comment. She never liked my taking the instrument away from camp; she didn't trust me not to bang the delicate skin along the ground—the skin my dead father had so painstakingly stretched and smoothed. But today she held her tongue. I was approaching adulthood and knew more mysteries than she. The drum was my inheritance, and I'd brook no arguments about its treatment. Besides, Ataata merely smiled at my antics, and it was not Puja's place to question him.

On the hills above the camp, far from curious eyes and listening ears, I flung my song into the sky. The new words came easily to my lips. I sang all through the long twilight, until the sky grew black as peat and spangled with stars. Clouds swirled in, ghostly white in the Moon's glow, and I danced with them, knowing that Sila the Air moved to the rhythm of my drumbeats.

The howls of dogs pierced my song—a storm approached. If I didn't return soon, Puja would worry. Yet no storm would stop tonight's celebration. In the distance, I could see the camp springing to life. The glowing qaggiq beckoned to me, the oil lamps inside pouring light through the seams around each snow block. Ipaq had promised to bring the char he'd dragged through an ice hole. Ataata would contribute a bearded seal. My fox meat would be a paltry offering in comparison, but my song would serve as my true gift. They said I was descended from a line of great songsingers whose words could inspire any hunter, chasten any enemy. Tonight I would make my ancestors proud. I would prove myself as much a man as anyone born with a man's parts.

⬩━◆━⬩

Inside the qaggiq, my confidence fled almost immediately. Puja pointedly ignored me, but Kiasik beckoned me to join him with a tilt of his chin.

"Are you ready?" I'd rarely heard my milk-brother speak so

gently. Certainly never to me. He gestured to the drum in my lap, but I knew he meant something more. Puja must have told him about my conversation with Ataata.

He knows, I realized. Perhaps he'd always known. No wonder he so often cautioned me not to show any weakness. *We will be great hunters together*, he'd said when we were children. Great hunters couldn't act like girls.

I ran my finger around the hoop, checking the skin for tautness. "Ataata taught me to sing. Ipaq to drum. Puja to listen. And you... you taught me not to fear."

He held my gaze for a moment, the softness quickly vanishing beneath fierce pride. Then he passed me a portion of seal meat. A lower vertebra. He returned to his own meal, as if the gesture meant nothing. But I understood it perfectly: only *men* ate from the bottom of a bearded seal's spine.

Ququk sat between his wife and daughter on one of the snow benches that ringed the qaggiq. As usual, his thick mustache and tuft of beard only accentuated his perpetual frown. Even on this night of celebration, the old man didn't smile. I'd never asked Ataata where Ququk's anger came from. Perhaps he'd known joy before his son died upon the ice. But unlike Ipaq and Ataata, Ququk had no grandchildren to adopt. Saartok was the only child left to him. And he didn't want to let her go.

As I stepped into the center of the qaggiq, I could barely bring myself to look Ququk in the eye. Saartok couldn't, either; she kept her gaze on the small upper vertebra in her hands. But the bright fox fur spiraling around her long braids gave me the courage to raise my drum.

The women kept passing meat and fish. Ipaq had just finished dancing in his owl mask with its carven face and feathered ruff, and there was much talking as everyone praised his skills.

I began to beat the drum, spinning it in time to my own sway-ing body, my stamping feet, striking one edge and then the other. I found the patience Ataata taught. I waited until every face turned toward me. Until the chattering ceased and their exhalations rose in a silent, white fog.

Finally I took a deep breath and began to sing.

"This is the story of Taqqiq and Malina."

Everyone smiled, eyes wide. Ataata had told this story many times.

"This is a tale of the time before time, but their camp was not so different from our own, and the laws they broke still hold sway." I didn't give more exposition than that, trusting the story to work its magic.

"Taqqiq and Malina were brother and sister, both very beautiful, with full round faces and great shining eyes." I circled the qaggiq as I spoke, my words drawing my listeners into the tale.

"In the winter, the men entered a qaggiq much like ours. For days they ate and sang, while the women stayed in their homes. One night, while Taqqiq feasted, his sister Malina lay naked in her empty iglu. She was so lonely that she let her lamp go out, and she lay in darkness, not bothering to relight the wick."

I heard Puja's disdainful snort—she had no patience for lazy women. I repressed a grin: already my most exacting critic was caught in the net of my tale. "Malina heard a sound above her. She tried to sit up, but a man's hand fell across her mouth, and a man's body pressed her against the ground. In the dark, she could not see his face. 'No,' said Malina. 'I do not want you. Beware, for my brother Taqqiq is a strong hunter and he will surely kill you.' But the stranger would not listen, and he took the girl against her will.

"The next night, Malina tended her lamp with care, but a strange wind blew through the vent in her roof and again the man came to her in the dark. This time he grabbed at her breasts and bit them with his sharp teeth until they bled."

Millik gasped. My cousin's fear only made me slow my song. I would drag out the horror like a hunter slowly unspooling a fishing line before jerking his catch ashore.

"But when he came to her on the third night, Malina dipped

her fingers into the lamp and smeared her attacker's forehead with black soot. The next day, she gathered with the other women to welcome the men as they emerged from the qaggiq. Malina peered at every man, looking for the black mark, so she might know her attacker. 'I will tell my brother, Taqqiq, what has happened. *He* will avenge me.'"

I slowed my song still further, letting every humming drumbeat fade to silence before I struck the hoop again. "Finally Taqqiq crawled from the entrance tunnel. Malina opened her mouth to beg him for help." I held my mallet poised above the rim for a single long breath. "Taqqiq's forehead was smeared with black soot."

I continued drumming, faster now, pacing the qaggiq until I stood before Ququk and his family. "Malina screamed at her brother, accusing him before the whole camp of breaking this most sacred agliruti. For no man shall lie with his sister, or his mother, or his daughter, or even with his sister's daughter."

Ququk shifted on his bench, his jaw clenched tight. I stared at him, daring him to protest as I sang an old song suddenly made new.

"Malina took up her *ulu* and cut off her breasts. She handed them to Taqqiq. 'If you enjoy my body so much,' she said, 'if you want so much to bite at my breast, then take these!' Her brother's face was pale with fear and shame. He ran toward Malina to stifle her cries. But she broke from his grasp and began to run, grabbing a lamp to light her path as she sprinted away."

I angled my mallet against the rim so my drumbeats echoed the crunch of Malina's footsteps in the snow, the rhythm of her pounding heartbeats. I turned my gaze inward, watching the story fly before me like a cast harpoon. I moved to follow it, my feet carrying me swiftly around the qaggiq. "Her brother took another lamp and struck out after her. But Malina was faster. Taqqiq's lamp slipped from his grasp and sputtered in the snow. He picked it up, the flame faltering and weak. But still he could see his sister's lamp, and so still he ran." I was panting now, my words barely squeezing through.

"On and on they ran, until great Sila the Air took pity and lifted Malina up until her feet touched only clouds—higher and higher into the sky, until she became the Sun, red with her woman's blood. But Sila does not play favorites: It lifted Taqqiq, too, with his weak flame. He became the Moon."

Finally my drumming slowed. "Even now they run above our heads." One more drumbeat. A long, resonant boom. "Brother and sister, suffering for their wickedness." Another beat. "An eternal chase." I struck the drum one last time. "Now and forever." I finished as I'd been taught: "Here ends this tale."

"Alianait!" Ataata led the shout of approval from the crowd.

My milk-brother took in my delighted audience with a furrowed brow, and I worried his old jealousy would return. But when Tapsi turned to him, gabbling my praises, Kiasik merely grinned and lifted his chin as if to claim some of my success for himself. I did not begrudge him that. I had pride enough to spare.

Ataata smiled broadly; he'd never doubted I would be as great a storyteller as my parents. Only Ququk did not cheer. His usually somber face looked positively thunderous.

Soon my uncle Ipaq quieted the crowd with an upraised arm. "Omat has told us a great and true story!" More cheers. "One we must remember as our children grow older and look for mates. My son, Tapsi, has come into adulthood." This was true—barely. My cousin had killed one small, maimed walrus cow, though not without a good deal of assistance from his father. "It is time he had a wife."

No one seemed more surprised than Tapsi himself, who looked past his mother and sister to the available women. There weren't many—he looked first at Puja, thrice his age, then, only slightly more hopefully, toward Saartok. Finally, although our mothers had been siblings, his eyes rested on me. He looked somewhat pleased at what he saw. I scowled at him fiercely while my heart thudded against my ribs in sudden terror. That would teach me to meddle in other people's affairs—to have Ipaq choose *me* for his son's wife.

I need not have feared, however. My uncle grinned at Ququk's daughter, reaching for her hand. "Saartok is still young enough to have children, and she has grieved too long. I ask Ququk to give her to my son, so our camp may once again ring with the laughter of children!"

On any other night, Ququk would've flatly refused. Since Saartok was his only living child, he would keep her in his household, even after her marriage—but he would have to take Tapsi, too. Accepting the camp's weakest hunter into his home meant that Ququk would assume the heavy responsibility of feeding the couple and any children they might have. But he looked briefly at his daughter, and then at me, and I knew he understood my warning. Either he'd allow this, or I'd tell everyone that he'd wanted to lie with his own daughter. The wrath of our entire camp and all the spirits would fall upon him.

Ququk grunted his acceptance of the match.

Saartok and Tapsi joined hands in the center of the circle. She stood half a head taller than he, and many years of chewing hides had worn her teeth, but the fox fur in her braids gave her a youthful air, and Tapsi's hesitant smile matched her own. Perhaps his cheerful nature would wipe away some of her perpetual sadness.

That night, a young man and his wife would lie together in our camp for the first time since before my birth, and hope for our people would spring anew.

Leaving the qaggiq, Saartok broke away from her new husband and rushed to me. She lay her cheek against mine. "I'm sorry I said you were just a girl," she whispered. "You've helped me more tonight than any grown man could."

I felt my face burn at the compliment and couldn't contain my smile as the new couple slipped off into the night.

I headed back toward our qarmaq, my step light, the worries of the day forgotten until Puja stopped me with a hand on my arm. She glanced around to make sure no one else was near. "I thought you were going to tell the story of the Orphan Boy."

"I changed my mind."

"After you spoke with Saartok."

I shrugged, but she wouldn't be put off so easily.

"I know what you and Ataata talked about today."

My heart drummed in my chest. Was Puja going to say Ataata had lied? That I would indeed become a woman one day?

"I don't always agree with him," my milk-mother went on. "I would've taught you more about being a woman. Just in case. But I think now Ataata was right. I don't know what part you had in what happened tonight..."—I braced myself. This would not be the first time she accused me of acting above my age—"but you did a good thing."

She looked around slowly at the surrounding qarmait full of uncles and aunts, cousins and siblings, each generation more closely interwoven than the last. Saartok and Tapsi were not just the first new couple in our camp—they would likely be the last. Any other pairings would break the aglirutiit and bring the spirits' anger down on us all. "If we are not careful," Puja murmured, "we will destroy ourselves like a bear trapped in a collapsed den, who eats its own young to survive. Tonight, you've given us a way out. At least for now."

CHAPTER SIX

⅃

A walrus has hips like a fat woman, big wide hips that sway when she swims. Ataata taught that if you look carefully, you can see the woman the walrus used to be. The flippers don't join together until far up her body, as if her legs have been slow to transform. Or perhaps the walrus has always been a walrus, but is now on her way to becoming a woman. It wouldn't be the first time a sea animal changed to a human, or a wolf to a whale, or a man to a woman. These things happen all the time.

The walrus swimming beside my kayak was still a walrus, for now. A big female with long face bristles, as if a sea urchin had perched upon her snout, enjoyed the view, and decided to stay. As a child, I'd thought walrus whiskers would be venomous like urchin spines, and that an angry walrus might spike me with them. But Ataata said they merely served as the walrus's eyes and ears on the dark ocean floor, where it rooted for the countless clams it needed to fill its enormous belly. The tusks were the real danger. Yellow tusks, scored with claw marks—like those of the female near us— meant the walrus hunted seals, not clams at all. She'd probably lost her mother soon after weaning and never learned to scour the

ocean beds; she might charge my kayak, hoping to knock me into
the water and spear me upon her tusks. I kept a safe distance from
her, careful not to arouse her anger.

Three springs after my first performance as a story-singer, I was
still a boy—not yet a man but not a woman, either. Perhaps, as
Ataata had said, I was something in between.

My nightly prayers had so far worked, and I hadn't bled. With
my grandfather, I hunted everything from ptarmigan to seal pups,
but I had yet to kill a full-grown seal or walrus. The previous
summer, Ataata had deemed me too young, although Kiasik had
returned from the seal hunt with his harpoon proudly bloodied.
I'd grown over the long winter, and though still far smaller than
Kiasik—shorter even than Tapsi—I no longer looked quite so
foolish holding a harpoon. When Ataata pulled me forward the
morning of the walrus hunt and placed the weapon in my hand, I
couldn't repress a grin. Once I proved my manhood, no one could
take it away from me.

Crouched in his own kayak, Ataata raised a hand for silence,
his eyes following the path of the walrus beside us. We must not
scare her, lest she panic and try to sink us. I'd heard that even clam-
eating walruses could swim on their backs beneath our boats, ripping holes through the bottoms with their sharp tusks. Revenge,
I thought, for we covered our boats with walrus hide and braided
our ropes with the spiraled skin of their calves.

The length of her tusks branded her a young animal, perhaps my
own age. I couldn't suppress a feeling of relief that she wasn't our
target; she reminded me too much of myself, an orphan trying to
survive in a dangerous world. She coursed through the clear ocean,
waving her big hips at us, each hind flipper paddling in turn, as if
she swaggered sideways through the water. I stifled a laugh at the
image, careful to remember Kiasik's warnings: I must not show
any weakness in front of the other hunters. They had all been born
with a hunter's most precious weapon. I had not.

The walrus dove beneath the surface. Ataata whispered a chant to Taqqiq the Moon Man and Sanna the Sea Mother, and then motioned us to ready our paddles. We scanned the horizon for a sign of the walrus surfacing. Her skin was very light, a sure indication that she'd been in the cold water for a long time—an auspicious sign. Soon she'd head back to the haul-out, and we need only follow her to find the entire herd. But her light skin also made her harder to spot among the scattered icebergs and the bright, sun-spangled ocean swells.

Finally the Moon Man must have heard our prayers, for I spotted the pale walrus and jerked my arm toward her excitedly. Ataata's weak eyes couldn't see that far, but he trusted me and motioned for us to head that way.

As the Sun crept her slow path across the sky, the unmistakable rumble of the walrus haul-out rolled across the water, a sound more like a calving glacier than like roaring beasts. A moment later, we spied the dark smudge on the white landscape. The mass of animals lay on one of the season's last large expanses of ice, surrounded by plenty of open water—the perfect location for a hunt.

I unfastened my harpoon from my boat and checked the knots: one that tied the long rope to the handle, another that fastened the toggle head to the foreshaft. Striking a walrus and then letting it slip away beneath the waves because a rope came loose would be a great affront to Sanna. The Sea Mother doesn't take kindly to a hunter who wastes her children.

Our young walrus guide struck the ice with her tusks, using them like claws to pull herself out of the water and up the slippery edge. Even surrounded by her kin, I could still pick her out, her skin light among the dark brown bodies of the others. Soon, as her body warmed, she'd become one more indistinct animal among many.

Kiasik didn't need to ask me if I was ready. Our eyes met; he smiled. We'd done this over and over on walruses sculpted of snow.

I followed his kayak to a stretch bare of animals on the far edge of the ice. We tethered our boats and clambered onto the floe. The strips

of seal fur on our boot soles quieted our tread as we paced closer to
the herd.

Eyebrows lifted, Kiasik signaled toward two young males side by
side. I raised my own brows in acknowledgment, hoping the beasts
wouldn't hear the pounding of my heart.

We tied the ends of our long harpoon lines together, with plenty of
slack so the joined ropes wouldn't impede the weapons' flight. Kiasik
readied his harpoon, and I hefted my own shaft above my shoulder.
We locked eyes and matched our breaths, just as we'd practiced.

Then, at the same instant, we let our harpoons fly, the long hide
ropes unfurling behind like smoke on the wind. Kiasik's blade pierced
his target in the ear, a killing blow. My harpoon struck the neck of
the other animal, only wounding it. The injured walrus roared in
anger, alerting his neighbors to danger. As one, the herd lifted their
heads and swiveled their massive bodies in our direction. Kiasik
tensed, ready to turn and run for his boat if they charged us.

"Go away," I called to the herd in the angakkuq's tongue. "We
are almost done here." I willed my voice to stay calm, although my
knees quaked. A charging walrus would crush me easily. But the
beasts understood me; they lumbered to the ice edge and slid into
the water, disappearing beneath the waves. Still connected to Kiasik's
kill by our rope, my wounded walrus remained behind. He rolled his
red eyes toward me; pink foam flew from his lips with every panting
breath. His flippers beat the ice, and his body thrashed like a worm's
as he tried to reach the sea, but the toggle head had done its work,
swiveling into place so it wouldn't come loose. I longed to deliver
the beast from his torment, but approaching him now would get me
gored. *Patience*, I reminded myself. *Patience*.

A few other walruses surfaced near the ice, unwilling to abandon their kin. Ataata, still in his kayak, readied his own harpoon
and let it fly, striking a young walrus in the side. He quickly strung
an inflated seal float onto his harpoon line, then tied the end of the
rope to his boat. When the walrus tried to dive, the float kept it
from going too deep. It tried a different form of escape, swimming

frantically toward the horizon, unwittingly towing the hunter behind.

My own walrus finally showed signs of fatigue. I approached cautiously, keenly aware of the foam-flecked tusks. He watched me with beady black eyes nearly hidden in folds of brown skin. His bristles jerked in time to his spasmodic panting, his nostrils flaring and closing, flaring and closing. The misty cloud of his breath smelled of clams and salt and darkness. When I was just close enough to reach him with a thrust of my lance, I stopped and planted my feet as firmly as I could on the slick ice. I aimed for the back of his head, where a small cross in the wrinkles of his flesh marked the killing spot. With the force of my whole body, I plunged my weapon through his tough outer skin, through his blubber, and into the top of his spine.

Kiasik, already starting to prepare his own kill for butchering, laughed and tossed back his hood. The wind ruffled his gleaming black hair. "You're so small, Omat, you had to lie on top of your lance!" he teased. He was right—I stretched prone across the hulk of my kill. I laughed with him as I slid down the side of my walrus and back onto my feet like a child playing on an iglu roof.

Ququk, who should have been fishing by a safe ice hole at his age, not joining in the dangers of a walrus hunt, had successfully killed his own beast the traditional way—slamming an anchor into the ice to keep his walrus from escaping, rather than pinning it to its neighbor. He silenced us with a curt gesture. "Your walrus's spirit hovers nearby. Would you show it such disdain with your boastfulness? You prove yourself too young to join the hunt if you can't respect the hunted."

"I do respect—" I began.

"Some would say you shouldn't even have come. If we were not so desperate for hunters, you wouldn't be here in the first place."

I knew he spoke not of my unusual hunting technique, but of the lack between my legs. I wanted to fly at him, but such was not our way. A young man did not attack an old one. I turned aside instead, hiding my flushed cheeks.

Kiasik would not question his elder, either, but I could tell from the tightening of his jaw that he was angry. Without looking at Ququk, he let out a long sigh. "I'm glad *I* didn't harpoon Omat's walrus. It was much fiercer than mine—I'm not sure I could've given it a good death."

The old hunter's mouth tightened in annoyance at Kiasik's implicit reproach. He stalked away, leaving us to our bloody task.

Kiasik flashed me a bright smile.

I smiled back, warmed by his regard. In response he puffed out his chest, just a bit. *Like a male ptarmigan*, I thought. *Preening under his mate's attentions.* Fear gripped my stomach. Was Ququk right? At the moment I finally claimed my manhood, why did I suddenly feel like a girl?

For the rest of the hunt, I concentrated on the task at hand, ignoring Kiasik. I dribbled fresh water into my walrus's mouth, quenching its soul's thirst so it might be reborn. No matter what Ququk said, I knew well how to respect my prey.

After towing its attacker in circles, Ataata's walrus finally exhausted itself. He easily dispatched it with a blow to the head. We all worked together to butcher the animals—they were too heavy to drag home in one piece. With our slate knives, we peeled away the skin and blubber in long pieces, each as thick across as my palm. Next we chopped off the heads and tusks and set aside the flippers to ripen. In a moon's time, they'd be everyone's favorite food. Finally we pulled the innards from the stomach in one long ribbon.

With the butchering finally complete, Ataata stood at the ice edge, dropping the bloody entrails into the water. They'd sink to the bottom and feed the tiny creatures, who would in turn feed the walrus, who would later feed us. The hood of his parka was thrown back, his chin-length gray hair floating in wisps around his weathered face.

"Calm water," he said softly to the bottom creatures, asking them to allow us a safe journey home. "Calm water."

He handed a piece of dripping organ meat to me. The blood was warm on my bare hands, a reminder of the life that pulsed beneath the ice in our frozen world. Ataata placed his hand under mine, as if to heft the weight of it. "Your hand is small for a hunter's, Omat." Before I could protest, he continued. "But you wield the harpoon with skill." He turned to look out over the ocean, following the flight of a puffin that skimmed low across the waves. "My eyes grow dim. I should be fishing. In another camp, I'd be useless. Soon I would take myself out onto the ice."

I couldn't stop myself from interrupting. "Then we must be thankful that we are not in another camp. We could not do without your wisdom."

"That's what I'm afraid of." He paused again, his hand still on mine. The blood cooled, the wet trickles now chilling my hand rather than warming it. "Very soon, you must meet your helping spirit. Then, when I'm gone, you must speak to the spirits for our people. Promise me, Omat."

I met his eyes in silent assent. He guided my hand over the water, and I released the entrails. They drifted down into the dark, leaving spirals of blood rising in their wake.

"Calm water," I murmured, my voice breaking. "Calm water."

We paddled back to our hunting camp under a still-light sky, our kayaks low in the water with their heavy bounty loaded on top. As we pulled up to the edge of the landfast ice, the women left the *igluit* to meet us.

"Omat's first walrus!" Kiasik announced, holding up the flipper from my kill. Puja beamed. As the woman of my family, she sliced the dark-red meat and distributed it to the other women present, so that every family could benefit from my good luck. Custom dictated I be the only one not to taste my own walrus. My generosity in sharing would bring me goodwill from the other families, more valuable by far than mere meat. Puja kept only the animal's penis bone for me. All men envy the bull walrus his mighty penis, so much longer and stiffer than an Inuk's. I pitied the poor walrus cow who found herself pierced by such a staff.

I severed the tip of the bone and gave it to Ataata, who would carve it into a tiny walrus totem for my amulet bag. The summer before, when Kiasik had killed his first large bearded seal, he had earned a seal carving. Many times, he had taken it from his bag so I might admire it. We would talk of the day when I could join him, and together we would become the next generation of hunters to provide for our camp. All boys dreamed of such a future, but few as intensely as I. The walrus totem was more than proof of my hunting skills. It made me, finally, a man in the eyes of my people. And no one—not even crotchety Ququk—could take that away from me.

We held a great feast inside Ataata's iglu. We slurped the raw blubber until the oil ran down our chins. For two full days, we did not sleep, but the Sun kept us company, never dipping far beneath the horizon, and we scorned exhaustion. When our bellies swelled with meat and we could eat no more, Ataata took out the drum. The circle quieted around him, preparing for a tale.

"To thank Sanna for this bounty, tonight we sing her story," he began. I shifted uncomfortably. This story always filled me with a sense of foreboding.

"In the time before time, Sanna was a young girl from a camp far to the west, where our people first entered this world. When they came, they found only summer animals to eat—fish and birds and caribou—so our people went hungry every winter. Sanna's father could not provide for his daughter, and so he was eager to marry her off. Many times, hunters offered to marry the girl, but Sanna refused every one." Ataata kept the rhythm of his song on the drum, a careful, even beat. There was nothing frenzied in his telling, no wild pacing or violent flourishes such as so often accompanied my own songs. Yet his voice resonated with a power beyond his aged body, and his words carved the images into our minds. We'd all heard the story many times; that didn't make it any less dramatic.

"One day, a new man came to their winter camp. He stood so tall he could barely crawl through the entrance tunnel. Sanna's father knew right away that he was no ordinary Inuk, and he begged her to be careful of the stranger. But the girl ignored her elder's advice. She saw only a handsome man who would bring her pleasure. The girl's mother wailed and her father begged on his knees, but still she would not listen. And so Sanna, who had refused all other suitors, left with the stranger. He took her far into the north, where nothing grows even in summer. The Sun shines only on a land of ice and water, nothing more, so bright that Sanna had to wear eyeshields every time she stepped outside.

"The man built an iglu and told Sanna to go inside. He warned her not to leave it while he was away hunting, for her woman's spirit might disturb the animals. And then he left for many days. Before too long, Sanna decided she could stay inside no longer. She yearned for the wind upon her face. Hearing no one around, she crept outside. 'Aii, I am safe! There is no one here but a great black petrel circling in the sky!' And so she stood up and looked around. Just then, the bird dove into the ocean and surfaced with a large, shiny fish clutched in its beak. With a flap of its black wings, it landed on the ice far from Sanna. The petrel was much larger than any bird should be, nearly as tall as a bear. And when it turned its dark head to the summer Sun, its eye glinted red.

"Sanna had started to run back inside the iglu to hide from the evil bird when she saw an astonishing thing. The creature's silhouette stretched and grew until it transformed into the figure of a man. Sanna screamed in alarm. The giant petrel was her husband!"

I didn't notice when Ataata began to speed up his drumming—only that now the drum blurred before him as he spun it back and forth against his mallet. I realized I was holding my breath. Next to me, Puja moaned and rocked. Even Kiasik, my bold milk-brother, sat transfixed.

"The bird-man looked up when Sanna screamed, his eyes still glowing red. She could feel their heat boring into her even across so much ice. And so Sanna ran, calling for her father to rescue her from her bird-husband.

"She ran and ran for days, her husband never far behind, but Sila gave strength to her legs and filled her lungs with Its wind. Finally she approached her old home and saw her family in its *umiaq*. She leapt into the water and swam to the boat. When she reached it, she grasped on to the side with her cold fingers, crying, 'Save me from the bird-man, or I shall be killed!' She was sure that since she had reached her family, she would finally be safe.

"But the bird-man was right behind her, standing on the shore. He called out to Sanna's father, 'If you take back your daughter, I will kill you and all your family! Make her let go of your boat!'

"The father could not look his daughter in the eye. 'You must let go, Daughter! Go back to your husband before he kills us all!' But still, Sanna clung. On the far shore, her husband crouched down and raised his arms above his head. Sanna looked over her shoulder just as her husband rose off the ice, his nose a hooked beak, his arms wings.

"'Pull me into your boat and take me home!' she begged, but her father refused. With every beat of the giant petrel's wings, storm winds swirled, faster and faster. Water poured over the sides of the rocking umiaq. At any moment, the whole family would drown.

"Sanna's father pulled out his long hunting knife and raised it above his head. Sanna thought he would fight off the bird.

"'Daughter, you must let go!' he cried once more. And with that, he brought down his knife upon her hands, slicing off the tips of her fingers to the first knuckle. The fingertips fell into the ocean and drifted toward the bottom. But still Sanna clung. The father struck again, slicing through her second knuckles. The middles of her fingers dropped into the waves. But still Sanna clung. 'Go back, Daughter!' he cried one last time as he cut off her last knuckles. The roots of her fingers fell into the ocean. Sanna fell from the side of the boat, leaving trails of blood on her father's umiaq, marks that would never come off."

The drumbeats slowed again. Tears shone in Puja's eyes. Even Ipaq looked downcast. But the story was not over.

"Sanna did not try to swim, for she had no hands. She drifted down through the water, down into the darkness where the sunlight never reaches. As she sank, the blood streamed up in curls from her mangled hands. The lines of blood split and twisted, branched and stretched, until they became seaweed. The pieces of her fingers floated before her eyes, and her pale fingernails broadened into ice bears. Her tiny fingertips grew flippers and whiskers and became seals. Her middle finger-bones swelled into long-tusked walruses. Her strong finger roots floated to the surface and became whales, blowing their hot breath skyward. Sanna finally came to rest on the ocean floor, no longer pursued by the bird-man, finally safe from all danger. She lives there still, guarding the sea creatures. And when she pleases, she gives them to Inuit to hunt, so that her people will not starve." The drum stopped. "Here ends this tale."

A communal sigh of relief broke the silence. This had been a good story.

Ataata did not look at me when he finished. Nothing in his manner revealed that he had meant it for my ears. I was not disobeying my elders by living as a hunter and refusing to take a husband; Ataata had agreed it was the proper course for me. Still, I thanked Taqqiq that with my initiation into manhood finally secure, I was one step closer to never succumbing to Sanna's fate. Yet I took the story as a warning.

Desperate families did desperate things.

CHAPTER SEVEN

A winter had passed since my first walrus hunt. Once again, Sun and wind had opened the sea, carving the remaining ice into fantastic bergs. Though snow still covered most of the ground, the first flowers of spring dotted the steeper slopes, and I was finally ready to become a full angakkuq.

It was the Moon When Animals Give Birth, a perfect time to begin my new life. I knew what I needed to do. Ataata had given clear instructions: find an isolated spot where I'd be invisible to all but the spirits, perform the necessary rituals, and wait for my guide to appear.

"No weapons, Little Son," Ataata said, taking the bow from my hand.

"How will I hunt?"

"Your spirit journey is a time for thinking, not hunting. If you need food, you'll find it. If you need tools, you will make them. An Inuk can always make something from nothing. And Puja," he added, turning to my milk-mother. "You may not give Omat any food to take." She scowled at her father and tried unsuccessfully to hide the sack of dried fish she had prepared for me.

"Give it to me," he said. Puja handed him the bag, which he proceeded to dump onto the ground. She opened her mouth to protest, but thought better of it and busied herself instead with gathering the fish into the apron of her parka.

Ataata handed me the empty sack. "This is all you may take with you. Something to hold whatever you may find."

I slung the bag over my shoulder.

"Find your guide." My grandfather's face, usually so gentle, was stern. For his own initiation, he had waited for Uqsuralik in a cave of piled ice on the frozen sea. I, however, sought Singarti, the Wolf Spirit, who'd guarded my infant grave; I would go inland.

Behind our camp loomed the mountain shaped like a whale, its black flanks bared by the wind. In the summer we would leave the Land of the Great Whale, journeying through the narrow pass between the mountain's ribs and tail to the low valley beyond, where caribou came to eat lichen and wolves came to hunt the caribou. This early in the season, I'd find neither caribou nor wolves in the valley, but I hoped the Wolf might still favor the place with his presence.

"Go now, Omat. We'll await your return."

I turned to the distant mountains.

"Older Brother!" Puja's voice stopped me in my tracks. "Return to us safe!" Her voice, usually so steady, held a hint of fear. After all, I'd never been on such a journey by myself—few Inuit had. Always we traveled as a family or with a hunting partner.

I turned back to where she crouched on the ground amid the fish. Hunching down beside her, I gave her a quick hug and pressed my nose upon her cheek, breathing in her familiar scent. When I pulled away, I could see the tears pooled in her lower lashes. We didn't need words, my milk-mother and I. I knew she feared not only that I might fail—return without my spirit guide or, worse, never return at all—but also that I might succeed. When I was a full angakkuq, she'd lose her little boy for good. I offered her a confident smile; her own lips twitched upward in return.

When I finally began my journey, I didn't turn around again. But I knew Puja would be sitting there still, watching me go.

I hadn't gone far when Kiasik appeared on the horizon, a small ringed seal thrown across his shoulder. He caught up with me quickly and fell into an easy lope by my side.

"So, you're off for lands unknown." He grinned down at me. "Spirit journeys and angakkuq secrets?"

I kept my expression solemn. "You can't come, Kiasik. I must do this alone."

"Come? Me? Why would I?" he asked a little too sharply. "I'm doing just fine without any angakkuq magic to guide my steps." He patted the head of the dead seal.

"It's a fine catch," I conceded.

He smacked his lips. "I can't wait to eat it. Too bad you'll miss the feast."

"You know I won't be eating much of anything for a long time. Are you trying to torment me?"

Kiasik only laughed. "That's the sacrifice you make for magic," he teased.

"It's worth it," I insisted.

"I hope so, Little Brother."

"It is, Sister's Son."

"Then when I see you again, and you're even skinnier than you are now, I won't worry."

"Since when have you ever worried about me?"

"True. I don't." He flashed me a bright smile to cover the lie, rumpled my hair despite my protests, and strode off toward the camp. As always, both love and envy swam within him like a pair of horned narwhals. I never knew which one would surface first.

But I couldn't worry about my milk-brother today.

I walked the whole of the morning. The spring rains had melted and frozen the snow in turn; my feet either slipped on ice patches or broke through into soft drifts. Sweat pooled beneath my parka. The Sun slid lower in the sky; my shadow stretched out behind me like a long cloak, weighing me down. I stopped, bending double to rest my hands on my kneecaps. I longed for a walking stick to steady my steps, a stream to quench my thirst. A gentle wind brushed my cheek, and I heard Ataata's words on Sila's breath: *An Inuk can always make something from nothing.*

I stuffed a few hard-packed handfuls of snow into my sack and wedged it beneath my bare armpit. As I walked, the snow melted into a few mouthfuls of water that would sustain me until I reached a stream.

When darkness fell, I had no shelter on the open tundra. I had neither knife nor enough hard snow to fashion an iglu, so I stomped on the slushy drifts until they were solid enough to form into a rough wind block. Before I slept, I drew the sinew cord from my boot top and fashioned a small snare. Then I pulled my arms inside my parka and spun my hood around to cover my face. With one mitten beneath my shoulder and one beneath my hip so the parts of me pressed against the cold ground might not freeze, I slipped into unconsciousness.

By dogsled, the journey to the valley would've taken one day, or two at most—on foot it took me nearly four. In that time, I caught only two mewling lemmings in my snare—pitifully small meals, more bones than fat.

By the time I arrived, exhaustion and lack of food had left me dizzy.

Now the hardest part of my journey began.

I found the perfect place—a deep cave on the western side of the whale mountain, its entrance facing the valley. Small, dry pebbles covered the floor. A far corner of the cave held signs of an old wolf habitation—swaths of fur and the scattered bones of caribou and hare. The pack might return to this place later in the spring or summer, but for now, I had it to myself.

I drank the last of my water; I wouldn't drink again until I'd fulfilled my quest. Searching the rocky ground, I chose two stones, one small and white, the other larger and orange-red, both as close to perfect spheres as I could find. With the setting Sun before me and the Moon rising behind, I used my left hand to rub the white stone in a circle atop the red, mirroring the endless orbit of brother and sister in the sky. Three times I completed the circles, and for three days I would await their response. Sun and Moon would send me a helping spirit, and I'd emerge from the cave an angakkuq. Or they would not—and I'd return a failure.

I did not leave the cave for those three days. I did not eat or drink; I did not relieve myself. I sat with legs outstretched, my back to the cave, scanning the long valley before me. The cave protected me from the worst of the wind but also hid me from the Sun's warmth. I sat on my water sack to protect my backside from the ground. I pulled my arms inside my parka, slipping a bare hand up through the neck hole to warm my cheeks and nose. It would be a sad thing indeed if I returned to camp a full angakkuq—with half a face.

I drifted into dreams and visions for much of those three days, and soon I could not tell reality from imagination. *Perhaps*, I reasoned, *in the end they are one and the same.*

In the wind, I heard the voices of the dead—Saartok's beloved, Puja's husband, my own father. I couldn't understand the words, only their despair.

Above my head, the ravens circled, their harsh cries like the screams of women learning of their menfolk's deaths. In the shadows on the face of the faint Moon, I saw Taqqiq's grim visage, and as the Sun sprinted across the sky, I stared straight at her, blinking as visions of Malina flitted across my closed eyelids—a round-faced woman with yellow flowers in her braids and blood where her breasts had been. Even Sila revealed Itself to me—I could see the eddies of the wind, the swirls of cold air and warm forming the hazy outline of a human figure dancing across the snow-covered valley.

Other visions came, ones far beyond my understanding. A one-eyed man with a raven on each shoulder. Another cloaked in lightning bolts, who strode across the surface of the frozen sea, each step drumming like thunder. A third who wavered and shifted like windblown snow, his face always hidden from view. Yet somehow I knew—his eyes swirled with rainbows.

On sunrise of the third day, I no longer felt my hunger. I watched the purple-gold clouds move slowly across the bloody sky, my skin prickling. Something approached.

Still, I didn't notice the Wolf until he was right before me. A huge animal who'd walked straight out of the burning Sun.

Like most wolves in my land, he was pure white, but no one could mistake him for a regular animal. Normal wolves didn't meet a man's eye. Normal wolves didn't stand as tall as an Inuk. From where I sat, he towered above me, looking down with bright yellow eyes, head cocked.

"Singarti...," I breathed, my voice faint and ragged from disuse. The being lowered its snout in acknowledgment. I'd found my spirit guide. What next? Ataata's instructions had ended here.

Suddenly it didn't matter what I wanted to do—all I could do was scream.

Unimaginable pain stabbed through my chest, my gut, my groin. Toppling over, I curled into a tight ball. The Wolf sat back on his haunches and watched me impassively, following my movements with his glowing eyes. Tears coursed down my cheeks, and I reached up to brush them away, embarrassed by my weakness. My hand came away covered in blood.

"What's happening to me?" I gasped. Blood seeped from my eyes, my nose, my ears. When I tried to wipe it away, my skin sloughed off in great sheets, like flesh deadened from frostbite or sunburn. Another sharp stab of pain in my gut, a wetness on my lap. I lifted up my parka in alarm; the red and white coils of my intestines squeezed forth from my navel. Other organs slipped from between my legs, thick lumps of hot kidney and liver and spleen stretching me wide. Only my heart stayed put, each beat pumping another gush of blood down my cheeks and throat, blinding, choking, deafening. I could no longer scream, or see, or breathe...

I awoke to a large tongue laving my face. Through my closed eyelids, I saw a vision from my own past.

I am cradled in the snow, wrapped in white fur. A huge wolf is the whole world. It licks my face, my neck, my stomach, scraping away my mother's blood. Then Puja comes, eyes red with tears, to raise me to her breast and take me home.

A part of me had always wondered if my aunt had exaggerated the story of my birth—now I knew she had not.

I opened my eyes. The blood had vanished not only from my body but from my clothes and the ground as well. I raised a hand to my stomach; everything was in place, as if the events of the morning had never happened.

Singarti lay with his head on his forepaws, his nose close to my own, his yellow eyes searching mine.

Omat.

His mouth didn't move, yet I heard his voice in my head, a noise meant only for a fellow wolf, too high-pitched for humans.

You have died. You have been reborn. As your father was before you. And your grandfather before him. Look around.

I did as I was told, getting unsteadily to my feet. The great Wolf rose beside me, lending me his broad back for support. When we both stood, his head was level with my own.

Breathe out. Breathe in. Release your human soul. Take in the spirit of the wolf.

I obeyed, pushing out my own spirit on a shaky breath. I inhaled: it felt like breathing fire. My neck lengthened, my ears moved, but this time I felt no pain. When I looked down, my feet had become wide-splayed paws. Next to Singarti, I looked a pup, but I was a wolf full grown.

Twilight spread across the valley like the shadow of a raven's wing. The Sun set behind the mountain, turning the snow the purple of new-blossomed saxifrage. Although I'd seen the sight many times before, something had changed. Things didn't look different, exactly; they *smelled* different, the scents sharp and clear enough to taste. The air seeping from the cave behind me was mold and blood, excrement and musk. The air around the Wolf was lightning.

I lifted my nose to the valley. Willow leaves and lichen. A stream carving a tunnel beneath the snow. A whiff of lemming, fox, ptarmigan. What to my human eyes had looked like a barren valley now revealed itself to my wolf senses as a land full of prey.

Though I burned with curiosity, I knew not to ask my guide foolish questions. Only in the direst of circumstances, when survival lay in the balance, might we ask the great spirits for advice, lest they get impatient and refuse to come to our summons. For now, I'd simply follow his lead.

With a single thrust of his powerful hind legs, Singarti left the cave entrance and bounded out across the valley—I followed in his wake. I'd never run so easily on snow. My broad feet did not sink in the drifts nor slide on the ice, but silently skimmed the surface as we dashed along, tails outstretched.

We headed toward the smell of the ptarmigan; as we approached, the odor of its blood lay thick on my tongue. Singarti slowed to a careful stalk. I followed him behind a snowdrift, hiding from our prey. With my wolf's ears, I heard the bird scratching through the thinning snow for food.

We will capture it between us.

His words didn't resound in my mind as they had before. Instead he spoke in the wolves' true tongue: a mixture of gesture, posture, sounds, and odors as intelligible to me as human speech.

Yes. I surprised myself by responding in kind, bowing my head and averting my glance in a gesture of submission.

As one, we leapt from behind the drift and pounced on the skinny bird from either side. A sorry specimen, ragged in the patchy beginnings of its brown summer plumage, but my first kill as a wolf. To kill a bird with my teeth, to feel the hot blood spurting into my throat, was a pleasure beyond anything I'd known. For once, I didn't need to preserve the feathered skin for mitten linings or the fragile bones for sewing needles. An Inuk planned for the future; a wolf lived in the now. Saliva dripped from my jaws as I prepared to tip the bird down my throat, but one direct stare from Singarti froze me in place. The big Wolf seized my muzzle with his teeth, hard enough to hurt but not to draw blood.

I flopped to the ground and dropped the bird at his feet.

Singarti released me. I whined softly, sidling up to him and licking his jaws, tail tucked. *I am sorry for not offering you the kill first, Great Wolf.*

He ate a few bites of the bird—more for show than anything else, I suspected, for how could a spirit wolf feel hunger?—and left me the rest of the carcass. I coughed a bit on the feathers sticking to my tongue, and Singarti's jaws hung open in unmistakable wolf laughter.

Above me, a raven cawed once, looking for a taste. A cunning bird. A pest and a thief. I placed a paw over my kill, but Singarti looked at me sharply, his pupils narrowed in displeasure.

The raven is our ally in this world. We watch where it flies to know where the prey is, and in return, it eats from our kills.

A few scraps of meat still clung to the narrow bones; I grudgingly moved aside. The raven alighted on the carcass, cawed its gratitude loudly in my direction, and began to tear the meat off with its sharp, black beak. White wolf, black raven, an eternal partnership.

When the bird finished its meal, it launched into the sky, rising in lazy circles toward the clouds. I marveled at the ease with which it conquered the bounds of earth.

Go ahead. You are an angakkuq now. You are free.

I breathed out. I breathed in. I became a raven. Legs turned to wings. Snout to beak. My hearing was no longer so acute, but I could see each strand of fur on Singarti's back. Without pausing to think, I swept my wings downward and pushed off with my scaly legs, pressing each talon against the snow. I was aloft.

For a moment, I wobbled in the air, afraid I'd plummet back to the ground—then instinct took over. A warm updraft lifted me higher, and I angled my tail to steady myself, each feather bending and twisting of its own accord. The wind rushed in my narrow nostrils, blowing my feathers tight against my face. Another pump of my powerful wings, another, and I flew as high as the clouds.

Singarti no longer looked so big. Only his black nose distinguished his white form from the white field beneath him. I turned my eyes to the sky. The other raven cawed out. I couldn't understand its tongue, but I knew it wanted me to follow.

We flew over the valley, leaving the Wolf behind. We passed over the entrance to my cave. My time of starvation seemed many winters behind me. The wind off the whale mountain blew cold, pushing us forward. I did as the raven did, allowing the eddies and currents to lift me up and over the highest peak, so we might swoop down the other side. I'd never been up the mountain's flanks. My people always skirted the bottom, for little life existed on the rocky slopes. Even with my raven's vision, I saw no animals. Still, the mountain had a magnificence all its own that I'd never bothered to notice before. From above, its towering flukes were flexed fingers reaching toward the sky. The first meltwater of spring cascaded from the cliffs like poured sunlight.

Beyond the mountain lay the long glacier-carved valley that led to my own home, pressed up against the icy shore. I could see the low mounds of our few qarmait, even see Puja staking a sealskin out to dry and Ataata shaving a caribou antler into a new runner for his sled. And around them—endless expanses barren of humanity. Our home had never seemed so small, so lonely to me. And I had never felt more powerful. Powerful enough, even, to help my people finally escape their solitude.

The Moon had risen, and his wide crescent beckoned me like an outstretched arm. *I will go farther than Ataata ever has*, I decided.

I would visit Taqqiq himself, as the greatest *angakkuit* of my people once had. I would demand that he send other Inuit to our camp.

I pumped my wings and headed for the Moon.

My raven companion slammed against me.

We tumbled downward for a heart-stopping moment before the wind once more caught our wings.

The other bird cawed angrily, nipping at my wing tips. I cawed back and turned sharply to dodge its next blow. It chased me back over the mountain, down its slopes, into the snowy valley. Before me, I could see the cave where my journey had begun. I felt a moment of apprehension: I hadn't bound my limbs as Ataata did during his trances. Would I even have a body to return to?

Swooping into the cave entrance, I landed heavily on unsteady bird legs, relieved to find my slumped form just where I'd left it.

The other raven landed gracefully nearby. I stepped away from it hurriedly, anxious to avoid another attack, but it simply preened its feathers, suddenly content to ignore me.

Taking advantage of the sudden respite, I looked at my human body. Unlike Ataata, who thrashed and trembled in his trance state, I lay motionless. My skin was pale, my breathing invisible, like that of one stripped of his soul. But my fascination subsumed my concern: I'd never seen myself clearly before.

Sometimes, on a summer day, a glimpse of my reflection might waver in a pool of meltwater. A young man had always looked back; despite my lack of a mustache, no woman's tattoos decorated my face or hands, and my parka's small hood and short hem made my sex clear. Now I hopped closer to my body, peering up at this stranger. My jaw was strong for a woman's but still far smaller than a man's. My feathery brows, too large for beauty, looked just like Puja's, and something of Ataata showed in the way my nose met the divot above my lips. The thick lashes that swept my cheeks like a raven's wings must've been a gift from my mother. Tiny moles lay scattered across my high cheekbones—markings no other Inuk in my camp possessed. Puja always claimed her tears had left these shadows on my infant face, but I wondered now if the great spirits themselves had marked me, signaling their favor. I was the chosen of the Wolf, of the Raven, of the Moon himself. How else could I have so easily transcended my human form?

Maybe I don't need to return to my body at all. Why continue life as a man trapped in a girl's body when I could just as easily fly into the heavens or run with the wolves? Then the figure before me twitched, a faint frown passing across its lips, and I recognized Puja's expression in the gesture. My family needed me. Why learn the angakkuq's magic if not to use it for their benefit? The raven stopped its grooming and cocked its head at me. It let out a final croak to push me along.

All right, I thought, *I hear you.* Reluctantly I breathed out the raven spirit and breathed in my own once more. I opened my eyes and found myself back in my own body, disoriented and weak from hunger. Everything seemed darker than I remembered it. The Sun had set, and without my animal vision, I felt nearly blind. Still, I couldn't mistake the approaching glow of yellow eyes.

Singarti growled low and stalked into the cave, his white form aglow in the starlight.

The bird says you tried to fly to the Moon.

"With raven's wings, what's to stop me?"

You are a visitor to the spirit world. You are not of it. Do not journey where you are not wanted. This is the only warning I will give you.

"I can still be a better hunter than any other man. With the power of wolf and raven, I can see farther, run faster—I'll be unstoppable."

Again that rumbling growl, more felt than heard. *Does your grandfather hunt as an ice bear?*

I bowed my head, afraid I knew what he was about to say.

The gift of transformation is a precious one. Do not disrespect it—or it may be taken away. The raven cawed its agreement. I couldn't help scowling in its direction. When I looked back toward my helping spirit, Singarti had disappeared. No footprints marked the snow.

The raven cawed again. I could've sworn it laughed at me. I swiped at the pest, but it hopped backward, easily avoiding the half-hearted blow, croaking all the while. Then it swept up into the sky, its black form quickly dissolving into the surrounding night. I longed to follow it—to fly on my own wings back to the camp and transform before my family's eyes. Once and for all, I could prove to Ququk and Kiasik and anyone else who doubted me that I was strong enough to lead them. But Singarti's words echoed in my mind: I must save my powers for the direst circumstances.

I collected a tuft of wolf fur left on the ground. White as new snow. Carefully I placed the fur in my amulet pouch, where it curled around the walrus carving.

Closing my eyes, I breathed deeply. No longer could I smell with a wolf's nose or hear with his keen ears, but my own senses felt more acute. I remembered Ataata saying that at the height of his powers, he could hear the ice forming from far away and the caribou moving across the tundra.

I listened with my whole being—I heard only a hare scratching through the snow outside the cave's mouth. I lunged to catch it, but my human speed couldn't match a wolf's. I sighed. Right now, the hunger in my belly and the exhaustion behind my eyes prevented further exertions.

It was a long way back to camp on tired human feet.

CHAPTER EIGHT

For the next three summers, as the old men of my camp grew weaker, and we all waited in vain for Saartok to give birth, I honed my skills as an angakkuq. I collected the bones of the animals from the hunt—the feet of the hare, the tusk of the walrus, the beak of the raven—and I felt the spirits of the earth within them. A few times, when starvation loomed, I entered a trance state and flew through the air, seeing my camp spread out below—the hide tents in summer, qarmait in deep winter, igluit on the spring sea ice. When I was a wolf or raven, my senses heightened just as Ataata had once described. I could hear the thunder of caribou, smell the return of spring, feel the slow swell of the tides. I could call upon the animals to surrender themselves to us for a good hunt, or upon the wind to calm while we traveled by kayak and umiaq along the shore of the great ocean. The spirits didn't always obey my commands, but more often than not, they did. Ataata grew older. More and more, the angakkuq's duties fell upon my shoulders.

These were joyful seasons for me, although the lingering cloud of Saartok's barrenness shadowed all we did.

At least Tapsi and Saartok seemed happy together. I felt my first act as a leader of the camp—bringing them together—had been successful. They remained childless, but not for lack of trying. They slept in their own tent, but we could all hear their exertions long into the night. A new sound in the camp. The older men and women rarely touched each other anymore. Occasionally, as had always been the tradition, one of the other hunters' wives would offer herself to Ataata for a night, but whether out of lack of interest or lack of will, my grandfather rarely accepted.

Sometimes, in the morning, as we all crawled naked from beneath the hides, I noticed Kiasik's erect penis. Puja and Ataata would tease him about it until he disappeared somewhere and returned in a much happier mood. Sometimes I'd roll over in the middle of the night to find him beside me, stroking himself. There was no shame in this. Better he satisfy himself than try to take one of the women in the camp, disobeying the agliruti against close relatives lying together.

As I had never reached womanhood, my breasts remained quite small, but neither was I completely a man. Always I felt myself balancing between worlds like a hunter on an ice floe, worried I might tip off and drown at any moment. I soon started wearing my light atigi and trousers to sleep. With my entire family crowded nearby, I found the sleeping furs unbearably hot, but I couldn't lie naked beside Kiasik. I was too scared of what he might be thinking—and what I might think in return. Finally I astounded everyone by building my own small qarmaq so I might sleep alone. No one understood.

"Won't you be cold?" asked Puja.

"And lonely?" asked Ataata.

"It's better this way," I assured them.

As we traveled on foot across the tundra on the summer caribou hunt, I tried to avoid walking too near my cousin. A full-grown man, Kiasik towered over me. His broad shoulders strained the

confines of his atigi. Puja would soon have to make him a new one
from the caribou we killed. He had a thick mustache for so young a
hunter, and he pulled at it when angry or impatient.

He was still the first to leap at any prey, the first to jump upon
a floating ice pan. Sometimes his impulsiveness secured him the
day's best catch—sometimes only an empty game sack and a wet
parka. While Ataata watched with a mixture of pride and dismay,
the women of our camp, old and young alike, watched his loose,
confident gait with the keen interest of falcons tracking their prey.
To my shame, more often than not, I found myself doing the same.

Kiasik was more than my cousin. He was my milk-brother.
Wanting him was little better than Ququk's desire for his own
daughter. And though Kiasik could be brave and generous and
kind, he was also a vain fool. With my man's spirit, I shouldn't
think of such things in the first place. I knew I should want Millik;
her woman's walk, smooth and swaying even over rough ground,
had drawn the other men's attention of late. The radiating lines of
her recent tattoos accented her cheeks and eyes. Her neat braids
reached nearly to her waist, and her father had given her a handsome wolverine pelt for the cuffs of her parka and the border of her
hood. Yet while Kiasik looked at her—I looked at him.

For most of the trip inland, I avoided the problem by walking
far from my milk-brother. Following the signs of foraging, we'd
taken a different path than usual. As we came upon new valleys
and skirted unfamiliar hills, the same thought obsessed us all: perhaps we'd finally discover other Inuit. Then the heat in our bodies
could be released, and children would play once more amid our
tents. Hope made us giddy. The dry ground made us swift. The
long days were filled with laughter, and even when we stopped to
rest, we disdained sleep, spending the sunlit nights telling stories
and playing games instead.

Ipaq, even in his dotage, usually won the strength contests,
although Kiasik occasionally bested him. I excelled at the balance
games, perching on one foot and hand while holding the other leg

extended, walking on the knuckles of my toes, fixing a knife hilt-first in the ground and bending over it backward until my body arched a mere handbreadth from the point.

Only one of our games involved striking another person: the head-butting test. After Ataata and Ququk had competed, gleefully ignoring the women's admonishments to be careful of their old bones, Kiasik rose to choose a challenger. Had he chosen Ipaq, he might have lost; the old man's weight alone would have bowled Kiasik over. Tapsi always flinched away too early; Kiasik would find no joy in defeating him. So, as usual, he chose me.

We faced each other on all fours. A lock of hair fell across Kiasik's flashing eyes; he pursed his lips to blow it away. That just made me stare at his mouth. I'd never noticed before how full his lips were.

Sensing my distraction, he charged toward me, slamming his head against my chest. I grunted but held my ground. He backed away, looking impressed.

"My turn," I said, barreling forward. My shoulder crashed into the hard planes of his stomach. He wheezed through his laughter, staying firmly planted on the ground.

Tapsi shouted encouragement to Kiasik. Saartok cheered for me instead. The others joined in, crowing for more. Back and forth we went, taking turns slamming into each other like musk oxen in rut. My chest ached. I knew I'd wake tomorrow covered in bruises. Kiasik's good cheer had grown thin. He hadn't expected to have to work so hard.

His turn. He pawed the ground and lowered his head.

I forced myself not to flinch as he hurtled toward me. His attack lifted me clear off the ground. My breath knocked away, I crashed onto my back—Kiasik landed on top of me. I could feel his hardness against my leg, even through our trousers. Perhaps only the excitement of the match caused his arousal, but for a brief moment, his eyes burned with a strange fire. More disturbing still, something between my legs twitched in an unfamiliar spasm of pleasant pain.

"A'aa! I give up!"

Kiasik released me quickly, blinking away the interest in his gaze, and I rolled to my feet.

From that moment, he seemed as uncomfortable around me as I did around him. We never spoke of it. No one else noticed the exchange. But I grew even more convinced that we needed to find other Inuit.

As we continued toward the caribou's calving ground the next day, the night's warning hung in my mind. I kept a wary eye on the earth, looking for any sign of other travelers. I found only lichen, fox scat, and the occasional patch of yellow poppies, spinning on delicate stalks to turn their petals to the Sun.

Ataata walked nearby, leaning on his harpoon shaft for support on the uneven ground. He could still walk all day without complaint, but he'd lost much of his speed, and without something to test the ground before him, he became even more hesitant.

"Tell me the story of how our people came to be here, alone on the edge of the world," I asked as we traveled, more to distract him from his aching joints than because I needed to hear the story again. Even if he was tired, I knew he'd comply. An angakkuq never refuses a tale.

He licked his lips, as if considering the story's flavor. A single deep breath, then he began. Even without his drum, his voice took on its old resonance. "My father was a great angakkuq. Some say he could even travel to the Moon itself. When he was still a young man, the whales started moving toward the sunrise. Qangatauq the Raven told him to follow them. The others said only ice lay in that direction, ice so solid it could not crack to allow the animals to breathe. But though Raven is a cunning bird, known for trickery and mischief, he was my father's helping spirit. So he and a few companions set out with their families to follow the whales. Ipaq had just learned to walk, and I was a mere babe beneath my mother's hood. The ice opened before the hulls of our boats, and we traveled that whole summer. When the ice froze again in winter, we were farther than any Inuk had ever been. With every warm season, my father paddled farther, until finally we came here, to the edge of the open sea, where there were no more islands on the horizon. He thought perhaps he'd circled back to the sea of his fathers. But the Sun rose above the waves rather than set, and so he knew this was a different ocean. The waters teemed with life, and his women were tired, so finally he stopped."

"Why do we no longer hunt the whales?" I asked, not for the first time. We saw them spouting sometimes in the distance, but no one from our camp ever ventured after them.

"The knowledge is lost to us. Ququk's father died young. Before I could walk, my wife's father and your mother's grandfather were lost when their umiaq capsized on a whaling trip. And by the time Ipaq and I learned to hunt, our own father had maimed both his arms after falling down a cliff. He described it to us—but that's no substitute for showing. Ipaq and I tried it once, when we were very young and very foolish. The first time we got close to a whale, it nearly knocked over our boat with its head. We knew that if we drowned, there'd be no one left to hunt for our families. Better to take the seal and walrus Sanna offered us freely and not court disaster."

I looked over the tundra, imagining the open ocean instead. "Maybe if we meet other Inuit, they can show us how to hunt the whale."

He smiled gently. "Perhaps."

"And do you ever think of journeying as your father did? Going far to the west? Or south perhaps? Maybe there are rich hunting grounds there as well. Maybe there are even other Inuit?"

"No." Ataata frowned. "My father made many journeys. To the west there is no sea and to the south there is no ice, and so the seals cannot be caught. Uqsuralik doesn't venture there. They are barren lands promising nothing but starvation. No Inuk can live there."

We walked on in silence, his sadness palpable.

In my distraction, I nearly tripped over a large rock in my path. I chided myself for not watching where I was going, then sucked in a breath when I looked more closely. The rock was part of a large, nearly rectangular border around a shallow depression in the earth. Other stones lay in neat rows, dividing the rectangle into two parts, and I recognized the soot-stained slab in the center as a hearth, though I had never seen one inside a qarmaq before. There was no sign of the turf-and-whalebone walls that should've risen above the rocks. Every one of our own qarmait sat upon similar stones, with one vital difference. Our dwellings were circular. Surely my own ancestors hadn't built such a strange straight home.

I knelt down eagerly beside the depression. "Do you think it could be an old campsite built by strange Inuit?" I asked excitedly. Ataata approached more hesitantly, reaching down to touch the flat rocks briefly with his palm.

"No, not Inuit," he said slowly. He raised his palm a hairbreadth above the stones, as if to feel the heat rising from them.

"Do the stones speak?" I whispered.

He winced and withdrew his hand. The rest of our family had stopped to watch us. Before he answered, Ataata looked up at their curious faces. Straightening, he said in a loud, clear voice, "An old dwarf camp."

Everyone hurried over, curious to see a trace of the creatures we'd only ever heard about in stories.

"I thought the dwarfs were like animals," Puja said, crouching beside the neat row of stones.

"Not animals. Not Inuit." Ataata, for once, sounded impatient. "Creatures that look like small men—but are not men at all. Or so the Ice Bear Spirit has told me. They disappeared long before real people came to this land." He lay a hand on his daughter's shoulder. "Come. Don't disturb their spirits."

Never before had I ignored Ataata's wishes, but as everyone

moved away, I couldn't resist lingering at the site a moment longer. The pattern of stones looked like the bones of a fallen animal, moss growing in the crevices where the joints would be. Flowers no bigger than my smallest fingernail dotted the interior with white. So it had always been—life attracted life. Plants grew in the remains of our fires or midden heaps, creating soil where before there was only gravel. More plants would come, then hare and caribou to eat the plants, then Inuk and wolf to eat the caribou, then raven and fox to clean the bones.

I glanced up—everyone had moved on, their backs to me.

I stepped very carefully into the ruin, sending a silent plea to the spirits of the place to pardon my trespassing. One side of the depression was still covered in a pallet of dried willow twigs and moss, just like a sleeping platform in our own sod qarmait.

I placed my hand upon the border of stones; it gave back the Sun's heat, but more than warmth coursed through me. I felt what my grandfather must have: a deep sadness, a great fear. Then I saw it—a shard of ice buried among the moss where no ice should be. I pulled it free. Clear as a frozen stream, but warm to the touch. Not ice at all, but a perfect triangle hammered from a vein of clear quartz, the kind I'd seen running through darker stone like a river through silt. It was shorter than my smallest finger, but a quick touch of its edge proved it as sharp as any slate blade. Unbidden, a vision flashed before my eyes: *blood . . . screams . . . the howling of dogs.*

No dog's howl had ever scared me before, but my gut clenched at the sound.

A pack of wolves moves at the command of men, I knew, *coming to tear me to pieces, coming to kill my child—*

I dropped the quartz blade to the ground, my throat raw with unshed tears, my breath burning my nostrils. The spirits of the dead had possessed me—I heard through their ears.

"Omat!" Kiasik called. His figure was small against the vast mountains, hanging back to wait for me.

"Coming!" I cried back. I bent to pick up the blade, begging its secrets to stay silent for now, and slipped it into my amulet pouch before any more memories could overcome me.

All day, the visions swam through my head. Around me, the faces of my family seemed like those of strangers, as if I saw through the eyes of long-dead dwarfs. Yet the emotions swirling through me were certainly those of a human, not just a small, man-shaped creature. A growing uneasiness twisted my stomach.

Black Mask, laden with tent poles and bundles of hides, came to trot beside me. She'd remained smaller than most dogs, still completely white but for the black that stretched from nose to ears. After surviving that first terrible summer in my childhood, Black Mask had shown such intelligence that she'd become Ataata's lead dog. She was his favorite, and mine, too, yet with the strange memory of snarling dogs still so sharp in my mind, I couldn't bring myself to smile at her or scratch her ears. I could only shudder.

By picking up the strange blade, I'd ignored Ataata's warning and disturbed an evil spirit. I knew I should toss it aside at once. But I didn't. It had a story to tell.

As we walked, I wrestled with the understanding that this land had not always lain empty. Others—not Inuit, perhaps, but some kind of humans nonetheless—had walked across this tundra before us. A sudden hope surged through me: if we were not the first, then surely we would not be the last. We wouldn't be alone forever.

Then again, I realized with a jolt, *if one people can disappear—so can we.*

BOOK TWO

WHALES

The old Inuk stands vigil on his qarmaq roof, watching for the stars that herald the Sun's return, his gaze constantly drawn to the birthing iglu outside his camp, where a child named Omat will soon be born. But he does not watch alone.

Taqqiq the Moon Man also watches the child's birth.

His ascendance is coming to an end—soon he will share the sky with his sister Sun once more. For these last solo journeys, he revels in his power, but he is restless and lonely as well, bereft of the eternal chase.

The Moon sees much from his perch among the stars. He wishes he could see even more. Only for these few days each winter does he circle the earth at full strength without setting. At other times, as his white eye waxes and wanes, so too does his vision.

The Moon does not watch as a man watches. He is not limited in his sight to the Inuit struggling below, calling out to him for help. Instead, he sees the present, the past, and sometimes even the future, all melded into one. He sees far to the west, to the edge of a great ocean, where many Inuit thrive. He sees far to the east, where one lonely band makes its home on the edge of another great ocean—and he knows that they are only the first of many who will one day come to hunt there.

But when he peers across that vast eastern sea beyond the Inuit camp, his sight fails him. He feels a deep dread of this unknown realm. He feels something approaching. Something that threatens his reign. Something more powerful than anything he has ever encountered.

For many seasons Taqqiq has watched the little band of Inuit on the eastern shore with pleasure, for their worship of him spreads his power to the very edge of the known world. But now he looks upon the frozen land and sees a future he did not expect. A future that lies within a tiny girl child born with her mother's dying gasp. Taqqiq cannot see all—he does not know what role this child will play—but he knows that her fate is tied to the unknown evil across the sea. Such a little child, so pale and weak, covered in blood, but containing the potential for untold destruction.

She cannot be allowed to survive.

For nine wanings and nine waxings, he has done his utmost to prevent the girl child from ever being born. First he sent a great tide that shook the ice itself, so the young hunters of her camp would slide to their deaths, joining the Sea Mother's watery realm as her consorts. Then, although the old angakkuq, her grandfather, has worshipped him faithfully, Taqqiq stole away his powers. Now, as the girl is born, he commands the stars themselves to withhold their spirits. The dead, living in the night sky, waiting impatiently to be reborn, will have to wait a little longer. This girl will be born with no soul at all.

The Moon watches as the woman Puja carries the baby girl into the snows. His cold eye gleams on the bloody form. Soon, he thinks contentedly, the child will be no threat to him.

><< >++ +—<

As the Moon looks down from above, Sanna the Sea Mother looks up from below.

Around her the ocean sings. Seals bark and moan. Walruses roar and grunt. The whales whistle and click. The sea ice itself squeals and groans in its slow collisions. But Sanna has ears only for Omat, the handsome young hunter who sits beside her.

His tears shadow his sister Puja's. "My wife is dead," he grieves. "Her spirit ascends now to the stars while I wait here below the sea. Will you let the Moon take my child as well?"

Sanna places her fingerless hand upon his soft cheek, so different from the taut, slick skin of a whale. She longs to scrape her tongue across it and feed on his warmth. Even after three moons with him beside her, she has not sated her hunger for him. The salty-sweet taste of him is like a current eddying just out of reach—if only she could lose herself in its flow, perhaps it would carry her back to her own humanity.

"The Moon sent you to keep me company here in the deep," she reminds him, licking her lips. "Would you have me disdain his gift?"

"Sanna, most beautiful and powerful of all spirits, mistress of the seal and creator of the whale, surely you're more powerful than the Moon!"

Some part of her knows Omat flatters her for his own purposes. She enjoys it nonetheless. Still, he is only an Inuk. He does not understand the ways of the spirit world. "The Moon controls the tides," she explains. "Even I must bend to his will."

"Can no one stop him?"

"Sila the Air, which has always been and will always be. But It does not involve Itself in the world of men."

"And so my child is alone."

She runs her palm across his cheek once more, catching the hot tears before they dissolve into the cold deep. "You cry now. I have cried for an eternity." She sweeps an arm at the dark ocean around them, her movements slow in the weight of the water. "Do you see my tears? So many they cover the world. Your few will be lost amid the boundless depths of my grief."

Yet Omat's weeping does not cease.

Sanna frowns, growing impatient. He is supposed to bring her pleasure. To be a companion whom she controls, not a bird-husband who brings her nothing but misery. "You have no right to be sad in my realm. No grief can compare with my own." She turns her eyes up to the surface. "The Moon has foreseen that your daughter will bring great destruction to this world. Would you ignore his warnings?"

"She's just a child," Omat begs, passing his fingers through her tangled seaweed hair.

Sanna sighs and closes her eyes at his touch. He plays with her—she doesn't care. She has been alone for so long. The waves swell with her quickened breath.

"I will speak to the whales, who will speak to the wolves," she says finally. "The Moon Man has ruled since there were men to worship him. But Wolf and Whale were here long before. They will help the child."

"Thank you, great Sea Mother."

Sanna brushes away his thanks with her fingerless hand, and the ice cracks on the frozen sea. "It is a small thing. What do I care what goes on above when I have you with me here below?"

With another wave of her hand, Sanna restores the old angakkuq's powers so he might protect his camp. Then she whispers to the Whale, who speaks to the Wolf, and Singarti guards the child from the Moon's baleful eye.

The baby breathes the Wolf's hot breath, sucking the life-giving spirit into its breast.

For an instant, the young man smiles at the Sea Mother, and her lips curve in response. He is happy—truly happy—for the first time since he arrived in her realm. His joy is even more delicious than his skin. But in that moment, the baby pulls its father's soul from beneath the waves.

Deep beneath the frozen sea, a cry rings out. A shrill scream more piercing than any whale's whistle. The seals scatter in fear. With useless palms, Sanna clutches at her pale breast and seaweed hair. She has restored the old man's magic. She has allowed the Wolf to save the child. And for all her generosity, see how she is repaid! Omat is gone, returned to the surface to live again in the body of his child.

The waves swell, tumbling Sanna across the sea floor like an empty shell. The Moon has called his tides to punish her for her treachery. She raises her palms in supplication. "Taqqiq, Moon Man, I too am angry! The hunter lied. I will not be so easily deceived again."

"You have let the child live!" he cries. "Now you must help me hunt it down."

The Sea Mother promises to be loyal, shouting her oath through the rocking waters until the tides finally calm and her realm is her own once more. Then, before Taqqiq's ever-turning wrath renews, she flees to a cave deep beneath the waves, out of his reach.

She is alone once more.

⋯ ⋇⋈⋇ ⋯

Inside his iglu, Taqqiq paces. "I long for the day when my sister and I need not share power with creatures such as Sanna and Singarti," he fumes. "They do nothing but stand in our way."

He does not know yet how to rid himself of the other spirits—and with the Wolf to protect it, the child is also beyond his grasp. The Moon fears that his doom draws nearer with each journey he takes across the sky.

But he has ruled for as long as Inuit have dreamed.

He has learned patience.

CHAPTER NINE

𝄐

Ipaq left us. My large uncle, always laughing, had lost all his teeth long before. It was hard for him to eat. The flesh sagged on his frame. He grew weak.

One winter morning, he came back to the camp from fishing through the lake ice with his parka frozen stiff around him. He'd lost his balance and fallen into the water. No Inuk can swim; he'd survived only by grabbing on to his dogs' traces so they could haul him out. After that, he never really recovered. For many days, we brought him what food we could spare and tried to keep him warm. Ataata and I used our medicines and amulets, trying to summon the helping spirits to his aid. But finally Millik came running to our qarmaq, her face wet with tears, and told us her father had disappeared. We found him later that day, sitting up in the lee of a tall ridge, his body as cold and hard as the ice at his back. He'd taken himself there with the last of his strength.

We placed his body, feet facing southward, on a high platform of snow, so it might be safe from the fox and the bear. We walked slowly three times around it in the direction of the Sun.

Day after day, the ravens came and took pieces of Ipaq with

them as they flew into the sky. There, they'd reassemble his spirit as a star. I knew he'd watch over us in the long winter night, but still—I missed his laughter.

Without Ipaq, the spirit of the camp grew heavy. Ataata seemed older, using his walking stick to make sure of himself rather than of the ice beneath his feet. Ququk's frown was etched upon his face, as deep and permanent as a scar.

The Moon of the Sun's Rising failed to bring the usual relief. Despite the increasing daylight, we felt spring would never arrive. We built snow igluit on the landfast sea ice and readied our dog-sleds and harpoons, but the seals didn't come to us as they usually did. Ataata said our grief for Ipaq kept the animals away; seals always refused to give themselves to those who didn't enjoy the hunt. Not everyone believed him. We knew that bad luck came to those who disobeyed an agliruti. If the seals stayed away, then someone must be to blame.

I stood beside my seal hole, staring down at the piece of dark feather on the slim probe until my back ached and my feet grew numb, watching for the slightest movement that might indicate a seal's breath. Never before had hunting on the sea ice seemed so torturous. I'd seen more than eighteen winters; I understood the importance of patience. But something in me knew this hunt was hopeless.

Every time the dogs sniffed out a breathing hole, I closed my eyes and whispered the seal's secret name. If the animal had swum nearby, I'd have heard its response. And yet I heard nothing.

No ice had covered my breathing hole when we arrived, a sure sign that a seal had recently gnawed its way to the air. Standing on a square of bear fur to protect my feet from the chill, I bent low, resting my elbows on my knees and gazing fixedly at my feather. But even as I watched, the frost began to spread. Wind no longer rippled the surface. No seal came to break the thin crystal skin. Soon the hole would disappear entirely.

I glanced up at the Sun; it hung low in the sky, its shape distorted, flattened like a wavery egg yolk. I rose finally, rubbing the small of my back, and looked over at the other three hunters crouched over their own holes. Ataata saw my movement and stood, moving slowly. Even to his weak eyes, my defeated posture spoke volumes. But as badly as my own back ached, I could only imagine his pain.

"Come," he said to the others. "We go back to camp."

Kiasik looked up in shock. No one ever spoke during a seal hunt, for the slightest sound would scare off animals alert to the ice bear's footsteps. He glared at his grandfather, then at me, and then at the Sun. Of us all, only he didn't look tired. He always believed a fat seal was wending its way toward him. "There's still light enough."

"But there are no seals," I said wearily.

"You can't know that." He clutched his harpoon, his knuckles white.

"I've listened, and they're not here."

"Then call them! If you're so wise that you can speak to seals, tell them to come to us." Hunger made him angry. Like the rest of us. We'd had no fresh meat for many days, and our supplies of frozen caribou and dried char ran low. We missed Ipaq, our most able fisherman.

"They're not here to be called," Ataata said softly, walking back to his sled. "We cannot fight what we cannot change."

"I'm not giving up!" Kiasik shouted at his grandfather's departing back. I turned to stare. A grown Inuk should never raise his voice to an elder. I'd never wanted so much to shake him.

Ataata didn't turn, simply continued to load his sled. When he spoke, I could hear the smile in his words. "Little Grandson, go ahead and stay if you want. We will still have no seals to eat, but we may have frozen Kiasik to fill our bellies." He laughed at his own joke, and I managed a grin for my grandfather, but Kiasik, who knew well the reproach hiding in Ataata's words, now refused to back down.

"You and Ququk are old men, Grandfather. If your bones are cold, go home."

"You go too far, Sister's Son," I warned him. "You don't know what you're saying."

"I'm saying *I* won't let my mother starve."

If I were a sled dog, the hair on my back would have stood up straight. Puja's survival was as much my responsibility as his. "You cannot catch a seal with foolishness," I snarled.

"Foolishness!" He snorted. "I call it strength. So go on back to camp, Omat—if your woman's flesh is too weak."

I knew he spoke thoughtlessly, driven by desperation and hunger. That didn't stop my heart from thrashing inside my chest. I felt like a storm-tossed raven, helplessly flapping my wings against Sila's merciless breath. There'd never been violence among the members of our band—we made our harpoons to pierce the skin of beasts, not men—but my hand balled of its own accord.

"Come," Ataata said, his voice still composed. "We'll return to camp, and Omat and I will call upon our spirit guides to help us."

"I'll stay," Kiasik insisted. "Maybe the seals will return once you're gone."

Blood flushed my cheeks. To say the seals would come once we left meant that our presence brought bad luck—that somehow the spirits punished us. I waited for Ataata to refute him. Instead, Kiasik's words hung in the air like a heavy fog that refused to lift—until even I had to admit he might be right.

We were used to the threat of starvation. Sometimes we caught prey easily; sometimes the prey made us wait patiently for many days. But never before had it seemed as if the seals avoided us on purpose. Whenever we found a breathing hole that looked newly visited, no seal returned to it. I'd set traps for fox, but the bait remained untouched. Even the lemmings somehow knew to avoid our snares. Something—or someone—had told the animals to stay away from us.

We left Kiasik next to a breathing hole, a small, dark form bent at the waist against the white expanse.

Ataata's dogs seemed eager to get home again, and the journey was short. I felt a spark of hope that Uqsuralik or Singarti might have the answers we sought.

I never got the chance to find out.

As I staked Ataata's team for the night, I watched for Kiasik's sled. Despite the tension between us since the summer games, he remained my closest friend—my only friend, in truth.

In the last glimmers of twilight, the sky gleamed like a cluster of wet blueberries ready for picking. Soon the Moon would shed enough light for traveling, but no sane Inuk would choose to journey at night if he could avoid it. This was a familiar feeling— waiting for Kiasik to return home so I might tell him all would be well—and yet I didn't resent my role. He had done the same for me when we were children. He was my milk-brother, after all, and my cousin and my sister's son, too. Sometime, in the not-too-distant future, the two of us would have to provide for the whole camp. We needed each other. No Inuk hunts alone for long.

I pulled off Black Mask's harness and ran my hands through her thick fur, scratching at the base of her tail until she pressed her flank against me in pleasure. Although gray now flecked her muzzle, she still led Ataata's team. "How do you do it?" I asked. "Leading all the other dogs even though you're half their size?"

She panted at me and blinked. Not much of an answer. On my spirit journey, I had understood Singarti, but wolves and dogs do not speak the same tongue. Still, as I unfastened the other dogs' harnesses and combed out their tangled traces, I started to understand. The lines all led to the fan hitch at the front of the sled. Black Mask had the longest rope so she could run in front. The other lines were each a different length to distribute the weight among the dogs. And although the lines all fed through the same hitch, although all pulled the same sled, no dog was tied to another. Fanned out across rough ice, each had enough slack to move at its own pace, to find its own way, to avoid its own obstacles. If a dog stopped to shit or sniff or scratch, the momentum of the sled would eventually yank it forward. Black Mask's job was simply to keep the team headed in the right direction.

"I can do that," I murmured, more to myself than to the dogs.

Black Mask yipped. Not agreement, but alarm. I followed her gaze to the horizon.

The long-awaited sled appeared. First just a speck; then, as it turned to skirt the base of an ice hummock, the shape stretched out into a ribbon of dogs and cargo. My breath caught in my throat; too many dogs, too long a sled to belong to Kiasik. And then, instead of one strange sled, there were two.

"Strangers!"

I ran toward the iglu, stumbling in my panic, and ducked my head inside. "Ataata! There are strangers coming!"

By now our dogs had caught the scent of the strange teams and joined their frantic howling to my own cries. They pulled at their leads, cracking the ice that held the stakes in place. Ataata and Puja crawled out of the iglu to join me. The other families hurried close behind.

Puja clutched her arms across her chest. Never had she looked so thunderstruck—or so excited.

Ataata grinned broadly. "The Ice Bear has answered my prayers before I could even speak them. Our luck has changed!"

Ququk whipped the dogs until they quieted, then turned brusquely to Ujaguk. "Go. Prepare what food we have for the visitors. Or has it been so long that we've forgotten our hospitality?" His wife scurried inside their iglu.

"Ququk is right!" Ataata clapped his mittens together. "They'll be hungry after their journey. Bring fish and meat to my iglu. We'll feast them properly."

"Can we spare the food?" I couldn't help asking.

"The spirits wouldn't send us such good fortune if they weren't pleased," he chided me. "We must light our lamps and put them close to the windows so our guests will see the glow and know where to come."

Soon I was alone again outside the igluit. Everyone else had hurried inside to prepare. I waited, watching the strangers approach across the flat white expanse. Distance is deceiving on the frozen ocean; though I could see the two sleds clearly, I had a long wait before they arrived. By the time they reached us, the Moon, already full and bright above the horizon, would rule the sky.

The dogs paced on their leads, tails up, noses sniffing the wind. Black Mask whimpered a little, and I put a hand on her head.

"I know. I'm excited, too."

Ataata often told tales of life in the distant camp of his birth, before his father had led his family on their long journey. It sounded like a magical place to me, full of children and hunters. Sometimes they met other families for a season, allowing the young people to play and mingle—and sometimes to marry. If their hunting failed, Inuit from a neighboring camp would bring them food from their own caches. And every Moon When Birds Fly South, many families would come together at the shore so the men could ride out in their umiaq and hunt the whale.

As a child, I often dreamed of strangers appearing over the crest of a hill. I imagined running to greet their sleds, then feasting them long into the night while they shared new songs and dances. In the morning, they'd announce a whale hunt, and Kiasik and I, of course, would go with them.

I could hear them coming now, their runners squeaking over the ice, their dogs panting, the rough voice of a man calling commands to his team.

As my family emerged once more to meet our visitors, clouds scudded across the Moon, dousing his light, but the women had added extra moss to the lamp wicks; a warm yellow glow poured through the ice windows and limned the chinks between the snow blocks. Puja stood beside me, her lower lip pulled up in a familiar half smile, half frown that meant she was happy and concerned all at once. Ataata's expression held no such ambivalence. Clutching his bear claw in his fist, he murmured his thanks to Uqsuralik.

The strangers arrived through the darkness as if through a heavy fog. At first we saw only the lead dog trotting toward us with its tongue lolling. A whip whistled past its ear. Then the other dogs appeared in a wide fan, straining at their traces.

And then, finally, the sled itself came into view, laden with furs and meat. Among the cargo, two women huddled close together beneath a thick bear pelt. Last, the hunter, running behind with the whip. Long white fox tails streamed from the neck of his parka.

"Hoa!" He called his dogs to a halt and slammed the ice hook into the ground. His team jerked to a stop out of reach of our own tethered dogs. All the animals yowled and whined as if tormented by evil spirits.

We barely knew where to look first: The sled laden with caribou and seal meat that promised an end to our hunger? The fine parkas and large dog team that would bring prosperity and luck to our own hunting? The strangers themselves, future wives or husbands who might allow the continuation of our people? Then all our attention snapped toward one sound: a whimper, a cry. A puppy, I thought. Then Puja gasped and took a hurried step forward. One of the women on the sled reached behind her head, into her voluminous hood, and drew out a squalling infant. The first baby I'd ever seen.

"Anaana?" A high-pitched voice rose above the infant's wailing, a child asking for her mother. "Are we going to rest now?" A little girl peered out from behind the other woman on the sled.

I was no judge of children's ages, but she looked only a few winters out of her mother's hood. Two children in our camp, when for so long there had been none.

Ataata raised both hands overhead, letting his sleeves fall away from his wrists to show he had no weapons. "You arrive," he greeted them. His broad smile belied the formality of his words.

The hunter, his face still shrouded in darkness, stepped out from behind the sled, raising his arms in return. "I arrive." His voice rasped as if he'd once been caught by the throat and had never recovered.

Ataata introduced himself and then the rest of us. When he got to me, he said proudly, "This is Omat, my grandson, also an angak-kuq." A sudden sound caused him to lift his head. Two more sleds, the first one familiar. "Aii! And this is Kiasik, my other grandson. A great hunter! Look at the fine seal he caught. I knew our luck had changed!" Indeed, a large male bearded seal lay across the sled. On any other occasion, Kiasik would have grinned with pride, but tonight he simply stared dumbfounded at the strangers before us. When he finally tore his gaze from them, he looked to me, his slow smile of astonishment matching my own. Our argument at the breathing holes meant nothing now. We would face these new arrivals as we faced everything else: together.

Wobbling under the weight of a small, fat umiaq, the other new sled finally arrived. Two more young men—one spindly as a crane, one stout as an owl—ran beside it. They looked to the driver of the first sled, waiting for him to speak.

The leader finally pushed back his hood, smoothing the fox tails at his throat into a handsome symbol of his hunting prowess. The clouds moved from the Moon as if Taqqiq had blown them aside with a mighty breath, and cold white light illuminated the man's face. A long, drooping mustache made his pointed chin even lon-ger. High cheekbones and low, thick brows crowded his narrow eyes. He was a man, I thought then, defined by his mouth. His lips were dark. On that first night, they looked almost black. But in the sunlight, they would shine bright and red, like those of a man just finishing a feast of fresh-killed meat.

"I am Issuk. We come following the whale."

CHAPTER TEN

⨏

The press of bodies kept Ataata's iglu warm, and everyone, except me, sat naked or nearly so. We ate Issuk's caribou carcasses frozen, barely stopping to wipe our lips with ptarmigan wings. Never had meat tasted so good.

Our fears seemed at an end.

The stouter of Issuk's companions, Onerk, seemed more interested in his meat than anything else. With his insatiable appetite, small eyes, and dim expression, he reminded me of the fat sharks we sometimes saw prowling the coast: slow and stupid until they ripped the prey from our nets. Issuk's other hunting partner, Patik, was younger. He moved well despite his gangly frame, and a ready smile revealed a gap between his two front teeth. Millik glanced constantly in his direction, flicking her long braid from one shoulder to another like a dog in heat wagging its tail.

Issuk claimed both the strange women as his wives, further proof of his great skills as a hunter. The younger one, bright-eyed Kidla, wore her hair looped in two braids around her ears, showing off the roundness of her cheeks and jaw. She popped one large, dark nipple from her baby's mouth and shifted the child to her other full breast. The older, more homely wife was the mother of the little girl who now scampered around the iglu, garnering the cooing praise of everyone in our camp. Saartok's eyes followed the child as a hunter's might follow a hare.

We ate and rested and ate again. The blood dripped across our chins; we licked it greedily from our fingertips. The meat satisfied the hunger in our bellies—the strangers eased an ache much deeper.

I watched them with an intensity usually reserved for the shifting sea ice, as if by observing I could come to understand. Their clothes were like ours—except where they were not. Heavy fringe bordered the women's parkas; the men wore ivory circles in their earlobes. Their words were familiar, but I didn't always understand the intention behind their speech. I had to decipher their gestures and expressions as I might those of a caribou or wolf. Exhausted and exhilarated by the effort, I finally dragged myself outside to piss. The Moon had already journeyed halfway across the sky. He hung above me now, full and heavy.

"Thank you, great Taqqiq," I murmured, "for ending our solitude."

After the cold air outdoors, the iglu felt unbearably stuffy when I returned. Issuk wiped a drop of meltwater off his forehead and looked up with concern. The ceiling above him shone wetly, reflecting the lamplight. "Aren't you afraid this snow house of yours will melt away on top of you?"

"Of course not," Kiasik replied. "We don't usually have so many people inside, so it's weeping a little, but it'll freeze back up soon enough."

"How did you build it?"

"The same way we always do," said Kiasik, confused.

"We've never seen anything like it," tall Patik explained, running a finger down the iglu wall. His fingertip came back stained with soot, leaving a bright streak of clean snow behind.

We all exclaimed in wonder, unable to imagine hunting on the sea ice without a snow iglu to shelter in, yet Issuk's band had done so for many moons.

"What do you build when you travel in winter?" demanded Kiasik. He was rude to interrogate our guests, but they didn't seem to mind.

"We make a windbreak of ice or snow," Issuk answered. "We turn our umiaq upside down, or use our sled for shelter."

"Nothing as secure or warm as this," Patik interjected.

"Come!" my milk-brother crowed. "Come outside so we can show you!"

"Alianait!" the cry went up. "Come and see!"

Heavy with food but invigorated by the chance to show off our skills, we clambered from the iglu. Kiasik explained our building process eagerly, with interjections from all. I was content to let him brag a little, grateful that our conflict was over. How could Kiasik accuse me of bringing bad luck when the spirits had finally granted our most fervent wish?

Soon we were all wielding our long snow knives to build an iglu for Issuk's family. Before we could finish, however, Tapsi drew forth our old ball—a fist-size globe of sealskin stuffed taut with moss—and we began the kicking game. For many winters, since the old men had grown too frail for such pleasures, only Millik, Tapsi, Kiasik, and I had played. Now a whole herd of us kicked the ball back and forth under the moonlight, trying never to let it touch the ground. Both of Issuk's wives joined in. Saartok stood to the side, Kidla's little baby snug against her back, its round face peeking from beneath her capacious hood. She bounced on her toes to soothe its whimpers. I couldn't decide if she cried from sorrow or joy.

Puja watched over Nua, the little girl, offering her a doll of carved antler that once belonged to Millik. I hadn't seen it since I was a child, when Kiasik had chided me for playing with it. Nua happily built her own tiny approximation of a snow iglu to shelter her new friend.

Despite the darkness, we acted sun-mad—as if we'd stayed awake for days of unending summer light, our energy boundless, feeling no fatigue.

The kicking game soon degenerated into a chaotic contest of tag. Millik squealed as gangly Patik seized her around the waist and swung her in a wide arc. Together they collapsed onto the ground, breathless with laughter. Kiasik grabbed Issuk's younger wife, Kidla, by the sleeve of her parka. She spun into his grasp, flashing a broad smile of white teeth before wiggling loose and dashing off across the ice.

While we played, Ataata and Ququk patiently completed the new iglu. Puja showed little Nua how to pack loose snow into the chinks so no wind could get inside. I remembered well her teaching me to do the same thing. I went to help, fitting a clear ice window into the spiraling pattern of snow blocks.

When it was done, Ataata and I sat atop the roof, watching the others play. His hand drifted to the black bear claw at his throat, and his lips moved in a soundless murmur.

"You're thanking Uqsuralik for sending us visitors?" I guessed.

"I've already done that," he said with a chuckle. "Now I thank the dwarfs for teaching our family to build igluit from snow. It's good to offer Issuk such a fine gift in return for the meat he brings us."

"The dwarfs taught us?" This was a story I had never heard. "I thought they disappeared long before our ancestors arrived here."

But for once, Ataata didn't offer me a tale. He didn't even seem to hear my question.

The game had slowed now, everyone panting and laughing, their eyes still bright even as their limbs dragged. Issuk's older wife collected her daughter and headed back inside Ataata's iglu with Puja. Soon Kiasik and Kidla followed, chatting merrily.

"This reminds me of my father's camp," Ataata said to me, smiling. "The nights were long and full of play. No one would decide to start a game, it would just begin. Just as easily, it was over. We ate, we talked, we played, we slept. When we awoke, if the weather was good, we hunted. If not, we would sleep again, or talk, or play some more." He turned and took my hand in his own. "Your life hasn't been so simple, Little Son. Too few hunters. But now, it'll get easier. You'll see."

That was the last time I trusted Ataata's words. It was the first time he'd been wrong.

CHAPTER ELEVEN

꒔

We followed the others back into the iglu. Ququk drowsed through half the conversation and even Puja's eyes drooped with weariness. But the younger people showed no sign of needing rest. We were eager to learn as much from our guests as we could. Issuk told stories of the whale hunt, interrupting even my grandfather to brag of his exploits on land and sea. I found such boasting unsettling but reminded myself that much these Inuit did was strange to me.

Although she'd seemed cheerful enough with Kiasik, Kidla never spoke a word in her husband's presence. Silently she pulled meat off the bone and handed it to him in generous portions. Her enormous, dark eyes followed his every move.

When Issuk leapt to his feet to demonstrate his technique with the harpoon, his young daughter flinched and shrank back. Though more composed, the girl's mother, Uimaitok, also sat silently, her eyes trained on the sewing in her lap.

Still, the ways of women were not my concern. They must be bored by stories they'd heard before. I, on the other hand, dreamed of the whales we might hunt with Issuk at our side. Finally we'd have new jawbones to strengthen our qarmait's walls, baleen to fasten our tools, and, best of all, the delicious whaleskin the elders spoke of so wistfully. The hand of Taqqiq must have guided Issuk and his men to us.

"We traveled east for many moons, always following the black whale," explained the hunter. "In the summer, we found them in great numbers, far to the north. Then, in the fall, they began to move south. We followed."

"Where are they now?" Kiasik asked.

Issuk waved a hand. "At the ice edge."

"Where's that?" Kiasik spoke for us all. In the Moon of the Sun's Rising, we had never seen the end of the ice. The whole sea lay frozen before us, and we wouldn't see open water again until late spring.

"I haven't seen it yet." Issuk's mouth twisted on the words, as if he were loath to say them. "But that's where whales always live in the winter, and they were swimming south when we saw them last. We thought to move quickly and follow them, hunting as we went. But the ice buckled and rose, and our sleds were slow. I didn't understand why the spirits would punish us, but now I think it was so we could teach your people to hunt the great whale." Murmurs of excitement all around. Issuk looked pleased. "The ice here is smooth. The traveling will be easy. But we must hurry or the whales will be on the move again."

"Open water…in winter?" I asked, remembering Ataata's story of his own father's journeys to the south. His warnings of a barren land without ice. "You will find nothing but starvation there."

Issuk frowned. "I know the sea and the whale, boy. Better than you. You should not—"

"No ice means no seals, no seals mean no bears, no bears mean no fox, no raven, no wolf. There will be emptiness. Stone and snow. That's all," I insisted. He glared at me and I glared back; suddenly the warmth of the iglu felt suffocating.

"Who are you to question—"

"I am an angakkuq—"

"Omat," Ataata interrupted. His tone, soft but firm, silenced me. Issuk was our guest and a gift from the spirits. "Come," my grandfather continued, "we should have more games to celebrate our new friends."

"Head butting?" proposed Kiasik brightly, hoping to show off his skill.

"Maybe a song-singing competition?" offered Puja. I silently thanked her for suggesting something I was good at.

"We play a good game among my people," Issuk declared. "I'll teach you."

The rules were simple. One man would hit the other as hard as he could upon the temple. They would take turns until only one remained standing; then the winner faced the next challenger.

I shrank back against the iglu wall, remembering my discomfort during our summer games when Kiasik's body pressed against my own. I felt even more keenly that I didn't understand these new Inuit. Issuk's proposal—and our brief confrontation—left me uneasy. One might emerge from the head-butting game with a sore chest and an aching scalp, but we never tried to injure each other.

Issuk went first. "I'll challenge every man here, and I will win every time."

Kiasik leapt to his feet. "I'll do it!"

Issuk eyed him doubtfully. "And what will you wager?"

"Wager?"

"Don't you bet on your games? You're missing half the fun! You bet something, and if I win, I get it. If you win, you get what I wagered."

Kiasik looked confused for a moment, but then he opened his amulet pouch and removed his tiny seal carving. He had nothing else to call his own.

"This carving was made by our great angakkuq after my first hunt. It brings me luck and calls the seals."

I placed a hand protectively on my own amulet, feeling the tiny tusks of my walrus carving pricking through the sealskin. I would never surrender it.

Issuk's eyes narrowed. "You must be very sure of yourself to wager such an item." He cocked his head, thoughtful. "If you win, I'll lend you Kidla for the night to warm your bed."

My stomach clenched. Kiasik's lips parted as he stared at the young woman.

We pulled our legs up onto the sleeping bench to make room on the floor. Kiasik and Issuk stood a few feet from each other. As the host, Kiasik would hit first. The stranger calmly pushed his hair behind his ear, baring his smiling profile and bracing his legs for the impact. Everyone leaned forward eagerly, the lethargy of the long night extinguished. Kiasik pulled back his fist and took a few practice swings at the air in front of Issuk's nose. He didn't flinch.

Finally Kiasik threw his entire weight behind a blurring punch that cracked squarely on the other man's temple. Issuk's head snapped to the side. He stood staring at the ground for a breath and then straightened, still smiling, seemingly impervious to the pain. A murmur ran through the crowd. Puja's hand crept into mine.

Kiasik looked shaken, but he braced his feet for Issuk's punch and turned the side of his face toward his opponent. Issuk didn't need a practice swing. With one swift jab, he laid Kiasik flat on the ground, unmoving. Puja's shrill gasp sounded above the excited clamor. My own fear forgotten, I hurried to my brother. Shallow breaths lifted his bare chest. I slapped him lightly on his uninjured cheek. His eyes fluttered open, and in the moment before he hardened his gaze, I saw fear—and shame—cross his face. He pushed away my help and heaved himself to his feet. Dizzy—but alive.

Issuk held out his hand, palm up.

Slowly Kiasik removed the seal carving from his pouch and handed it to Issuk.

My voice rose over the shocked chatter. "That amulet won't work for you."

Issuk lowered his brows. "Who are you to know such a thing?"

"An angakkuq," I insisted, aware that I was repeating myself. Frustration crept into my voice. "That amulet was carved for Kiasik and will protect him alone." I deepened my tone and stood as tall as I could, willing myself to seem wider than my slim frame, suddenly aware that he might see me as something other than a hunter like himself. Ataata coughed, warning me to proceed with caution.

Issuk stood silently a moment, then let out a laugh. "I am the favorite of Taqqiq himself, the Moon Man! I don't need an angakkuq's amulet when *he* guides my harpoon. Sanna quails when she sees me coming, and the Ice Bear hides his nose in the snow!"

His own band laughed with him, but my family shifted nervously to hear Issuk deride the great Uqsuralik, to whom we owed our very survival.

"Would you like to wager to get it back?" Issuk demanded. "You'll be an easy challenge."

"I accept," I said quickly. I stepped to the front of the iglu.

Ataata spoke. "Omat—"

"I'm ready." I tensed the muscles of my stomach and planted my legs firmly. *Help me, Singarti*, I prayed. *Give me your strength and swiftness, your keen eyes and fierce bite.*

Issuk raised his arm, his fist clenched. In the lamplight, his red lips shone wetly.

I looked away, awaiting the strike.

From the corner of my eye, I saw the oncoming punch whirring toward me—and I knew in that instant that Issuk would bring us nothing but grief.

I swiftly shifted my weight and raised my own arms, grabbing his fist in my hands to stop the blow. The iglu erupted in protest. This was not how the game was supposed to be played—I shamed my whole camp through my cowardice.

I met Issuk's wide eyes as I pried his fingers open. Too late, he realized my intention. He tried to pull away, but I'd already yanked the short piece of antler from his closed fist. I held it aloft.

"This is why his punch is so powerful. This man must cheat to win!"

Issuk lunged toward me, but I stuck out a foot and let his great weight fly harmlessly over my outstretched leg. Patik and Onerk sprang to his defense, but my own people, their faces pale with anger, restrained them from joining in. Issuk grabbed my leg and I crashed beside him. My grandfather didn't intercede; when I'd accepted the role of an angakkuq, I also accepted its challenges. Ataata wouldn't protect me.

We rolled across the fur-covered floor, each scrabbling for the other's throat. From afar we must've looked like lovers wrestling in their sleeping hides. Issuk let go for a moment, just long enough to punch me hard in the face. Even without an antler in his fist, the blow brought stars to my eyes. I rolled away, attempting to gain my feet, but Issuk caught me by the corner of my atigi. When I rose up, the sinew threads ripped, and the caribou hide flapped open, leaving one breast—small and high, but unmistakably female—exposed.

A shocked inhalation from Issuk's band. He dropped my atigi as if it were covered in boiling seal oil.

"Woman!" he spat through gritted teeth, the word a curse. He rose to his feet. "*Now* who's the coward here?" He glared around the iglu. "You need a woman to fight for you."

I clutched the ends of my torn atigi across my chest and somehow found my voice. "I carry a man's spirit," I began, but Issuk cut me off with a short, derisive laugh.

"If all men had tits as nice as yours, I'd lie with them more often!"

Patik and Onerk roared with laughter. Kiasik did not. But neither did he defend me.

Leaning heavily on his harpoon shaft, Ataata stood. Silence fell. "Omat is an angakkuq." His voice was stern. "Beware the spirits who protect my son."

"One angakkuq is a woman, the other an old man who barely uses a harpoon anymore," Issuk scoffed. "I'm not worried. Does this camp have no one who can bring down a whale?" He thrust out his chest. "Tomorrow I go to hunt. Who will come with me?"

"Sanna will not yield up her gifts to one who doesn't respect the angakkuq!" To my shame, my words squeaked out. A woman's high-pitched complaint.

Issuk spun toward me. "And one who doesn't respect the balance of man and woman, but tries to be both at once?"

He didn't wait for my response, but turned instead toward Kiasik, Tapsi, and Ququk. "You—men of this camp. You've been too long hungry and too long weak. Come with me tomorrow, and I'll show you rich hunting. We'll load our sleds high with seal. Then whoever is brave enough will come with us to the whale hunting grounds. When we return, our umiaq piled high with bones and baleen, Onerk and Patik will marry your women." Millik clutched her hands tight, as if to stop from clapping aloud. Puja looked to me, eyes wide and scared. *She's the only other unmarried woman here,* I thought. *And she doesn't want to share Onerk's bed.*

But Issuk wasn't done. "And I'll finally teach this angakkuq of yours how to be a real woman!"

I choked on fear. *He's not talking about Puja,* I realized. *He's talking about me.*

Issuk tossed Kiasik's seal amulet at my feet. "Here! You can have it back. I don't need it—but you will." With that, he strode across the iglu and crawled swiftly through the tunnel. His wives and companions quickly followed. To my horror, Kiasik and Tapsi rose to join them.

All my childhood dreams of whale hunting lay shattered like slate. But I refused to give up the role I'd fought so long to assume. "Issuk will bring nothing but woe to us all," I warned, steadying my voice. "We must not go south, to the iceless lands."

Kiasik rounded on me. "Would you have us surrender the

chance of surviving through the winter to save your own pride? We're too many women and too few men. The seal meat's almost gone. Grandfather"—he softened his tone as he turned to Ataata—"you were a great hunter once." This time he didn't say the rest. He didn't need to.

Ataata just stood there. He'd known this day was coming for a long time. No man too old to hunt could lead a camp for long. But he'd thought I'd be the one to replace him—not this strange whale hunter from the west.

"Listen." Kiasik addressed the entire gathering. "We went today to hunt at the breathing holes, but the seals swam away the moment we arrived."

I felt suddenly unsteady, like a child trapped in a rushing stream, fighting a current that could rip me off my feet at any moment. *No,* I begged silently, *please stop talking.*

Kiasik went on, merciless. "But when the others returned to camp, I stayed behind. As soon as Omat left, a giant bearded seal rose through a breathing hole at my feet and offered himself to me. And now Issuk has come, another gift from the spirits, to teach us to hunt the whales and to bring us more good fortune."

"What are you saying?" I spared a glance at Ataata, at Puja, but both were silent, their eyes on Kiasik.

He took a breath. "Perhaps Issuk is right. We've let you live as a man too long—every time you throw your harpoon, you break the agliruti against women hunters."

Before I could find the words to respond, Ququk broke in. "I always said as much. Our lives are perilous enough already—we should never have risked the wrath of the spirits by allowing her to hunt."

I tried to stand tall. But keeping my atigi clutched across my chest forced me to hunch forward like a weakling. "Do all my seasons bringing you seal and walrus and caribou count for nothing?" I managed. "You'd turn against me now—because of a stranger?"

"We haven't turned against you," Ataata said quietly. How could I have doubted he'd defend me? "But...perhaps Kiasik is right. Perhaps you should stay behind. Just for tomorrow."

My tongue felt thick in a mouth suddenly dry, unable to form words of anger or entreaty.

"The seals have stayed away," Ataata went on gently. "Now they're back. And Issuk says he has the ear of Taqqiq."

"And you believe him? A cheater? A braggart?"

"I don't know," he admitted with a sigh. "But we must be careful with things we don't understand. He follows the whale, a creature we gave up hunting long ago. I don't ask," he continued, taking a step closer to me, "that you change who you are—just that we be cautious."

I wouldn't challenge him further in front of the others, but my fury was clear.

"Tonight you will speak to the Wolf Spirit," he offered in consolation. "We will do as he advises."

That was good enough for Kiasik. He left the iglu to prepare for the morning's hunt, followed by Ququk, Tapsi, and the others. Puja, Ataata, and I remained, the sudden silence broken only by my own ragged breathing.

Finally Puja said, "Issuk laughs, but his eyes are cold. He won't forgive you for embarrassing him."

"I can defend myself," I answered shortly, still stung by my family's betrayal. "I'll call upon the spirits to help me."

"And if they don't heed your call?" She'd never questioned my abilities before.

"They can't refuse me." Though I felt as wobbly as a new-fledged chick, I forced my voice to remain calm. "Ataata. You promised me that as long as I didn't bleed like a woman I wouldn't have to live as one. Even then, you said, I'd have a choice. Now you turn your back on me."

Never before had I accused him of failing me. My grandfather flinched as if from a blow. "But Kiasik may be right. The spirits may be angry. All I ask is that we be careful."

I couldn't stand to look at them. I crawled into the tunnel and pulled on my over-trousers, boots, and outer parka, raising the hood over my head and pulling it close across my cheeks. The pale moonlight illuminated the sea ice, lighting my way back to the small iglu I called my own. Kiasik stood not far away, icing his sled's runners so they'd glide straight and true for tomorrow's hunt.

"Here," I said, thrusting his seal totem toward him.

He glanced at it, and then turned back to his work. "Keep it." He took a slow mouthful of water from a musk ox horn cup, then let it dribble through his lips onto the runner. I couldn't help feeling that he was spitting at me.

"I fought to get it back for you." All the anger I'd felt at Ataata now burst forth, aimed squarely at the man I called friend. "Would you throw away our grandfather's gift?"

"Issuk's right." For once, Kiasik kept his temper better than I. I found his coolness more infuriating than his anger. "What good is the Ice Bear Spirit? We're always starving, even with his help. Issuk said he's met the Moon Man face-to-face. *That* is power."

"Issuk's a liar." I clenched the seal-bone carving tighter to hide the trembling of my hand. "Only the most powerful of angakkuit could journey to the Moon. Even Ataata has never tried it."

"Because he's old, and weak, and scared." Kiasik spoke the words not as an insult, but as a tragic fact. "We should've hunted the whale ourselves long ago. Or journeyed back to the west to find other Inuit. His fear has kept us alone. If not for Issuk, we'd be alone even now. He's brought us a future."

I laughed harshly. "What kind of future? He threatens to make me his wife!"

Kiasik put down the cup of water and turned to face me. His words were soft, conciliatory. "Would that be so terrible, Omat? To be a mother and hold a babe to your breast? To help secure the future of our people? To love a man?"

I looked at my handsome milk-brother. He'd noticed how I avoided him. How my eyes sparked with a fire like his own.

I tried one last time. "I thought we were going to be great hunters. *Together.*"

He turned back to his sled. "That was because there was no one else." Another sip of water. Another long trickle onto the runner. "Now there is."

I turned and ran, my boot soles squeaking on the hard-packed snow, my breath coming in short, panting gasps. *He doesn't understand. None of them do. I have not bled. I am not a woman at all.*

I'd never give up the joys of the hunt for the dubious pleasures of motherhood.

Once inside my iglu, I removed my clothes and sat naked in my womb-like home, the oil lamp casting a red glow on the surrounding furs like sunlight shining through my mother's stomach.

I looped a rope around my big toes and secured it to my wrists to keep my human body in place, closed my eyes, and began to chant.

By the time I finished my song, my soul flew high over the camp on raven wings.

I hadn't left my human form for many moons; it felt good to be free once more. For a moment, I allowed myself to revel in the strong air currents beneath my wings, the awareness of each feather shifting so I might stay aloft. Surely, for all his bluster, Issuk couldn't do this.

I spiraled down to the strangers' newly built iglu and perched next to the ice window. Inside, Issuk celebrated his humiliation of me—or compensated for my humiliation of him—by violently thrusting into Uimaitok, the older wife. Or perhaps their coupling looked violent only because I'd so rarely seen it done. Maybe I saw hatred in Uimaitok's stony face because I felt it myself. Whatever the cause, my bird's heart beat with the frenzy of an insect's wings in midsummer.

When Issuk finished, he moved to Kidla. He bit and licked at her nipples, milk drooling down his chin. The sight disgusted me, terrified me. Yet I couldn't look away.

Soon he sprawled across the sleeping platform, snoring loudly.

The women crept to the other side of the iglu, careful not to disturb their husband. They dipped handfuls of moss into hot water. Squatting, they strained until the drops of his seed rolled down their legs.

I watched them wipe away every trace of him.

CHAPTER TWELVE

♪

I spread my raven wings and caught a wet ocean-borne wind that carried me high above the camp. With each circle, I rode the wind closer to the stars. Below me, a small wolf ran across the white plain, chasing its moonshadow. A reminder that I could follow my grandfather's advice and seek the Wolf Spirit. But no—Ataata had failed me. Besides, I knew what Singarti would say: He'd warn me that I was a visitor to the spirit world. Not of it. He thought me too weak to journey to the Moon.

I'd prove him wrong.

Above me, Taqqiq's shadow-carved face promised power beyond my imagination. Revenge on Issuk. Vindication of my strength.

Ataata had once admitted that he'd tried such a journey in his foolish youth. *My owl wings grew stiff*, he'd said, *and the moonbeams felt like hailstones upon my shoulders*. Finally Uqsuralik himself had summoned Ataata back to earth, warning him not to venture farther.

No such heaviness pinioned my raven wings, and the wolf below me was just a wolf. Ever upward I flew, my pride spurring me on until the air grew thin and the breath burned in my beak's nostrils. The full orb grew larger as I approached until it filled my vision.

The dark night dissolved into a field of pale white, the Moon's familiar face now only a patchwork of gray.

Then, slowly, the shadows shrank, merged, solidified into the figure of a man.

Suddenly, although I have no memory of landing, or even descending, I stood before him in raven form. He was bald, his skin as white as the large snow iglu behind him—except for the thatch of dark hair between his legs and the smear of black soot across his forehead.

Taqqiq. Moon Man.

"Who is this raven who intrudes on my domain?" His voice was sharp, brittle. High-pitched, like the squeal of stone on slate. He spoke in the tongue of the angakkuq.

Ataata taught me never to hide my true form from the great spirits, so I breathed out slowly through my beak, expelling the raven soul and inhaling my own with the dry, icy air. Human once again, I stood clothed only in a cape of raven feathers, the moon-ice burning against my bare feet.

I swayed for a moment, dizzy from the transformation, but then squared my shoulders, willing my shivering to stop.

"I am Omat, son of Omat."

The Moon raised one hairless brow. "Come to me, finally... after all this time."

"I wanted to come before."

"Hnnnn... and why didn't you?"

"I was told not to."

A smile played along his lips as he moved closer to me. No scent drifted from his ice-smooth skin, only a palpable chill that raised the hair on my arms. I tugged the raven cloak more firmly around my body, trying in vain to hide my woman's flesh.

"Told? By the animal spirits, no doubt. They wanted to keep you for themselves. But you finally sought me out. Were they not help enough?"

"I face a danger greater than any I have known before."

Again his hairless brow quirked upward. He slanted a smile at me. "Yes?"

"There is a man, Issuk, who would lead my family south, into the barren lands. I tried to warn them not to go, but he has bewitched them all. He claims to be a follower of yours, but you would never favor a man so arrogant and cruel."

"You are not being honest with me. I grow bored." He yawned hugely, the inside of his mouth as pale as the rest of him. "Why did you really come?"

"I have told you the truth."

"All the truth? You come all this way to help your family, like the good angakkuq you have trained to be, yes? You fear nothing for yourself, only for them? Good Omat, totally selfless."

I swallowed. "I am afraid for myself as well." I spoke reluctantly at first, then with greater urgency. "Issuk threatens to hurt me." Everything rushed out at once. "He blames me for our hunger. He says I've disobeyed the agliruti against female hunters. But I am not a woman! I have never bled!"

"Because the animal spirits have protected you. Your ancestors in the stars as well."

I lifted my chin. "They want me to remain a man, so I might give food to my people."

He rolled his eyes slowly upward, as if scanning the sky. But there was no sky, only whiteness. "Do you see any stars here?"

He knew I did not.

"Do you see any animals?"

I said nothing.

"There is only me. If you come to my world, then I am all that matters. Did your grandfather never teach you that all an angak-kuq's powers come from the Moon Man? I, who control the tides themselves, who give you light in the darkness, can also give you the power of flight, the power to speak with the animals." He paused, his eyes narrowing. "And I can also take those powers away."

"You can . . . but you would not."

"I do it all the time. I took the magic from your grandfather before you were born, but that fool of a woman, Sanna, insisted on giving it back. She learned her lesson, though. Your family has caused her nothing but grief. The Sea Mother bears you no love, Omat. It is she who withholds the animals from you now."

Cold fear tightened my chest. My whole life, I'd thought myself blessed by the spirits. Now I felt their curse like a blade against my throat.

"Why?" I finally croaked.

"Your father's soul once kept Sanna company in the deep. But your birth returned it to the world above. He was her . . . special favorite. You took him away from her. She is lonely now. And you know how childish she can be." He thrust out his pale lower lip. "She won't rest until she gets what she wants. Every step you take across the frozen sea in winter, she shadows you beneath the ice. Every stroke of your paddle in summer, she paces beneath your kayak, waiting to strike."

"Then you must help me!" I begged. "I have done nothing to deserve her rage! Why would she hunt me so?"

He smiled briefly. "Because I told her to."

His words, so casual, felled me like a blow. I crashed to my knees on the ice, clutching at the raven cloak until the quills cut the flesh of my palms. I wanted to melt into the ground like an iceberg beneath the summer Sun. If even Taqqiq had turned against me, then I no longer knew who I was or what purpose I served. Better simply to disappear.

"Why now?" I asked weakly.

"I told Sanna to bide her time until my plan was in place. Now your family is desperate. They question you. They long for a real hunter to provide for them. They will listen to Issuk—they will let him take you far away, where you will no longer be a threat to me."

I knew I should run. Turn back into a bird and fly far away. I had always thought myself wise—a wise Inuk would flee. But despite everything Taqqiq had said, I could not yet admit that I'd failed so utterly. "I only came to ask your help with Issuk. Please, I beg you, I will never bother you again—"

"That is the first true thing you have said. You will never even *see* me again. You are only dangerous as an angakkuq. If I take that away from you—"

"*No!* I have disobeyed no agliruti—"

An unfamiliar warm wetness slid from between my thighs, and the words caught in my throat.

"You did not think, when you came here. Did you forget? It is I who make women bleed. I have watched you scuttling across the earth, puffing out your too-flat chest, pretending to be a man. I have tried to reach you before, but Wolf and Raven protected you, kept you from my realm." He spoke of the animal spirits with loathing. "But now"—he stepped closer to me, cold rushing off his body in waves—"you have come to me. Naked. Powerless."

I rose shakily to my feet, pressing my legs together. Hot liquid trickled to my knee. A warm flush, part mortification, part rage, suffused my cheeks. I opened my mouth to scream at him, my fingers tight on my cloak, resisting the urge to strangle the malevolent being before me.

Taqqiq remained maddeningly calm. He placed an icy finger on my hot cheek. "I have not seen my sister in an age. And yet I remember her face. Rounder than yours. And pink, as pink as a child's. She was beautiful. Not like you. Long hair in braids twined with yellow poppies, a parka with fringes round the neck. Now she drapes herself in clothes so bright no man can stand to look at her." He sighed. "My sister is forever out of my reach. But so the world may remember that I still have power over womankind, I make you bleed with my every passage from sliver to circle and back again. The world works in balance. I lost my sister—I have been given all women in return."

"I do not want to—"

He slipped his finger from my cheek to my lips, stopping my protest. "Did you never desire to be a woman? Did you never want, for just a moment, to lie beneath a man? To take in his seed?"

The raven cloak lay puddled at my feet, although I didn't remember letting it go. I glanced down at my naked body. A streak of brilliant red painted my left leg. My blood was the only color in the world.

His finger drifted from my lips, tracing the curve of my chin, the smooth line of my neck, the sweaty hollow between my breasts. I could not move as he trailed his finger over my flat stomach, the crease at my hip—all the way to my wet thigh, his touch like ice. He finally raised his finger, staring at the thick coating of red. "Every passage is one of blood, little girl. Birth and death, you are torn apart and re-created."

I tried to run then, but a pool of frozen blood trapped my bare feet.

"You are a woman." He rubbed my blood between his thumb and forefinger, sniffing at it hungrily. "You always have been. You have flouted the aglirutiit all your life. Now you will suffer the consequences."

I was sure that he'd kill me. But no—he was incapable of such mercy.

"You are no longer an angakkuq."

"Don't!" I begged like a child. Too scared to remember the sacred tongue, I spoke like a common Inuk. "Without my magic, my family will starve."

"Only if you continue as you have been, foolish girl. If you stay and hunt, no animals will come. Your family will know it is your fault. You bring despair."

I blinked back tears. "You wouldn't do that," I insisted. "You're a friend to Inuit."

"That is why I must protect them—from you." His words stung like a slap.

"But I'd never do anything to harm them." My breath hitched.

His soot-smeared brow drew low. "From my perch in the sky I see the past, I see the future." He sucked in a slow breath, as if preparing himself for the next words. "You will bring about the end of the world."

I stared at him for a long moment before I found my tongue. "Not just my family? Now the whole world?" Sobs turned to laughter. Then back to sobs. It was all so absurd that I felt suddenly dizzy. "Then why not just kill me now?"

He frowned. "I cannot kill a mortal in the spirit world. Your body lies safe below. If I wanted to kill you, I would have to send a mortal messenger to do it."

"Issuk—" I choked.

"He is a great hunter, is he not?" He quirked a smile, as if speaking of an old friend. "You would do well to be his wife."

"Never."

My vehemence amused him. His chuckle sounded like icicles shattering on stony ground. "If he does not make you a woman now, someone else will. Raven, Wolf, Bear—all the dim-witted spirits who might seek to stand in my way—will be deaf to your pleas."

"I still have my harpoon." I bared my teeth at him as Singarti would.

Taqqiq heaved a sigh of regret. "It will not be enough." He stepped away. "You may fly from here, but when you return to the earth, you will be grounded on your own two feet. No wings. No paws. No hooves. Only your own weak woman's flesh. Remember that what I do, I do to protect your people and your world. It is for the best, Omat."

His words barely registered. I thought only of escape. I bent to retrieve my cloak; the bloody ice around my feet had melted. I pressed my face into the feathered cloak and breathed in the raven spirit. My arms rose as the wind caught my wings.

I was a bird again, no blood leaking from within, no flesh bared to Taqqiq's sight. Yet I could still feel his frigid breath on my skin, see his bloody fingers before my eyes.

I rose into the whiteness, Taqqiq now a mere pale speck on a paler world, but I heard his words: "It is for the best, Omat. For the best..."

I flew once more amid the stars. Below me the lights of the igluit beckoned. Once I returned to camp, if Taqqiq spoke true, my body would never again escape its human form. But where else could I go? I wanted to stay in the sky all night, joining my brother birds on the wing, but, foolish as I was, I thought my family needed me—even without my magic.

With a tilt of my wings, I spiraled down through the vent hole of my own iglu and alit on my bed of furs. With no woman to tend my lamp, the weak flame spluttered and hissed, casting more shadow than light. But I could see my body. It remained where I'd left it, bent double with toes tied to wrists, eyes closed, breathing so slow and deep it might not have breathed at all. A naked woman's body with shoulders too narrow and limbs too slender. A boy's face, too delicate to be a man's but lacking a woman's tattoos across chin and forehead. My lips, even in a trance state, pressed thin and pale as if to hold back any semblance of smile or frown. The tiny birthmarks on my cheeks looked less like a woman's tears than like dirt. Or insects. Or scars. Taqqiq spoke true: I was not beautiful. And I was not strong.

I croaked a grim raven's laugh.

So why does Taqqiq fear me so much? I wondered. *Perhaps his lonely exile among the stars has driven him mad. Why else would he think I can endanger the world, when I've never felt more powerless?*

Footsteps crunched in the snow outside my iglu, and I knew my time as a bird had ended. If the visitor awoke me before my soul had returned to my body, I might never get it back.

The world darkened around me as I breathed out the raven. When I breathed in again, the sweet smell of a burning moss wick warmed human nostrils.

I felt it then. The warm trickle.

A hunter never cries at the sight of blood, but cry I did. Black in the quivering lamplight—blood upon my thighs, dashing any hope that I had bled only in the spirit world.

Smearing the tears across my cheeks, I pulled on my trousers and atigi, too hurried even to wipe away the blood from my legs.

I didn't register the change at first.

But when I settled back onto the furs, I realized that the scent of the burning wick had faded. The textures of the pelts felt less distinct. My body was stiff, awkward, overlarge—like a new parka sewn by a careless woman.

Closing my eyes, I reached out with my angakkuq's senses beyond the walls of my home—but I had no senses with which to reach.

My body trembled with a dawning fear.

Ataata crawled into the iglu, bracing hands on knees to stand upright. When he saw my face, he hurried toward me.

"What is it?"

If I spoke, I knew I'd cry out.

His brow creased with concern. "What did Singarti say?"

"I didn't…," I managed. But then I stopped, knowing that I couldn't tell him the truth. Ataata had worked too hard to train me. His greatest joy, his only comfort, lay in the knowledge that I'd protect our family when he was too old to do so. So I lied. "You were right. The Wolf told me to stay behind tomorrow."

He laid a gnarled hand on my shoulder. "Perhaps you'll come on the next hunt. And then we'll see if the animals stay away." He seemed very old in the light of the oil lamp, his eyelids sagging as if he'd tired of looking into the bright Sun of life and was ready for the dark. "I know this isn't easy. I didn't raise you for a woman's role. Perhaps I was wrong. Did Singarti say you'd bleed? Will you be a woman?"

"No." Another lie.

"Then Issuk will soon realize the spirits have chosen you for a man's life." He squeezed my shoulder. "All will be forgotten."

I remembered Puja's warning: Issuk wouldn't forgive, because he'd never forget. For once, I wondered if a woman held more wisdom than an angakkuq.

"You'll run beside my sled again before long," Ataata continued. "And for now, I'll tell Issuk that you'll enter a spirit trance to help the hunt." He smiled at his own cleverness. "Then, when Kiasik and I return with our sleds full of meat, we'll share the glory with you."

I forced an answering smile, though my stomach clenched with shame. I wouldn't be entreating the spirits, but hiding from them. "And Tapsi and Ququk?" I asked, trying to shift the topic.

"Ququk's too old for a long hunt. Tapsi, though, has asked to come along. We'll need his help to carry home our heavy loads."

So Tapsi, a man who could barely throw a harpoon, would go, but I'd stay behind with the women and the old men.

"You'll be careful tomorrow on the hunt?" I begged.

"You shouldn't ask that!" His smile broadened. "Am I not a great hunter still?"

"Of course. The best."

"Then you don't need to worry. It's all in Taqqiq's hands."

That, I thought, *is what I'm afraid of.*

CHAPTER THIRTEEN

The hunters are coming!" Millik's shrill cry carried across the valley long before she appeared in the camp, gasping for breath like a beached fish. Every sunrise since the men had left, she'd climbed to the crest of an ice ridge to watch for their return. Inside the igluit, my aunts spoke of her furtive glances at Patik, the gangly one who laughed at everything Issuk said and wore a wolf tail at each shoulder.

Now, as she bounded down the slope toward us, I knew Millik dreamed of the meat the hunters might bring. Without a wife of his own, perhaps Patik would let her butcher his portion and feed him morsels of blubber off the end of her own ulu. The other women stopped their tasks to gather around Millik and hear the news. Even Puja, who'd stayed quiet in deference to my own gloom, rubbed her hands in anticipation of the meat to come.

I watched them from just outside the entrance to my iglu, where I sat in the short-lived sunlight, carving a harpoon head. I yanked at the seam of my trousers, sharply aware of the wadded moss tied between my legs. I'd told no one of the blood, not even Puja.

Perhaps I could keep Taqqiq's mark hidden forever—could go on living as a man.

Even from far away, we could tell the sleds bore towering loads. Despite my distress, I couldn't suppress a sigh of relief: we'd last the winter without starving.

But a moment later, I knew something was wrong. My grandfather's sled, which should've led the group, trailed far behind. Black Mask kept stopping to growl at the two dogs behind her, who stumbled and skipped over their tangled traces. The sled kept moving, nearly running down the team, before Black Mask jerked forward again, yanking the others with her. From this distance, the sled's driver was merely a bulky silhouette against the pale sky. But I knew it was not Ataata.

The other three sleds slid to a stop within the camp. The women rushed up to marvel at the vast piles of dark-red seal meat and thick white blubber, their thoughts consumed by the feast ahead. Issuk cuffed his snarling dogs with the handle of his whip before unlashing his bloodied harpoon from the sled. He turned to the gathered women as if ready to recount his exploits. But before he could begin, I pushed my way through the crowd and grabbed him by the arm. His face darkened.

"Where's my father?"

"On his sled," Issuk said shortly, wrenching his arm from my grasp.

The crowd quieted as the women finally noted Ataata's absence. I turned to Kiasik, who stood beside his own heavily laden sled with shoulders hunched. Busy untying his dogs, he kept his gaze on his hands. But Tapsi met my eye. For the first time, I noticed that his face glistened with ice. Even as I watched, another slow tear froze upon his cheek.

I felt Puja's mittened hand on my shoulder, saw my own growing panic reflected in her eyes. Together we walked to meet Ataata's sled as it finally jerked into camp.

Patik knelt upon it. No pile of meat lay before him. Just a low pallet of gear, covered by a familiar white sleeping fur. I pulled it back.

Ataata, his face blackened and bloated, eyes open and dull, stared up at me.

Puja fell to her knees, keening. Black Mask sat back on her haunches and began to howl.

Despite the blood flowing from my body, I still didn't feel like a woman. I couldn't show such grief.

"What happened to him?" I asked softly. The rest of the camp gathered around, the women shaking, the men silent and stoic.

Kiasik answered me, his voice quavering as it never had before. "He fell through the ice."

"Ataata has spent his whole life judging the thickness of ice!" Issuk interrupted. "His eyes were weak. The old cannot judge as well as the young." Nonchalantly he began unloading the heavy slabs of meat from his sled. As he bent over, something slipped from the neck of his parka to swing slowly on its thong. He grabbed the pendant quickly and shoved it beneath his clothing, but not before I saw the single dark bear claw.

"You killed him." The moment I said it I knew it must be true.

Kiasik stood very still, looking down at the ice beneath his feet.

"Sister's Son!" I demanded. "What did you see?"

"I heard a shout and looked behind me." Kiasik spoke without inflection, as if afraid even a sliver of emotion would slice him apart. "He was already in the water. I rushed back to help him—I was too late."

"And where were you, Issuk?"

"The ice would've cracked beneath me, too." His raspy voice held no regret. "There was nothing I could do."

"I don't believe you," I hissed. "He was not too old to tell strong ice from weak. And if he *had* fallen into the sea, the spirits of the ocean would protect him. The seals would lift him upon their backs and bring him out of the cold!" I knew my words made little sense, but the sight of my grandfather's cold, black face drove me to madness.

Issuk drew himself up a little straighter. "Who are you to accuse me of murder, little girl?" His red lips curled back. "You've ignored so many aglirutiit that I'm surprised the ice doesn't crack beneath your feet right now. Although perhaps this is a sterner punishment—to know that the old fool's death was your own fault."

I drew my knife from my belt and, for the first time in my life, hurtled forward in anger.

"Omat!" Puja screamed, clutching at my leg from where she knelt in the snow. Kiasik grabbed me around the waist. His breath on my cheek smelled of blubber and blood.

Issuk laughed, but his eyes were cold. "If you're as powerful an angakkuq as you claim, why don't you ask the old man yourself? He'll tell you what happened."

"Yes, Older Brother!" Puja cried. "Leave your body—enter the spirit world and speak to Ataata, so we might settle this."

My eyes bright with pleading, I wrenched from Kiasik and spun toward her. "Don't ask me to do that."

"But you'll find the truth," she begged. "Isn't that why Ataata taught you the ways of the spirit?"

Shame heated my cheeks.

"Yes, go ahead," scoffed Issuk. "Show us your magic."

The others stood silently, watching me with reddened eyes. Tapsi balled his fists in futile distress. Saartok clutched at his arm, her cheek pressed against the sleeve of his parka. Millik, all her morning's dreams dashed, stared hopefully at me while sneaking distracted glances at Patik, unwilling to believe anything terrible of her chosen man or his friends. Only Ququk, his face as hard as carved antler, ignored me, staring instead at his old friend's blackened corpse. Issuk's wives stood in the shadow of the laden sled, their expressions blank. Clearly they'd seen their husband pick such fights before. Maybe they knew the inevitable outcome. Maybe they didn't care.

"If you're no angakkuq, then you're just a woman like any other woman," Issuk said. "Although a fierce one, I'll grant." Glancing back at his wives, he looked thoughtful for a moment—a very short moment. "There's no need to wait until the whale hunt. I'll take you as a wife now. I'm sure your grandfather would've wanted it. You won't starve, and you'll finally learn a woman's ways."

"Never." I shot the word at him like a stone from a sling.

He remained as hardheaded as a caribou bull. "Come now. All women must be wives. Unless"—he laughed shortly—"you're an uiluaqtaq who needs no husband and never bleeds. Is *that* what you are?"

I swallowed, unable to admit the truth. "I've lived as a man my whole life."

"Then go and ask your grandfather how he died. If you speak to him, then you're truly an angakkuq, and perhaps the aglirutiit don't apply to you in the same way. I'll leave you alone."

I looked to Puja, to Kiasik, for help. My aunt looked back with blind faith, as if all her trust in Ataata had already transferred to me. But Kiasik avoided my gaze. My whole life I'd believed his love for me outweighed his envy. But after only a few days with Issuk, he, too, believed I couldn't lead our camp. Unless I proved that my magic exempted me from a woman's usual role, Kiasik wouldn't stand in Issuk's way.

"I will speak with Ataata." I had no choice.

I entered my small iglu. Everyone crowded in behind.

"Tie my limbs," I ordered, "so my body might remain here, even as my spirit takes flight." The more preparations I made, the longer I could postpone my inevitable failure. Puja dutifully looped a narrow rope from my toes to my wrists, bending me double.

Issuk squatted an arm's length away, lazily stroking his long mustache even as his eyes sparked with hatred. Puja was right: he hadn't forgiven me for proving him a cheater.

I closed my eyes to block the sight of his face and deepened my breath.

I don't know how long I lay there, listening to the sad remains of my family chanting around me. Puja's voice rang sharp and clear; Kiasik's was hesitant. The others of my camp tried their best. The strangers stayed silent, but they did nothing to prevent my success. Still, I could feel Issuk's gaze upon me, hot as a new-fed lamp.

I called upon Singarti to lift me into the sky where I might speak with my grandfather among the stars and learn the truth of his murder.

But nothing happened.

I remained trapped in my own body, my soul tethered to the ground.

The voices died away. Puja's went last, hoarse by the end.

"Enough." Issuk chuckled low in his throat, more growl than laugh. "Can't you smell it?"

Silence.

"You're no hunters, then." I heard a small sound of protest from Kiasik, but Issuk wouldn't stop. "I can smell the blood of a wounded seal beneath the ice. I can smell the blood of a harpooned whale beneath the water. I can smell the blood of a woman beneath her clothes."

I squeezed my eyes shut, willing myself to disappear.

"Omat, tell him that's not true," Puja pleaded. But I wouldn't lie, not anymore.

Again, that low laughter. "You wonder why you don't succeed at the hunt. Why your angakkuq fell through the ice This woman has deceived you—played a man's part despite the blood on her thighs. She doesn't have the ear of the spirits. She is nothing. With every harpoon she throws, she defies the agliruti." I heard him rise. "Come. We feast tonight on the meat that men have brought."

Hot tears leaked between my lashes; I turned my cheek against my knees so no one might see. One by one, I heard the members of my own camp leave the iglu.

"Come, Anaana," Kiasik said to his mother. I had heard my cousin speak with annoyance, with envy, even with anger. But never before with contempt. "Leave her."

My milk-mother's tears fell warm against my hands as she untied the ropes at my wrists and feet.

Released from my bonds, I curled into a ball like a snail seeking its shell. Puja didn't touch me again. Instead I heard the familiar *tap tap tap* as she shaped the moss wick in my lamp. Giving me light. Keeping me warm. Before she left I heard her inhale sharply, as if she might speak, but whatever words she wanted to say, whether of comfort or accusation, she bit back.

I pressed my fingers against my face and breathed heavily, so that my whole world shrank to the resonance of air between my nostrils and hands—to the rushing inhalation, the quavering exhalation as I tried desperately not to scream. *I control nothing. Not the spirits, not the hunt...not my own flesh.* For so long, I'd felt like a spider standing astride a web of life. I could feel the tremors of the whole world—wind, sea, sky, animals—in my own flesh. Now Issuk and Taqqiq had torn the web asunder, leaving me dangling from a single silken thread, spinning helplessly above rocky ground.

Eventually my body took pity on my dizzy brain, and I sank into sleep. Even then, I remained rooted to my human form, unable even to dream, blind to the spirit world.

When I woke sometime later, I thought for a heart-stopping moment that I'd lost my sight in the mortal world as well. Without anyone to tend it, my lamp had gone out. Then a cloud moved aside, and Taqqiq's eye blazed through the ice window. His cold beam illuminated the iglu for an instant before another windblown cloud doused the light once more.

Only then did I realize why I'd woken. Someone had entered my iglu.

"Puja?" I called softly into the dark. No one else might seek to share my twofold grief—for my grandfather and for myself. "Is that you?" But I knew my mistake before the words had left my lips.

I needed no angakkuq's nose to smell my visitor's excited sweat. "What do you want, Issuk?" I asked, somehow keeping my voice steady.

"I won our little bet after all," the darkness answered me.

Without my heightened senses, I couldn't tell his exact position, but his voice came from very close by, and I could feel the cold air still clinging to his parka. Carefully I shuffled a little farther away. *No matter what*, I vowed, *I won't scream*. In that, at least, I was a hunter still.

His voice rasped on, grating like fine gravel on my skin. "The elders say the best wives are those who fight the hardest. I've always wanted to bed a woman who didn't shrink before me."

Even in the dark, I knew every part of my home, knew exactly where my knife lay. Its grip was cold and smooth in my palm.

"Leave now, Issuk. This is your only warning."

"You think to defend yourself against me?" His voice grew moist, as if he sucked the saliva from the corners of his too-red mouth. "Good. I hoped you would. I could've tied you up while you slept, but I wanted to see you fight. Wanted to bed a woman with the heart of a man."

I lunged toward the sound of his voice, leaping off the sleeping platform with my knife outstretched. In my fury, I forgot all Ata-ata's long lessons on patience. I landed on nothing but fur-covered snow.

His laughter rose from somewhere behind me. I spun to face him, and felt his hands, as cold and hard as the Moon's, seize my wrists.

"You may not be able to see in the dark," he said softly, his breath damp and hot on my face, "but I can. They say my father was the Moon's demon son, for my mother died when I was born, and her husband claimed I wasn't his. You and I have more in common than you think. Dead mothers, lying in pools of their own blood. The spirits and demons, wolves and ravens, creatures of this world and the other—they waited in the cold, listening to our infant wails. I may not be an angakkuq, may not speak the sacred speech or have the Wolf's ear—I may even need to cheat at games—but that doesn't mean I'm powerless."

Perhaps it was a trick of the dark, but his eyes sparked red, more animal's than man's. As he spoke, he tightened his grip on my wrists until my hands grew numb. My knife dropped with a dull thud.

I had told stories of rape all my life. Sanna and the bird-man, Malina and her brother.

That night, I became one more story.

Never before had I felt my female flesh more acutely or resented it more. I won't tell the details here, for they're hard to tell, and I've told them only once. Enough to say that he bound and gagged me with my own ropes, the same ones I'd used to secure my body as my mind flew aloft. That I fought with all my strength, but it was not enough. Too long had I relied on my angakkuq's senses, my spirit helpers. My own skills were weak. He ripped me apart as easily as he would split a seal carcass. And some time in the middle of it all, I simply left. Not to the spirit world, but to a dark corner of my own mind.

When he finished with me, I lay bloodied and torn, inside and out, too weak even to drag myself beneath the furs.

Puja found me in the morning, I think, but the visions of that time are hazy, as if I looked at the world from beneath the dark water, drowning in Sanna's black lair. I don't know if Puja cried or screamed. But I imagine she did.

When Issuk left our camp a few days later, he took me with him as his third wife.

He tied me to the sled to make sure I couldn't run away, though I'm not sure why he bothered; I would not move or talk. Puja begged him to leave me behind, saying that I'd be a burden, that I might never recover my wits—that he himself had said I brought bad luck. But perhaps Issuk knew me best of all, because he felt sure that before long I'd fight him again, just as he wished. As for bad luck, he merely laughed. "The spirits are done with her. They no longer care what she does."

The others simply stood mutely. They might not like what Issuk had done, but punishing him would mean losing the food he promised to bring them. The camp's need to survive outweighed any desire for vengeance.

Kiasik would travel with us, leaving only Tapsi and Ququk to provide for our women. But Issuk had left a large cache of meat behind to supplement my family's dwindling supplies. Plenty of food for two moons. With Ataata's dogs divided among the other teams, Issuk assured them his sleds would move swiftly across the sea ice. The hunters would return.

My people finally had hope for the future. I did not.

CHAPTER FOURTEEN

⚡

As a very small child, I once hid inside the prow of my grandfather's kayak, desperate to go with him on a walrus hunt. He got in and paddled around the bay for a while, pretending not to notice the boy curled tightly between his feet until he came back to shore with a laugh and deposited me with Puja. I had to wait many more seasons for my first walrus hunt, but I still remember that short trip inside the kayak.

The dim light that penetrated the thick hide created a soft, orange glow. If I stretched my hand above, the skin felt warm from the Sun; beneath me, the ocean chilled the boat's hull. The driftwood frame curved around me, the slats silhouetted against the light like the ribs of some great sea creature seen from within. I used to imagine a narwhal had swallowed me whole. The thought didn't distress me—I felt warm and safe in its belly, protected from the cold sea water that lapped and sloshed at its sides, with Ataata to guard me from the monsters of the deep. His feet, encased in his sealskin boots, were all I could see of him. The rest of his legs disappeared into the darkness, and the seal-intestine anorak tightly tied to the cockpit hid his torso. But even from that angle, I didn't find the view frightening. I knew every inch of him, even the soles of his feet.

Lashed onto the back of Issuk's sled, heavy pelts covering my body and face, I willed myself back into the belly of Ataata's kayak. But the sled careened over the rough ice with far more violence than a boat rocking on the waves, and the darkness beneath the furs suffocated me as the orange glow inside the kayak never had. Even if I could've snapped the ropes that held my arms in place, I didn't want to move the pelts from my face. As much as I might long to breathe fresh air, I couldn't bear to see the man running nearby.

Occasionally the sled jerked as Issuk climbed on board, and my body stiffened in response. Not soon enough, he'd leap off again to whip his dogs and push at the sled. The ice piled around us in great heaps, buckled and jagged where the currents slid the great frozen pans against each other, creating teetering blue mountains that would last only until the next strong current mowed them down, or until the summer Sun melted them back into the sea.

I knew the strain of running beside a sled. Boots slipped on the ice, shortening every step, lungs burned with exhaustion, and sweat rolled beneath heavy parkas despite the winter air. Yet I would've given anything to run beside Ataata's sled right now, rather than lie helpless and bound on Issuk's.

I'd lost count of the days on our journey—everything was darkness and sleep. One of Issuk's wives would shake me when we stopped and press some meat or blubber to my lips, forcing me to eat just enough to stay alive. Then I'd sink back into oblivion, burrowing beneath the furs on the sled like a bear in its den.

Issuk's young daughter rode beside me, as silent and still as a seal carcass or a pile of hides. The women ran with the sled, helping to push it over the hillocks. Like Issuk, they took turns hopping back on board when the ice smoothed, their breathing rough and labored as they stole a brief rest. When round-cheeked Kidla drew near the sled, I could hear the thin cries of the baby rising from the warm embrace of its mother's hood. The two women said little, but when they did, they spoke of me.

"Why'd he bring her?" Uimaitok complained under her breath.

"She's nothing but a burden," Kidla agreed. "In my camp, we'd leave her to Sila."

My body still sore, I drifted in and out of sleep. Even if they hadn't tied my arms and legs, I was too weak to escape or to rail against my captors. Something deep inside me felt torn and bruised. When I tried to move, pain pierced my gut. So I didn't try.

Exiled from the spirit world, I wanted only to return to my own dreams—where Ataata lived and I was a child in his care. I'd nearly blocked out the crack of the whip and the hissing ice beneath the sled runners when Issuk ripped away the fur blanket covering my face. The sled skidded to a stop, the dogs yelping in their tangled traces. Kidla stood nearby, bent with exhaustion. Her baby rested against the nape of her neck, a long line of mucus running from its nose into her hair.

Issuk slashed the ropes from my limbs. "We're far from your camp. There's no use trying to run."

I didn't move.

"Did you hear me? You don't have to be tied anymore, and the sled's too heavy. Get up!"

I raised my eyes to him slowly—I had no intention of obeying.

He prodded my shoulder with the butt of his whip. "You like being tied up, is that it?" A sneer tugged at his red mouth. "Or are you so weak you can't even leave the sled? What happened to Omat, the strong man? You're like an old woman, or a very young child. Even Nua could run if I made her." He gestured disdainfully toward his daughter; I could feel the child trembling through the furs between us. "Nothing's wrong with you." His voice and whip rose as one. "I've done nothing to you that I don't do to my other wives nightly!"

Other wives. I was one of them now.

"Get up, dog!" The handle of his whip cracked against my

shoulder. I cried out and curled even tighter. Had he come at me in my previous life, I might've reached up and grabbed the whip from his hand, swinging the long strands through the air until they hissed down upon his flesh. But I'd lost the will to fight. I wanted only to hide—one step away from wanting to die.

Issuk dragged me from the sled, heaving my limp body upright until I swayed on my own feet. Erect, I could feel the pain more sharply, and hot blood leaked against my leg—whether from his violence or my own body's betrayal, I didn't know. And I was too weak to care. The fringed woman's parka they'd dressed me in felt awkward, the long front and back flaps cumbersome against my legs, the weight of the huge hood heavy on my back.

Issuk flicked his whip at the lead dog and shouted hoarsely for it to move on. I looked back at the other sleds—two dark dots on the horizon. But the thought of Kiasik's nearness only made me feel worse. If I couldn't even turn to my own milk-brother for help, then I was truly alone.

One foot in front of the other, I made my way across the ice, following the sled tracks blindly like a newborn pup grappling toward the teat. Only the movement mattered.

With each step my thighs rubbed against my wounds. Every motion reminded me of my shame, my womanhood.

We came to a brief stop so Issuk could scan the surroundings from a tall ridge of crumpled ice. I stood panting, chin on chest, eyes closed against the snow glare. A slight pressure on my mittened palm and my eyes flashed open. A familiar grizzled muzzle.

I pulled off my mitten so Black Mask might lick my bare hand, her tongue warming my cold flesh. Uimaitok, the older wife, jerked on the harness line. The dog growled low.

"Go on, girl, go on," I whispered hoarsely—the first words I'd spoken since I'd left my home.

Uimaitok tugged on the line again, and Black Mask plodded back toward the front of the sled as the team moved out once more.

I watched the black-and-white dog moving among the rest of

the pack, enduring their nips and growls, always pushing forward.
Issuk had demoted her from lead dog to one of the pullers in the
back. In my camp, three or four dogs would pull a sled, but Issuk's
sled was nearly twice as long as one of ours, and eight animals
stretched ahead of us, their long traces fanning across the whiteness like dark cracks in the ice. Still, Issuk should've taken one
of our bigger, male dogs if he wanted more power. The choice of
Black Mask made sense only as a warning: he'd killed my grandfather, taken my body, and now debased our dog. He demanded
she fill a role she hadn't been bred for. If she kept falling behind,
he wouldn't hesitate to leave her on the ice. No doubt he'd do the
same to me.

A sudden spark of defiance kindled the ashes of my heart. Black
Mask had survived worse days than this. I would, too. I thought
of Ataata's face, black and swollen, and fixed my gaze on my feet,
willing them to keep moving. *If I die now*, I realized, *I'll never have
my revenge*. I had found something to live for.

I lifted my head only when I saw Issuk coming toward me with
the fur-clad baby dangling from his outstretched arms. Its legs
pumped weakly, its face scrunched as it looked everywhere for its
mother.

"Take the child. Kidla is tired of carrying it."

The young wife slipped her own carrying harness from her
parka and handed it grudgingly to me. I stood stupidly, the leather
thongs dangling from my hand.

"Help her." Issuk snorted with disgust. "She doesn't even know
that much."

Kidla secured the harness to my shoulders and chest. Uimaitok's
hands were cold as she dropped the baby into the carrying pouch
inside the back of my parka, while Kidla cinched the straps tight to
distribute the weight and keep the squirming baby from slipping
free. She pulled the large hood over my head to create a warm cave
where the baby might look out past my shoulder. Its tiny fists beat
against my back.

The whole procession began again: Issuk running, his long whip cracking at the panting dogs, his two wives trotting after him, the silent little girl sitting wide-eyed on the sled, and me—walking even more slowly now with my extra burden. Kidla had been tired, true, but I knew Issuk had given me the baby more to shame me than to please her.

As I walked, the baby mewled in my ear and grabbed my short hair with surprisingly strong fingers.

"Stop that!" I shrugged my shoulders violently, hoping to jerk it into silence.

Its wails only grew more insistent.

"I have nothing to feed you," I said, trying to sound reasonable. I'd seen Kidla simply pull her arms inside the parka's wide shoulders and swing the baby around her body to nurse, but my own flat breasts contained muscle—not milk. I learned quickly that babies are difficult to reason with.

It continued to cry and grab at my hair like an evil spirit on my back, a tangible reminder of my newly imposed womanhood. Yet I couldn't escape to the past while the babe slobbered so prodigiously onto my present. Its crying and clutching grounded me in my own body—a body I wasn't happy to be in, to be sure, but mine nonetheless.

We didn't stop to eat. The ice wouldn't melt so deep in the winter, but at any moment the currents could break it beneath us—we kept moving while we could. I dimly remembered that the journey had started on landfast ice and followed the shoreline south. Now no land appeared either behind or before us, only the desolate landscape of the frozen sea and the piled ice mountains.

The Sun wouldn't last much longer—the overcast sky already grew dark. The lack of bright light made the ice a treacherous, uniform gray, with no shadows to warn of crevasses. Our pace slowed. Eventually I caught up to Uimaitok.

"Do you know where we're going?" I asked diffidently.

"South," the older woman grunted.

Even a babe would have known that. "But how much farther?"

"We go until we find enough open water for whale hunting," she answered without looking at me. "We've already spent two days on the pack ice. I don't know how many more it will take."

"We slept on the pack?" I asked incredulously. From winter to winter, some leads—or open channels—in the ice reappeared at predictable spots, but others formed and shifted without warning. Ataata always taught that a wise Inuk camped only on landfast ice, lest he float away in the middle of the night, lost forever on the ocean.

"You didn't notice?"

I didn't reply, too ashamed of the weakness that had kept me so dim-witted.

Uimaitok lifted her chin. "Issuk doesn't believe in hiding in the ground like a lemming when good hunting waits farther out."

I ignored the insult to my family. "Aren't you afraid the ice will crack or move while we sleep?"

"We trust the Moon to guide us. We travel across the pack ice because it's faster than sticking to the landfast ice at the shoreline. Issuk doesn't wait in camp like others for the whales to pass by. He chases them down, no matter what stands in his way."

I'd never heard her speak so freely. Although she clearly bore little love for her husband, she spoke of his daring with pride. She owed the wolverine fur that edged her parka and the strong baleen twine that fastened her bags to her husband's audacity. Peace reigned in my sad little camp, but we were slowly disappearing on the edge of the world, starving and childless, while Issuk led his people to rich hunting grounds. *There's more than one kind of leader,* I realized, *and sometimes it's the worst of men who make the best of situations.*

We camped on the pack ice that night, just as Uimaitok had foretold. Issuk ventured in a wide circle from his chosen spot, looking for cracks that might break the pack into smaller drift ice. Satisfied with the relative safety of our camp, he signaled his wives to unload the sled. I could barely lift my own feet to take another step, let alone help with the heavy sleeping furs and the soapstone lamp. Panting, I sat down on the snow, the baby finally motionless against my back. Kidla roughly flipped back my hood and retrieved her child. Soon the babe nursed loudly at its mother's breast.

The other two sleds skidded to a stop. Onerk and Patik stood beside one, checking the lashings around the small, fat umiaq wobbling on top. Kiasik unloaded supplies from the other, his familiar dogs sniffing in my direction. One let out a cheerful yip and wagged its tail. I got no such greeting from my milk-brother.

No. He is not my brother, I realized. *Not anymore. Only a cousin.*

While Kiasik staked his team, he watched me from the corner of his eye. I didn't recognize his expression at first. It was one I'd never seen him cast in my direction before: pity.

"You've been sick," he said finally, his voice carefully neutral. "Get some meat in you. Get some sleep tonight."

Kidla looked up from her nursing babe, and an easy smile flashed across her face. "We've slept warm and well since you've joined us, Kiasik."

Smiling in return, my cousin ran his tongue along the blade of his long ivory snow knife, creating a thin coating of ice. Glowing with pride, he bent to carve large blocks from the hard-packed ground. He tried to catch my eye; he hadn't yet lost the habit of sharing his triumphs with me. I looked away.

Together the men propped the snow blocks upright in a large circle. Tall Patik and hulking Onerk came to assist, and the iglu quickly took shape, the walls slowly spiraling upward until they met in a neat dome over the men inside.

As Kidla and little Nua pressed loose snow into the cracks between the large blocks, Kiasik cut a small vent through the roof and erected a miniature windbreak around it. The other men dug out an entrance passage. Uimaitok procured a translucent square of scraped caribou hide to serve as a window.

Throughout, they left me alone. Kiasik laughed and joked,

securing the window into the domed roof and waving through it at the women, who'd already lit the oil lamp inside.

Night had fallen when they finally completed the iglu. Issuk crawled out to where I sat beside the sled. He stood and stared down at me, his long mustache mirroring the frown on his too-red lips. "Kiasik has carried you inside long enough. Tonight you walk."

I didn't remember my cousin helping me every night. The thought brought me no comfort, only disgust at myself. I hurried to my feet.

Inside the iglu, the women had already hung the men's boots on the drying rack above the lamp. I missed Puja. Ever since I'd reached manhood, she'd removed my boots and warmed my feet.

I crawled onto the farthest corner of the fur-covered sleeping bench and looked down at my own boots. I didn't want to pull them off, afraid of what I might find underneath. Sitting motionless on the sled had likely led to frostbite. To stay warm in winter, I needed to move, to run, to build.

I pulled my hands slowly from my large seal fur mittens and bent my fingers until the feeling returned. Gingerly I pulled off my boots and the fur liners underneath. The ends of my toes were white and swollen but not yet black. Frozen, not dead. The iglu air wasn't warm enough yet to help, and I couldn't ask Uimaitok to add more moss to the lamp wick—if the oil burned too hot, the iglu would melt above it. My numb toes felt like meat in my hands, and my cold palms couldn't warm them. All those nights I hid in my dreams, I must've slept in my boots, never drying my feet. Each day on the sled, my toes had frozen a little more. Tears pricked my eyes—only the youngest or stupidest of hunters got frozen feet.

My flesh has become ice, I thought, *earthbound and heavy and hard as stone, but so brittle it will shatter with the slightest force.*

I rubbed the white flesh gently, careful not to snap off an entire toe. Still I felt nothing.

"Here—" Uimaitok crouched beside me, offering a piece of

thawed seal from her cooking pot. She took one look at my stricken face and my white toes and let out a loud humph. Sitting with her back to me, she grasped one of my feet with surprising gentleness, raised her own parka, and placed my foot in the warm hollow of her armpit. She squeezed her arm against her side to hold my left foot in place and did the same with my right. I fell awkwardly onto the sleeping furs, this strange woman clasped between my legs. Slowly I chewed my own small meal, holding back cries of pain as the feeling gradually returned to my feet, burning and stinging like splatters of hot seal oil against flesh.

The others ignored me, busy with their food. All except Kiasik. A faint, relieved smile touched his lips as he watched me eat. *So he cares if my woman's body survives,* I realized. *But not my man's spirit.*

When he lay down beside me on the sleeping platform, I looked away from him, my heart as numb as my toes.

By the time I drifted toward sleep, my icy flesh had melted, and with it my resolve to survive and seek revenge. I was water. Formless and vulnerable. I wanted to sink deep into the earth, or turn to vapor and disappear into nothingness. Wishing for death. Wishing for escape. Not sure if I could have one without the other.

CHAPTER FIFTEEN

ᛉ

That night I dreamed that Issuk took me, only to wake to the sound of his rhythmic grunting coming from the far side of the sleeping platform. I did not move. The others slept on.

When it was over, Uimaitok whispered, "Will you let Kiasik lie with Kidla?"

Issuk grumbled, "All my men want to lie with my wives. After I lent Kidla to Patik, he followed her around like she was his seal mother and he wanted to suck at her teat."

"Kiasik has never lain with a woman," Uimaitok urged. "It's not right. Easier to lend him Kidla—otherwise he may try to take her without your permission."

"Let him try. Now that we know how to build his snow iglu, we don't need him. If he doesn't respect me, then he has no place with us."

They were silent for so long I thought they'd fallen back asleep. Then, more softly, Uimaitok asked, "When will you lie with Omat next?"

"I should do it soon, just to remind Kiasik whose wife she is. He lies next to her each night, and I don't like the look he gives me—like he's built one of his igluit around her and won't let me through the entrance tunnel."

"So you *will* claim her again?"

Issuk snorted. "Let Kiasik have her for now. I'm not interested in one who can barely walk or speak. When she acts like a person again, I'll take her. Until then, even *you* please me better."

Next to me, Kiasik didn't stir, but his broad shoulders rose up like a wall between me and my new husband. I hadn't noticed his efforts to protect me. Or perhaps, in my blindness, I'd actually seen the truth: my cousin couldn't save me, even if he wanted to.

The next day I walked beside the sled rather than lay upon it. I forsook the sure hunter's step I'd learned from my grandfather. Nor did I move like Kidla and Uimaitok, with the knees-inward gait of a woman. Instead I shuffled a little, tripping often, as if every step hurt—which was not too far from the truth. If Issuk wanted me to act like a person, then I would be a walking corpse.

Even with my awkward movements, I easily kept pace with the sleds. The men stopped frequently to hunt at breathing holes. Occasionally we saw the telltale frost smoke of a lead, a cloudy haze where the warmer water of the open channel met the frigid air. None of the leads were large enough for a whale, but Issuk stopped us with a raised hand when his keen eyes noted a tiny dot on the horizon—a basking seal.

Watching from afar, I had to admire his skill. Long before the seal would notice him, he lay down on the ice and scuttled forward on his stomach. He wore a set of seal claws tied to each mitten, and he scratched the ice as he went, turning himself sideways to mimic a seal's length. The seal strained its head upward to watch his progress, its body tense and ready to flee back into the misty lead. Issuk lay perfectly still, unthreatening, convincing his prey that he was just another seal. It lay back and closed its eyes. Only then did the hunter leap up in one swift movement and thrust his harpoon through its neck.

The wounded animal humped across the snow and splashed into the water, but Issuk had wrapped his harpoon line around his waist, and the bone cleats on his boot soles kept him from sliding after it. He used his whole body to anchor the seal as it thrashed in the lead, kicking up fountains of spray. Finally, when the water welled up red over the ice, and the line ceased its jerking, Issuk hauled up his prize.

Uimaitok offered me an upper vertebra. A woman's portion, but nourishing nonetheless. I gorged myself on the dark, hot meat. I was not too proud to enjoy Issuk's bounty.

An Inuk survives.

→ ⊷ ≡◊≡ ⊶ ←

One night a howling, snarling clamor awoke us. As the only one to sleep clothed, I made it through the entrance tunnel first. While the others pulled on their parkas, I alone witnessed the cause of the uproar.

All the dogs remained tied up, their eyes trained on the swiftly departing shape of a scrawny white wolf. He was almost invisible against the ice; only his moonshadow gave him away.

The slavering dogs growled in chorus. There is nothing a dog despises more than a wolf. Having once been a wolf myself, I couldn't share their distaste. But I thought perhaps I understood their anger: the dog and the wolf are cousins, yet the dog remains tied while the wolf roams free.

Black Mask alone lay peacefully in the snow, tongue lolling, jaws slightly agape in a gesture I recognized from my wolf journeys as a sign of pleasure. I thought little of it at the time. The men came outside and busily whipped the dogs into silence. They never saw the wolf, and I didn't enlighten them.

Black Mask wasn't the only one finding pleasure in the arms of a stranger.

It happened naturally enough. After another long day of

traveling across the ice, Kiasik settled himself on the iglu's bench beside Kidla on the pretense of playing with her baby. Never having seen a mother and infant before, I wasn't prepared for the glow that lit her face when someone praised her son.

Kiasik lifted the baby's arms, crowing, "Such a strong little man! He'll grow to be a great whale hunter!"

The little boy smiled and gurgled. My cousin threw the child into the air as if he were a ball for games, catching him and tossing him aloft once more as the baby screeched with laughter. Kidla's smile broadened as she watched Kiasik. With only old men and soft Tapsi to compare him with, I'd never realized quite how handsome my cousin really was.

Patik's nose sat crookedly in his face, and his habit of holding his gap-toothed mouth open reminded me of a dumbstruck walrus. Onerk, with his tiny eyes and broad frame, still reminded me of a shark. Or perhaps his heavy brows and shaggy mustache were those of a lumbering musk ox. Kiasik's oval eyes, on the other hand, glimmered beneath arching eyebrows, his nose flanked by wide, expressive nostrils. I'd seen him flare those nostrils at me with both anger and humor—and, occasionally, with something akin to desire. When he met Kidla's frank gaze, they flared anew.

The women trimmed the lamp wick for the night, and Kiasik took his usual place next to me on the sleeping bench, still holding the baby. An innocent enough reason for Kidla to slip beneath the furs beside him.

I awoke to giggling. Kidla and Kiasik, whispering to each other. Then the distinct sound of flesh sliding against flesh. I stiffened, willing myself not to turn around, not to hear it. I didn't want to witness their transgression, lest Issuk somehow read it in my face later. They were taking a terrible risk; Issuk slept on Kidla's other side, a mere handbreadth away. *He sleeps heavily and snores loudly*, I reminded myself. *If he wakes, they'll know.*

The sounds continued. Not rhythmic enough for sex, but from

the twitching motion of the sleeping furs, I knew their hands were all over each other. The heat from their bodies sent sweat running in rivulets down my own.

The snoring stopped.

The pace of Kiasik's panting breaths only quickened. He was too wrapped in his own pleasure to notice. I wanted to scream a warning. To kick him into silence. I lay frozen instead, bracing for the worst.

A harsh intake of breath from Kidla, followed by a sudden quiet. I felt Kiasik's body tense beside me. They knew Issuk was awake.

I expected shouting. Blows. Instead, Issuk merely rasped out Patik's name.

"What?" the gangly hunter slurred sleepily.

"Tomorrow night, you may borrow Kidla."

Unable to restrain my curiosity, I rolled over slowly to face my cousin.

Eyes wide and full of hate, Kiasik lay with his back to Kidla and Issuk. I met his gaze for an instant, but he looked away and locked his fists on the sleeping fur at his chin. In my camp, hunters asked their wives' consent for such an arrangement; Issuk had said nothing to Kidla—and she had said nothing to him. I peered over Kiasik's shoulder at her. She stared upward, the fur pushed away from her body, the sweat on her breasts shiny in the dim light of the oil lamp.

At the far end of the platform, Patik sat up and rubbed sleep from his eyes. "Hnnnn?"

"Kidla will lie with you tomorrow, yes?"

Patik grinned hungrily, now completely awake.

He did not wait long. As soon as we'd chosen our next camp and finished our iglu, he took her inside. The rest of us stayed on the ice, skinning the men's latest catch and feeding scraps to the dogs. The two returned before long.

Issuk snorted. "You're as quick as a lemming."

"Yes, in and out of your hole so fast it's over before it began," Onerk added with uncharacteristic humor.

Patik managed a gap-toothed smile and mumbled, "It's been a long time."

Kidla didn't look particularly upset. This wasn't the first time the men had shared her. Still, I caught the glance she cast at Kiasik, who stood frozen beside the butchered seal with blood coating his clenched hands.

"I haven't lain with a woman in just as long," Onerk reminded Issuk.

"I haven't forgotten," Issuk replied. "You can have her tomorrow—you've hunted long and loyally by my side. It's what one friend does for another." He turned his back on Kiasik, his meaning clear.

The next morning, I awoke to the sound of Onerk's moaning. The coupling had ended by the time I came fully awake. Kiasik lay stiffly beside me, his narrow gaze fixed on the ceiling as if he would punch right through the snow blocks. *Does he truly want her?* I wondered. *Or does he just want her all to himself?* Most men didn't feel possessive about their wives. A woman was like a weapon or a sled or a seal—an Inuk shared everything with his partners. Whoever needed it used it. Even children could be shared. My adoption by Puja wasn't unusual; even if my parents had lived, another childless couple might've reared me as their own.

Issuk didn't offer his wife to my cousin the next day. The stolen glances between Kidla and him ended. But I remembered Kiasik's jealousy when Ataata had shown me special favor.

My cousin always liked to win.

I could only hope that Kidla had sated the men's appetites, not whetted them. I spent the next several nights in a state of constant vigilance. At any moment, one of them might come for me. Kiasik hadn't saved me from Issuk the night Ataata died; he wouldn't be able to save me now. I felt like Black Mask, curled up outside with her nose under her tail, one ear pricked for the approach of the other dogs.

During the day, the ice beneath my feet only added to my unease. Sometimes I would catch sight of land again, far to the west, but Issuk stayed upon the frozen ocean where our path was smoother. Still, every time I slept, I worried we might awaken on a piece of drifting ice, carried to a whole new world with no hope of ever finding our way back home. But when I woke each morning, the ice remained firm, and Black Mask sat outside the iglu, unharmed. Her tail thumped weakly in greeting. Unseen by the others, I would slip her whatever meat I could spare.

We'd made it through another night.

CHAPTER SIXTEEN

♪

We traveled for another moon before the sleds started splashing through turquoise pools of meltwater. Issuk guided us closer to the shore, finally consenting to stay upon the safer landfast ice.

But when the shoreline curved sharply westward, he kept heading south. I thought we were simply crossing a deep inlet, as we had several times before. Yet no more land appeared, and the ice grew steadily softer beneath us. The narrow leads we were used to became chasms too wide for the sleds. For the first time on our journey, we used the small umiaq. Patik and Onerk stowed their sled and dogs inside the boat and paddled it across the stretch of open water. They returned for Kidla, Uimaitok, and the children. It took several more trips and most of the daylight, but eventually everyone—including all our dogs and supplies—had crossed the channel, and the men lashed the dripping umiaq back atop their sled.

"There are more big leads like this ahead," I heard Patik say to Issuk as we harnessed the dogs once more. "The farther we get from land, the more dangerous this becomes. I've never seen ice so soft this early in the spring. What happens if we hit wide-open water—with no ice at all?"

"Then we will use the umiaq again and paddle for as long as it takes to find land." Issuk sounded unconcerned.

"It's not big enough to take everyone at once." The gangly hunter glanced at me and Kiasik.

"Then some will get left behind." Before Patik could protest, Issuk went on. "The faster we move, the farther we get before it all melts." His whip licked over his lead dog's flanks, and the sled jerked into motion. "So if you want us all to cross, then stop complaining and start running."

And run we did. We splashed through deep pools of water. We helped the dogs drag the sleds through slush. Often, whole pans of ice would crack beneath us, forcing us to leap from one floe to another just to keep going in the right direction. When the leads grew too wide, Patik and Onerk would paddle one group across in the umiaq while the rest of us waited our turn, hoping the ice wouldn't crumble away beneath our feet.

Never had I seen such recklessness. We should have turned around and headed back to shore. Instead, we found ourselves in the middle of a quickly melting sea, struggling just to stay alive. If we lost the ice before we reached land, everyone who didn't fit in the umiaq would drown. I was too angry and afraid to say much, but when Kiasik ran beside me, I couldn't help myself. "This is what Ataata's father warned of," I hissed at him. "A sea that never freezes fully, not even in Seal Birthing Moon. Issuk will find no whales here."

"You're right." A quick, confident smile. The kind he had always reserved for me, and that I'd never thought to see again. "*I* will find them all. So many I'll build a huge umiaq from their ribs and paddle us all back home through the summer sea." He laughed at his joke.

I did not. "You know better than to boast like that."

His smile vanished. "And you know better than to sulk."

"So my sorrow is my own fault," I retorted. "Then go ahead, stop sleeping between me and Issuk. Why protect me from something you think I should enjoy?"

"I have always protected you," he shot back. "Ever since we were—"

"Then where were you?" I had never asked him. "When Issuk came into my iglu that night? Where was my older brother?"

He stiffened. "No one knew—"

"And did you still not know the next morning? When he tied me to his sled like a dead seal?"

"Our grandfather always taught us not to fight what we cannot change."

"And you chose *now* to listen." I wanted to laugh at the absurdity. "I remember a different lesson: Ataata taught me to be a man. One better and smarter than *you*."

I wanted him to snap back at me. Once, he had done more than protect me—he had thought me an equal worth wrestling with. Now he merely flared his nostrils and picked up his pace, leaving me to sweat and struggle alone.

Night and day we moved. We took turns sleeping on the sleds, but the sleds never stopped. The men rotated the dogs, tossing some into the umiaq to rest while the others kept pulling. At any moment, I was sure we would all crash through the ice and drown. None of us knew how to swim, and the weight of the sleds would pull the dogs under, too. But Issuk kept moving, never complaining, never showing any sign of fear. *The Moon guides him indeed*, I thought. There was no other explanation for his confidence.

Black Mask struggled to keep pace. Unable to compete with the stronger dogs for meat, she lost her flesh over the course of the moon—but gained a belly. She was unmistakably pregnant. The others assumed another dog had mated with her before anyone noticed she was in heat. Only I had seen the wolf. Only I knew the truth.

Normally we'd leave a pregnant bitch behind in camp, but we had nowhere to leave her. She was too weak to run for long, and we needed room in the umiaq to rest the other dogs. Finally Issuk pulled his harpoon off the sled and splashed across the melting ice toward her.

She sat back on her haunches and began to howl. The hunter stood, arms crossed across his chest, staring down at her; she stared right back, panting a little, then lifted her head to howl again. He stepped closer, his harpoon in one hand and his whip in the other.

She growled and bared her teeth. He slammed the whip down hard, but she ducked out of the way, moving faster than she had in many moons.

I knew full well that Issuk had little choice. He couldn't keep her; she slowed us down when we needed all our speed to cross the ice before there was no ice left. To free her would waste good meat and fur, from both her and her unborn pups. Either Black Mask must die, or we all might. Yet I found myself leaping to her defense. "You don't want to lose a whole litter!"

"I have too many dogs already."

A blur of fur and fangs, Black Mask lunged forward; her jaws snapped around his leg. Issuk yowled in pain, slamming the butt of his whip onto her head and shoulders.

Knife drawn, Onerk rushed forward and grabbed her by the ruff, yanking her head back as he swung his blade toward her throat. At the last moment, Black Mask jerked aside, sending Onerk's knife slicing neatly through her lead.

The dog bounded away.

"Aii!" Issuk launched his spear at her. Too late. Black Mask was long gone.

Issuk's wounded pride clearly hurt worse than his injured leg. The dog's sharp teeth couldn't penetrate his double-layer sealskin trousers. Watching from the iglu entrance as Ataata's favorite dog disappeared southward, I cheered silently. But I couldn't help feeling that I'd lost my only remaining friend.

◆━◆═◆═◆━◆

Not long after Black Mask's escape, we saw our first sign of a whale passing through a distant lead: a plume of wet breath exploding into the air. We heard the great exhalation, then the patter of drops falling into the water. Our first sighting of many. But always, when we finally reached the open lead, the whales were gone.

On the third morning of our journey across the melting ice, the dawn haze lifted and the shadows of mountains appeared in the distance, looking more like clouds than stone. But as the real clouds shifted, the mountains stayed put.

The black peaks remained visible for a full day before we reached the snowy shore. Steep sided, limned by the trailing tongues of glacier ice—not so different from the mountains I knew.

When we finally dragged the sleds onto shore and began to unload, Uimaitok and Kidla glanced at the mountains only briefly. Like my own family, Issuk's people preferred to stay by the shoreline or in the valleys. They might scramble on the lower slopes where the birds nest and the lemmings burrow, but they'd never ascend onto the slick glacier, where our knowledge of sea ice couldn't stop us from plunging into a glacier's hidden abyss.

Nevertheless, I found myself staring at the mountainside rather than at the tasks before me. As the Sun sank, the stark black-and-white cliffs softened into shades of gray. Thick clouds hid the summit, and wisps of white vapor encircled the slopes. Once, I'd flown above a mountain on raven wings. Invincible. Omniscient.

I still have my legs, I reminded myself. *If I could climb to the very peak, I might reach the sky. I could beg the Moon Man to give me back my magic.* But my legs were too sore and Taqqiq too stubborn.

I kept unloading.

CHAPTER SEVENTEEN

ϟ

Not like that, Ilisuilttuq," chided Uimaitok, yanking the seal-skin away from my clumsy hands. I've had many names in my life—Son, Grandson, Brother; now I had another, and every time I heard it, it stung. Ilisuilttuq. Stupid One.

To me, it was still Seal Birthing Moon, when the Sun and Moon finally split the day between them. At home, the ice bears would stomp on the sea ice to break into the seals' dens and steal their pups. But I hadn't seen a bear since we crossed the melting strait, and when I mentioned it to Uimaitok, she laughed and corrected me. "Ilisuilttuq, this isn't Seal Birthing Moon. This is Whaling Moon!"

In preparation, we spent our time strengthening the walrus-hide harpoon lines and repairing the damage the umiaq had suffered on our crossing, patching it with new sealskins and waterproofing the seams. It was tiresome work, and my jaws ached from chewing the hides until they were pliable enough to stretch around the drift-wood frame. The women laughed at my efforts.

The first time they placed a crescent-shaped ulu in my hands, I stared at it dumbly. This was a woman's blade. I yearned for my long, straight hunting knife. But when Issuk had packed me aboard his sled, he'd left my weapons behind. And even if I'd had my hunting knife—would using it break an agliruti? Would using an ulu? A woman carried one tool. A man another. But what if I was both? Or neither?

The women watched me impatiently.

"I don't know how to use it," I finally admitted. "Will you show me?"

A successful hunt would let us return to my family's camp. If that meant scraping hides and learning to sew, then so be it.

Little Nua, expertly working the walrus skin with her own small ulu, giggled at my plight. But Uimaitok wrapped my fingers around the blade's handle and set it to the hide at the proper angle.

"Gentle," she chided, rocking my hand back and forth. "You clean, you soften. You don't tear."

We continued along the shore. The mountains loomed to the west, and an unending expanse of sea stretched to the east. Landfast ice hugged the coast, but beyond it floated great pans webbed with wide leads. Further out, towering bergs and broad floes churned past. A perfect feeding ground for whales, but far too treacherous for a dogsled. To my relief, we stayed on the beach. But we did not stay in one place. Every morning, we packed up our camp and moved farther south in our perpetual search for the whales.

While the women continued to work on the umiaq, the men left every afternoon to seek out food. They ventured onto the narrow landfast ice looking for seals or traveled inland tracking fox and musk ox. Most of the time, they came back empty-handed.

My lessons continued. The women taught me to sit as they did, legs tucked beneath me, so I might bend over needle and scraper and ulu more easily. But Kidla's son made a mockery of my efforts, crawling into my lap just when I'd finally gotten the knack of separating the strands of caribou sinew for sewing. I suffered his attentions only because staying in his good graces ensured I stayed in Kidla's as well.

He clambered onto my pile of sinew, clearly thinking he'd found a very comfortable place for a nap. I gently pushed him off my work and back onto the small fox fur his mother had set out for him. He crawled right back, reaching one chubby hand toward me.

"He wants to be picked up," Kidla said mildly. I sighed in exasperation, hoping she'd volunteer to distract her son. But with no help forthcoming, I slipped him into the pouch in the back of my parka, where he promptly began to play with my hair. It'd grown long enough that Kidla had insisted on fastening it into a small tail at my neck.

"Soon," she said with a smile, "I can loop your hair in braids like mine."

For once, the baby knew my mind; he began to pull each hair out by the root.

When the men returned from yet another hunt with only a skinny white hare for their efforts, I was in the midst of a familiar—and fruitless—argument with the evil spirit on my back. Kiasik laughed and settled down beside us. "You have a new friend. Next thing you know you'll be having a child of your own. You're a good mother."

I gripped the ulu tight, my knuckles whitening. The baby, sensing my anger, began to whimper. Kidla hastily pulled her son from my parka and placed him on her breast.

"What?" Kiasik persisted. "You're still angry with me?"

"I should be hunting," I said finally. "I'd bring back more than that hare." Pride—an emotion I'd thought lost—welled once more beside my bitterness.

"I see." He was angry now. Defensive. He picked up our argument where we'd left off, as if he'd been chewing over my words for days. "Because you're a better, smarter man than I. Is that it?" He threw his own small catch onto my lap. "Clean it, Little Sister," he said, rising to go.

"I remember my father's words better than you do, Sister's Son," I spat back, my voice rising now. "Our ancestors warned that this land was barren. You follow Issuk into nothingness! We'll starve here. And if we all die, hope for our people dies with us. We're going the wrong way! The seals are in the north with the ice. Why do we go south?"

Issuk's calm rasp interrupted my tirade. "Because, Ilisuilttuq, the whales are south. So south we go." He looked at me keenly, and I felt the flush of life upon my cheek drain away. I dared not let him see my spirit return. I slumped my shoulders and willed my eyes to grow dull. Only once he released me from the pressure of his stare did I breathe easier once again.

The next day, we completed the repairs on the umiaq. We walked more quickly now, sure that when the next whale appeared, the men would be ready to chase it. I still didn't understand why they didn't just hunt from kayaks and spare themselves the trouble of hauling the larger boat, but Uimaitok laughed when I mentioned it.

"You can't hunt a whale from a kayak! One breath and it'd blow you out of the water!"

She turned to Nua and exhaled loudly through her mouth, making a sound surprisingly like that of a whale. The little girl giggled. Uimaitok swept her up as we walked and blew again, vibrating her lips against her daughter's belly until they both convulsed with laughter.

As if called by Uimaitok's mimicry, a great plume of water burst offshore. We stopped walking and stared, inhaling as the whale exhaled, sighing out as it sucked air. A round hump of black rolled amid white ice, then sank once more into an open lead. I was sure it was just another lone whale like those we'd seen before. One that would disappear long before the men could gather their harpoons and paddles.

Instead, another wet rush of air, and another. The quiet plash of bodies curving through water, the loud thump of their strong heads against the floes, the sharp crack as they broke the lead wider to help their calves breathe.

For the first time, a true grin split Issuk's face.

To my surprise, I found a smile to answer his own.

CHAPTER EIGHTEEN

♩

Issuk steered us to a bowl-like valley where two low hills would shield our new camp from the worst of the seaborne wind. From the hilltop the men could see all the way across the ice to where the whales fed along the floe edge. I wondered that they didn't leap into the umiaq right away, but Uimaitok assured me that, having found the whales' feeding ground, we must prepare carefully for the hunt ahead. A reckless chase was bound to fail.

Kiasik, Patik, and Onerk built a roomy iglu for us while Issuk readied the umiaq for its voyage. Revived by the hope of whales to come, the men laughed at their tasks, the sound echoing off the surrounding hills in a cacophony of overlapping voices. *Our own camp must've sounded like this before the death of my father and his age mates*, I realized.

The women caught the joyful spirit, smiling and giggling as they chinked the iglu cracks and set up the stone lamp and the drying rack.

Nua, arms outstretched, ran in tight circles around the outside of the iglu, despite her mother's efforts to get her to help set up the camp. She cawed like a raven, laughing in delight as the sound bounced back to her, mistress of a whole flock of invisible birds.

"I'm protecting our iglu from danger!" she cried, imitating the ritual of an angakkuq she'd seen in days gone by. At one time, I might've taken offense that a child would claim to have magic, or worried that her actions might thoughtlessly offend some spirit, but now I simply shrugged when the little girl turned to me and asked, "Am I doing it right, Ilisuilttuq?"

"I wouldn't know." I had no desire to relive my own failures. I continued searching the ground for a frozen pond, seeking clear ice for our window and drinking water.

"I'm trying to summon a raven," she explained, her lips pursed like a serious old woman's. I looked up at the empty sky, a flat expanse of dull gray cloud. She followed my glance, frowning. "It's not working yet."

"Ravens come where there's food. They follow the wolves, or sometimes the bear. They don't come when you call them."

"You never summoned a raven?" she asked.

Kiasik, coming around the iglu with a snow block for the entrance tunnel, interrupted. "Don't ask Omat about such things."

Immediately Nua's expression closed into the same solemn, frightened mask it always wore when a man came too close. Her hands dropped to her sides like the wings of a wounded bird.

"She's no angakkuq," Kiasik went on, oblivious to the girl's discomfort. "Omat has no more magic than I do." I hadn't heard such spite in his voice since we were children, fighting for Puja's affection.

He hadn't spoken to me directly since our last argument. My words had clearly wounded him more than he'd let on, and he'd sought friendship elsewhere, following Kidla's every movement with bright eyes.

To my surprise, Issuk came to my defense. "*All* women influence the spirits, Kiasik."

My cousin turned quickly toward the hunter like a shamefaced boy caught shirking his chores.

"If our women are not very careful to obey the special agli-rutiit," Issuk continued sternly, "the whales won't give themselves to us."

I wasn't sure which rules he spoke of, but a lifeless woman like me wouldn't bother to ask.

Tensions in the iglu that night ran high. The men sharpened their harpoons while the women checked the hide ropes for fraying. Kiasik and Kidla sat apart from each other, eyes averted, yet I could feel the heat between them, as palpable as if it rose from my own body.

Excited about the forthcoming hunt, I woke many times to find the others also rolling beneath the sleeping furs, sighing heavily or choking on interrupted snores. Had his desire not so clouded his judgment, Kiasik never would've chosen such a night to steal what belonged to Issuk.

I didn't realize I'd fallen asleep until a sudden draft pulled me awake; the place beside me on the sleeping platform lay empty. No Kiasik. No Kidla.

Only her sleeping baby remained, his mouth open in a wet circle. I lay still for a moment, listening, but heard only the steady drone of Issuk's snores.

I don't know why I went to look. I was as stupid as Kiasik. Even as I rolled silently off the platform and tiptoed across the iglu floor, I told myself I was Ilisuilttuq indeed.

I bent to glance down the tunnel—empty. I should have stopped there.

I slid my boots from the drying rack and crawled outside.

A whispered moan stopped me at the iglu entrance. I thought they must be coupling in the snow. Yet when I peered out beyond the rim of the tunnel, I saw no bodies writhing in the moonlight. They simply stood there. Holding each other. Nose pressed to cheek. Kiasik stroked Kidla's hair gently away from her temple, his fingertips light on her skin. She moaned softly and wrapped her arms more firmly around his back, her fists grabbing at the fur of his parka. He whispered something to her, too softly for me to hear, and I saw her smile before she nuzzled her face into his neck.

I backed up slowly, more upset than if I'd seen them straining together. I'd never seen Kiasik so gentle, so caring. His rare flashes of affection for me had never involved caresses. Had he simply taken Kidla's body as Onerk and Patik had, I would have felt no jealousy. I had no desire to lie with any man. But Kiasik did not just *want* Kidla—he loved her.

Uimaitok rolled over when I crawled onto the sleeping platform. Perhaps she too had spied on the couple, perhaps not. I couldn't bring myself to care. Envy burned in my gut like a sparking willow fire. I lay with my head under the furs, my eyes burning, until the dawn.

⊷ ▆◆▆ ⊷

The next morning, I'm sure only I noticed the new softness in Kiasik's glance when he looked at Kidla. Everyone else was too busy readying for the hunt.

Finally, when the men set out across the ice carrying the umiaq on their shoulders, I found out just what Issuk had meant about the power of women to influence the hunt. I started to leave the iglu, planning to walk to the floe edge to watch the chase. On the way, I might kill a bird or a lemming before my skills faded from disuse. Sanna's curse would keep me from capturing any sea animals, but I might have more luck with the creatures of land. I picked up a length of sinew and an ulu, hoping to fashion a crude spear if I could find driftwood or an antler.

"Ilisuilttuq!" Uimaitok screeched. "Don't touch that ulu! Don't you know anything?"

I dropped the knife in shock.

"You're a whale hunter's wife! If you cut anything, even a length of sinew, the harpoon line will be sliced and the whale will escape!"

Though Nua played at string figures, the women had been strangely inactive all morning. I'd assumed that after so many days of ceaseless work on the umiaq, they were simply enjoying a rest.

Uimaitok patted the furs beside her. "No wife should work while her husband is at a whaling camp. Better to sit quietly and wait for him. The whale will learn from us, and be quiet and still when the hunters approach."

"Who told you such a thing?" In Ataata's story of Sanna's marriage, the bird demon told her to stay inside while he hunted, but I'd assumed this rule applied only to spirits, not to Inuit.

"That's always been the way," Kidla chimed in. "No one needed to tell us. We watched our mothers." She glanced worriedly around the iglu and whispered conspiratorially: "I remember once when the men were whale hunting, we heard a dog whining outside our qarmaq. It sounded so pitiful that my mother sent me to check on it. It was caught in its traces. The more it struggled, the more the traces tightened around its throat. I was very young—I didn't have the strength to cut the dog loose. Finally my mother couldn't take the crying."

"Your mother was always too soft with her dogs," Uimaitok muttered.

"She went out, made sure no one was looking, and cut the dog free with her ulu."

"The Moon Man always sees," the older woman interjected.

"Uimaitok is right. When my father returned, he told us they'd harpooned a whale. It dove, but they watched the drag-float and followed its path. They waited and waited for it to surface again, but eventually they realized that the float wasn't attached to the whale anymore. The line had been cut, and the beast had swum away. My mother never told him it was her fault—but she never again disobeyed the agliruti."

The women's caution extended even to trimming the lamp wick, and with only Nua to mind the flame, the iglu grew smoky and hot. Drowsily, the women spoke of what they would do when the men returned. "I haven't eaten *maktak* in many moons," Uimaitok said wistfully.

Kidla smiled softly, her eyelids drooping. "With Kiasik to help," she mused, "I'm sure they'll bring back a bigger whale than ever."

I looked at the young woman sharply, but she was already asleep. Soon Uimaitok drifted off as well. Haunted by memories of last night, I could find no such escape. I longed to do something with my hands. I reached over to help Nua with a string figure she was creating, but she yanked it out of my reach and whispered, "You mustn't! The Moon Man will tangle the harpoon lines."

I lay back on the sleeping robes and threw an arm over my face. Kidla's baby cried for a moment; she rolled over, still half-asleep, to offer her breast. Again, all was quiet.

I couldn't bear it. I slipped off the edge of the sleeping platform, careful not to disturb the women.

"Where're you going?" Nua whispered.

I held a finger to my lips.

She turned to wake her mother, and I grabbed her arm, hard. "Don't say a word," I hissed, "or I'll transform into a wolf and bite you in your sleep!"

The little girl trembled in my grasp. Obviously she didn't trust Kiasik's assurance that I'd lost my magic, because she stayed quiet as I pulled on my boots and crawled outside.

As an angakkuq, it was my solemn duty to prevent my people from disobeying the aglirutiit. Yet all that time, I'd been the worst offender of all. It felt somehow liberating to finally break a rule of my own volition, to spit in the faces of the spirits who'd destroyed my life.

If the harpoon lines snap in punishment, I decided, *Issuk should blame Taqqiq. He's the one who created such a stupid rule in the first place.*

CHAPTER NINETEEN

ʃ

I slipped past the tethered dogs and scrambled up the low hill that separated our bowl-shaped valley from the sea. The glaring sunlight bounced off the ice, lightening the lower edge of the scattered clouds so they glowed like the bottom of a stone pot above a lamp. Farther out, the clouds darkened into water-sky, where the black water in an open lead reflected less light than did the ice surrounding it. The men had seen it, too, for they moved in that direction. Carrying the umiaq over their heads, they looked like a fat, many-legged beetle scurrying across the ice.

I squinted against the glare, wishing I'd remembered to bring my eyeshields. A true hunter would not have ventured out on so bright a day without them. I dared not go back to retrieve them for fear of waking the women. For a moment, I felt paralyzed.

Then, with a grunt of disgust at my own helplessness, I remembered Ataata's words: *An Inuk can always make something from nothing.*

In one of my favorite tales, a little boy lost his family and had to find his way down a mountain without a sled or dogs. Alone amid the ice and snow, he had no driftwood, no bones, no tools. So he shat onto the ground and formed his warm dung into a small, flat disk. It froze moments later—he had a sled. He peed along the bottom, and his piss froze into runners. He slid all the way down the mountain and into the safe arms of his family.

Trotting down the hill and onto the shore, I felt the crunch of gravel beneath my feet. The ocean winds had blown away much of the snow. I knelt and brushed away the white dust, uncovering a bed of stones and mostly unfamiliar shells. Using my ulu, I scraped a narrow slit, like the horizontal pupil of a musk ox, into two shells. Carefully I spun the corner of the blade to create ragged holes on either side, then threaded the sinew thong from my hair through the holes and tied the rough goggles onto my head. The ungainly contraption pressed into the bones of my face, but at least I wouldn't go snow-blind.

I must look like Sanna, I mused. *With shells for eyes and my hair loose and windswept.* I needed only frozen seaweed around my neck to complete the picture. Yet I couldn't help a surge of pride; my accomplishment, however small, proved I'd not yet lost my wits or skills.

I walked across the ice not with a woman's glide or an affected stumble, but with my own sure step. A hunter's walk. I longed to pull off my woman's parka and move without the encumbrance of the fringed tails and heavy hood, but some shred of common sense remained. The spring Sun warmed my face, but the cold air still nipped at my cheeks and nose. I had no spiked harpoon shaft with me to test the ice, and I remembered the lessons of my father's and grandfather's demise. As buoyant as I felt, I moved carefully. Still, this close to land, the ice would be quite solid, and I didn't intend to get near the dangerous edge. I'd walk only far enough to see the hunt.

Large ridges of pressure ice rose up to block my way time and again, slowing my progress. Yet I thanked Sanna for sending them—the ice hid me from view. I heard the hunt before I saw it. The splash of paddles in water, the low murmur of men discussing their plans.

Creeping behind a jagged tower of ice, I looked toward the small umiaq floating high in a wide lead. Hunting whales in the wide-open ocean, I'd heard Issuk explain to Kiasik, was nearly impossible. The whale could simply dive below and emerge too far away for even the swiftest paddlers to reach. But in a lead, the whale had few options. No matter where it surfaced, the men waited nearby.

Kiasik, Onerk, and Patik sat with paddles poised, their eyes scanning the surrounding water. In the bow, Issuk knelt with his long whaling harpoon raised. Its ivory head gleamed in the sunlight as if already wetted with blood. A good sign.

When the whale surfaced, I almost cried out in surprise. A loud exhalation, like the roaring of the wind. A sudden torrent of wetness thrust up into the air, a rainstorm reversed. The glint of slick black skin rolling through the water. This far away, I couldn't see its pair of yawning blowholes, but as the wind blew the whale's breath toward me, I could smell it—not fishy like a seal's, or bloody like a man's, but deep and dark like the sea. As I imagined Sanna herself would smell.

"Alianait!" Kiasik cried as the whale dove.

Issuk gestured sharply for silence, his eyes never leaving the spot where the whale had vanished. He pointed to the north.

The others paddled furiously. I watched, awestruck; the next time the whale appeared, the umiaq waited a mere boat-length away.

I scurried along the ice, dashing from ridge to ridge, trying to follow the hunt's progress while remaining hidden. The eyeshields I'd been so proud of became more burdensome than helpful, jostling when I moved.

Just as the whale rose again, I untied the sinew thong and let the eyeshields drop to my side. The shells slipped from the dangling cord, clattering onto the ice. I had no time to gather them—I dared not turn away from the hunt.

This time, the great animal rose farther from the water, revealing the black curve of its skull, its white, barnacle-stubbled jaw, even its small brown eye. Issuk hurled his harpoon. The blade struck true, right above the eye socket, and sank deep into the corrugated flesh.

The harpoon head twisted inside the beast like an anchor, while the driftwood pole fell away to float nearby, a narrow line still connecting it to the fore-shaft. A longer harpoon line unfurled behind as the animal disappeared once more beneath the water. Attached to the end of the rope, the inflated corpse of a seal bobbed on the surface. Even when the whale dove, the sealskin would stay afloat, marking the animal's location and preventing it from swimming too deep. But then, even as Kiasik shouted congratulations to Issuk, the float came loose from its line, bobbing quietly on the current to bang against the side of the umiaq like a seal begging to be killed. The harpoon line, which the women had spent so long carefully strengthening, floated for a moment longer, empty and loose, then slid after the whale.

As Issuk's angry voice carried across the water, I looked down at the empty sinew cord dangling loosely from my hand.

"Pull in the float!" he ordered Onerk. "Tie another line to it, and this time, make sure it's tight!"

He picked up Onerk's paddle and drove the boat forward, no doubt hoping for one more chance. Just as Onerk finished securing the new line and passed the last harpoon to Issuk, a blast of red spray shot up before them, raining droplets of blood. Issuk leaned back for an instant, then pitched forward to hurl the shaft. The rope streamed behind the harpoon, uncoiling like a whip; Onerk held up the seal float, ready to throw it overboard.

I've never forgiven myself for what happened next. Onerk had never paid me any mind, never been particularly cruel or kind. I didn't seek to harm him. I wasn't even aware that I wanted him dead. And yet at the sight of the excited grin on his broad face, envy surged through me, so raw my throat burned.

I should've been in that boat.

Before I even understood my actions, I'd tied a small loop in one end of the sinew cord.

The seal float still clutched in his hands, Onerk flew overboard, his feet yanked out from under him by a loop of the quickly vanishing rope.

For a moment, I could still see his arms wrapped around the drag-float as it tore through the waves behind the whale. The blood from the whale's spray stained the sleeves of his parka, and his thick hands gleamed red.

The whale, enraged by the second harpoon, thrashed and rolled, rocking the umiaq violently in its wake. With a slap of its massive tail, a wall of water swelled skyward and crashed onto the boat.

I tore my gaze from the foundering umiaq and searched for the bobbing seal carcass among the peaks and troughs of the roiled sea. The small gray float soon reappeared, moving swiftly southward as the whale made its final attempt at escape. Onerk had vanished.

"Keep paddling!" Issuk's voice was rough with anger and fear.

"There he is!" Patik called, pointing ahead with his paddle.

Onerk's black head floated on the dark waves, his body buoyed by his clothes. The men grabbed him by the hood of his parka and dragged his limp form into the umiaq. Even from my distant vantage point, I could see his skull lolling upon his snapped neck.

The bobbing seal float had finally stopped moving.

Slowly the water near the float swelled upward like broth in a pot. The whale's body rose to the surface. Issuk leaned from the boat to slam a long lance just behind its huge head, into a heart that had already slowed its beat. After a moment, the whale rolled to the side to expose its long white jaw, its glazed brown eye. The bloody lance protruded like a lonely inuksuk on an empty plain.

I'd seen enough.

My easy stride gone, I staggered back toward the camp, heavy with the weight of my guilt. For so long, I'd wanted nothing more than the return of my magic. Instead, I'd been given a power I never knew existed, much less thought I could possess.

And I didn't want it.

CHAPTER TWENTY

↱

I'd left my makeshift eyeshields in a tumbled heap on the ice when I fled, and I returned to the camp with my throat burning from the cold air and my eyes stinging. The tethered dogs raised their heads, tracking my passage as if they smelled blood upon my skin.

The iglu was cold. The lamp had sputtered out under Nua's inexpert care. In the faint sunlight streaming through the ice window, I could see her eyes glinting in my direction from beneath the sleeping furs. Before she could say a word, I whispered fiercely, "You let the lamp go out." She shrank back as if I might strike her, huddling close to her mother's sleeping form.

"I tried," she murmured.

"If I light it for you, and I don't tell anyone what you've done, will you stay quiet about my leaving?"

She widened her eyes in agreement. I moved toward the lamp and reached for the bow drill and the moss.

"Wait!" she hissed. "Don't tear the wick, only light it." I grunted my acknowledgment. Nua couldn't know it was too late to worry about breaking an agliruti.

I went through the motions of starting a fire like one asleep, my mind elsewhere. I took up the bow drill—a small, pitiful copy of the hunting bow I could no longer wield—and twisted its sinew string once around a short antler shaft. Pressing the bottom of the shaft into the moss on a board of driftwood, I slotted the top into an indented piece of bone clenched between my teeth. With the board in one hand and the drill in the other, I sawed briskly, the twisted bowstring spinning the shaft one way and then the other, the antler squeaking as it scraped against the bone in my mouth.

"Ilisuilttuq!" Nua put a hand tentatively on my arm. "You'll burn through the board!"

Smoke rose in low gray billows, threatening to suffocate us all. I stopped abruptly, my mind restored, and carefully tipped the black coals onto a flat stone.

Nua blew on the ball of moss tinder to create a flame while I stumbled onto the bed platform and wished for sleep.

The ceiling above me glistened wetly in the lamplight as the air warmed. In the flicker of ice crystals, I imagined the midnight stars.

Somewhere, in the limitless reaches above my head, Ataata's spirit inhabited one of those points of light. Beside him flickered the spirits of my parents and all my ancestors, looking down upon me. Upon this thing, this monster. Not woman. Not man. Just a murderer too obsessed with power to be trusted to wield it.

I lay on the sleeping bench for the next full day while we waited for the men to return. I tried not to imagine the worst. I knew the men had caught a whale, and it would take a very long time to drag it back, yet I worried that my magic had continued its evil work. Perhaps they all floated as Onerk did, dead on the waves.

Finally a holler echoed through our small valley. Racing from the iglu, we scrambled up the low hill. The landfast ice was weaker than we thought; a wide lead had opened nearby, allowing the men to tow the whale through the water right up to the shore. Kiasik sat in the prow, a wide grin on his face. Once I might've derided my cousin's smile as a sign of arrogance. Now I welcomed it. At least I hadn't killed him, too.

The giant whale carcass, three times the length of the boat, floated calmly behind like an obedient dog on a leash. Uimaitok and Kidla let out a bellowing cry, welcoming the men. The older woman licked her lips, anticipating the taste of fresh whale flesh.

Soon they would notice Onerk's body. I could see it already, wrapped in sleeping furs in the back of the umiaq. Nua's quick eyes had noticed the corpse, too; her smile evaporated. She turned to me. She knew.

I scowled at her until she looked away.

As Kiasik and Patik lifted Onerk's body from the boat, the women pulled their hoods over their faces, their joy dissolving into grief. Issuk stood before us, glowering. "Twice our lines failed us on this hunt. First one came untied, and then the next caught Onerk by the foot and dragged him off the boat."

"Ia'a!" Uimaitok cried. "We did no work, husband! We lay on the sleeping platform and neither cut nor untied string or wick!"

Issuk glared at each of us in turn. Kidla slashed the air with her hand. "No, no, not me."

"And you, Ilisuilttuq?"

"I lay in the iglu, as you asked," I murmured humbly.

Nua squeaked. Her father rounded on her and she flinched backward. "Yes? Speak!"

The little girl's eyes glistened with tears. Her mother whispered, "Have no fear, child. You're no woman yet. You can't be blamed."

But Issuk stepped toward his daughter and grabbed hold of her parka. Her head barely reached his waist. "Your face is open to me. What do you know?"

Nua didn't spill my secret, but I had no delusions: she didn't wish to protect me, only to avoid whatever punishment she feared I'd mete out. Still, her eyes betrayed her, shooting in my direction. Her father spun to follow her glance.

Before I could raise my arms to defend myself, Issuk struck a cracking blow against my jaw. My body twisted; my knees buckled; the earth rushed up to meet me.

Kiasik caught me just before I slammed into the ground.

Issuk bent toward us, close enough that I could smell his stale breath. "We called you Ilisuilttuq for your clumsiness, but we should've known you were still a danger."

Kiasik's arms tightened around me. "Issuk, she doesn't know your ways. She didn't mean—"

"Quiet! She knew full well what she did." Even then, Issuk knew me better than the others. "So, *Omat*," he growled, speaking my name like a curse. "You pretend to be a humble wife, but you think yourself an angakkuq still, meddling with forces better left alone." I clutched my throbbing jaw and wouldn't meet his eyes.

Uimaitok spoke. "Husband. The whale..."

Issuk grunted and stepped back from me. "First we mourn Onerk. Then we butcher the whale. This woman's folly must not disturb the joy of the hunt. To let it do so would insult the whale. Then...then we will deal with her."

He moved away, back to Onerk's corpse, and the others followed. Only Kiasik remained.

I said nothing for a long moment, just let myself slump within his arms. I had forgotten what it felt like to be held.

"What did you do, Omat?" he asked finally, his breath warm in my ear.

"I didn't mean...," I murmured. "I didn't realize."

He sighed. "I know. You're no murderer."

I glared at Issuk's back. "But *he* is."

Slowly he released me from his embrace and stepped away. He, too, stared at Issuk, his eyes narrowed. "I didn't see him push our grandfather into the water."

"But you didn't see Ataata slip, either."

"No," he admitted.

"So why don't you help me confront him? We could avenge—"

He spun back to me. "For the same reason I didn't fight Issuk just now, when he hit you! For the same reason I let him tie you to that sled!" His nostrils flared. "He and his men are our only chance to learn how to hunt the whale. Have you already forgotten how the seals fled from your harpoon? You brought ill luck to our camp. You must admit that!" He sounded more desperate than angry. He wanted me to agree with him.

When I remained silent, he lifted a hand, as if he would lay it on my cheek. "Everything I do," he murmured, "I do so I can help provide for our family when we return."

"Everything?" I demanded, flinching away before he could touch me.

He let his hand fall. "There is pleasure," he said, "in being good at something."

"At being better than me, you mean."

I expected him to grow angry. To lash out—or walk away.

Instead he simply stared at me for a long moment, his eyes full of pain. "Our grandfather, Ququk, Ipaq—even my own mother—never thought I was good enough. Too rash, too impatient, too arrogant. Here...they like me."

"Some like you very much," I said without thinking.

Kiasik's jaw tightened.

I moved close to him, nearly as close as Kidla had been. "I saw you the other night."

"You won't—"

"No, Sister's Son. I won't." He had tried, in his own way, to help me. I would not throw him on Issuk's mercy.

Kiasik darted close and pressed his cheek to mine. I did not pull away. "I would never have survived my first caribou hunt if it weren't for you," he whispered. "I'm sorry I never thanked you for that." I felt some of the frozen space between us begin to thaw, the long winter giving way to the first trickles of spring. "You and I," he went on, pulling back so that his eyes met mine, "we have always saved each other. We always will."

"Kiasik!" Patik's call sent my cousin jogging back to the umiaq. I wanted to reach after him, to drag him into my arms and tell him that he didn't need Issuk or Kidla to tell him he was worthy. I had always loved him. That should have been enough.

But I had no time to worry about Kiasik or Issuk or anything else. After we laid Onerk upon a pedestal of snow, where the ravens could take his spirit to the sky, we returned to the whale. Only butchering mattered.

Under Uimaitok's direction, we sewed every available line into one long rope and threaded it through a hole in the whale's tail. We harnessed the dogs to one end and reached for the middle of the line ourselves.

"Up!" shouted Issuk. We all held the rope at waist level. "Now!" Straining as one, we leaned back against the rope, using the weight of our bodies, the strength of our arms and legs and hearts. Issuk shouted commands at the dogs and at us with equal ferocity. "*Hut! Hut!* It's moving! Don't stop!"

Kidla slid to her knees, threatening to bring us all down, but was soon up and hauling again. I imagined myself as Black Mask, pulling beyond her strength, pulling until she nearly collapsed, but never giving up.

When the whale lay halfway on the ice, its bulk looming over our heads, Issuk finally cried, "Good! Stop!"

Gratefully we all sank to our knees and released the rope. Like water poured from a skin, the rope slid past us as the whale carcass slipped backward, dragging the helpless dogs yelping and squealing toward the sea. As one, we threw ourselves on the line, digging with our heels into the rough ice, but the beast's momentum was too great. The whale slid back into the water with a loud plop. It floated meekly, the rope line now slack, the team safe. We lay on the ice beside the dogs, panting along with them.

Once more we picked up the rope. Once more we pulled with all our strength. This time the agony lasted longer, for Issuk wouldn't take any chances. He was as merciless with us as with the dog team. Finally he deemed the whale secure. Patik loosed the dogs and led them back toward the iglu, where he could tether the team far from the tempting whale carcass. Issuk and Kiasik tied extra lines around the whale's flippers, staking the lines deep into the snow onshore so that even if the sea ice broke, we'd save our catch. We stood back to admire our handiwork.

It was a massive beast. I'd never seen one out of the water before. Once, when paddling along the coast, I'd seen a whale burst from the sea, flinging its body in an arc through the sky, rainbows forming in the spray and then disappearing just as fast. But that quick glimpse paled next to seeing it up close. The towering head made up a full half of its length; even Patik could reach the top of its skull only on tiptoe. Its bowl-like lower jaw, striped white and gray and encrusted with barnacles, curved up like an umiaq to join a long, narrow upper jaw that sat like a lid on a cooking pot.

Issuk pried the beast's mouth open: long, brown spears of baleen hung like seaweed inside. Tiny sea creatures moved about in the feathery curtain, unaware that their rescue from the jaws of the whale would be short-lived. Uimaitok eyed them with interest, no doubt wondering how best to prepare them for a meal.

But Issuk had other meals in mind. Why settle for tiny creatures when we could have rich meat and blubber? With his longest knife, he sliced deep into the whale's skin. Using a hook, the women pulled back the long strips of thick black hide backed in even thicker fat.

"This isn't just skin, like you get from a narwhal or white whale," Uimaitok corrected me when I admired it. "This is maktak."

All day and into the night we pulled the maktak from the beast, the blubber faintly pink and as deep as a man's forearm. We cut slivers of it and ate it raw, our exhaustion tempered by the sustenance. It melted on my tongue, rich and mellow and delicious. Yet every time I thought of my family, it turned to ashes in my mouth. _Puja has never tasted maktak, and if we don't make it back to her, she never will._

Soon the whale lay in a bloody heap on the reddened ice, scrawny and pitiful without its fat. We dared not stop to rest: if we abandoned our kill now, foxes and bears would happily steal it.

We cut away the meat, storing it in ice pits, and chopped off the flippers and tail, laying them in the sun to ferment. Finally only the skeleton remained, dripping with strips of tissue and organ. The skull, as big as an iglu, still supported the wide curtain of baleen.

"We have to harvest it soon," Uimaitok told me. "Once the baleen dries, it's no good for bending into tools and containers." Tireless, she prepared to cut it off, but Issuk laid his hand on her shoulder, a gesture of surprising warmth.

"Later," he said, his usually raspy voice made even rougher with fatigue. "Now we sleep."

When we woke next, Malina's rays once again crept steadily above the horizon. A mist rose off the water, shrouding the whale carcass in filmy cloaks of swirling white, as if its own breath once again sprayed forth in a cloud. Soon we'd finish the butchering. By then Issuk might have forgiven me for breaking the agliruti. Perhaps Kiasik and Kidla would cool their passion, or find a way to love each other without risking Issuk's wrath. The southern lands weren't barren after all. We would take the meat north, returning home to my family. Soon. Soon.

Then we heard the sound—a strange, uneven creaking. We knew the sounds of all the animals—the wavering bugle of caribou, the rising howl of wolves, the percussive rumble of musk oxen. This was none of those. But it was loud... and growing louder.

We stopped dismembering the whale skeleton. We tried to peer through the mist but saw only swirling white.

None of the men considered hiding or running. They were hunters, and whatever appeared must be prey. The fearsome ice bear would fall beneath enough arrows. Even the great whale fears our harpoon. Only the ice was unconquerable, and this new sound bore none of its familiar rhythms or melodies. We knew its growls, screams, groans. It could even creak. But never was that creaking accompanied by the sound of a loose hide flapping in the wind and the splash of countless flippers hitting the water.

Though Issuk looked more curious than afraid, I found myself suddenly shivering. As surely as if I'd heard the warning from Singarti himself, I knew danger approached. A danger far worse than cracking ice or blinding fog. Worse than jealous husbands or straying wives. It would tear our lives apart more swiftly than any woman's thoughtless string magic.

And nothing would ever tie them back together again.

CHAPTER TWENTY-ONE

γ

As the strange creaking and splashing continued, Issuk gathered his bow and arrows and motioned for the other men to join him. Another gesture sent the women and children scurrying back over the hills toward the iglu, the whale carcass abandoned.

I stood my ground. Kiasik frowned at me.

"You might need my help," I whispered.

That look again. Pity. "This is man's work. You might get hurt, Little Sister."

Sister. The word drove me away as swiftly as a lash. *If this is what he means by saving me, I would rather he didn't even try.*

Seething with anger, I returned to the iglu but remained outside. No matter what Kiasik believed, I was a hunter still. I would stay ready to rush back over the hill if something threatened our catch—or my brother.

It might be a spirit, I thought, squinting toward the distant sound. *Or a giant, or some creature half walrus, half bear, created in the womb of Sanna herself.* This was a new land—perhaps it held new monsters. But it never occurred to me that the sound could come from other men. The only other Inuit besides my family were those far to the west, where Issuk and his people had lived. Here, in the south, no other men existed.

Patik had taken his bow and a sheaf of arrows but left a harpoon stuck in the snow beside the iglu. If the men came back and saw me with the weapon, I'd be punished—but I'd rather face their wrath than meet a strangely creaking animal unarmed. I pulled it from the snow, comforted by the solid shaft of driftwood in my hands.

A scream pierced the air, high and shrill, like the cry of a bird. It came from the water's edge. I tensed, ready to run.

Shouting. Several voices speaking nonsense. A loud splash, like a boulder falling into water. Another scream. This time, a voice I recognized.

Kiasik.

I ran forward, an instinct deeper than self-preservation urging me toward the sound of my milk-brother's cry.

Up over the first low hill, over the rise beyond it, my legs slapping against the heavy apron of my woman's parka. Out of the mist loomed the whale carcass, a third hill. I skirted the bloody pile, past the beast's gaping maw.

A few steps past the carcass, Patik materialized from the whiteness, nearly bowling me over.

"Run!" His last word.

As I lurched to the side, slipping on the frozen puddle of whale blood, an arrow flashed from the mist. With a thud, it sank between Patik's shoulder blades. He tumbled to his knees.

The fletching of a second arrow slashed across my face like a knife.

With blood trailing down my cheek, I ducked low and scuttled behind the looming whale head. Footsteps crunched toward me across the snow. A slow man, or one with an impossibly long stride. I dared to move my head so I could peer between the whale's jaws, hoping the curtain of baleen would obscure my face. The mist thinned—I could make out the dark shape of a man striding toward the fallen Inuk, who lay facedown, his own blood mingling with the whale's.

The stranger was tall, taller even than Patik. A spreading beard covered his pale face like an animal's pelt. In the light of the foggy evening, his hair looked white, like an old man's, yet he moved with the sure stride of youth. He pulled a weapon from a sheath at his waist—a short spear, or a very long knife, I couldn't tell which. Though it glinted like obsidian, it was the light-gray color of normal stone. But no stone blade could have so easily severed Patik's head from his body.

I stifled a gasp.

The tall stranger turned at the sound of my breath, but I ducked just in time. He stood still for a long while, looking in my direction, but finally a shout from the beach drew his attention. I heard him turn on his heel and move back to the shore.

I dared to peek out once more as he walked away. The clouds parted, and thick rays of sunlight quickly dissipated the remaining mist. I could see his form clearly now. His clothes hugged his body in a way no fur parka ever could. His limbs were long and lean, his shoulders broad beneath a flapping blue cloak that fell to his ankles. The sun struck his hair, dispelling the white, and it glinted back like fire, orange and gold. This was no Inuk. He must be a giant.

Only a giant could ride in such a boat. I could see it now, the great beast that made such strange sounds. Its paddles jabbed the sky like the limbs of a grasping insect. The head of some spirit— part wolf, part bird—loomed above its prow. The boat was longer than any umiaq and three times as wide. Strangest of all, a tall pole soared from the middle of the boat, hung with a great white wing. On board, four men stood crammed against the rail, looking down at the shore. One aimed a bow. Each of the others held a spear or long blade. The wide lead had opened even farther; the boat drew close to the shore.

The flame-haired giant who'd killed Patik hurried back toward two prone figures lying at the water's edge. I recognized one of the bodies: Kiasik.

I wanted to scream his name, but at that moment, the sun flashed off the strangers' drawn blades, and I snapped my mouth shut. I'd be of no use against such a force, and my milk-brother might already be dead. If both of us died, who'd take care of Puja?

Kiasik lay motionless, his face obscured by the wolverine ruff of his hood. Next to him lay another stranger, slighter and shorter than the others, but clearly no Inuk. His hair was as pale as dead leaves, and, like his companions', his strange garments were blue, red, and yellow. Even in that moment, consumed by fear, I found myself staring at the colors these giants wore. They looked like spring flowers bursting from the winter soil.

The flame-haired giant knelt and gathered the thin stranger in his arms, propping him gently against his chest. Blood trickled down the smaller man's shoulder, turning his yellow shirt red. The stiff black feathers of Patik's arrow protruded from beneath his collarbone.

From the boat, the surrounding crowd spoke loudly. At least I thought they spoke; they didn't say words, just a string of strange sounds. Sometimes melodic, sometimes grating, always as incomprehensible as the roaring of the ocean.

One man, taller even than the flame-haired giant, began beating his long gray blade against a round wooden board and chanting the same few coarse sounds over and over: *"Drepa! Drepa! Drepa!"*

A hood as hard and gray as his blade covered his head and most of his face, more like a shell than a hat. Long hair, the dark yellow of old piss, streamed from beneath his headpiece, some hanks flowing loose to his back, some tied in intricate braids like a woman's. The sunlight picked out carven monsters glinting across the headpiece, spirits like the one on the prow of the enormous boat. Only his mouth was clearly visible, a gaping red maw in a jaw as long and thin as a fox's snout. His full yellow beard hung in a loose braid a handspan beneath his chin.

The other men soon joined in his chant, their voices thrumming like a chorus of angry walruses.

I scanned the rest of the camp and the surrounding hills but saw no other bodies—and no sign of Issuk. The flame-haired giant didn't join in the chanting. He was too engrossed in comforting the injured man in his arms, speaking to him in soft murmurs as he ripped strips from his own blue cloak to tie around the man's wound. What sort of hide could split so easily? Or did he possess the power to hunt blue beasts and tear their skin with his bare hands?

Kiasik stirred briefly, his head rolling toward me so I could see the blood trickling from a wound on his forehead. My heart shuddered beneath my ribs—he was alive.

And yet, without help, he wouldn't be for long.

I tensed, ready to rush to his rescue despite the near certainty of my own capture. Then the fierce hooded giant leading the chanting vaulted over the boat's rail and onto the ice. He sprinted toward my hiding place, his long yellow hair streaming. The others followed, their chant devolving into a hoarse cry of rage.

I ducked farther behind the whale's carcass, willing myself invisible. I felt rather than saw the crowd rush by me, their feet kicking snow and gravel. When they were past, I dared to peek toward the boat. I couldn't believe my good fortune. Only the injured stranger and his flame-haired protector remained at the water's edge. Kiasik lay motionless beside them.

Despite his swift murder of Patik, the giant seemed far less intimidating now. He pressed his cheek against his companion's. As any Inuk might do for a hunting partner, he stanched the smaller man's wound with one hand while grasping his limp fingers with the other.

I dared to slip out from behind the whale, my harpoon ready.

A child's scream ripped the air.

I froze. The flame-haired giant hunched forward as if to shield his companion from the sound.

The dogs, still tethered beside the iglu, soon drowned out the child's scream with a discordant chorus of yips and howls. One by one, those yips strangled into whimpers, then silence.

I clutched the harpoon so tightly I thought it might splinter in my grasp.

In my concern for Kiasik, I'd left the women and children to fend for themselves. *If Issuk were in my place*, I knew, *he'd let my family die.*

At the little girl's next scream, the giant glanced up. Revulsion and anger flashed across his face, and for a moment I thought he'd rise. But then his gaze met mine. He bared his teeth like a cornered animal, tightening his grasp on the wounded man like a woman protecting her child.

I thought of Uimaitok and Nua. Kidla and her infant son.

I took a step back, lowering my harpoon.

I cast a last glance at Kiasik. His eyelids fluttered; a single line of blood ran from his forehead down the side of his nose, sliding between his parted lips. His arms and legs splayed like the limbs of a fallen caribou.

I sprinted back to the iglu, slipping and sliding on the bloody snow beneath my feet.

CHAPTER
TWENTY-TWO

↯

I remembered bitterly how carefully Issuk had picked the location of our camp. The two hills that had sheltered us so well from the harsh sea winds now stood between his family and the only rescue they were likely to find.

Nua screamed once more. Circling overhead, a raven cawed harshly in reply.

The little girl's cry ended in a gurgle.

The bird's cry went on.

I couldn't understand the raven's tongue, but I knew these were bird curses—whether cast upon the strangers or the Inuit, I didn't know.

Up and over the rise of the first hill I ran, then the second.

I saw the dogs first. Scattered heaps of bloody fur, each body pierced by arrows. A few still whimpered. One kicked its legs spasmodically, unable to rise.

Then Nua. Her tiny body lay in a pool of red slush by the iglu entrance—her head lay a few paces beyond. I staggered at the sight, the bile rising in my throat.

I couldn't see Uimaitok's body, but her legs, twisted and still, protruded from the tunnel. Kidla crouched in front of the tall yellow-haired leader, sheltering her squalling infant with her body.

"Please!" She grasped at the man's trouser leg. "Don't hurt him!"

He shook her off, throwing back his head and laughing while the sunlight glared from his hard gray hat. He said something in his guttural language; his comrades laughed. Their own blades remained sheathed, their arms full of stolen furs. Only the leader's weapon was wet with blood.

With his free hand, he wrenched the baby from Kidla's grasp and suspended it by one tiny arm over his head. The infant swung like a haunch of meat, his mewling drowned out by his mother's hysterical screams. The giant raised his impossibly long gray knife and pressed the tip against Kidla's throat.

"Stop!" I screamed. I didn't think—if I had, I might've held on to my harpoon. Instead, I threw the shaft with all my strength. It whirred through the air, a streak of white death, and struck the man's ribs. The driftwood shaft clattered to the ground, but the head remained embedded in his flesh.

He didn't scream, merely stumbled for a moment, the breath gone from his body. He dropped the baby as his hand flew to his side; the child landed with a sick thud on the icy ground, whimpering.

Through the holes in the strange headpiece, the giant's eyes met mine. The men around him turned toward me, their voices raised in shock and anger.

I looked around frantically for some new weapon. *An Inuk can always make something from nothing.* But what good was snow and gravel against these men's long blades?

Kidla gathered up her unconscious child, rocking it desperately.

"Run!" I shouted. "Don't just sit there! Run while they're after me!"

She turned dazed eyes toward me and staggered to her feet. She made it only two steps before the yellow-haired giant's blade cut into her neck. She sank to her knees, her blood spilling over the clean white pattern on her parka.

He raised one foot above the baby. Its skull cracked open as easily as an eggshell.

"*NO!*" The scream ripped from my throat.

The men drew their weapons and closed on me.

I sent a silent vow to the spirits of my ancestors. To Ataata and my parents and all Inuit who'd come before me. *If I live, I'll follow the giants to the ends of the world for what they have done. And if I must die, make me an avenging spirit to haunt them unto madness.*

A single shouted word from the yellow-haired leader stopped the oncoming men in their tracks. With his hand pressed against his ribs and blood seeping between his fingers, he hobbled toward me.

"*Skraeling minn,*" he growled. "*Vig mitt.*"

The men came no closer. They formed a loose circle, their blades pointed at me. I could only assume the giant wanted to finish me off himself.

I wanted to cower. I squared my shoulders instead. I'd only ever fought Issuk, that night he came for me in my iglu. And I'd lost. This giant was taller, stronger—but I'd already wounded him once. I'd killed walruses that were larger. Caribou that were swifter. I might have a chance.

He lunged toward me, swinging his blade in an awkward overhead arc. I sidestepped the blow easily. With the wound in his side, he could barely stand, much less strike quickly. Yet still he fought.

He grunted something to his men. One of them hurried forward to remove the leader's headgear. I hoped it would rip off, tearing at his flesh like a shell torn from a sea creature. Instead, a man's face lay underneath, hard boned and thin, the flat cheekbones covered in hair. His long yellow braids whipped in the wind. His eyes, gray as a thunderhead, burned with anger.

Sheathing their blades, two of the men moved to grab me, one young, with a puckered scar across his cheek, the other older, with grizzled hair cut short against his scalp. I ducked beneath the scarred one's outstretched arm and swung my leg, hoping to catch the older man in the chest. The apron of my parka hampered my movement; I managed only a glancing blow to his thigh before I tripped and fell to the ground.

The yellow-haired giant laughed at my clumsiness. He stumbled toward me with his blade raised. I forced myself not to wince, not to cry out.

An arrow whined past my ear.

A near-silent thunk of blade slicing through flesh.

The grizzled man I'd kicked fell to the ground, clutching at an arrow in his throat. White gull feathers on a caribou-bone shaft. Issuk's arrow.

Before the men could turn to find their attacker, another arrow, another man wounded, white feathers drenched red as the scarred one's arm spurted blood.

"Begone! Gone! Gone!" Countless Inuit shouted from the hills, the shore, the distant mountains.

"Leave us! Us! Us! Us!"

The remaining men spun around, searching for the invisible horde. Another arrow whistled by the yellow-haired giant's head. He dropped to the ground beside me. The shaft clattered onto the hard snow a few paces away, but the giant's fall had driven my harpoon head deeper beneath his ribs. For a moment, Kidla's murderer and I lay eye to eye, our faces pressed into the frozen ground. He blinked very slowly, his eyes glazed with pain, but I knew he saw me. Hot and rank, his breath brushed my face.

The other men shouted to each other, their voices pitched high with fear. The scarred man with the wounded arm scooped up the leader's headgear and blade. Another flung the body of his dead comrade over his shoulder. The other two grabbed the leader under his arms and struggled toward the shore. The yellow-haired giant's feet left long trails in the snow as they dragged him away.

I lay still until I could no longer hear their crunching steps. Until the slap of oars grew fainter and fainter and finally faded into nothingness, replaced only with the beating of my own blood in my ears. Only then did I dare stir.

"OMAT! Omat! Omat..."

My name echoed off the hills. A desperate, pained cry for help. Then it too faded away.

I knew that all the voices had been the echoes of Issuk's voice, and all the arrows had been shot from his bow. And now he needed me.

The first cry came from inland, beyond the iglu. I ignored it.

I ran back over the two hills toward the sea. I could still see the boat, very small and very far away, its massive white wing reflecting the last of the Sun's rays. But the shore itself was empty. No flame-haired giant or his wounded friend—and no Kiasik.

I knelt beside the snowy rocks that had cushioned my milk-brother's head. I rubbed my hands into his blood. It outlined the whirls of my fingerprints, as if an angakkuq had turned my flesh to a carven totem, adorned with spirals.

"Kiasik!" I screamed his name at the retreating boat. But my voice did not echo, did not carry. The wind drowned out my cry.

"Omat."

Issuk stumbled toward me. A long arrow shaft protruded from his gut. Two more sprang from his back. Blood poured down his parka, staining him red from waist to feet. He dragged his bow across the ground, pressing one hand against the wound in his stomach.

Instinctively I backed away from him. "Where were you? How could you leave them alone to die?"

It took him many shuddering breaths before he could speak.

"They shot me and I ran. The next thing I remember..." He paused, a bubble of bloody spittle growing and shrinking with every labored breath. "I was lying on the ground, and I heard their voices near the iglu. I crawled to look...and I saw them around you."

"Your family is dead." I couldn't bring myself to thank him for saving my life. Not after he'd destroyed it in the first place.

He moaned faintly, swaying where he stood.

"You were too late." My voice was hard, merciless. "Too late for your family. And too late for mine."

His bow clattered to the ground. He fell to his knees.

"Help me."

Responses pounded through my mind like a herd across the tundra, so fast and so many they blurred before me. I could try to save him despite his terrible wounds. I could take the knife from his belt and plunge it into his heart, killing him as he'd killed Ataata. I could tell him to call upon his grandfather, the Moon Man, for aid.

But in the end, I chose to do nothing.

Standing over him, I watched him die. Watched the light fade from his eyes and the blood pump more slowly across his fingers and between his lips.

With his head lolling to the side, Issuk's long mustache fell unheeded into his open mouth, black and wet with blood, heavy like a leech crawling between lips now pale.

I didn't touch him until his blood ceased to run and his chest no longer moved. Only then did I reach to close his eyes; I couldn't stand for them to look at me ever again.

I pulled off his boots and trousers, as I had seen Uimaitok do so many times after the hunt. His penis lay white and shriveled on the dark mat of his hair, a root rotting amid wet soil.

If this were a story like those we tell on winter nights, rather than my own tale, I'd have cut off that root and buried it in the ground that it might grow into something finer than the plant from which it sprang. But it was getting cold and the Sun was low, and I had no time for grand gestures.

I yanked out the arrows, then straightened Issuk's arms over his head so I could pull the parka from his body. His skull smacked the ground as it came free.

The arrows had destroyed the careful pattern of black and white fur, all his wives' hard work ruined. I cut Ataata's pendant from around his neck. Carefully I placed the black bear claw, worn shiny by my grandfather's fingers, into my own amulet pouch. I dragged Issuk's corpse across the ice to the edge of the open water.

I kicked it into the lead and watched the current carry it away. His naked body glowed white on the dark waves, growing smaller and smaller until it disappeared.

"The seals will feed on your flesh," I whispered. "The fish will feed on your eyes and the whales on your blood. Your bones will drift to the bottom of the sea—they will fall as a feast for Sanna's lair, and she will count me again among her favorite sons."

I felt an echo of the old power in my words, and for a moment, I wished I could take them back. I'd sent Issuk to my old enemy, hoping to placate her. Had I instead sent the Sea Mother a new ally? If Issuk's soul didn't rise into the stars, but instead sank beneath the waves, would he have even more power than before? Ataata might've known the answer. All I could do was wait and see.

I slit the throats of the suffering dogs. I dragged Patik's body to lie beside Onerk's. I laid the bodies of the women and children on their own tall mound of snow that they might be given to the ravens.

When I returned to the whale's carcass, Sanna had answered my question.

The umiaq was gone. The fragile sea ice had split asunder, leaving only fast-moving water in a wide lead where the boat should've been. The Sea Mother still punished me.

Even if I could build a new umiaq, I knew I couldn't travel across the sea—not with Sanna hunting me at every step. And a sled was little use without a single dog to pull it.

I had to walk.

But walk where?

Standing before the slain, I'd vowed to follow the strange giants and have my revenge. But the task now seemed impossible, the stuff of legend, not life. Far easier to simply wait for winter and then return home as I'd longed to do for so many moons. Once the wide strait froze again, nothing would stop me.

I looked north, to where my family waited. Soon their meat caches would be empty. Long ago, I'd promised to take care of them. But if I returned, I'd be a hunter who scared off the seals, an angakkuq who angered the spirits. All my life I'd had such pride in my skills—now I faced the truth of my own worthlessness.

With no dogs and no boat, I couldn't even carry the maktak to my family. They didn't need me. They needed Kiasik.

How he'd strut to hear me say that, I thought, laughing hoarsely through my tears. We had always saved each other, he'd said. I wanted him to be right. I just didn't see how.

I had two options. Walk home to starve beside my kin. Walk south to certain death chasing the giants who had captured my milk-brother.

I looked out once more over the water. There was a third option. I could do as Ipaq had done—take myself onto the ice to die. With no babies born to my camp, my soul wouldn't return to this world for a long time. Yet I didn't mind the prospect of leaving this life for a while.

I was very tired.

I sat on the ice and closed my eyes. I didn't try to summon the spirits; I knew they wouldn't listen. Instead I offered myself to Sila the Air. It would do with me as It wished.

As You raised Malina and Taqqiq into the sky to become Sun and Moon, I prayed, *so too might You guide my path.*

When I heard a wolf howl, I felt my own spirit crack open in lamentation. Stripped of my magic, I couldn't understand the wolf's words, but I knew it sang of my loss: Never again would I see Ataata's face or little Nua's. Never would I fly like the raven or run like the wolf. And now I'd lost Kiasik as well.

I opened my eyes. Far across the open lead, a wolf ran toward me, a distant blur of white fur on white ice. It came from the ocean, a place no wolf should be.

The wolf galloped straight toward the water's edge, never slowing. It leapt—so high and long I thought it might never come down. But the crack in the ice gaped wider than any wolf could ever jump, even a wolf such as this.

The wolf didn't fall into the water—it merged with it. One moment the animal hung in midair; the next an ocean swell covered it completely. I got to my feet, squinting to see if the wolf might survive and swim to shore.

A burst of wet air shot from the sea, the setting Sun painting rainbows in the droplets. A whale's breath.

I could just make out the top of its glossy dark head. A moment later, a tall fin, as sharp and black as a raven's wing, pierced the water. An *aarluk*. A whale with teeth like a wolf's.

The aarluk surfaced to suck another slow, wet breath. For just a moment, I could see its eye, small and dark beneath a bright oval of white skin. Then it slid beneath the water, first its head, then its tall, sharp fin. I watched until the fin appeared one more time far down the lead, waving slowly in the distance. Beckoning me south.

There is a very old story, rarely told, of a wolf that runs into the ocean and becomes a whale. It is said that the two animals share a spirit.

I'd been sent a vision, though I didn't know by whom. Sila, perhaps. Or Singarti. Maybe even Ataata. I couldn't speak to them, couldn't summon them—but I could watch. I could listen. And I thought I understood their message.

The wolf is not bound to its shape. It can change form at will, transforming to a whale when it must swim in the sea.

Seeing the whale, no one would ever suspect it had once been a wolf.

———— ✦ ————

Asking its pardon, I undressed Onerk's corpse. Flouting the agliruti, I dressed myself in the dead man's clothes. I'd killed him. Now he would be my rebirth.

Garbed once more as a man, I entered the blood-soaked iglu. I sawed at my hair so it brushed the tops of my ears as a man's should. I filled a pack with sleeping furs, a tent, a few tools and weapons, the smallest stone lamp and pot, and as much maktak as I could carry. I lashed the pack between Issuk's bow and a harpoon shaft and slung the frame onto my back. A carrying strap braced the weight against my forehead.

I wore a man's knife in a sheath looped across my chest. I carried a woman's ulu in my pack.

The wolf in the whale had gone south, following Kiasik. Following the yellow-haired murderer with his bloodstained hands. Following the flame-haired giant with his gentle touch and wicked blade.

The wolf in the whale had gone south. And so did I.

BOOK THREE

WOLVES

The old Inuk stands vigil on his qarmaq roof, awaiting the heralding stars and the rebirth of his son.

The Moon looks down from above. The Sea Mother looks up from below.

At the other end of the world, a great one-eyed god with a long gray beard sits on a high silver throne. With a raven perched on each shoulder, he looks westward across the wide ocean toward the land of ice, where the Frost Giants, his eternal enemies, live amid the black mountains and the frozen sea. But he does not see the child born amid its mother's cries and a wolf's hot breath. He sees only his own fear.

Long ago, he slew the greatest of the Frost Giants. He made the earth from the Giant's eyebrows, the rivers from his blood, and the sky from his skull. To the small, dark folk who live in homes of snow, the Frost Giants are gods still—gods of moon and sky and sea. And one day, those Giants will return to take their revenge on the one-eyed god and his kin.

He has spent an age readying for the prophesied battle. At his command, the gods have forged weapons of iron and gold, clothed themselves in armor, and gathered armies both human and divine—all in preparation for the Ragnarok, the Fate of the Gods. Even the one-eyed god cannot tell who will be the victor.

Thus, since the time before time, he has stood vigil, his one eye sharp, watching the West for the Frost Giants' approach. Until now.

The god turns away from the Giants' icy realm and toward the searing heat carried by a strange new wind. A desert wind that saps the strength from his limbs, the keenness from his mind. A wind that carries word of a new god upon the land, a god without spear or hammer, without wife or child, a god more powerful in death than in life.

A new enemy threatens his rule. One he did not prophesy. One he cannot defeat with arms or armor or armies.

—————✖————

The one-eyed god summons his divine family, who call him Odin, All-Father. They stand tall and stately, with hair in streaming braids of yellow and orange and brown, their gowns of silver cloth and armor of beaten gold so bright no mortal can live in their presence.

The All-Father's mightiest son comes forth, red bearded and broad shouldered, his hammer—so heavy no other god can lift it—held loosely in one armored hand. "Father," Thor begins, his voice rumbling like the thunder he wields, "the new god walks among his followers, barefoot and radiant, with blood coursing from his hands. Always north and west, spreading like a pestilence. He saps the strength and courage of our people. No longer do they dream of joining us in Valhalla, where the walls echo with the clash of glorious battle."

The old All-Father nods weakly. He rubs at the socket where his eye once lay. A shiver runs through the others as they watch Odin diminish. His wife, Frigg, shudders with grief, and the mothers on earth tremble in turn. Tyr, one-handed god of war, strikes his fist against his thigh—far below, warriors strike their swords upon their shields in unconscious imitation of their lord. Freya, beautiful goddess of love, hides her face behind her golden hair—the flowers wilt as mortal maidens sing songs of death.

The Thunder God raises his hammer, and lightning sparks from his fiery beard. "Let us march to the East and kill the desert god! Let us banish him as we banished Loki!"

"Patience, Thor," Freya's brother, Frey, urges. Barley sheaves bind the brow of the god of growing things, and his eyes are mild.

Red-bearded Thor strikes his hammer against the walls of the golden palace. Lightning flashes. Storm clouds roll. "You are a coward, Frey—you who gave away your sword an age ago! What know you of battle?"

Frey merely nods. "True, I am no warrior. I give men food, not rage. I do not wield a hammer, like you, or a sword, like Tyr, or a spear, like the All-Father." He raises his empty hands, and a soft yellow light fills his palms. "I bring sunlight, not war. I seek fertile land, not the plains of battle."

Beautiful Freya steps between her brother and Thor. Flowers bob in her hair, but her voice is fierce. "Listen to Frey. Peace is what we need now. Force of arms will accomplish nothing against this new god. He is dead already, and yet lives on."

"So what would you have us do?" demands Thor.

"Where our people go," she answers, "where their skalds tell our tales and their warriors sing our songs, so, too, do we. Perhaps we can live on . . . after a fashion."

"You are saying we stop fighting?" Thor roars the words, his voice shaking the hall. The others shout and gasp—to a god of the Norse, there is nothing worse than surrender. A slim goddess, handmaiden to Freya, nearly faints in shock. One-armed Tyr helps her to a nearby bench.

Tall Frigg, Odin's wife, silences the assembled gods with a single raised finger. "Why are you shocked? You know our immortality has always been a fragile thing." Deep shadows circle her eyes. She has already mourned the death of her youngest son, lost to foul trickery and murder despite all her efforts to keep him safe. This new threat is just one more grief to bear. "We chained Loki for his crimes"—she touches the heavy keys that dangle from the brooch on her breast, the ones that keep her son's murderer imprisoned—"but we are the ones who are trapped. Bound in place beneath a serpent's fangs as its venom trickles on our heads without cease. Drop by slow, poisonous drop, until we are eaten away to nothing."

No one speaks. No one breathes.

The All-Father finally rises from his throne, leaning on his spear. The gods wait, sure their wise king will know how to defeat this new enemy as he has defeated all the others. But when he speaks, his shoulders hunch. Odin has already surrendered. "Soon there will be no place for us here.

Freya and Frigg are right. The bleeding Christ will conquer our lands without striking a single blow. He will chase us away just as he chased Athena from Athens and Jupiter from Rome. Now those gods wander homeless, forgotten, all their powers lost. The same fate awaits us. The Ragnarok I envisioned will never come to pass. No final glorious war with the Frost Giants. No battle to end all battles."

He gives his arm to his grieving wife, and they walk slowly from the chamber. One by one, the other gods depart.

Odin's high silver throne sits empty.

Only one goddess remains: the fainting handmaiden, still propped upon her bench. Her eyes flutter open, spinning with rainbows. Then, suddenly, she is not a she at all.

The others name him Trickster, Shapeshifter. Loki, the god of mischief. Born a Frost Giant, but so cunning that he convinced the gods to let him live among them. Until he murdered Frigg's favorite son, of course. They think he suffers his punishment even still, but he long ago escaped his bindings and wiped the serpent's venom from his skull. Now he takes his seat upon the throne so that he, too, might see across the vast distances of space and time.

He looks across the ocean to his birthplace, far to the West. Wise Odin thinks he sees the future. But the earth is round, and so is time. Loki gazes over the horizon. He sees what farseeing Odin did not.

Between the ice-girdled mountains and the frozen sea, a newborn child is warmed by a wolf's warm tongue. She is small and still and covered in blood. Yet within her tiny breast lies the power to end the world.

"She is like me. She contains multitudes," he murmurs. "I am man and woman, giant and god. So Omat, too, will live between worlds, speaking to men and gods alike, containing two souls." A single tear forms in the corner of his rainbow eye. "Like me, she will be torn between the people she was born into and those she will grow to love."

The Trickster wipes away the tear before it can fall. "Odin thinks the final battle will never arrive," he whispers to the empty hall. "But the Ragnarok is already in motion."

He raises one arm and points toward the child in her cradle of snow, a smile dawning across his face. "There. There it begins."

CHAPTER TWENTY-THREE

⚡

I hated Issuk. But I missed his hunting.

Taqqiq the Moon Man grew weaker as summer approached, often disappearing from the sky for days at a time. Yet I still felt the weight of his curse upon me.

This was a barren land indeed—no seals basked along the floe edge. No caribou trotted across the tundra. The few animals I saw vanished before I could even ready my spear—as if fleeing from Taqqiq's shouted commands.

Once I finished the maktak, I contented myself with setting snares. Sometimes I caught a lemming. Sometimes other small, unfamiliar animals. At one creek I managed to spear a fish. But for the most part, I went hungry.

The straps of my pack cut into my ribs and forehead. Without meat to sustain me or dogs to help carry my load, my limbs grew tired quickly, and my back bent over the hollow curve of my stomach. Soon I walked with the faltering step of the very old. I discarded Uimaitok's heavy stone pot first. There wasn't meat or blood enough for a proper soup anyway. The lamp next. I had no seal fat to feed its flame.

I kept my weapons. And the ulu.

My boots wore out, my weight thinning the sealskin until the stark white imprint of my foot appeared on the dark sole. A wise hunter always carries an extra pair of soles, but in my haste to begin my journey, I'd left all the spares behind. I couldn't afford to destroy my few sleeping furs to make new ones, and lemming skin would tear too easily, so I cut the hem from my sealskin tent instead. As I walked, I chewed the stiff hide until it was soft enough to work, the taste of flesh—no matter how dry—taunting my tongue and wringing my stomach. I stretched the lemming hides, too, unwilling to let any furs go to waste. I never stayed in one place long enough to dry them properly, but I built a small driftwood frame to carry on my back so they might stretch as I traveled. Though the women's work made a mockery of my reclaimed manhood, I sent thanks to the spirits of Uimaitok and Kidla for teaching me to prepare hides. I would use what skills I had, no matter if they were men's or women's. Above all else, an Inuk survives.

When I finally had enough softened sealskin to repair my boots, I made clumsy work of it. Without new caribou sinew for sewing, I had to rip out a seam from my tent. I softened the old sinew as best I could, but it still snapped far too often. I tied the shreds together; the thick knots tore holes in the boots faster than I could sew them closed again.

The farther south I went, the less snow squeaked beneath my ill-shod feet—too little for a proper iglu despite the frigid weather. My ever-smaller summer tent sheltered me from the wind, but not the cold. The lemming hides became misshapen socks and mitten liners. Better than nothing, but not nearly as warm as caribou or wolf fur. I was, in short, miserable. Worst of all, I was completely alone for the first time in my life.

The Sun barely set at night, but the length of the days only made them lonelier. I didn't even know what moon it was. Could it be the Moon When Rivers Flow if they'd never frozen completely in the first place? Could it be the Moon When Animals Give Birth if there were no caribou calves? I knew only that many days had passed, and still I saw no sign of the strangers' boat.

I walked along the snowy shore with only the driftwood to keep me company. At home I'd learned to save every precious log that washed ashore for kayak frames or harpoon shafts. But here, trees lay piled upon the beach like tide-tossed seaweed.

I'd never seen a plant taller than my knees—these massive driftwood trunks soared over my head. They lay in great tangled nests, their roots pointing skyward, each limb a withered arm crooked toward me, each sea-polished trunk as smooth as skin. I considered making a kayak frame from the wood, though I didn't have the proper hides to cover it. Then I thought of Sanna—I wouldn't be safe upon the sea. Better to stay on land, out of her grasp. So instead, I did the unthinkable: I burned the logs.

One night I made my camp in the lee of a massive tree, sheltering from the ocean-borne wind. I paced the shore, seeking the needle-point breathing holes of clams, then digging through the icy sand to rip them from their slumber. Without a pot to boil them in, I shoved them into the fire, then plucked the hot shells free the moment they popped open.

I fell asleep glad to have found a meal, however small. But it would take more than clams to sate the hunger that never stopped gnawing at the flesh between my hipbones.

I awoke the next morning to a faint whining. I fitted a spearhead into the foreshaft of my harpoon, hoping for more food, and followed the sound to a dark crevice in the driftwood log. Cautiously I bent to peer inside.

Two very small yellow eyes flashed back.

A wolf pup. I might no longer speak its language, but I knew its gaze.

I backed away, wary of a wolf parent ready to defend its young. But Singarti's face flashed through my mind. Wolves were the only family I had left. Even just a glimpse of one might relieve some of my aching loneliness. So I waited.

Before long, a tiny black nose appeared, followed by two paws, one gray and one white. Then, amid much clambering and whining, a whole pup tumbled from the tree. She sat on her haunches and stared at me.

A moon old. Perhaps a little more. Young to have eyes already so yellow. Not yet big enough to wander from the den on her own.

"I'm going to eat you, you know," I warned her.

She padded over to me and began gnawing contentedly on my bootlace, as if enjoying the best meal she'd had in days.

"Stop that." I pushed away her little body, her ribs as sharp as my own. "You'll get me in trouble." I expected a wolf parent to arrive at any moment.

Again the gray pup attacked my boot. Again I pushed her away. She began to howl. I sprang to my feet, sure the mother would come running. But still nothing. The wolves in my land always left one grown animal to guard the litter, but perhaps these southern wolves were more negligent parents.

With no adults nearby, this pup and her siblings were completely at my mercy. Little meat padded her bones, and her soft fur would provide scant warmth. But my belly growled anyway.

She stopped howling and cocked her head at me, as if listening to the sounds of my hunger. I moved carefully toward the den; she scrabbled at my legs in an effort to play.

"I apologize for entering your home, wolf," I said in the angakkuq tongue. No response. Afraid to stick my hand into the dark trunk, I pulled off a mitten and waved it inside. Sure enough, I felt a tug. The gray pup grabbed the mitten on my end, helping me pull. When I withdrew the mitten, two more pups came with it. A small black female, her eyes screwed shut, clamped needlelike teeth onto the thumb; a larger white male with one bent ear worried the palm.

"I've only got one set of mittens. Bad puppies! Get your own!" I pried open the wolves' jaws, then looked down to examine the three forlorn specimens at my feet. Their coats were strangely colored for wolf pups, but much was strange in this land.

Then the small black female opened her eyes. I caught my breath at her dark brown gaze. A dog's eyes. Not a wolf's. Warm and rich as summer loam.

I dangled a stick of driftwood in front of the pups. The gray one with the white paw gamely swiped at it, leaping back and forth. The other two, weaker, followed it with their eyes, their straight tails wagging hesitantly. I tossed the stick. The gray puppy ran after it, her tracks in the thin snow staggered like a dog's, not single file like a wolf's. She trotted back with the stick in her mouth, flopped to the ground, and began to gnaw.

A new whimpering floated from the den. Deeper and longer than the pups' cries. Very slowly, I felt inside with the blunt end of my spear. The whining turned to a low, weak growl as I hit something soft and yielding. The mother.

Using my knife, I widened the opening in the log until a dim shaft of sunlight pierced the den, illuminating the pale form of a dog. She turned weakly toward me. Grizzled black fur covered her face.

"Black Mask!"

Tossing aside my knife, I pulled Ataata's dog from the tree. Her puppies gathered around her, eager to nurse. A long gash ran along her flank, oozing blood and pus—an animal bite. From her own prey, perhaps. More likely, the wolves she'd joined had attacked her when she gave birth. No pack would tolerate more than one litter at a time.

Only the force of her will could've kept her alive long enough to raise her pups. She followed me with the same warm brown eyes that had watched me lying half-dead on Issuk's sled.

The puppies sucked noisily, although such a ravaged dog could provide little milk. A shudder passed through Black Mask's body. I placed a hand on her head and tried to stroke away her pain and fear. She choked; a trickle of blood slid through her jaws.

"Go, run with Ataata. Pull his sled amid the stars. May you guide me from the sky as you did upon the ice."

I drew my knife across her throat swiftly, ending her pain.

I let the puppies nurse until the milk stopped flowing. They curled up next to their mother's still-warm flank and fell asleep. One by one, their heartbeats fluttering against my hands, I placed them back in the driftwood trunk. I didn't want them to see me butcher their mother.

When I'd cut her flesh for eating and stretched her fur for drying, I turned back to the puppies. They'd never survive alone, and I didn't have enough meat for myself, much less for three hungry wolfdogs.

I reached into the tree for the gray female with the white paw. I pressed my knife under her soft chin.

"You'll be spared death by starvation and cold," I murmured to her. "And I'll have meat. It's a fair trade. I can offer you no better."

She looked up at me with Singarti's yellow eyes, guileless and wise at the same time.

I put away my knife.

I placed the pup in the small hood of my man's parka. Her wet nose brushed the nape of my neck. I slipped the other two puppies under the hem, next to my skin. Their wriggling subsided as they fell asleep against my heart.

For one more night, I camped beside Black Mask's den. With the puppies warm against me and my belly full of meat, I finally conquered the cold.

I awoke to a wet nose snuffing my ear. The short night had given way once more to dawn, and the gray puppy was already awake. I rolled over to look at her, careful not to crush the two other wolfdogs curled inside my parka. I offered her a finger; she began to suck ravenously, her teeth like shards of slate. I pulled her away and dropped her back in my hood.

As I packed up my rough camp, White Paw—for so I'd begun to call her—whined next to my ear. The other puppies soon joined in. The little black female, with her striking brown dog eyes, wriggled her way through the neck hole of my parka, licking my throat and chin with more hunger than affection.

I chewed some dog meat for my own meal while the puppies whined and snapped, trying to get a piece for themselves. I'd thought to share—chew the meat until it was a soft pulp as I'd once done for Black Mask—but when it came time to feed them their own mother's flesh, I balked.

"I can't, little ones. I know your mother would want it—she gave her life for you once already. But it would break an agliruti even I dare not flout..."

Dogs had no aglirutiit, of course, and wolves followed their own unknowable laws, but eating the flesh of a fellow man was an unpardonable crime. I suppose I'd begun to think of my little wolfdog pack as nearly human even then.

So I set off, Malina's yellow rays guiding my steps ever southward while I looked for possible prey to feed my new family. The white and black puppies settled into my parka, whining occasionally when I moved too suddenly, but little White Paw kept me company, her forepaws planted on my shoulder, her twitching ears soft on my cheek. She'd ceased her own crying, intent on scanning the desolate beach around us from her high perch. Every time a bird chirped in the distance, her ears swung toward the sound. Her nose followed. Sniff sniff. Tongue out. Taste the air. Pant. Sigh. Sniff sniff.

"Are you trying to help me hunt?" I teased. "You're too little." I felt like Ataata, reminding his grandchildren not to grow up too fast.

Another sound caught White Paw's attention. Her jaw snapped shut, and her tiny body tensed against my shoulder. I followed her gaze to a large, rotting log of driftwood. I could hear a slight scratching from within.

I pulled the wolfdog from my hood so I could reach my spear. White Paw tensed, ready to spring toward the log, but I placed a hand on her back, pressing her into the ground.

"Stay," I whispered firmly. She couldn't understand me; it took months to train a puppy to listen to such commands. But White Paw turned her yellow eyes toward me, listening, then stood motionless, nose pointed once more at the log, stubby legs tensed.

The log was too small for a wolverine, much less a bear. What other land animal could be any threat to me? I crept up to the opening in the near end of the driftwood, cursing the crunch of dry seaweed beneath my feet. The scratching stopped.

Now it'll never come out. I couldn't break the sturdy log, and its massive length meant the animal could easily avoid my spear point. It need only stay inside to escape my clutches.

A blur of gray flashed past the corner of my eye. White Paw dashed toward the far end of the log, barking maniacally, and scuttled inside. Just in time, I readied my spear—our prey hurtled toward me from the other end of the trunk.

I hurled my weapon before I even recognized what we'd caught.

The animal stumbled at my feet but kept coming. I drew my knife and slashed downward. Its dying yowl matched my own scream of pain.

I snatched back my hand, leaving my knife planted in the animal's ribs.

The strange creature lay in a pool of its own blood like a large brown sea urchin, its back and tail covered entirely in spines. Five slender black needles, each only a little shorter than an arrow, protruded from my palm. I flexed my hand against the pain; the spines wormed farther into my flesh.

Now wide awake, the puppies inside my parka struggled to get out. With my uninjured hand, I spilled them to the ground in a tumble of white and black. They headed toward the spiny carcass, smelling fresh blood.

"Hoa!" I shouted, commanding them to stop. When they ignored me, I grabbed them both by their ruffs, groaning with the increasing pain in my wounded hand. A growl rose in my throat—a sound I hadn't made since I'd run with Singarti across the tundra. The two puppies looked at me sharply, the white male tilting his head in disbelief. I stared them both down until they lay on their backs, soft bellies exposed. "Good. Stay," I added.

As I turned to examine the needles piercing my hand, I heard a familiar whine from the tree.

I bent to peer into the mouth of the log. A spine-covered face stared out at me. "Ia'a... You're in even worse shape than I, White Paw."

She cried as she crawled out, her every movement driving the needles deeper into her soft snout. Finally she was free and shaking her face.

"You're making it worse. You look like a walrus!" I grabbed her firmly by the ruff and yanked the longest needle from her black nose. A good chunk of flesh came with it. White Paw yowled. The other puppies ran over, eager to help, but mostly getting in the way.

"It can't be that bad! I'll do it, too." I yanked one of the spines from my own hand. I screamed.

The gray pup stopped howling. All three of them turned to me in amazement.

I laughed at their expression. Then my laughter slipped into tears, as if the pain had cracked open a shell I'd crawled inside the day Issuk tore me from my family. Kiasik would have warned me that a great hunter doesn't cry. I let myself weep anyway. For him, for Black Mask, for Kidla and Nua. For myself. The tears were no shame with only wolfdogs to see them.

The black female raised her front paws to my knee and reached to lick the tears from my cheeks. In her familiar brown gaze, I saw Puja's concern, Ataata's love.

I wept until I realized that White Paw's cries outmatched my own. I worked the rest of the needles from her snout before removing them from myself. With bloody red patches dotting our skin, we looked diseased. The other pups didn't seem to mind.

The white male, whom I decided to call Floppy Eared for his bent ear, set to work cleaning White Paw's wounds with his overlarge tongue. The black female cleaned mine far more delicately.

"I hope you two aren't just enjoying a meal," I said as they lapped the blood with more hunger than solicitude.

Floppy Eared just kept licking White Paw's snout, but the small black female stopped to stare at me, all wide-eyed innocence.

"I should call you All Black," I said. We always gave our dogs such names. Descriptive. Practical. The puppy let out a tiny whine. "No?" She pawed at the air until I lowered my face, then reached up to sniff my cheek, pressing her nose against my own as I'd so often done to Puja in my childhood.

"You're a sweet one, aren't you?" I murmured. "Sweet One, then. Is that better?" A sloppy lick of agreement across my lips. I spluttered, pushing her away. "Glad you approve."

I rolled our strange kill onto its back with the butt of my spear. No spines here, just dark brown fur. I sliced open its stomach, mashed the entrails in my own mouth, and let the wolfdogs suck the hot morsels of meat pulp from my fingertips.

You were right, Kiasik, I admitted. *I do make a good mother.*

CHAPTER
TWENTY-FOUR

𝄽

Blue is the color of the summer sky. Of autumn berries. Of winter ice. But not of men.

In the late days of summer, when orange cloudberries and magenta fireweed swirled across the ground like oil in water, a fluttering stripe of brilliant blue danced on the horizon. White Paw's low growl brought me from my tent. My three wolfdogs stood stiffly, ears pricked and guard hairs raised. I didn't have to reach down to place my hand upon my lead dog's head—White Paw's ears reached my waist, and she grew taller every day, the pace of her growth beyond that of any normal wolf, much less a dog.

The blue apparition flapped like the wings of a great bird. Perhaps the red-eyed petrel-man had finally come to take me away. But as the figure climbed above the crest of the hill, I saw it was only a man, wearing a cloak the color of sky.

With the glaring Sun casting the man's face in shadow, I allowed myself to imagine Kiasik had escaped his captors. *Or perhaps Issuk's ghost has come seeking vengeance. After so long alone, I'd welcome even his face, if only to have the pleasure of watching him die all over again.* But I knew the truth: no Inuk would wear such a cloak. For three long, lonely moons, I'd followed every tortuous curve of the shore in my search for the strange giants who'd stolen my milk-brother. They had found me instead.

My fingertips pressed cold, damp palms. The southerly wind had hidden his scent from my wolfdogs; I'd had no warning.

Heart knocking against my ribs, I ducked into my tent. I pulled my heavy parka over my atigi, then retrieved my slate hunting knife, my last antler-tipped arrows, and Issuk's bow.

Outside again, I called my wolfdogs close. Their tails wagged in apprehension—they'd never seen another person. Much less a giant.

I motioned them to sit. They obeyed instantly, ears swiveling between me and the approaching stranger. White Paw's tail lowered slowly; her upper lip drew back from her fangs as she sensed my fear. Floppy Eared raised a hesitant paw, as if unsure whether to lunge forward or run away. Sweet One whimpered between her panting breaths.

"We stay," I told them. "If we cower—if we hide—I'll never find Kiasik." I nocked an arrow to my bow and pointed the sharp tip at the approaching form. *Let there only be one of them*, I prayed. A single giant perhaps I could manage to wound or capture. Then I would make him lead me back to his camp.

The figure paused at the crest of the hill—paralyzed, I hoped, by the sight of my wolfdogs and my bow—but he didn't stop for long. He glanced over his shoulder, then stumbled down the hill toward me, favoring one leg. The rocks skittered beneath his feet as he floundered, and the hood of his blue cloak slipped from his head. His hair and beard glowed in the afternoon light, orange as the clouds in a long summer sunset.

I knew this giant.

He'd sheltered his wounded companion the day the other strangers murdered Issuk's family. I remembered the long knife in his hands. Its blade glinted more like water than stone, yet it had struck Patik's head from his shoulders in a single blow.

I took a deep breath, willing my arrow point to steady.

"Stop!" I aimed my arrow at his throat.

White Paw growled, her snout furrowed above her teeth. My pack formed a loose arc before me.

The giant ignored the warning, but the earth itself protected me: he slid on the wet moss and lost his footing, falling awkwardly on his injured leg. With a grunt of pain, he hit the ground. The long knife flew from his hands and landed many paces away. He twisted awkwardly, looking not toward his fallen weapon or toward me or even toward the wolfdogs but behind him once more—to the crest of the hill. I followed his gaze.

Silhouetted against the sky stood a brown bear, its long neck stretched forward to sniff its prey. This stranger had led it straight to my tent.

For a moment, I froze, uncertain which threat to face first. I'd seen a few of these animals from afar on my journey; they seemed far tamer than their white cousins, eating berries and fish where Uqsuralik hunted seal.

As if to protest my assumptions, the brown bear rose onto its hind legs, opened a mouth full of long, yellow teeth, and roared. Crashing back down on all fours, it swung its massive head toward me, then back to the stranger, snuffling wetly.

The giant pulled himself across the moss toward his fallen knife, dragging his injured leg uselessly behind.

The bear lumbered toward him, lifting one massive paw at a time. I could see its claws now. White and curling and impossibly long. It snorted and chomped its jaws, teeth clacking.

"This giant is mine, great bear," I said in the angakkuq tongue, keeping my voice as firm as the grip on my bow. "You cannot have him. Not until I have followed his trail to my brother."

But whatever power I'd once had to speak with wild animals had disappeared with Taqqiq's curse. Only my wolfdogs would listen to me now.

"Go!" I ordered them. "To the bear!"

With Sweet One and Floppy Eared blurs of black and white at her heels, White Paw galloped up the hill. My pack surrounded the beast, growling and snapping. The bear took a step back, clearly cowed.

I moved toward the fallen giant, who'd continued his desperate crawl toward his long, gleaming blade. "Stop," I insisted, deepening my voice.

He glanced toward me but kept up his struggle. My arrow whistled past his ear, pinning the hood of his cloak to the ground. I was close enough now to hear his sharp intake of breath, close enough to see that his hand still crept toward the weapon. I slung my bow over my shoulder and dashed forward, snatching the long knife away from his reaching fingers. The tip of the blade, far heavier than I'd expected, dragged on the ground for a moment before I could lift it properly.

"I said *stop*." I pointed the blade's tip at his throat.

His eyes, wide with fear, glinted the same bright blue as his cloak, and his face, burnt pink above his heavy beard, was as young and unlined as my own.

One of my pack yelped in pain, and I turned to look. I barely glimpsed a whirl of motion on the hillside, the bodies of the wolf-dogs leaping and lunging around the now fast-approaching bear, when I fell to the ground with the giant's hand around my ankle.

I jerked free and rolled to my feet, but I'd lost the long knife. A blur of brown in the corner of my vision became a wall of fur before my eyes. A black shape leapt between me and the bear. Before I could react, I heard the sound of ripping flesh.

Then I was flat on my back again, pinned to the ground by a weight on my legs, the wind knocked from my lungs. I raised myself to my elbows, expecting to find my body half-crushed by the enormous bear. Instead the mound of fur at my knees was black—Sweet One lay across me with blood pouring from a bear-claw wound on her flank.

I fought the urge to tend to her pain; if I didn't bring down the bear, more of my family would die. Sucking a breath into my burning lungs, I managed to shift her off my legs. I tried not to hurt her, but her quavering whine proved I'd failed.

Staggering to my feet, I fumbled my slate knife free of its sheath. Nothing, not even a cousin of the great Uqsuralik, could hurt my pack and live.

My wolfdogs did my work for me. White Paw clung to the bear's back, her claws and teeth turning the brown fur black with blood. Floppy Eared leapt forward with a snarl, then just as quickly sprang back to avoid the bear's swiping claws. Amid the fray, the empty blue cloak, still pinned to the ground, snapped and twisted in the wind like another attacker.

The giant had found his feet. He stood upright between me and the bear, garbed only in white and brown. He didn't stumble this time, or run. He held the long knife before him with both hands. The sun winked off the blade, casting a needle of light into the bear's eyes. It blinked, shaking its head.

The giant lunged forward awkwardly, his weaker leg nearly folding beneath him. His long knife slid into the thick meat of the bear's foreleg. It roared its anger, foam flying from wide jaws, and reared onto its hind legs once more, shaking off White Paw and Floppy Eared like mosquitoes. Before the towering bear, the giant no longer looked so tall.

The bear waddled forward, walking like a man on its hind legs. It swiped at the giant, long claws extended. I rushed forward and thrust my own knife into the taut skin between its foreleg and chest, the bear's most vulnerable spot. The tip of my blade stuttered against bone—and then slid cleanly between the ribs. The bear crashed to the ground, nearly catching me in its embrace. I snatched back my knife and leapt away, its hot spit splattering my cheek.

It charged me, just as an ice bear would have, bowling the stranger out of the way as it came. I was ready. I ran, knowing the wound in its heart would soon drain its strength. Overconfident, I slowed to look behind me just as the bear came to a skidding halt. Its eyes rolled to white, and it plummeted forward, sending me flying with one glancing blow from its massive shoulder.

For a long moment, I lay with my head pillowed on my arm, my breath raw, willing my heart to slow. I shifted just enough to look into the cloudless blue sky, wondering what Sila must think of the strange constellation of figures sprawled across the mossy rocks. An arm's length away, the enormous mound of brown fur blocked my wolfdogs from sight. But I could hear Floppy Eared and White Paw snarling at each other as they fought over the bear's innards. I had to stop them before they ate any: raw bear meat could kill a man or a dog. But I couldn't yet find the strength to rise. Somewhere beyond the beast lay a strange giant with flames in his hair. His presence was a weight on my chest, stopping the air from my lungs. I clutched my knife more tightly, my fingers chilled by the bear's quickly cooling blood. The thought of using it again so soon—this time on a person—made me all the colder.

I pushed myself slowly to my feet and walked around the bear. The stranger lay sprawled and unmoving, clearly unconscious.

I grabbed White Paw and Floppy Eared one at a time by their ruffs, dragging them away from the bear carcass. They twisted in my grip, desperate to return to their meal, but I calmed them with the piercing stare Singarti had once used to warn me away from a fresh-killed ptarmigan. I found the leashes I hadn't used since my wolfdogs were puppies and staked them beside the tent entrance. They watched me with reproachful eyes as I walked to the top of the hill to scan the ocean beyond.

Nothing.

No wooden boat on the sea. What had become of the giant's wounded friend? Where was his camp? Where was Kiasik? I needed answers.

But first I had a wolfdog to save.

Sweet One's tail thumped weakly at my approach. I couldn't see the gash itself, only weakly pulsing blood and matted fur. When I reached to touch her flank, her lips trembled in the semblance of a snarl. In our moons together, my pack had shown an uncanny understanding of my wishes, rarely growling or snapping at me the way normal dogs would have. But an injured animal was a dangerous one, and Sweet One's long teeth would tear my flesh as easily as they had the bear's.

"I'll come back," I assured her, unable to keep my voice from cracking.

Black Mask had been in better shape when I slit her throat without hesitation. My world has little room for the weak.

I've already broken most of the other rules of my upbringing, I reasoned as I hurried toward my tent. *What's one more?*

From the corner of my eye, I saw the giant twitch awake. His eyes were open but glazed—whether from exhaustion, pain, or starvation I didn't know. Belatedly his gaze focused on me. His long knife lay loose in his grasp; he moved to raise it and made a half-hearted effort to stand, but his leg wouldn't hold him. He was one threat, at least, I could afford to ignore for the moment.

"Don't bother with your knife," I said, conspicuously placing my own blade back in its sheath. "I have more important animals to worry about than you." I gestured back toward Sweet One's limp form. He looked at me blankly, oblivious to the insult. Perhaps he was stupid as well as injured.

I went inside the tent to gather my waterskin and a handful of dried moss. When I emerged moments later, the giant had disappeared. Then I heard his voice, strangely gentle despite the mad gibberish on his tongue. I walked around the bear carcass and found him sitting next to Sweet One.

"Leave her alone," I barked, imagining him slicing her apart as he'd once done to Patik.

He backed away, dragging himself over the ground with his hands. His long knife lay nearby, but he didn't reach for it.

Careful to stay clear of Sweet One's bared teeth, I washed the blood from her wound so I could see how deep it went. I could feel the giant's eyes on me as I worked, but he didn't move or speak. His was not like an Inuk's silence, patient and watchful. It was like that of a trapped fox, waiting to bite as soon as the hunter reaches into the cairn.

Sweet One's gash was worse than I'd thought. Too wide to simply bind closed with a strip of bear hide as I'd planned. I would have to sew it shut. I had made a hooked needle from the spines of the strange urchin-creature I'd killed that first day with my wolf-dogs; it would sew living flesh much more easily than the straight bone needle I'd taken from Uimaitok's kit. But I still had no sinew thread. The bear's leg tendons would be too fresh, a strip of hide too thick, and I'd long ago torn most of the seams from my tent to repair my own clothes. My shelter was half the size it had been at the start of my journey.

With the point of the needle, I tried to pull the seam from the side of my parka—I loosed a scant finger's length before the thin sinew snapped. I tried again but got only another useless fragment for my efforts. Sweet One whined, the cry as plaintive and weak as a new-fledged chick's. Blood painted the stones beneath her.

I slipped my bow from my shoulder in desperation.

Gravel clattered as the stranger started in alarm—probably afraid I would turn the weapon on him. But Sweet One didn't snarl. She just rolled her eyes toward me, narrowed in pain. She trusted me. Trusted me to end her misery.

She knew me well.

I lifted my knife instead of an arrow and placed my blade against the bowstring. I knew where I could find a length of sinew.

A shout from the giant stopped me.

He gazed at me steadily, his eyes as sharp and cold as ice. In his palm he held a length of white string, one end floating and curling in the soft breeze, the other attached to the cuff of his sleeve.

I stared at him for a long moment before I slowly lowered my bow.

One slow step at a time, I moved toward him. His shoulders

rose at my approach; his bearded jaw clenched. But he still didn't reach for his blade. Instead his long-fingered hands kept moving, unraveling more string from his sleeve even as his eyes stayed fixed on mine.

He raised the cuff to his teeth, bit the string free, and lifted it toward me. I darted forward to snatch the offering, as cautious as a raven plucking meat from between a wolf's paws.

The string was light and soft in my hand, more like the long hair of a musk ox than the strong tendon of a caribou's leg, but I had no time to marvel at its strangeness. I could see Sweet One's injury clearly now, a long, straight gash, so deep that the white bone of her ribs glistened among the red flesh. Thankfully, the wound had missed her lungs. There was still hope. It took me three tries to pass the string through the eye of my spine needle, but I finally managed it.

"This will be over soon, Sweet One. Just hold on. I know what to do." I was unsure whether I feigned such confidence for the sake of my dog, myself, or the young stranger sitting nearby. The needle went in easily, but sewing living skin was not like sewing seal hide. The wound was too wide to pinch shut with one hand, and the thin string sliced through the delicate flesh as I tried to pull it closed. Sweet One twitched with pain. I was making it worse.

The giant still watched me. I looked down at the white string. A gift. A gesture, perhaps, of goodwill. Issuk had brought gifts, too. Meat and men and hope. Then he had taken it all away again.

Still, I had always made use of my surroundings. I could make use of the giant as well.

"I can't do this with only two hands."

His mouth opened, but only a quick sigh escaped. After a long while, he made more of his unintelligible sounds.

"Come here," I said, motioning to him as I might to a dog.

When he didn't move, I raised my arms so my sleeves fell back, showing that I held only the needle. He finally crawled toward me, dragging his leg behind. I looked away from his halting progress.

Let him suffer for a while, I thought. No matter what useful gift he offered, this stranger who had killed Patik and stolen Kiasik had no claim to my sympathy.

"I need you to hold the wound together," I said to him, demonstrating with my hands. "But keep her still." I pressed my body against the wolfdog's to show him. He did as I asked, bracketing her head with his knees. His fingers were long, exceptionally dirty, and surprisingly steady as he pinched the gash closed. Halfway through my stitching, I gestured to the stranger to release the wound. He complied immediately and placed his hands along Sweet One's neck, stroking gently. I'd never seen a grown man treat a dog with such compassion. Most hunters whipped and beat their dogs; there was no other way to control an unruly team. My pack had never needed such discipline—but how did this stranger know that?

As I worked on the wound, I finally noticed the shape of the gash. Long and straight, too deep for a bear's claws.

I paused in my sewing, my cheeks flushing with anger.

From the corner of my eye, I saw the man shoot me a concerned glance, but I wouldn't look at him. I had no time for accusations while Sweet One bled beneath my hands.

I finished the stitches and packed dried moss around the wound. I wished for the egg-like mushrooms that could stop her flesh from sickening or for dried willow to ease her pain. But I would use what I had. I sliced a narrow strip of skin from the bear carcass, peeling it free of the thick fat. I wrapped it around Sweet One's ribs—when it dried, it would shrink and help bind the wound together. Then I trudged back to my tent and grabbed a sleeping fur. A small hole in one side, a rope looped through it, and I had a sled. I pushed Sweet One's body onto it, trying not to hurt her further.

The giant tried to help.

"Don't," I snapped. "You've probably killed her with your long knife. Swinging it around like a fool. Don't come near her again." My voice was low and deadly. There could be no mistaking my tone, even if he couldn't understand my words. I cast a disdainful glance at his wounded leg. "Clearly you're no match for a bear. You had to hurt a puppy instead." I passed by him without another word, dragging my dog behind me.

I pulled Sweet One onto the piled furs inside the tent, safe from scavengers. She lapped greedily at the spout of my waterskin.

Her thirst was a good sign; she hadn't given up. Before long, she fell asleep, legs twitching weakly. I wanted to curl up along her back and join her, but I had work yet to do.

With my knife in hand, I returned to the bear. Floppy Eared pulled at his leash and snarled, desperate to start his feast. White Paw yipped her own complaint.

"Enough," I shouted. The two quieted instantly at my command, then settled complacently to watch my work. I needed to butcher the carcass quickly before it spoiled in the summer sun. A bloody, hot task. I started to pull off my outer parka—brushing blood from caribou hide was tedious, especially now that Puja wasn't around to do it for me—and then caught the stranger's eye. I'd kept my hair short; my forehead and chin remained free of tattoos. I walked with a man's gait, carried a man's weapons, and lived alone. How could he think me a woman? But if I disrobed, he'd know I had a woman's body. He might be unlike any Inuk, but his hairy cheeks and coiled muscles were clearly male.

I kept my parka on.

CHAPTER
TWENTY-FIVE

𐍈

While I butchered the bear, the blood ran in thick rivulets over my wrists and under the sleeves of my parka. I could feel the giant's eyes on me still. I glanced over occasionally. Wounded and underfed, he no longer seemed threatening—but I couldn't forget that he'd nearly killed Sweet One. Nor could I forget the violence of his long blade.

The weapon lay across his lap now, but his grip on it was slack. His eyes crept shut, then sprang open as he fought to stay conscious. I let myself become absorbed in my bloody task, trying to ignore him. By the time I'd cut the bear meat into large strips, hung them to cook above a seaweed fire, buried the poisonous liver beneath a cairn of stones, and staked the remaining pelt out to dry, the stranger had fallen asleep on the hard ground.

I paced quietly toward him and slowly lifted the long knife from his lap. He didn't stir. I needed both hands to wield the blade, and even then I could do little but swing it in a clumsy, aimless arc. It was far too long to butcher a carcass and too heavy to throw like a harpoon. What kind of hunting could one do with it?

I wrapped the blade in a scrap of bear fur and buried it far from my camp.

Finally, in the pink light of sunset, I washed the blood from my face at the shallow creek that ran beside my tent. A silver fish swam just beyond my cupped hands. I'd chosen the campsite for this very reason, hoping to stock up on fish. I never knew when I'd find any more on my journey through this barren land. But I didn't have the strength to snatch any more prey today. The long line of split fish I'd hung on my driftwood drying rack that morning would have to be enough for now. Besides, with all the bear meat, I would have plenty to eat while I waited for the fish to fully dry. For so long, I'd lived only on small prey. My wolfdogs helped me hunt, but they ate nearly as much as they caught. And even they couldn't procure a caribou or a seal when there were simply none to catch. Now, finally, I wouldn't go hungry.

I sat back on the mossy bank, wondering at the unfamiliar feeling warming my gut. *Hope*.

My travels might be over. The other strangers must be nearby. Kiasik would be with them.

I would rescue him, and together we could make our way back home. Sweet One wouldn't be able to carry anything on her back for a while, but with the bear meat to build their strength, Floppy Eared and White Paw would easily carry the full load of dried fish. Kiasik and I could start our journey north without fear of starvation. Puja, Ququk, and Tapsi would've found a way to provide for the others in our absence. My family would survive long enough for us to return. I had to believe that.

I walked to the crest of the hill, scanning the water again for sight of the giants' enormous wooden boat. Still nothing.

I headed back to the tent, passing the sizzling strips of bear flesh. White Paw and Floppy Eared lay nearby, muzzles on paws but eyes fixed on the meat. I unfastened their leashes. "Make sure no foxes get it. And don't even *think* about stealing it yourself while it's still raw," I added with a growl when they pranced forward. "Ataata always said bear is the one animal we have to cook." Floppy Eared cocked his head at me, dubious. I'd watched him eat everything from a maggot-covered hare to an entire nest of owlets—feathers and all—without suffering any ill effects. "Fine. Maybe *you* won't get sick, but you still can't eat the bear. You'll get so fat I'll have to build an umiaq and row you home."

Teetering slightly from exhaustion, I passed by the prone shape of the stranger. Pain creased his brow even in sleep. He pillowed his head upon his arm as an Inuk would. His trick with the string had somehow shortened his sleeve, revealing a thick tattoo spiraling around his wrist in a series of knots and braids more intricate than those in a woman's hair.

The sprawl of his length upon the ground still made him seem a giant to me, but perhaps he was human after all.

White Paw whimpered softly and padded over to him.

"I told you to watch the meat," I said sternly.

Usually so fast to comply, my gray friend simply sat next to the body of the man and stared at me, her tongue flopping in a foolish wolf smile.

"If you want to sleep with him tonight, go ahead," I said, continuing on my way. "After what he did to Sweet One, I'm surprised you haven't tried to eat him."

At the mention of food, Floppy Eared pricked his ears toward me. "Don't get any ideas," I warned him. "I have to get some answers first. *Then* we can take our revenge on him for all he's done."

I thought once more of the empty expanse of ocean beyond the hill, and my newfound hope sputtered and died like an untended lamp.

If the rest of the strangers weren't coming, and this man died of his wounds, I had no chance of finding Kiasik anytime soon. I'd have to keep walking.

But if the stranger lived, he might lead me to his people—and to my milk-brother.

I nudged him with my toe. He didn't move. I kicked his shoulder lightly. He muttered something in his sleep and opened his eyes very slowly, as if dragging frost-sealed eyelids apart. After a long moment, he finally seemed to see me.

"If you can make it to the tent, I'll feed you," I said, speaking as if to a child and making the appropriate gestures. He lifted his hand to his mouth, copying my eating motion, and came fully awake. But when he'd hobbled to the tent and collapsed on the furs next to the wolfdog he'd nearly killed, he passed out again.

His hair looked almost crimson in the long finger of firelight that crept through the tent entrance. *Maybe it's not hair at all*, I thought, reaching for it tentatively. *Maybe it's a flower, like the summer blossoms that look like goose down.*

He didn't stir; I grew bolder. Through a tear in his trousers, I saw a dirty, blood-caked bandage tied around his injured thigh. The wrapping looked like the same strange material as his clothes— not hide, nor pelt, but something plaited like Uimaitok's baleen baskets. I'd never seen anything woven so fine—so tight it almost looked solid.

Illuminated by the fire, his colorless eyebrows and eyelashes glowed like tiny shafts of light on his rough cheeks. Such delicacy was unsettling beside his sharp, overlarge nose and too-square face. His beard seemed a living thing, like a small animal that had attached itself to his jaw and refused to leave. *Ugly*, I thought.

Gently, I pulled off his trousers and unwound the bandages from his thigh. Underneath, purple and black flesh surrounded a long gash that ran from above his knee to just below his groin. Pus and dried blood crusted the wound. Perhaps I wouldn't need to take my revenge on this man. His own body already had. His leg was sick, and the sickness would probably spread.

I knew a tale of an angakkuq who cut off his wife's leg when it turned black from an injury. He burned the stump with a hot stone until it ceased to bleed. The woman lived, but the very next winter she hobbled into the snow and disappeared forever. Her husband understood. He'd watched her limping around the camp, unable to complete the tasks a woman should, and knew she'd happily given herself to Sila. Just like the bear, she would die only to be reborn into a new body.

I dared not take such a risk. If I sawed off the stranger's leg, and he died from the blood loss, I'd never get the chance to ask him about Kiasik. Better to wait until he woke, ask him my questions, and then tell him to kill himself to avoid the agony of a slow death. Or I could do as Ataata would have: I could try to save him, leg and all.

I heated water and washed the wound with the last of my dried moss. With the blood and dirt cleared away, I could see the orange pelt of hair covering his thigh. I wrinkled my nose in disgust. He might not be a giant, but maybe he was not fully Inuk, either. Perhaps he was half man, half dog. That would explain a lot.

I turned away to wash my knife, and when I looked back, his eyes were open. His glance flew to my blade. His body tensed.

"Don't worry. If I wanted to kill you, you'd be dog food by now." I put the knife down with exaggerated care and spread my empty hands, palms up. His face relaxed.

I handed him a morsel of cooked bear meat. He sniffed it first, then ate with relish. I felt more at ease once he had—having eaten in my tent, he might think twice before trying to kill me.

I pointed at his leg. "I'm going to try to save it." I picked up my weapon again and slowly moved it toward his thigh.

He jerked away, wincing with the pain of the movement.

"I'm not going to fight with you. If you want to suffer, I'm happy to let you."

He propped himself on his elbows and looked down at his leg. His face drained of blood, as if he was seeing the festering wound for the first time in days. He made a few more of his strange sounds, as incomprehensible to me as a gull's croak to a wolf.

A brutal laugh ripped from his throat, and he lay back on the ground. This time he spoke without emotion, waving his hands at me. I couldn't tell if he wanted me to go ahead and cut—or go ahead and leave. But when I moved back toward his leg with my slate knife, he stopped me with a terse *"Nei!"*

Grimacing, he reached into his tall skin boot to pull out a small knife made of the same strange material as his larger weapon, as bright as the surface of a sunlit pool. He handed it to me, hilt first.

The blade drew blood when I tested it on my thumb, sharper than any weapon of antler or slate. Mysterious, spiraling beasts adorned the ivory handle, the carvings more intricate than my grandfather's but the shapes somehow achingly familiar.

When I first pierced his flesh, he gasped with pain. When I looked up a moment later, he was already unconscious.

I cut away the black meat until what remained oozed with clean blood. I pulled more string from the cuff of his garment and sewed the wound shut, then bound it all with strips of newly scraped bear hide, just as I had for Sweet One.

I worked the whole of the short, moonlit night. By the time I finished, the Sun had lifted above the horizon once more. I cleaned the stranger's small knife and slipped it into the sheath looped across my chest, where it rested beside my own slate blade. Though we seemed to have reached some sort of tentative peace, I'd sleep better knowing he was unarmed.

I finally found time to sate my own hunger. I took a hunk of bear meat and thrust it deep in the coals to make sure it was well cooked. My lonely feast held little joy. I remembered longingly how my whole camp would gather when we brought home an ice bear. We never dried the meat like fish, or froze it raw like caribou or seal. All of it had to be cooked and eaten before it spoiled, and so we would feast on thick chunks of boiled meat long into the night and tell stories about great Uqsuralik. The hunter recited a song he'd composed about the kill, and Ataata offered a prayer to thank the bear's spirit for its sacrifice. Somewhere another bear would be born with the same soul, and the animal would live on. I longed for the heat of our crowded iglu, the bubble of the pot, the smell of the bodies pressed together, the roar of the laughter and singing. I would eat until my guts ached, then fall asleep with my head in Puja's lap, then wake to eat some more.

Yet now I had to force myself to swallow more than a few bites of the bear meat. I'd left it too long above the fire, turning the rich, red flesh into a dry, charred husk. But my stomach knotted for a different reason. For the first time since I'd discarded my woman's parka and followed the aarluk's waving fin, I felt truly uncertain. Not just unsure if I would live another day—that was an unknown I'd long ago come to accept—but unsure of what to do next. Until now I'd had only two goals: survive and find Kiasik. Now the stranger had roared into my life like the first rainstorm of spring, bringing both danger and hope. Only time would tell if a burst of green or a sheet of ice would result.

⊶ ⚜ ⊷

When I returned to the tent, Sweet One rested quietly. I tucked the sleeping fur I'd made from her mother's pelt around her flank. The stranger moved a little in his sleep, turning his face into the wolfdog's neck so his breath moved her fur.

An angakkuq would enter a trance to ask the spirits for aid in healing the wolfdog and man. Even if I still had such powers, which spirit would deign to help? Singarti might show pity for Sweet One, but what spirit guarded giant dog-men? Taqqiq, who saw all from his high perch, must know of them. Maybe this stranger was the Moon's latest effort to thwart me. But somehow I thought not: his hair glowed more like the Sun than the Moon.

Perhaps the spirits who had so firmly laid hold of my life did not have such a tenacious grip on his.

CHAPTER TWENTY-SIX

♪

I dreamed of music. Of flying like a longspur over a valley of nodding yellow flowers, with melody lifting my wings. I heard the tune with a bird's ears, for it was more like birdsong than like the chants of men.

I woke to the same lilting tune dancing across the tent from where the stranger lay.

I didn't move—I didn't want him to stop. But I cracked open my eyes. He lay where I'd left him, his bound leg outstretched, his knee resting against Sweet One's shoulder. He held a narrow bone to his lips, his fingers pressing against a row of three holes drilled through the shaft. The whistling melody rose and fell, the rhythm unsteady, the tone clear.

When he stopped, Sweet One lifted her front paw a little, asking him to continue. I lay curled only an arm's length away—as far as I could get in the cramped confines of my tent—yet I felt left out of their cozy gathering of invalids.

I sat up and checked on Sweet One's wound; so far it was healing well. And she'd clearly forgiven the stranger for hurting her. I wasn't yet sure if I could.

"How's your leg?" I gestured toward his wound.

He gave a slight grimace, then shrugged his shoulders. It seems that in some ways, men of all worlds are alike—unwilling to admit to pain. I didn't embarrass him by pressing further. He made a motion toward his mouth and asked a question in his strange language.

"Yes, you must be hungry," I replied, keeping my voice purposely gruff, wondering again if this man thought me male. Would my short hair, tight hood, and straight knife mean the same thing to him that they did to an Inuk? His own clothes were neither male nor female but something else entirely. He wore his flame-colored hair like a woman, some of it plaited into narrow braids, most falling loose to his shoulders. And I had never seen a man with tattoos. For a moment, I dared let myself hope that he lived between man and woman, as I did. Yet as I'd cleaned his thigh wound, it'd been perfectly clear that his body, at least, was very much a man's.

While he ate a portion of the charred bear meat, inhaling more than chewing, I hand-fed chunks to Sweet One. She sniffed at it tentatively, unused to cooked flesh.

"Eat it anyway," I scolded her. I found the charred meat flavorless compared with our usual bloody fare, but Sweet One and I choked it down. I didn't want a single bite of the bear to go to waste.

The meal done, we sat in awkward silence. I suddenly felt very certain that, despite my bulky parka, the stranger knew I had a woman's body—and that he, like Issuk, would never understand I had a man's spirit at the same time. I had to get out of the tent, away from his blue stare, and think of some way to convince him I was as male as he was.

I made to leave, but he stopped me, gesturing to his groin and making pissing sounds. I held the tent flap for him as he crawled, wincing, to the opening. He tried to stand, failed, grunted a few angry words, then managed to rise awkwardly to one knee and reach for the waist of his trousers.

While he gingerly maneuvered himself, I slipped my waterskin beneath my parka. When he finished, I walked a few paces from the tent, turned my back, untied my own trousers, and squirted a thin stream from the waterskin while sighing contentedly. Surely even among his strange people, women didn't piss standing up.

When I knew he slept once more, I finally left to remove my clothes. I scraped my bloody parka with my ulu and washed the worst of the blood from my skin in the swift, cold stream, keeping my back to the tent, just in case. High overhead, the Sun sent her beams to warm my cheeks. Still no sign of other strangers on the horizon.

Before my bleeding had begun, my chest had been little different from a man's. But in the moons since I'd left home, my breasts had grown larger and more tender. I had no more stretched hides to spare, so I retrieved the man's blue cloak from where it lay still pinned to the ground with my arrow. A seam ran along the bottom edge, easily ripped free with the small, glinting knife. The strip of blue was as long as my outstretched arms. I bound it around my ribs so I could remove my outer parka and still look like a man in my lighter atigi.

Far to the south I spotted a flock of geese flying toward my camp, too high to bring down easily—but I had to try. I couldn't grow complacent just because of my hoard of bear meat. When I returned to the tent for my bow and arrows, the man awoke. He pushed himself upright and started to rise.

"Brandr," he said, staring at me intently, pointing to his chest.

"You can't go with me," I retorted. "You can barely walk."

He frowned in concentration, pointed at me, and said haltingly, "Youcantgo..."

I nearly dropped my bow in astonishment. "You can speak! But what do you mean, I can't go? Are you ordering me to stay?"

"Brandr. Bran-duh," he repeated more slowly, slapping his chest. Then, pointing at me again, "Youcant." He said this a few more times, looking incredibly proud of himself, white teeth flashing through his orange beard.

"Brandr!" I cried in recognition, pointing at him. He nodded his head vigorously, a gesture that—from his smile—seemed to indicate agreement.

"*Já, já!*" He grinned, jabbing a finger at himself once more.

"Omat." I pointed to myself. "Omat."

"Youcant?"

"No." I moved my hand across my body dismissively.

"Uh-maht?"

"Yes." I tried to nod my head like he did.

"Uh-maht. Omat."

I hadn't heard my own name spoken aloud in many moons.

I turned away before he could see the emotion pulling at my face.

I looked to where Sweet One lay sprawled across his lap, completely trusting. If my wolfdogs approved of him, perhaps I had nothing to fear.

"I was there. I saw you on the beach, in the big boat," I said finally, trying to use easy words. "I need to know where my brother is." Clearly he didn't understand. I needed to start simpler.

"Are you all alone?" I ventured. No response. I tried speaking in the angakkuq's tongue.

He just shrugged, looking bewildered.

Finally I reached into my amulet bag and pulled out Kiasik's seal carving. "Brandr," I said firmly, pointing at the figure. He cocked a pale eyebrow at me in evident confusion but continued watching. Next I pulled out my own sacred walrus carving. "Other man," I said, pointing to it. I continued to place the other items from my amulet around the seal—the small quartz blade I had found amid the ruins, Ataata's black bear claw, the tuft of Singarti's white fur—naming each one as a new man. I prayed he'd understand.

"Brandr and many, many other men," I concluded, sweeping my hands over the assemblage. "Or..." I quickly removed everything except for the seal and placed them carefully back within my amulet pouch. I touched the solitary figure. "Brandr all alone."

"*Já.*" He pointed to the carving. "Brandr." He pointed to himself again. Was he saying he was alone, or that his name was Brandr? How stupid were these hairy dog-men? I began to put the other items around the carving again to make sure we understood each other, but he impatiently knocked them aside.

"Enough! I understand," I said. "You're all alone. Maybe hunting to bring back food? If so, you're not very good, are you?" Ataata would've warned me not to insult a guest lest I make him feel uncomfortable, but I *wanted* this stranger to feel uneasy. I needed him to be just scared enough that he would answer my questions. "You look like you haven't eaten in days, and you have no bow or spear." I spoke with more contempt than I felt. I, too, lived on the edge of starvation. "Where are the other giant dog-men?" I picked up the little figurines and placed them in a clump next to the seal I'd called Brandr.

"Here?" I asked before moving the grouping farther away from the carving. "Here?"

He looked blankly for a moment, his eyes following my motions as I moved the little grouping to the edge of the tent.

"Here?" He shook his head firmly—which seemed his way of saying no—and reached a long arm to pick up the penis-bone walrus. Without a glance at Ataata's delicate carving, he hurled it through the open flap of the tent. I heard it clatter dully against the gravel. He waved at it dismissively and reached for the next object.

"Hoa!" I shouted, just as I would to halt an unruly dog team. I stomped from the tent, scanning the ground for the tiny yellowed walrus. My frustration bled into anger. Why had I bothered saving him if my brother was still out of reach?

Ataata would counsel patience, I knew. I should try to seize the opportunity to learn about my enemy. By watching him, I might learn his people's secrets. Already I'd seen his weapon up close. If I could teach him real words, perhaps I could explain about Kiasik and finally get some answers.

Walking a wide circle before the tent, I spotted the walrus. I ran my fingers over the smooth, warm bone. One tiny tusk had chipped off. A reminder. *This man may seem helpless now, but he's still dangerous.*

I clutched the amulet in my fist and checked that the small knife he'd given me to clean his wound was safely tucked in its sheath and out of his grasp.

When I returned to the tent, I held the broken walrus in front of his face before thrusting it back into my pouch. He flinched, his cheeks flushing a brilliant red more suited to an unripe bearberry than a man. *That doesn't mean much*, I thought. *Even a dog can feel shame.*

He gestured toward the sheath looped across my shoulder. I moved my hands protectively over the knife's handle. "You seem tame enough now, but I'm not going to give you the chance to prove me wrong."

It felt awkward to deny him—I'd never refused to share a tool with another man. I expected him to rage at me for leaving him defenseless and taking away such a magically sharp weapon. Instead he simply nodded and reached to lay his hands on my own before I could pull away. His palms were as rough and calloused as an Inuk's, but his long fingers looked like tree branches beside my own. I listened carefully as he spoke, trying to pick out the words from the nonsense.

"Já. Nu thess er knífr thinn. Thu bargt mér. Takk."

I still didn't understand, but I somehow knew he was letting me have the knife. First the strange white string. Now another gift. I must've looked as confused as I felt, because he smiled and lay back down, gesturing weakly to his wrapped leg, then to me.

"Takk," he repeated. *"Hvar er sverthinn mín?"* When I didn't respond, he held both hands before him in an imaginary grip, as if swinging his long blade.

I motioned outside, shaking my head as I'd seen him do. "It's gone. You won't find it."

Rather than protesting, he merely closed his eyes. He looked both more exhausted and more at peace than before.

"*Takk*," he murmured once more.

Here he was, wounded and weak, yet seemingly content to put himself completely in my power. He'd given me his only remaining weapon. What kind of man was he? What kind of man could make music like a bird and kill like a bear?

I stared down at his gift. A small, sharp knife with a straight blade.

I didn't understand him.

But perhaps he understood me.

He'd given me a man's knife.

CHAPTER
TWENTY-SEVEN

𐌔

A knife and a whistle. I never ceased to wonder at them both. Brandr's small blade never chipped the way my slate tools did, and its keen edge put bone and antler to shame. The whistle stayed with him always. I didn't try to blow into it myself. I dared not steal the voice of the bird from whose leg the instrument was carved. Just because I didn't know the agliruti for such a thing didn't mean there wasn't one. Yet when Brandr played his music, I didn't tell him to stop. Instead I found myself pausing in my tasks, letting the melody carry my spirit into the sky as surely as the raven wings I'd once worn.

My body, on the other hand, stayed in one place. "I'll wait until the fish has dried," I told Sweet One. "Then we move on. Kiasik needs me." It seemed only fair to warn her. The moist wind slowed the drying. Five more days. Seven at most. And then she would have to be healed enough to walk. Perhaps she understood—she ate ravenously and grew stronger every day.

Brandr's leg healed more slowly—perhaps because he insisted on cooking all his meat, even the fresh prey I snared to supplement our dwindling supply of bear. He'd watched me swallow the raw red flesh of a small brown hare with a look of pinched revulsion; I watched him char his portion with similar disgust.

After two days of food and rest, he still couldn't walk easily, but he began hobbling around the camp, leaning on a staff of driftwood. His immobility had its benefits: I could easily avoid him, cleaning my clothes and relieving myself out of his sight.

I still hadn't learned anything more from him, although I didn't stop asking about my brother. I tried to teach him to speak like a real human, but he learned only a few scattered words. My own understanding of his tongue was equally poor. As I had with the Wolf Spirit, I learned to speak a different sort of language with him instead, watching the subtleties of his gesture, the way his brow would furrow or his mouth quirk. From his posture, I knew when he hurt and when he healed. From his music, I knew when he mourned and when he dreamed.

Eventually I felt comfortable enough with my new stranger that I let him show me how to whet the small knife against a stone, and sometimes I even let him use it. He always returned it to me when his task was done; he seemed almost glad to have it out of his possession.

As the days passed, I was desperate to keep moving, but I'd learned long ago that some things were out of my control. I waited for my dried fish as patiently as I'd once bent over a seal's breathing hole. The fish would let me travel much faster than I had before, giving me strength and, most important, letting me forgo the slow, uncertain process of snaring my food. Brandr, despite his weakness, seemed equally impatient to leave. He grew restless, gazing out across the tundra with something more than boredom. Sometimes in the night he cried out in his sleep and lurched upright, chased by some unknowable nightmare. I often woke with him, listening until his breathing slowed and he fell back asleep. I didn't let him know I heard his cries—no man wants to show weakness in front of another.

By the time the fish had dried into stiff, flaky hunks, Brandr

could finally walk without his staff—although he still moved haltingly. Sweet One, his constant companion, began to run and hunt
with her siblings again.

It was time to move on.

And I needed answers.

He sat beside the tent, whittling a scrap of driftwood with the
small knife. Malina, still low on the horizon, bathed his face with
her orange glow. The bear meat had filled the hollows beneath
his cheeks. His skin, though still roughened and pink, no longer
burned quite so bright.

"Brandr."

He looked up at me. I preferred him this way, sitting rather than
towering over me. He balled his hand loosely to hide the carving,
but I didn't worry. Whatever he was making, it was too small to be
a weapon.

"I need you to tell me where your people are," I began, trying
one last time to make him understand. "I promise I won't hurt
them if they release my milk-brother to me." He stared at me
blankly.

I crawled into the tent and packed my few belongings. When
I rejoined him outside, I dropped the pack beside him. His eyes
flashed from the bundle to me, his brow furrowing.

"I'm leaving," I insisted. I began to remove the rocks that
weighted the hem of the tent. He finally understood.

"No," he said quickly, using one of his few words. He scrabbled
awkwardly to his feet and placed a hand on my arm. "Stay!"

I pointed south. "My brother is with your people."

He shook his head violently, brow knit in confusion.

"Men. *Your* men." I raised a hand to his broad chest and then
pointed south once more. "I have to go there."

"No, no," he repeated. "No understand."

"My *brother*." I reached for the knife in his hand, and he gave it
willingly. I pretended it was long and heavy, like the weapon I'd

buried. I pointed once at Brandr and once at the imaginary blade in my arms. He nodded, understanding. Then I swung my phantom blade as I'd seen the yellow-haired giant do. Then, kneeling on the ground as Kidla had, I keeled over, feigning death. Brandr's eyes widened. Rather than help me up, he took a cautious step backward.

"I've tried to explain: I was there, that day on the beach. When your boat arrived." I scrambled back to my feet, searching through my memories until I recalled the yellow-haired giant's chant. Sticking out my chest as he'd done, I placed one hand over my forehead and nose to resemble the giant's horrible hat. "Drepa! Drepa! Drepa!"

Brandr stiffened, comprehension widening his eyes.

I gestured low to the ground, the height Nua had been. "There was a little girl." Then I slashed the air with the knife. "There was a baby." I rocked the imaginary child in my arms and flung it to the ground, crushing its head with the heel of my boot.

Brandr grabbed my hands, careless of the knife I still held.

"Stop," he said, his voice low. "Understand. You. Me. Understand."

I pointed at my forehead, the place where blood had poured into Kiasik's black hair. "My brother was wounded. You took him." Again I gestured to the south. "I need to go find him." Try as I might, I couldn't make him follow my words.

He released me and looked north hopefully. "Go. Yes? Good?"

I longed to do as he suggested. To travel toward the ice. Toward Puja and Saartok and Tapsi, and even crotchety Ququk. Toward home.

"No," I said finally. "I can't turn back now."

Brandr frowned, and for the first time since he'd recovered from his injury, fear tightened his face.

"Just tell me where they are. Where?" I repeated. I tried the simple words he knew: "Where. You. Camp."

"Much days," he responded hesitantly. "Much walk. Much

water." He grimaced. I thought him merely frustrated with his lack of words, but then his eyes narrowed again. He was scared. "Much walk. No. No."

I felt only hope. His camp was far, but for the first time, I knew for sure that it existed.

"Water?" I pressed. "Do you mean a river? The ocean?"

"Water," he said again, gesturing expansively. So, not a stream, but something larger. Maybe a lake. Whatever the obstacle, I'd find a way to cross it. I'd come this far, after all.

"Takk," I said, using his word for gratitude. It was barely more information than I'd had before, but it was all I was likely to get. It would have to be enough. The time for waiting was done; I wanted to start walking right away.

Brandr helped me take down the tent. We stood in the barren camp, the fish split between the panniers I'd rigged on White Paw and Floppy Eared's backs and my own heavily loaded pack. I gifted Brandr with a waterskin made from the bear's stomach and a sleeping fur made from its heavy pelt; he rolled the fur around his portion of fish and slung it across his wide chest. He tucked his whistle into his belt and draped his tattered blue cloak over his shoulders. He'd never questioned its ripped hem.

I heaved my own pack onto my back and secured the carrying strap across my forehead. I took a few steps, both chagrined and thrilled by the unaccustomed weight of so much dried food.

Brandr's gaze kept drifting from me to the north. I knew he'd leave me to continue his own journey, although I still didn't understand why he'd left his people in the first place, or why he insisted on traveling away from his camp, not toward it.

"This is where we part," I said, meeting his solemn blue gaze.

I waited for him to say he'd come with me. I *wanted* him to say it.

Not because I'm lonely, I assured myself. *Not because I've grown used to sleeping beside another human's warmth or listening to his music or meeting his smile with my own. I just need him to guide me to his people's camp.*

Otherwise I saved his leg for nothing. I might wind up wandering for many winters without ever finding Kiasik.

But I didn't know how to tell him any of that. I didn't know how to beg—and I'd long ago given up on the idea of forcing him to come. He was too strong, too large. He needed to join me of his own volition or not at all.

I stood, waiting for a moment longer for him to change his mind. Then I adjusted the straps of my pack one last time, ready to go.

"Tapvauvutit," I said to him. The word we always offered Ata-ata when he left our camp for a long hunting journey. Not "You are leaving," but rather "You are here." There is no final parting; even after death, the spirit always lives on in the body of the newly born, and so loved ones never really leave. But I could not know if Brandr's life followed the same rules as my own. While mine ran in a circle, perhaps his moved in a straight line. Had he been family, I might have placed my nose upon his cheek or held him in my arms, to express my wish that he stay well. But I'd never touched my stranger so intimately, never dared get too close for fear he might recognize the woman's body beneath my loose atigi. So I merely laid my hand briefly upon his arm, looked up once more into his eyes, and turned to leave.

I felt his presence behind me—silent, unmoving, watching my every step. I felt the emptiness of the path ahead, where I would be alone once more with only the wolfdogs for company. Then I thought of my milk-brother as I'd seen him last, bleeding on the beach beside the whale carcass, and my steps grew sure.

Still, I couldn't resist one final glance back at Brandr. I don't know what was in my eyes. I'd like to think it was courage. Determination. Hope. But if I'm honest, I know he saw my loneliness—and my longing. Perhaps that's what decided him.

With a deep breath, he limped toward me. I smiled encouragingly and saw his mouth quirk in response.

He placed a hand on my enormous pack as if to take it from me.

"You..." He gestured to the middle of his rib cage with the flat of his hand—exactly where the top of my head reached when I stood close to him. "Me..." He puffed out his chest.

"I can carry my own pack," I huffed. "I don't care how tall you are, you can barely walk." I limped around the camp in a perfect imitation of his halting gait. Among my people, such teasing was normal, but Brandr's already-pink face turned that deep shade of crimson no Inuk's could match; I worried I might've offended him. Instead he simply got down on his knees and pretended to be a very short person carrying a very large pack. I didn't quite understand until he started speaking in a gibberish version of my own tongue. Only then did I realize he was making fun of me. I laughed. A great gut laugh I hadn't enjoyed for many moons. No wolfdog, no matter how amusing, could make me laugh so hard.

Brandr grinned and made to get back on his feet, toppling unsteadily.

"Ia'a!" I lent him my arm, and he steadied, looking down at me from far too close. "No joke is worth undoing all my hard work." I pushed him gently away.

As we left the camp, I led my stranger to the cairn where I'd buried his long blade the day he'd arrived. When I unwrapped it from the fur and offered it to him, he took a step backward.

"Are you scared of your own weapon?" I teased. I could afford to be lighthearted; during the many days we'd spent in the same tent, surrounded by my spear and bow and knife, he could've easily killed me.

He took the weapon gingerly. Where I needed both hands to hold it, he wielded it in one. He rubbed at a speck of orange that discolored the blade like lichen on stone, then ran his thumb down the edge, drawing a single drop of blood.

"Takk." His brooding expression belied the word. This was not a gift he wanted, but he must have known it was one he needed; he rewrapped the weapon and strapped it against his shoulder blades.

Together, we set out southward. My stranger walked with a ponderous tread, bent with some burden heavier than the blade on his back.

I should've taken his reluctance as a warning.

Instead, despite the weight of my pack, my steps were light. Brandr would find the camp. I would find Kiasik.

And I would not be alone.

CHAPTER TWENTY-EIGHT

ᛉ

There are few sounds at night on the frozen sea besides the roar of the wind. No plants to rustle, no waves to crash upon the shore, no birds to caw. The white owl flies on hushed wings. The white fox walks with silent tread. Even Inuit move as softly as spirits, the snow too hard to yield and crunch beneath our boots. We hear little, but what we do hear is vital: the exploding breath of a surfacing seal, the shift and crack of drifting ice. But in the forest there is always sound. The trees, even in their shrouds of snow, are alive, and their voices—groans, creaks, screams—never cease.

Before, I'd seen tall trees only as naked trunks washed upon the shore. Now I witnessed them in all their terrifying glory. The farther south we walked, the taller they became, until finally we entered a forest of trees covered in sharp green needles like walrus whiskers. Above me the thick branches swayed with every breeze, nearly blocking out the sky. As autumn approached, we were constantly in shadow.

I was used to looking out across the expanse of tundra or ocean, scanning all the way to the horizon, my vision never impeded except by hill or iceberg. Suddenly I could see only a few paces in any direction, hemmed in by the towering trunks. I could hear the stirrings of life around me—a solitary bird skittering in the tree-tops, small animals running along the branches, the rare crunch of heavy paws on fallen tree needles—but I couldn't see it. If becoming a wolf had shown me the inadequacy of my human senses, the forest made me feel as if I had transformed from human to lemming. Everything was vast, overwhelming. The world moved too much and too fast and too loud. I wanted to crawl into a hole and hibernate for the season.

Brandr seemed to understand my unease but not to share it. He walked confidently through the woods, though the farther we traveled, the more frequently the shadow of fear crossed his face.

Without him I would've been hopelessly lost. All this time, I'd followed the nearby shoreline. When that failed, I navigated by the Sun or the wind or the stars. But now the trees blocked everything from view—even the sky itself.

By the third morning after we entered the forest, the trees stretched even taller. I stood directly beneath one and looked straight up, growing dizzy. From the outside, the branches seemed thick and unruly, an incomprehensible mass of wood and needle. Now I saw that they spiraled up the tree in neat, regular rows, thinning as they went. *Like the spirals in a seashell*, I thought, *each building on the one before. Like my grandfather and my father and myself, all springing from the same trunk.*

At least the trees gave me somewhere to hide when I needed to relieve myself. On the tundra, I'd managed to convince Brandr, through a series of gestures we both found highly humorous, that my people preferred not to watch each other piss or shit. Ridiculous, but he believed me. After that first trick with the waterskin, I took to ducking behind the nearest boulder or hummock, and he'd gamely turn around and occupy himself elsewhere.

When my moon blood flowed—not often and not regularly—I stuffed dried moss in my trousers. At first I worried he'd smell the blood on me as Issuk had, but he never did. I kept hunting even while I bled. I disobeyed a great agliruti to do it, but I had no choice if I was to survive.

The forest screened me not only from Brandr's questions, but from Taqqiq's gaze. Even when the trees thinned, and I glimpsed his shifting white eye, I no longer felt his power. The farther south we went, the weaker the Moon Man became. The animals, though rare, no longer shied from my bow, and fresh meat supplemented our ever-smaller store of dried fish.

Yet we did not travel in peace. The spirits that had ceased to haunt me turned on Brandr instead. The nightmares that had always plagued him grew more frequent, and the longer we traveled, the worse they became. Still, I didn't mind being woken by his thrashing. The forest creaked around me like the footsteps of the bird-man coming across the ice to steal me away, and I was glad for Brandr's presence beside me in the night. I never removed my clothes, no matter how warm the tent. Following my lead, Brandr wore his own shirt and trousers. Perhaps he thought sleeping clothed was yet another strange custom he should follow. Sweet One slept between us, with Floppy Eared and White Paw curled at the tent entrance.

All of us had been loosely stitched together from mismatched parts. An Inuk with a man's spirit and a woman's body. Three animals caught between dog and wolf. A stranger with a giant's frame and a man's heart. Yet somehow, we were becoming a seamless whole.

——◆——

We journeyed swiftly for many days before our surroundings changed again. Slender, white-barked trees nestled in clusters amid the surrounding darker forest. Their leaves, delicately pointed like the old quartz blade in my amulet pouch, fluttered in the breeze. Like children of Malina the Sun Woman, the bright yellow leaves continued to shield me from Taqqiq's eye. When a strong wind blew, they fell like rain, settling on our shoulders and hair like molten drops of sunlight.

We had eaten the last of the dried fish, and still we had not found Kiasik. But for once I didn't worry about food. Animals crowded this forest. Small, shy ones that looked like caribou calves. Great lumbering ones with antlers so wide and broad they reminded me of whale jaws. Brandr was no hunter, but between my bow and my wolfdogs, we ate well.

In the dappled shade of a white-barked tree, we feasted on one of the smaller creatures, stealing a brief respite from our hurried pace. I pulled the meat apart with my fingers and dropped it into my mouth, enjoying the rich blood. Brandr, as usual, made a small fire and turned his portion to an unappetizing gray lump, gnawing the meat off the bone with all the manners of a ravenous dog. After so long, he no longer stared at my bloody meal with surprise. I still couldn't repress my grimace at his strange way of eating ruined flesh—but I was getting used to it.

After finishing her own gobbled meal, White Paw didn't lie down beside us. She paced a wide circle, sniffing every tree and rock. Floppy Eared soon joined her, tromping through the fallen leaves with his broad paws, making more noise than any wolf should make. Sweet One watched them both carefully, but stayed in her favorite spot: sprawled beside Brandr, one paw resting on his leg. When he shifted, so did she, always touching him.

Brandr's eyes drooped shut, his back propped against the smooth trunk of the tree. The light played on his long orange hair. Strands drifted across his face like tiny sunbeams. His eyes were closed—he wouldn't see me staring. His thick beard and bony nose, once so strange to me, were more familiar now than the dimming memories of my family's faces.

The day was uncommonly warm for so late in autumn, and he sat with his outer garment unlaced, his white shirt open at the throat, and his blue cloak loose beneath him. This close, I could watch the slow, steady pulse between his collarbones, where pooled sweat glistened in the sun.

A short yip from White Paw shook me from my reverie. Brandr's eyes sprang open. I looked quickly away and went to join the wolfdogs. White Paw and Floppy Eared stood amid a cluster of trees, sniffing the ground. I crouched beside their discovery. Human footprints.

"Your people?" I asked, motioning Brandr over. As I waited for his answer, my heart thundered with anticipation. He knelt beside me, wincing slightly as he bent his bad leg.

"No. No Brandr men."

Then who? With Issuk's family dead, only one other group existed: my own family, far to the north. Then Ataata's words returned to me: *No land is empty.*

"Bad men." Brandr pointed toward my bow and spear and swept his hands around the forest. "Bad. They... they... *skít*! No words," he growled in frustration.

"You know these men?" I asked, pointing at the footprint. "But they're not your people?"

"Stay," he said firmly, more commanding than pleading. "Bad men."

"As bad as your own men?" My anger flared. I had not forgotten Nua's murder, or the baby's crushed skull.

Now, for all his long knife and his violent ways, Brandr feared facing these new strangers. But why should I trust what he told me? The enemies of his people were most likely the allies of mine. Besides, hadn't I waited my whole life to meet more Inuit? So far strangers had brought me grief. But maybe, just maybe, my luck was about to change. Maybe Taqqiq no longer controlled my destiny.

And so, ignoring Brandr's protests, I set out along the faint trail, looking for the scattered footprints that denoted the passage of men. Many different tracks dotted the ground. More than one family lay at the end of this path. My confidence began to waver.

I considered turning around, or at least pausing to rethink. But I could hear Brandr walking behind me, following despite his trepidation. I didn't want to admit any weakness to him. I pressed on. My spear and bow rested across my back, and Brandr's sharp knife lay secure at my side. This time, I would not be defenseless.

Suddenly I heard the laughter of children. Creeping forward as quietly as I could, I peered through the trees. A small camp nestled against the shore, round igluit made not of snow or sod but of narrow white sheets of curling bark. Between the huts, a band of children danced and played. At least, they moved like children, and were the size of children, but they did not look like children. They did not look like humans at all. They were bright red from hair to toes, like the belly of a trout. Only their eyes and teeth shone white. Were they demons? Ghosts? Red where Brandr's people were pale? My head whirled. How many types of humans were there in the world?

Despite their monstrous appearance, the boys shot toy arrows not unlike those Ataata had carved for me a lifetime ago. Mothers, equally red, sat outside the huts, pounding bark, sewing hides, butchering animals, while a few men lounged nearby, sharpening spears and tools.

I'd taken only a few steps toward the clearing when I realized that White Paw wasn't beside me. She sat on her haunches next to her brother and sister, staring at me, ears swiveled forward. Brandr stood beside them, his arms crossed.

"I'm going either way. But I'd rather not go alone." I directed my whispered comments to my wolfdogs. Brandr could make his own decisions, and I was loath to ask for his help. In the forest, I'd depended on him to guide me. I longed to make my own way again.

"Let's go," I ordered more sternly. White Paw didn't move. She simply lay down and rested her chin on her forepaws, her ears swinging backward in defiance. I could've tried to force her, grabbing her by the ruff, baring my teeth and growling. But she stared at me so fixedly that I felt she must have a good reason for ignoring my commands.

"You're staying. Fine." She didn't yip or whimper. If she had, I might've stayed. Instead, I walked into the clearing with my arms raised, letting the sleeves of my parka fall back to show I had nothing to hide.

A little girl saw me first, freezing in the middle of her dance with her arms upraised like wings, her knees bent. Her black eyes were round and bright in her red face as she opened her mouth and screamed. I stopped only a few paces from the woods, suddenly unsure, as the camp's men leapt to their feet, snatching bows and spears. Most wore trousers and nothing else, the muscles of their chests and arms taut and gleaming as they rushed toward me. There were more of them than I'd thought, spilling from the huts and the surrounding forest like wasps shaken from a nest.

I felt one of them rush up behind me and whirled to face my attacker.

Brandr. He didn't look happy.

I turned back to the red strangers before he could read the relief on my face. His long blade remained sheathed, but I was glad to know it was there. I hadn't forgotten his fearlessness when he faced the bear.

As they came within bow range, the young men slowed like a wolf pack stalking a hare, every step deliberate. Two older men stayed behind them, jabbering in an unknown language. Though they gestured angrily at my fur clothing, so different from their own light hides, they seemed particularly enraged by Brandr. They pointed and shouted at him. *What a pair we must be*, I thought. *Me dark and short. Him so red and hairy, a full two heads taller, with clothing from another world.*

I couldn't resist returning their scrutiny. Up close, the red was just paint, not unlike the dried clay that sometimes stained an Inuk's flesh after a day of digging for clams. The patches of flesh showing through the mottled ochre were the light brown of wet sand, just a shade darker than my own, and the hair beneath the caked red powder was black. They wore a crude mixture of hairless hides and woven bark.

Despite the roughness of their garb, the men, and most of the women, were taller than I—although few stood as tall as my companion. The men slid into a slowly tightening circle around us. I felt like a ptarmigan who'd walked blindly into a snare. A very stupid ptarmigan.

Just as I grew convinced that my journey south was about to meet an untimely end, a thin voice called out from behind the crowd, and the men parted for a stooped old woman.

She, too, was painted red; no white hair betrayed her age. But the ochre had settled firmly into the deep creases of her face, as if someone had drawn the wrinkles on with a bloodied brush. The little girl who'd first spotted me held the old woman by the elbow and guided her carefully across the uneven ground. The woman was barely taller than the child who led her, and her eyes were white stones on a red field, clouded with age and blindness. Despite her infirmity, the men fell silent at her approach.

She stretched a bony arm toward us. The little girl guided her hand to Brandr. He stiffened but let the crone rest a palm upon his chest. She stroked the strange woven material of his shirt, then crawled her fingers upward until they rested in the hollow between his collarbones. She was far too short to reach his face.

It took three red men to push Brandr roughly to his knees. My giant grunted as his injured leg slammed against the earth. Only I knew what it cost him not to cry out. Kneeling, Brandr was at eye level with the old woman. She explored his face with her fingertips, muttering to herself as she felt his heavy beard. She pulled on it experimentally.

"Ow!" Brandr sounded more surprised than hurt. The old woman gave a croaking laugh and spoke to the surrounding crowd. The villagers gasped and whispered to each other. I didn't like the fear I saw in their eyes.

Then she moved on to me. Her fingertips, soft as the pads of a puppy's paw, skimmed across my cheekbones, eyes, lips. Her touch felt like a bird's wing fluttering against my cheek. Then, as her hands explored the fur lining of my atigi's hood, her expression froze into a mask of terror.

She spoke tersely to the little girl, then hobbled off with her toward one of the huts. The red men seized Brandr and me and dragged us after them.

We ducked through the opening of her bark dwelling. Inside, a small fire crackled in the center, the smoke rising up through a hole in the roof. The crone eased herself down beside it, the flames turning her face an even more brilliant crimson. Brandr crossed his legs and sat awkwardly beside me, his frame filling up a full half of the tiny hut, his hair brushing the domed ceiling. The little girl knelt in the shadows behind the old woman.

The crone stared at us for a while with her sightless eyes, then said something to the little girl. The child moved around the fire toward me and began, without warning, to pull my atigi over my head. I grabbed the hem and snarled at her like a wolverine. If keeping my secret meant harming this little girl, so be it. She backed away, then spied my outer parka lashed to my pack and took that to the tiny old woman instead.

The crone stroked the thick caribou fur thoughtfully and lifted it to her nose to smell.

"Inuk?" she asked finally.

"Yes!" I replied. "You speak my language?"

The woman stiffened and didn't reply. "Where your people?" she asked instead, her words slow and strangely accented.

"North," I said, pointing. "Very, very far."

"Come find you?"

"No."

"No Inuit come?"

"No."

"Good."

"How do you speak like an Inuk?" I asked.

The old woman stretched an arm across the low fire. Faint tattoo lines crossed the back of her hand and ringed her fingers.

"You're an Inuk, too!" I said, reaching for her.

"No," she said firmly, snatching back her hand when I brushed her fingertips with my own.

"Then who are you?"

She shook her head wearily. "Too hard. No words." From a bark container, she pulled out a bundle of dried flowers and a small, swollen bag made from an animal's stomach. She tossed the flowers into the fire. The flames rose higher as acrid smoke filled the hut, stinging my eyes and throat. The old woman pulled the wooden stopper from the bag and passed it to the little girl, who scuttled around the fire to hand it to me.

"Drink," ordered the woman.

Brandr's hand rested on my arm. He stared at me, eyes wide with warning. I looked back at the girl, who crossed her arms impatiently. She spoke to the old woman, who laughed her strange croaking laugh, took the bag, and drank deeply, as if to show me not to fear. The girl passed me the bag once more. I offered Brandr a shrug—and took a sip.

I choked as the stinging liquid coursed down my throat.

As soon as the burning subsided, the dizziness began.

The last thing I heard before I passed out was Brandr calling my name.

CHAPTER
TWENTY-NINE

♪

A slavering mouth full of teeth snapped at my face. I thought White Paw had come to save me.

But I sat not in a bark hut, but in a sod-and-stone qarmaq. Dark and cold. The ceiling low with only lashed antlers—not whale bones—to hold it up, and the walls nearly straight rather than curved. The barking and snarling roared in my ears like thunder.

A gray dog stood atop me, its gaping maw a handbreadth from my face. Not White Paw. Its snout was too round, its legs too short. An Inuk's dog, yet somehow monstrous. Strange. Terrifying.

This was not my memory.

"Nooooo!" A man hurtled toward me from the corner of the qarmaq. He plunged a spear into the dog, the stone point a sharp triangle, just like the quartz blade I carried in my amulet pouch.

The dog howled in agony and fell to the ground, whimpering.

My savior crawled to me. He spoke in a language I'd never heard before yet understood perfectly. "Are you hurt?"

I sat up gingerly. My body felt small but strong. Indeed, my limbs were strangely thick and short, clad in rough furs and pelts.

"I don't think so," I said, surprised that the strange tongue came so easily to my lips.

The stranger clasped me to his broad chest for a moment. I wrapped my arms around him, my body beyond my control though my mind floated free.

"Stay here," he whispered.

"Where are you going? What's happening?" But he left the qarmaq, taking his spear with him. I crawled after him. As I reached the front of the tunnel he turned toward me.

"I said stay!" The sounds of terror drowned out his cry.

Another man in rough pelts lay sprawled in front of a neighboring qarmaq, blood seeping from an arrow wound in his chest. Beside him lay a woman and three children, their throats ripped out. A sled dog, oblivious to the chaos, feasted on their flesh. The man from my own qarmaq pushed me back into the tunnel and turned to the fray.

A small woman ran by, screaming, followed by a taller hunter with a raised spear. As my man bowled the hunter into the snow, I saw the taller man's parka and knew him for an Inuk. The two men rolled together, their long spears useless at such close range. The fleeing woman, safe for a moment, looked around her, searching for shelter. I crawled out just far enough to beckon her into my qarmaq.

She began to run toward me, but another Inuk grabbed her from behind. She screamed and fought before he thrust his short slate knife into her ribs. She melted at his feet like snow above flame.

I scuttled back into the tunnel's mouth, wondering how long before I'd meet the same fate. Before the entrance, the two men had ceased their struggling. The Inuk straddled the smaller man, his knife pointed at the man's throat. He spoke a few words in a language I'd known all my life yet that now sounded only like the rasp of gravel on stone.

"Why?" the small man demanded, breathless. "We taught you to build homes out of snow when you travel the sea ice, taught you the best places to hunt the seal! Why do you—" His voice cut off in a gurgle of blood as the Inuk's knife passed through his throat.

I screamed. The Inuk turned toward me. I scrambled out of the qarmaq, my feet churning through soft snow. Then all went black.

When I woke again, I thought I'd be back in the bark hut with Brandr at my side. Instead, I felt the familiar motion of a sled beneath me and an unfamiliar wetness on my scalp.

One more vision left to see.

A young boy sat beside me on the sled, patting my arm as if to soothe my fears.

He had Ataata's smile.

—◦—◄═╪═►—◦—

I woke again. Screaming this time.

"Omat!"

I was hot. Something held me down. I struggled, and the bonds loosed. My vision cleared—Brandr sat beside me, his face twisted with fear.

I took a deep breath. The fire had died. A single ray of dusty sunlight streamed through the smoke hole. My body was my own again, my limbs lean and long. I knew now why White Paw had chosen to stay outside the village. Her people had a history with the old woman.

So did mine.

The rectangular qarmaq, the terrifying dogs—I had seen it all before in a single flash when I found the quartz blade buried among the dwarfs' ruin. Ataata had told me the little creatures had taught our family to build igluit from snow, then long ago disappeared from our land. He lied. My own ancestors had killed some, probably chased away the rest. And they were not dwarfs at all—no more than Brandr was truly a giant.

"Where's the old woman?" I asked in my own tongue, knowing Brandr couldn't answer. I was too tired to act out what I wanted. I could hear men moving outside the hut. We were alone, but guarded. Who could tell what plans these painted men had for us? I knew now that the old woman had reason to hate me.

How long had she lived with my family before she escaped to join these red strangers? Long enough to be tattooed and learn some of our language. Not long enough to forget the harm we'd done her and her people. She would want me dead, and the villagers seemed equally suspicious of Brandr. Neither of us was welcome here. We needed to leave. Now.

The woman's bark container caught my eye. When I'd drunk with her, I'd shared her dreams.

I looked at Brandr.

If I could enter his memories, I might know more of Kiasik. I couldn't throw away that chance, no matter the danger.

I threw a handful of the flowers on the fire. Too many. The smoke rose up thicker and more acrid than before. Choking on the fumes, I took a deep swig of the bitter liquid, more than I'd intended, and handed it to Brandr, motioning for him to do the same.

"You have to trust me," I urged as the world began to spin around me once more. "Please!"

He looked at me, wide-eyed, but did as I asked.

— • —═╬═— • —

Ingharr doesn't heed the red man's screams. The knife sticks for a moment in the skraeling's rib cage, but Ingharr rocks it back and forth calmly until it moves again.

"He's the best," old Olfun whispers beside me. "Never kills the man until it's done."

Bile rises in my throat. At least Galinn's not here to see this. I never thought I'd be grateful for his injury, but I'd almost rather he suffer from a skraeling's arrow wound than witness this.

Ingharr's almost finished now. Gently, more gently than I've ever seen him do anything, he pries the ribs apart, his muscles bulging with the strain. The red man opens his mouth to scream again, but no sound comes out— Ingharr has just ripped the lungs from his body. He spreads them wide, one on each side of the skraeling's back, and nails them to the wooden cross.

Like the wings of a dying bird, the lungs pump weakly for a moment and then lie still. The red man, his mouth still open in a silent scream of agony, is finally dead.

"All glory to Thor!" Ingharr shouts, drawing his sword and raising it high.

"To Thor!" we respond.

This is not my first spread-eagling. Nor shall it be my last. There are two other skraelings left to be killed.

The other two die faster. Soon there are three trophies pinned to crosses, lungs spread wide. Blood courses down their bellies like paint, putting the streaked red of their stained skin to shame.

"Do you really think the red men won't try to avenge this?" I ask Ingharr as we walk back to Leifsbudir. Blood splatters the long blond beard he braids with such pride.

"You're worried about a group of skraelings, Brandr? You, who've seen the Vikings vanquish Picts and Celts and Slavs across the world?" He laughs and hefts his sword in his hand. His muscles bulge, engorged by the weeks of hunting seals, cutting timber, and rowing along the coast searching for grapes. "You're no better than our supposed leaders." He looks around us, suddenly cautious, but only Finnbogi the Icelander walks nearby. The other Greenlanders are out of earshot. "Thorvard Einarsson is a mewling coward," he mutters. "Freydis Eriksdottir is a greedy fool. He would run from the skraelings, and she would trade with them."

Ingharr's disloyalty isn't surprising. I've seen the way he watches the couple. He envies Thorvard his bed and Freydis her power.

"Brandr's right," Finnbogi says. The Icelander's pale face looks more drawn than usual. None of those from his house—myself included—have eaten well, and we have no one to blame but ourselves. Ingharr and his Greenlanders are flushed with health in comparison. Still, the hollows beneath Finnbogi's gray eyes are even darker than usual. "The skraelings will be back."

"And this time we'll strike them down before they attack!" insists Ingharr.

He doesn't mention that we struck the first blow, killing two skraelings when a trade went bad. He's not the type to see anything beyond his own pleasure and pride. Now there's a blood feud, no less dangerous than those I remember from my childhood in Greenland. One man kills another in a drunken brawl and there's a blood price to pay. Back and forth, spreading destruction from one settlement to the next until a meeting of the Althing finally settles it forever.

Ingharr is wrong to compare this war with the pillaging of a Celtic village. There are always enough Norsemen to overpower a village. We have the advantage of faster boats, stronger swords, and the berserker rage. But Ingharr, for all his bluster, is no Viking. Just a puffed-up Greenland hunter with dreams of a warrior's glory in Valhalla. And Freydis may be the daughter of Erik the Red, but she's only a woman. She had never even left home until a year ago, when she decided to lead this expedition of foolhardy Greenlanders. Her husband, Thorvard Einarsson, is a dullard. Ingharr is right about that. Thorvard carries a war hammer like a Viking, but I doubt he knows how to use it. Finnbogi and the Icelanders are mere merchants. Good sailors and ready for adventure, but they don't like to get their hands dirty with cutting timber and milking sheep, and they don't have the stomach for the sort of bloodshed a real Viking is used to.

If any of our leaders knew what they were doing, they'd seek out the skraeling village and kill them all. That's the only way to stop this endless cycle of reprisals.

But I don't have the heart to tell them that. I've seen enough bloodshed in my life. I thank the gods above that at least those fur-clad skraelings in the north are too far away for further strife. It's hard enough to worry about our red neighbors.

I'm almost back to Leifsbudir when I hear the shouting.

Ingharr starts to run. He's slow despite his massive strength, still cautious of his right side, where one of the fur-clad skraelings left a nasty scar. I pull ahead of him. I'm the first to see the battle.

Four of the red men's narrow birchbark boats are pulled up to the shore. Dozens of their warriors run through the settlement, brandishing bows and spears. Two Norsemen lie dead at the shoreline—I can't tell who. Another, Magnor Tyrkirsson, is screaming like a child, clutching a gaping wound on his arm. *We're in trouble. Magnor's one of the few Greenlanders besides Ingharr and me who knows how to handle a sword.*

The Icelanders' house is too far away from Leifsbudir. *The sailors there probably don't know what's happened. But where are the rest of Freydis's men? There should be at least twenty Greenlanders here to protect the long-house and the livestock.*

I'm running now, shouting in fury. I feel the berserker rage rise up, the blood rushing into my face, turning my cheeks to flame and my vision red. No. I push it away. I stumble to a halt. *That isn't me anymore.*

I did not come to Vinland to kill red men. I came to get away from the killing.

More screams.

I have no choice. I cannot let my companions die.

Running once more toward the shore, I can see the Greenlanders now, cowering like whipped dogs in the shadow of their wood-and-turf longhouse.

Then I see Freydis herself. Loosed from its wimple, her red hair twists about her head like angry snakes.

"Pitiful wretches!" she cries. Not at the attackers, but at her own cow-ardly men. "If I were a man, I'd fight more bravely than you! Why do you flee? You should slaughter them like sheep!"

Like a shield-maiden from legend, she strides through the settlement. She holds a dull weaving sword made of ivory, a tool for tightening cloth on a loom, but raised aloft in her hand, it looks like a Valkyrie's gleaming sword. She needs only a wolf-mount to make the image complete. She rips her green tunic with her free hand, baring one full white breast. She strikes her chest with the flat of the blade. "Come, skraelings! Fight ME!"

Freydis's men need no more urging. They burst from their hiding places, swords and axes aloft. Soon I'm caught in the crowd, my own steel sword unsheathed. Behind me the others raise a battle cry. *The skraelings won't know what hit them.*

One of them runs toward me, a crude stone ax raised to strike. His eyes and teeth are bright white in his red face. I don't think of right or wrong. Only of survival. I swing my sword with both hands. Steel connects with flesh, then bone. The stone ax flies from his grasp. I don't wait to watch him fall.

Thorvard Einarsson screams for help, swinging his war hammer uselessly at three skraelings armed with spears. A stone-tipped arrow whistles past my ear as I rush to Freydis's husband. The arrow thuds into the ground ahead of me, and I reach to yank it from the earth as I run by. I hurl the arrow toward one of the skraelings around Thorvard. It lodges in the soft flesh of the red man's upper arm and he drops his spear.

Before I can reach the group to finish the task, Freydis herself is there, still holding her ivory sword. She swings awkwardly with both hands, taking one skraeling unaware in the backs of his knees. He crumples to the ground.

Thorvard strikes out at the third skraeling, who dodges the blow with a disdainful sneer. But when the red man sees Freydis, breast still bared, gray eyes burning, he flees for the safety of his boats.

Soon all the skraelings are on the run, abandoning what loot they plundered from our storehouse. Bolts of cloth and iron nails drop to the ground as they leap into their slender boats and paddle for their lives.

A few of our men jump into our own rowboat to follow after, but the skraelings' nimble craft are far swifter.

I know we won't capture them.

The count of the dead is not large. Four skraelings. Two Norsemen. Magnor will join that number if we don't cut off his arm. Nothing compared to the carnage I've seen when we Vikings come to other lands. But still, our dreams are shattered. To men from a treeless world, Vinland has been a paradise of furs and timber and wild grain ready for harvest. Now it will never feel safe again.

As I've done so many times before, I clean the blood carefully from my blade. Sheathed on my back, my sword's a familiar weight I am both eager and loath to shed. The thought of the red skraeling I just killed reminds me of the fur-clad man whose head I took far to the north. I can still hear the screams of the women and children in their strange snow hut. I remember the skraeling who crawled from behind the whale to watch me holding Galinn. I can't remember his face, but I remember the way he held that harpoon—and the way he lowered it. I'd let the kid live. A small mercy in a day of death.

My blade is clean again. But blood still stains my hands.

Glory to Thor of the crashing thunder. Glory to Odin of the raging battlefield. Glory to Tyr of the flashing blade. So Galinn always says—my brother who speaks to the gods. He worships them with song and saga, not with sword. Would he still praise them if he knew what it felt like to kill? Still, I thank Odin that Galinn is safe in the Icelanders' house, a forest separating him from Leifsbudir and the carnage here. His wound heals, his hope grows—even as mine slips away as surely as the red men in their birchbark boats.

⊷━✦━⊶

"Omat, wake up. We've got to get out of here. Come on, kid. Come back to me."

I knew the voice. Now, for the first time, I understood the words.

CHAPTER THIRTY

ᛇ

The birchbark hut swam into view.

Brandr's face hovered above me, his relieved smile flashing in the dark.

"There you are. I thought I'd lost you." He sounded weak, as if suffering from the same dizziness I did. Then, in his halting version of an Inuk's words, he added, "Good Omat. Good. Go. Go."

"Yes. I understand," I whispered in Norse. My thick tongue struggled with the foreign sounds as they hadn't when I'd lived Brandr's dream, but I knew the right words. "We need to go. Where is your sword? My spear?"

"Odin's eye! How can you speak like that?"

"No time," I said, shaking my head. Even that much movement sent my brain spinning. "Your sword?"

"They took it, don't you remember? They left us our packs, but not our weapons."

So many other people's memories filled my mind that I barely had room for my own. I groaned in answer. "We must leave. Red men…" I searched my dream for the word I needed. "Are not dullards."

He grimaced. "True. Word of my people must've spread."

"They do not like my people, either."

"So I gathered."

With Brandr supporting my head, I sat up gingerly and leaned against the bark wall. "Hut can break. Can you make carnage? Red men are there." I gestured to the opening. "Not there." I motioned behind us.

He tapped the bark thoughtfully. "Carnage, huh? And then what?"

I shrugged. "We run."

"You can barely stand!"

"And you can barely walk."

"Not much of a plan."

"No," I conceded.

"What about your dogs?"

"Wolves," I corrected, remembering the word from the vision. "Wolfdogs."

"Oh." He looked at me with new respect. "Well, can you call to them?"

"Yes, but..."

"But what?"

I couldn't explain my hesitation to him. The old red woman's dread had lodged itself in my own mind—I couldn't shake the image of slavering sled dogs tearing her dwarf family apart. *No, not dwarfs*, I reminded myself. *People. People just like me.*

But Brandr was right: we needed my wolfdogs. We'd walked right into the feud between the painted men and the Norse. Our only hope was to fight our way free.

"I will call. Ready?" We didn't need more discussion than that. Despite our new words, we still shared our old unspoken understanding.

Brandr slung his pack over his shoulder, then hunched over in the low room. He braced his shoulders against the thin bark ceiling.

The support posts for the hut were sunk deep into the ground, but Brandr flashed a smile at me, all confidence. "Ready."

I shoved the old woman's bag of liquid and container of dried flowers into my own pack and lashed my parka back in place. Then I rose on unsteady legs, rubbed my face to clear my thoughts, and tried to remember what it felt like to run with Singarti across the valley. I took a deep breath and threw back my head, a howl tearing from my throat. Long and low it began, rising pitch by pitch. A wolf's cry of need.

At the same time, Brandr pressed up with all his strength. The hut jerked once, twice, then lifted clear off the ground. He stood to his full height, lifting the entire hut over his head, then bent his knees and tossed it away with a loud roar that nearly eclipsed my own call. Carnage.

Faint, but already getting louder, the wolfdogs' howls blended with our own. My pack was on its way.

Brandr ripped his sword from one stunned guard, and I toppled the other painted man to the ground, yanking my weapons free. In the twilight, White Paw and Sweet One's dark forms appeared mere blurs as they barreled through the village, but Floppy Eared galloped like a streak of white lightning, headed straight for us. They bounded through the camp, knocking over the flimsy bark huts, snapping at the red warriors and their outstretched spears.

Overwhelmed by the mayhem, our captors paid Brandr and me little heed as we made our escape. Still woozy from the dreams, I slung my arm around the Norseman, and he wrapped his around me. The wolfdogs protected our retreat, snarling at anyone who came near.

A sharp keening rose behind us. I turned briefly to see the old woman kneeling before my three wolfdogs, her hands tearing at her face, her voice rising in a wordless cry of rage and fear. Floppy Eared balked, whimpering. No human had ever screamed at him like that before. Sweet One, too, stopped snarling and tucked her tail. She lay down before the woman and offered her stomach, begging forgiveness.

"No! Come!" I screamed. Brandr added his own cries. White Paw nipped at her siblings, then turned and ran to us. The other wolfdogs leapt up and followed.

My fear for them cleared my mind. "I'm fine," I said to Brandr, extracting myself from his arm. I'd lost track of what language I spoke, but he understood. "Run?"

He nodded grimly. "I can try."

I reached my hand for his.

We let the wolfdogs lead the way, trusting their vision in the quickly darkening forest. Brandr limped, but he did not complain, did not falter. Spiked branches lashed our faces as we ran, hidden perils in the gloom. My oft-repaired boot soles offered little protection against the rocks and roots beneath my feet as we lurched through the forest hand in hand. But my wolfdogs bounded forward with ease, Floppy Eared's outstretched white tail darting before us like a guiding star. My panting breaths almost, but not quite, masked the sound of our pursuers. While we crashed through the dense forest, the painted men moved silently, but I could hear them calling to each other.

In the starlight filtering through the branches, I saw the black circles that shadowed Brandr's eyes. He gasped for breath between tight, pale lips. Even with his long legs, his limping strides grew shorter, slower. He wouldn't last much longer.

Suddenly the night darkened as clouds rolled across the sky, blotting out the stars. The gray world turned black. Floppy Eared's white tail disappeared ahead of us.

The voices of the painted men grew louder, angrier.

Slowing the pace of our flight, I squeezed Brandr's sweaty hand in my own. I didn't know which way to go. I pulled on him until I could feel, rather than see, his head bending toward mine. I pressed my mouth against his ear and whispered, "They do not see, but they hear."

His bearded cheek rasped my face as he nodded. Then a wet nose thrust itself against my free palm. I reached out, feeling White Paw's familiar skull butting my leg. I tangled my fingers in her ruff and bent to whisper, "Silent, little one. Be silent."

Very slowly, White Paw moved forward, her broad paws soundless on the forest floor. I trailed like a duckling, Brandr's hand still seized in my own.

The angry voices of the painted men grew fainter. Finally only the forest sounds remained: the whisper of wind in the branches, the hoot of an owl, the rustle of some small animal among the fallen leaves. The clouds rolled away; the starlight gave no sign of our pursuers. I still wanted to get as far away from the camp as I could before dawn. But even as I hastened my pace, Brandr's hand slipped from my own. He sat down heavily.

"I can't. My leg." He no longer bothered to whisper.

"Come," I urged, reaching out my hand to him. Leaning back and using all my weight, I hauled him to his feet. Standing, he towered over me once more, but his chin rested on his chest, his shoulders slumped. The wolfdogs stood in a loose circle around us, Sweet One and Floppy Eared with tails high, ears swiveling, listening for danger. White Paw looked only at me, waiting for instruction. I glanced behind us. Still no sign of the red men. No sign of the ocean, either. The wolfdogs had led us to safety—I could only hope they hadn't also gotten us hopelessly lost. We needed rest, a place to hide before the Sun came up.

A low overhang of rock promised shelter ahead. I beat aside a heavy thicket of undergrowth and urged Brandr forward. He shrugged off his pack and squeezed beneath the ledge. I crawled in behind him. What had seemed a shallow declivity broadened into a small cave, damp and rank. I tried to sit up and smacked my head on the low, sharp ceiling.

"A'aa!" I wiped a trickle of blood from my forehead.

"I tried that already," Brandr muttered. A sliver of gray starlight slipped through the cave entrance, enough for me to see the outline of his form lying a breath away. "The ceiling's too low. This is the back wall. It doesn't go any farther." His Norse words reached me like an echo. First the sound, then, a moment later, the meaning.

I grunted noncommittally, shifting my pack to form a rough pillow. My head ached from the aftereffects of the dream and my struggles to understand this new language. I just wanted to rest.

Brandr had other plans.

"Are you planning to explain to me what in Odin's name happened back there? Suddenly you can understand everything I say. You know Norse. You've been lying to me all this time?"

"Lying?"

"Stop pretending, Omat." He propped himself on an elbow so he could stare down at me, his blue eyes black in the faint light.

A bitter smile twisted my lips. If only he knew the true extent of my guile. He thought I'd been lying about the one thing I'd been perfectly honest about. A new fear crept unbidden into the pit of my stomach. *Or does he think I lied about something besides understanding his words?*

I'd lived his past—had Brandr lived mine? Did he know of my woman's body?

"You drank," I said in careful, hesitant Norse. "Then dreamed?"

"No, no dreams. I drank that awful stuff and passed out. When I woke up, you were still thrashing around and moaning."

I relaxed. My secret was still my own. "I dreamed," I explained. "I dreamed your life." The words started to come more easily to me now that I was too tired to fight the strange sounds in my brain. In the vision, I had fallen into the rushing stream of Brandr's mind, swallowing more of his language than I even realized. "I dreamed of you and many other men. The red men came. You fought. You killed. I heard you. Now I understand."

He laughed then, a bark of disbelief. "You came into my head, is that it, kid? You lived my life in a dream, and now you speak Norse as well as any Greenlander?" He settled onto his back once more. I breathed a little easier without his form looming above me.

"You don't believe me? Why would I lie?"

"No skraeling boy could do that."

"I didn't. The old woman had powerful magic. A powerful spirit. And I am not a boy," I added. "I am a man. A hunter for many winters."

"A small, beardless man, then!" he scoffed. "More dwarf than man, more like. Next you'll be telling me you're a seer, a priest. You have the ear of the gods? You're some magic man? Is that why—" He broke off abruptly, swallowing his next thought before it could emerge.

"Why what?" I demanded.

"Why... why you seem so familiar. Sometimes, even though I understand so little of what you're saying, it's like we can speak. Are you working some magic on me?" His voice had lost its laughter, a note of fear creeping in around the edges like a cold draft.

"No magic." I didn't yet have the words to explain my whole story to him, to tell him just how little magic I now possessed. I'd seen through his eyes, breathed into his lungs, felt the fear and courage in his heart. It felt wrong to lie to him, to hide my past. And now that I knew he bore no love for the tall, yellow-haired Ingharr who'd killed Kidla and Uimaitok and their children, I almost felt he might understand how I, too, had come to be alone in the world. Someday, perhaps, I'd tell him everything. But not now.

"No magic," I said again. "You know me because you saw me. When you came in your big boat and killed Patik. Women, children, all dead. I told you before."

His breath grew shallow. "You said you were there, but I didn't realize... that was you, hiding behind the whale," he said quietly. "I was so worried about Galinn... I let you live."

"You *think* you let me live. I could have killed you. You *and* your brother. I let *you* live."

"Omat, you haven't seen me when I'm not dragging this damn leg around. You couldn't have killed me." His voice was cold, colder than I'd ever heard it. "I'd *never* have let you kill Galinn."

"And I would *never* let you kill Kiasik!" I spat his own Norse words back at him, rolling onto my side to face him in the dark.

Brandr punched the low rock ceiling above his head. Had he been a different man, no doubt he would've punched me instead. "Kiasik? That man I killed? I had no choice—he shot my brother!"

"No," I said quickly. "Not Patik. Kiasik, my brother."

"*Your* brother? What are you talking about?"

"You don't even remember him, do you?" I said, my anger lending fluency to my words. All this time, I'd thought that if I could just explain, Brandr would have the answers I sought. "The last time I saw Kiasik, he was beside you, wounded. When I heard Nua's screams, I went to her. My brother was gone when I returned. You were all gone by then, fled like cowards from voices on the air."

"The skraeling…"

"Skraeling! What is this word?" I demanded.

"It means… 'savage one.' Dirty. A wretch. Like…you."

"*I* never murdered a child."

The silence between us grew thick.

"I didn't, either," Brandr said finally. "Ingharr Ketilsson did that."

"Where is my brother?" I demanded once more, impatient with his evasions.

"Look, kid, once Galinn got hit, I wasn't in my right mind. I don't remember much. I remember someone—you—watching us. And I remember Ingharr and the others coming back to the boat. Yes, there was a skrae—a man they'd wounded. They tossed him onto the ship so they could show him to Freydis Eriksdottir and her husband, Thorvard. Ingharr thought they might be interested in seeing what sort of people lived in the north. Your furs were so fine. Caribou and white bear. We thought the man…Kiasik… might eventually lead us to good hunting grounds."

"Just tell me if he lives."

"He was alive when we got back to Leifsbudir, our settlement.

He was alive when I left again, as far as I know. The Greenlanders kept him in their part of the camp. I lived in a different house with the Icelanders and Galinn. We didn't visit Freydis's longhouse often. I never saw your brother. They kept him locked up."

I didn't understand what Brandr meant by "locked up," nor did I care. Kiasik—my milk-brother, my cousin, my sister's son—still lived.

"I will get him out."

"There are dozens of Norse and *one* of you. You have no training with a sword."

"If I die, then I die trying."

I wished it were light enough to see his face more clearly. I was used to understanding him more from his expressions than his words. This new speech of ours sometimes felt like silence. "You are sorry you came?"

He lay back down, shifting his pack more comfortably against his side, avoiding my gaze. *He'll leave tomorrow*, I thought.

"You saved my life," he said. "I wouldn't have made it with this leg if you hadn't killed that cursed bear and sewn me up. If you and your wolves hadn't kept me fed. Among my people, debts are paid."

"So...you will come with me. To find Kiasik?"

"I never knew why you wanted to go to Leifsbudir, but I knew you'd been traveling as long as I had. I knew you had your reasons to go south. But I have to tell you, this is a fool's quest."

I sighed. "Your brother, Galinn...He is dead, no?"

Brandr nodded. He'd never spoken of his brother before this night. I could see the bright glimmer of tears in his eyes right before he turned his face away from me, digging awkwardly in his pack.

"But were he alive, you would search for him. Nothing could stop you. Even if only the smallest chance remained, you would still seek him out. No matter how far you had to travel."

He turned back to me for a moment, his breath sharp. Even in the dimness, I could imagine his expression—the same one he'd worn the day his people attacked mine: grief and rage and the fierce protectiveness of a mother bear defending its injured cub.

"Did he—" I wasn't sure I wanted the answer to this question. "Did he die from Patik's arrow? Did my people kill him? If we did, I—"

"No. You did not." He offered no further explanation. I nodded wordlessly, a great burden of fear—one I'd barely acknowledged—finally lifted. I need not offer him my apology; I could offer him only my empathy.

"I will look for Kiasik until I know he is dead. I don't know why you left your people—and I'm not asking," I added hurriedly, "but if you come with me...you would be a true friend." Impulsively, I reached out and placed my hand over his.

"I...," he stammered. "I..." Hesitantly, he turned over his hand and threaded his long fingers with mine. "I am no good as a friend. No good as a brother"—he took a shaky breath—"but I'll help you be a better brother than I ever was."

I looked down at our entwined hands, the tall peaks of his knuckles standing like ice-capped mountains among valleys. Suddenly the tiny cave felt more trap than shelter. He was too close.

"Thank you," I said, my voice coming out more hoarsely than I'd intended.

He fell asleep with my hand still clutched in his.

Only when I carefully loosed my fingers did I, too, find rest.

CHAPTER
THIRTY-ONE

♪

That night in the cave was my last peaceful sleep for a long time. Now that Brandr finally understood the urgency of my quest, we continued our travels with renewed haste. Leifsbudir, he explained, was still far to the south; it was already autumn, and if we wanted to reach Kiasik before the snows came and made walking impossible, we needed to hurry.

I crawled into the tent each night desperate for rest, yet found little. It wasn't the fear of the painted men that kept me awake at night, or even my worries for Kiasik—but my dreams.

Every night, Brandr's memories came to me unbidden. Though I hadn't touched the potion or dried flowers that I'd stowed in the bottom of my pack, the old woman's magic had tied a rope from my mind to his. And I couldn't shake it loose.

Usually the memories arrived in brief flashes of color and noise. Occasionally whole scenes unfurled in my mind. I woke knowing I'd seen some vitally important moment from his life but unable to remember more than a few stark images: dwellings the size of small hills, four-legged beasts carrying men on their backs, thin, pale-haired women wearing clothing the color of flowers, vast numbers of men with flashing swords and bloodied hands. Things I had no words for, things I knew must be pure fantasy.

Then, as we traveled, Brandr told me stories. Never the most important ones—never why he'd left his people or how his brother had died—but tales of his adventures across the wide sea. I never told him of my new visions, but he gave me words for them nonetheless: *buildings, horses,* and *cloth*—*armies, steel,* and *war.*

A few days after our encounter with the painted men, I woke to find the world outside my tent as unknowable and strange as the one I'd left in my dreams. A thick fog rolled off the ocean, shrouding the shore in white. I peered from the tent entrance but could see nothing beyond the dark shadows of Sweet One and White Paw lying nearby. Floppy Eared whimpered in greeting. I heard his tail thump the ground but couldn't see his white body in the mist.

White Paw picked up her head, ears pointed toward a sudden chorus of honking. My heart beat in time to the sound; I could nearly taste the rich goose fat on my tongue. Licking my lips, I ducked back into the tent.

"Brandr! Come! Before it's too late!" He groaned and sat up, his long orange hair a tangled mess. "Don't you want bird meat?" I urged.

"I want *any* meat," he grumbled. I'd been unlucky with my hunting of late. We hadn't had a real meal since I brought down two reddish, bushy-tailed little creatures—*squirrels,* Brandr called them—two days before. He moved to strap his sword onto his back.

"You don't need that. What good's a sword against a goose? Come!"

Barefoot, he followed me from the tent. "Don't you need a bow or a spear or something? And slow down! I can barely see in this fog. Where in Odin's name are we going?"

"You'll see. Quiet."

With the thick mist blocking my view ahead, I watched the

ground. Grass turned to rock beneath my feet, and waves crashed nearby.

"Here, this is good," I whispered. "Careful now. No sound until I say so. And then—scream as loud as you can."

"You're going to scare the geese to death?" I could hear the smile in his voice.

The honking grew louder. I'd always wondered where the geese went in the autumn—now I knew. My old friends brought the cold air of the north upon their wings. I longed to speak with them. *Did you look down from the sky and see my family? Is Puja angry with me? Did Saartok have a baby? Do they still live?*

The honking was deafening, the flock so close I could hear the slap of wings against air.

"Now!" I cried. I jumped up and down, waving my arms, screaming at the top of my lungs. Recovering from his momentary surprise, Brandr followed my lead, leaping and shouting like a man with a fish in his trousers.

A great flutter of wings and panicked honking sounded right above our heads. Then a large bird hurtled from the whiteness, its wide webbed feet swinging desperately as if trying to walk on air. It arced toward us, banking its black-tipped wings to gain height, but to no avail.

I grabbed it from the air.

The blood in its throat pulsed for just a moment against my fingers before I quickly broke its long, delicate neck, dropped the bird to the ground, and reached for the next white shape to come careening out of the sky.

"Don't just stand there!" I yelled to Brandr, who stood frozen in silent shock. He obeyed, making a mad dash toward another falling bird; he slipped on the rocks and missed. Recovering, he spun toward another goose, but the bird banked away from his outstretched hands just in time, disappearing into the fog.

With a loud honk of protest, a third goose plummeted toward us, landing on the ground with a scrabble of webbed feet. Brandr dashed toward it. The goose squawked in a most ungooselike way, batted at Brandr's hands with its wings, and nipped at his bare toes with its sharp orange beak.

"Skít!" Brandr cursed, kicking the goose roundly in the chest. The bird thrust its neck at him and honked in protest before successfully rising once more into the air. Brandr made a grab for it. A brief struggle, cursing from man and goose both, a shower of feathers. Then the goose was gone, winging disdainfully past us and into the mist. Brandr stood, glowering, with only a fistful of white quills to show for his efforts.

Standing with three dead geese at my feet, I tried to look sympathetic, but hilarity soon got the best of me. "No wonder you wanted a sword," I gasped out between peals of laughter. "I didn't know you were going to battle them!"

Brandr's grimace dissolved into a wide grin. "I didn't *really* think you were going to scare the geese out of the sky—clearly I should never underestimate you."

I wiped my eyes with my parka sleeve and carried one of my geese toward him. "You see the water on the wing? The heavy fog makes it hard for them to fly, so if you make them change direction quickly, they fall."

He raised his eyebrows in evident admiration. "I'm impressed. What else can you hunt with only your voice and hands?"

"Not much," I conceded. "How do your people hunt geese?"

"Not like that." He laughed, throwing the other two dead geese over his shoulder and following me back toward our tent. "Although perhaps we should. We get fogs like this, too, and the geese look the same. Greenland's not so different from where you come from."

"Greenland?" I'd heard the name in his dreams, but still didn't know quite what it meant.

"Where I was born. What do you call your homeland?"

"Our winter camp is at the Land of the Great Whale, because of the shape of our mountain. In the summer, we follow the caribou. In the spring, we live on the ice."

"But what do you call your *whole* land? As opposed to the lands claimed by other people?"

"There are no other people. Or at least...not anymore..." I wasn't sure what he was even asking. "It's all just... *nuna*. Land. What else would we call it?"

"I don't know. Something. My people named this Markland, the Land of Forests, when they sailed past. Just north of where I first met you, across the strait, is Helluland, because of the flat stones. Further south, where our camp lies, we call Vinland because Leif said he found grapes when he landed there, although I never saw any."

"Grapes?"

"Fruit. Round, purple, comes in bunches on a vine. We don't have any in Greenland, but I ate them in Rome. When you bite into them, they squirt juice into your mouth."

"Sounds like a clam."

"Ha! No, they're sweet. Delicious."

"Clams are delicious."

He laughed as if he'd never heard a better joke, then reached out a long hand to ruffle my hair.

I ducked my head before he could see my blush.

⊷ ▰◆▰ ⊶

Before long we sat beside a fire, enjoying our boiled goose as the Sun burned the fog off the waves.

"You know what?" Brandr sighed, licking the grease from his fingers. "Better than grapes."

I ladled the last of the yellow broth from the birchbark container I'd made in the painted men's fashion. "Maybe you should call this 'Gooseland' instead."

"Mmmm."

"Why is your home called Greenland?" *It's not very green*, I almost added, remembering a scrap of dream: Brandr as a boy, trudging through drifts of snow even deeper than those in my own homeland.

"People often ask that. It's only green for a few short months in the summer, when it's so bright it hurts your eyes. The fields are dotted with sheep and cattle."

Such animals, he explained, lived with men, like dogs. The cattle were for eating and milking; the sheep allowed themselves to be shorn of their fur to make wool, the close-woven cloth I'd found so strange. While he spoke, I busied myself with preparing the final goose. I cut off its long, proud neck and made a slit partway along its feathered underbelly.

"They say Erik the Red named it Greenland to lure colonists to its shores," he went on, stretching his long legs toward the fire. "But I met Erik once when I was a boy, and I don't think so. He was violent, arrogant—but no liar. I think it was green to him, for he always saw the possibilities in a place. Just like his daughter Freydis." I watched the angle of his jaw twitch as he spoke the name. It was a long moment before he spoke again. "I only returned to Greenland briefly before I left to come here. After so many years of traveling across the world, I thought perhaps I'd finally settle down. Find a pretty wife, work my own homestead, raise sheep like my brother. But I should have known I'd be traveling again before long."

"If working a homestead means sucking milk from an animal's breast, I don't blame you for leaving again. It sounds unnatural." While we talked, I kept one eye on him and one on the goose. I pulled back the skin; it came off inside out, like a feathery parka. As Brandr spoke, I scraped the blood and tissue from the skin with my ulu. I'd often performed such women's tasks in Brandr's presence—he never seemed shocked. Either he understood that I had no choice, or his people didn't make such distinctions.

"The world is full of things stranger than sheep's milk," he said with a laugh. "Arabia was all sand beneath my feet, soft and yielding like new snow and impossible to walk through. The air is so hot it burns your lungs, like sitting too close to a fire, and there's no water to quench your thirst. In Rome the buildings are so tall they block the sky from view. And in Iceland the earth's not earth at all—it bursts into flame and melts around your feet."

My head spun with all these names and places, each so different from the next. Brandr had traveled like this all his life. Yet if he felt lonely, he didn't say so. If he missed his brother, he never spoke of it.

"I'd like to hear about this 'Iceland,' but we've been too slow already this morning. We need to keep moving." I turned the goose skin right side out. It hung limp from my hands, a deflated mockery of its former bird glory.

"What are you going to do with that?"

"Make a waterskin for winter. The feathers will keep the water from freezing."

"The Romans would pluck the soft feathers and stuff a pillow with them," he said wistfully.

"I'd rather have water to drink than a soft pillow for my head. Come on, lazy man. You didn't catch a single goose. You don't get to rest."

We packed up our tent and sleeping skins, scuffed out the ashes of our fire, and continued on our journey. As we walked, I tried to keep Kiasik's face before me. Certain things I could call to mind: the way his hair waved in the wind, the movement of his muscles when he threw a harpoon, the reckless look in his eye. But when I tried to imagine his cheeks, his mouth, his hands, visions of the man walking beside me would intercede.

Without turning to look at Brandr, I could see the thin, dry lips that moved so quickly from tense line to broad grin, his wind-burnt cheeks shining red above the golden hairs of his beard. Even at night, when only a few embers from the fire served to illuminate the outline of his sleeping form, I could still see him. And I no longer found him ugly.

CHAPTER
THIRTY-TWO

ᛉ

The night after the goose hunt, we made our camp on a narrow ledge of rock overlooking a calm, black sea. Long before dawn, I woke suddenly from a dream of vast deserts and strange humped beasts the color of driftwood. I could tell without looking that Brandr was gone.

For a moment, I thought he'd finally left for good, returned to one of the many other lands he'd visited. I was surprised by the jolt of fear that gripped me. Would I miss him so much if he left?

When I sat up, I shivered in the frigid air. Winter was on its way. I pulled a sleeping fur around my shoulders and crawled outside. Brandr sat a few paces away, shivering in his blue cloak, looking out into the sky with his hands clenched on his knees. For the first time in many moons, the lights of the *aqsarniit* glowed overhead. The curtain of green light danced above the horizon, folding and unfurling like thick strands of bright kelp amid tide-tossed shallows.

"It's like old friends returning," he said softly at my approach. "I've missed this."

"The spirits want to play. They won't wait for winter."

He didn't turn to look at me as I sat down beside him, but I could see his eyes, and they were brighter than they should have been.

"Few men besides the Norse have ever seen these lights." His tone, so light the previous afternoon as he rambled from tale to tale of fantastical lands, had grown somber. "They think we're just telling tales."

He craned his neck, gazing up as a thick stripe of green flared across the dome of the sky. A raft of small, dark clouds floated past, breaking the green light into rounded patches—like pebbles humped on a stream bed, I thought. But Brandr traced the long green arc with his finger, murmuring, "A snake's scales. Jormungand the World Serpent, circling the earth with his tail in his mouth. If he squeezes just a little tighter"—he sucked in a breath, as if some great force pressed against his ribs. Then, as the arc faded from view, and he turned back to the curtain of green at the horizon, he managed a faint smile. "Or maybe my brother was right, and it's not Jormungand at all, but the fires of the Frost Giants in Jotunheim."

"You've never told me anything about Galinn," I said carefully.

I watched the knob of his throat rise and fall. "He was small, but stronger than he looked." His words came slow and soft, like a memory too fragile to touch. "Like you. But he told tales like a wise old man. He was no skald, no trained poet or bard, but he knew all the legends. And he was always dreaming. He saw the Aesir—the gods—in everything. He worshiped the three greatest ones, of course: Odin the All-Father, one-eyed far-seer with his raven companions; Thor, the red-bearded Thunderer; and Frey, the gentle god of growing things."

A one-eyed man with a raven on each shoulder. The image called to me, faint as a last dying echo bouncing in the bowl of my skull. *Another man cloaked in lightning bolts. A third with a hidden face—and rainbow eyes.* I'd dreamed of them on my first spirit journey. I hadn't thought of them again, yet now they drifted back into my life in

Brandr's wake. I shivered. The spirits of my own world had turned against me; I didn't have the strength to battle the spirits of his as well.

Heedless of my discomfort, Brandr went on. "But most of all, Galinn worshipped Freya." He kept his eyes on the sky. "The goddess of love."

We sat in silence for a few moments more. A cold breath of ocean air sneaked beneath his cloak, pulling it away from him. Shaking, he clasped the cloth closer around his shoulders.

The motion seemed to break him from his memories. He turned to me for the first time. "You said the flames in the sky were spirits?"

"Yes. Can't you see them running toward us?" Flashes of orange and purple now sprinted back and forth across the sky, streaks of green stretching behind like shadows in a long summer twilight. "The dead play games through the long darkness." The thought of Ataata and Nua and Kidla playing tag between the stars lessened the hurt of their loss.

He took a deep breath, uneven on the way in, but steadying on the way out, and tilted his face up once more. "Then, Galinn, I'm glad you found more joy in death than you did in life."

I wanted to touch his shoulder and stop his shivering. "My father and grandfather are up there with your brother," I said instead. "And in here." I pressed my palm against my chest.

Brandr flinched. "Don't say that. That's what they always say. That the dead live on inside of us. But they're no longer part of this world. Perhaps, as you believe, they still exist up there, out of reach, in the sky. Maybe Galinn was right, and he feasts tonight in the halls of Valhalla with Thor and Odin." He laughed harshly. "Or maybe, just maybe, although I hope it's not true, the dead live in heaven with the Christ, never to experience the joys of the flesh. But no matter what, Galinn is gone from here."

"You don't understand me. Up there, my father plays in the stars. But his soul has been reborn in me. I have his name, his spirit. We are curled one within the other, like the spirals of a shell." He looked dubious; I pressed on angrily. "You don't seem to believe in a world you cannot see. And yet, if I were like you, I wouldn't believe your stories of deserts and volcanoes and tall buildings of stone. I would say you made them up, since I've never seen them. But instead, I trust that there are many things beyond my understanding."

He didn't speak again right away. Perhaps he'd taken some comfort from my words. Perhaps he just didn't want to discuss it further. I tried to read his face, his posture, but I saw only ice. Whatever he felt, he wasn't yet ready to let me share his pain. Frustrated, I rose to leave.

"Here." He opened his hand to me. In the center of his calloused palm lay a tiny wooden object. I remembered how he used to hide his carving whenever I approached. I hadn't seen him work on it recently. In fact, I'd forgotten it entirely.

"It's for you."

I reached for it, my fingers brushing his hand. I held the carving up to the wavering green light of the aqsarniit. A tiny walrus figure with two perfect, intact tusks. Across its back, he'd carved a fine network of spirals and knots like those adorning the hilt of the small, sharp knife—like those of his own tattoo. I clutched it in my hand for a moment, then placed it carefully in my amulet pouch next to its one-tusked companion.

"I'm sorry about the other one," he offered. "I didn't mean to break it."

I nodded, eyes downcast.

"You say I don't believe what I don't see and don't understand. That's not true. I believe in you. I have no reason to, really—I know almost nothing about you. But I trust you." He turned his gaze back to the shimmering sky.

I breathed easier without his eyes on my face.

The aqsarniit streamed and swayed like silent tongues of green fire, stretching from one end of the sky to the other.

"I threw that little walrus out of your tent that day because I needed you to know how far I'd come, how alone I am. How alone I *was*," he corrected himself. In the starlight, his stony face melted—for a heartbeat or two, his mouth quavered into grief. Then, with a deep, hollow breath, his features calmed. "I don't feel alone anymore."

Afraid of what he might say next, I merely stammered, "You should come back inside the tent. The cold isn't good for your leg."

To my relief, he didn't press the conversation further.

When I finally fell back to sleep that night, with Brandr lying an arm's length away, my inherited dreams were more vivid than ever. Every time I rolled over, I rose from sleep like a drowning man sucking air, and in that instant of clarity, I remembered everything: a face not unlike Brandr's, but younger and beardless, with hair the color of dead grass. Blue eyes and a faraway stare. Galinn. I had last seen him pale and terrified, bleeding in his brother's arms beside the whale carcass.

Then another vision—a giant wooden boat surrounded by bearded men in iron helmets. A boat far longer and slimmer than the one that had brought Brandr to Issuk's camp. Ahead, a small village of stone houses with mossy roofs perched on a cliff overlooking the ocean. Even from far out at sea, the screams of the women carried across the water. They ran into their low houses, scooping up their children as they went. The screams grew faint as the women barricaded themselves indoors. A keening howl of an even higher pitch soon replaced their cries.

Ahead of the ship, three giant black wolves ran across the sea, their feet striking spray from the waves. On their backs rode three naked women, each holding aloft a sword shining with blood. The men on the ship paid no heed to these apparitions, but I saw them clearly, and my ears rang with their piercing screams. Above the village, three enormous ravens croaked out a harsh greeting as their mistresses approached.

I leapt over the side of the boat and waded to shore, my heart racing and my vision clouded with red haze. The part of me living within Brandr's memory wished only for blood. But my own mind shrank in horror.

With the other Vikings laughing beside me, I burst through the door of the nearest stone hut. A young black-haired woman with enormous eyes crouched in a corner holding out a crude spear. A Norseman wrenched the weapon from her grasp and broke it over his knee. He grabbed her by the hair and dragged her toward me.

"For you, Brandr," the man crowed. "Young and fresh. Just like you."

I awoke with a strangled scream. Beside me, Brandr twitched and moaned in his sleep. Did he wander in the same terrible dream?

Not Brandr, I decided. *He would never take a woman as Issuk took me.* With his brother, with an injured wolfdog, with me—he'd always been kind.

I laid a hand on his shoulder until he slept peacefully once more.

I will not believe it of my friend. I will not.

Still, I didn't sleep again that night for fear the dream might return. I could not bear to witness its end.

CHAPTER THIRTY-THREE

*H*ow much farther to your people's camp?"

I had asked the same question every morning since I'd learned Brandr's tongue. But today I shouted it over the howl of the wind. We'd woken to a frigid blast ripping our tent apart. A storm had roared in overnight, dumping snow as deep as my waist. It had taken all our strength to make our way from our camp to the nearby shoreline to check our location.

"I don't know exactly," Brandr shouted back through chattering teeth. He pointed through the whirling snow toward a small, rocky island perched in the center of a sheltered bay. "That looks familiar from when we explored up the coast, but we didn't reach it until at least two days into our journey, with a strong wind behind us. We may still be a week away by foot. Perhaps more."

I'd lost track of the moons. Brandr said the Norse called this time Slaughter Month—a useful name for the time when they butchered the sheep who wouldn't survive the winter—and the Romans called it November, "Ninth Month," which didn't seem useful at all. He said the days would continue to grow shorter for another moon. But if this was indeed the Moon of the Setting

Sun, why were the days still so long? The ice on the lakes still buckled beneath my touch, and the ocean still heaved and crested, completely liquid. Not even gray mush ice formed at the shoreline. From those signs, I'd thought we still had time before winter arrived in force. I'd been wrong.

The storm continued unabated, whipping the snow through the air with such ferocity I was surprised any had settled on the ground at all.

I pulled the hood of my parka tighter against my cheeks as we trudged back through the drifts to the remnants of my tent. It had only ever been meant for summer; I was lucky it had lasted this long. Brandr stood beside me, visibly shaking. His tattered blue cloak was no more substantial than the cloudless sky it resembled. By now the snow—wetter and heavier than usual—must have soaked through his cloth trousers.

Every day I tarried was one more day Kiasik lived alone among strangers. But we couldn't travel in weather like this. Brandr would freeze and I would lose my way. A wise Inuk would crawl inside his iglu and wait for the storm to pass.

I stabbed the butt of my spear into the snow, confirming what I already knew—it was far too soft to build a proper iglu.

"We build a qarmaq out of sod, or wood, or whatever we have," I announced. "Otherwise we freeze where we stand."

"Or drown in snow," Brandr added, brushing the heavy flakes from his beard.

So, with spear and sword and wolf paws, we dug a circular pit an arm's length deep through snow and earth. Brandr pulled up saplings to form a frame like those that supported the painted men's bark dwellings, and we used the remnants of the tent to cover it. On top of the skins, we piled a thick layer of snow. Without a lamp or seal oil, we made a fire pit in the center, as the painted men had done, and a smoke hole above it. A mound of pine boughs covered with pelts served as our sleeping bench. At my insistence, we also built a long entrance tunnel that curved into the earth before rising through the floor of our qarmaq. Used to turf longhouses, Brandr would've put the door in the side of the hut where the cold air would rush inside every time we lifted the door flap—but I convinced him of his folly.

As a final touch, I strung the wide brown bear pelt across one side of our new qarmaq, creating a private area where I might sleep and use the night bowl.

"Won't we need that fur to sleep in?" Brandr asked.

"We have others."

"Why do you want to sleep over there? It's going to get cold, kid. It'll be warmer if we sleep near each other."

That was precisely my fear. In a storm like this, he was likely to huddle close. I hadn't forgotten Kiasik's swellings. I didn't want to be anywhere near Brandr's.

"The qarmaq is deep; its walls are thick." I sounded more confident than I felt. "We'll be completely safe."

"No one is *ever* completely safe," Brandr huffed. "Galinn used to say that." As usual, his jaw tightened when he spoke his brother's name. "He'd tell me to remember Baldur and Loki."

"Who're they?"

"Gods, like Thor."

Thor I remembered. Brandr spoke of him often—the red-haired Thunderer, who wielded a war hammer. Many Norse, he said, wore little versions of this hammer around their necks, just as I wore my amulet pouch.

Brandr was no angakkuq, but he told stories like one. Confident and clear, as if he'd seen it all unfold with his own eyes. "Baldur was one of Thor's brothers," he began. "The youngest, handsomest, and kindest of the gods. And Loki...He's hard to describe. A trickster. A shapeshifter. Born a Jotun—a Frost Giant—in the icy realm of Jotunheim, but raised by Odin and his wife among the Aesir. He can turn himself into a gadfly, or an old woman, or a young man. Sometimes he's merely a mischief-maker, cutting off the long golden hair of beautiful goddesses. But he's got a dark side, too."

Brandr settled back onto our makeshift sleeping platform, propping his head on his crossed arms. His relaxed pose didn't fool me. His fingers threaded together, his knuckles white. For some reason, this was a story it hurt to tell.

"Baldur's mother, the goddess Frigg," he began, "received a prophecy that her beloved son would die. So she traveled the earth, demanding that every stone and beast and man and tree—everything living and not—swear an oath not to hurt him. They all agreed, and it became a game of sorts among the Aesir, tossing boulders and shooting arrows at beautiful Baldur, watching them bounce off his impenetrable skin, harmless as goose down."

"That sounds like a mean game."

"Mean games are what being a Norseman is all about." Brandr snorted a humorless laugh. "Loki transformed himself into an old woman and went to gossip with Frigg. 'Did you really get everything in the world to swear not to hurt your son?' And Frigg admitted that, no, she hadn't spoken to mistletoe. It was a small plant, young and green, too weak to harm a god. So Loki, of course, plucked a sprig of mistletoe, shaped it into an arrow, and handed it to Baldur's blind brother, Hod, saying, 'Join in! Throw this!' And Hod did.

"The mistletoe pierced Baldur's heart. The beautiful god was dead. As punishment, the Aesir imprisoned Loki deep beneath the earth, binding his limbs with the entrails of his own son. They placed a serpent above him, with its venom dripping on his skull for eternity."

"What had Baldur done?" I asked. "Why did Loki want him dead?"

"Baldur hadn't done *anything*. Innocents die all the time." Bitterness hardened his voice. "There's nothing we can do to save them. That's the point."

He closed his eyes, clearly unwilling to answer any further questions. To him the story was over, its meaning clear. But I knew better. Stories are ever changing, just like the gods. Assuming you understand either is a grave mistake. I'd seen the wolf-riding Valkyries crossing the water in Brandr's nightmares. I'd seen Odin and Thor in my own visions. It seemed to me that Brandr's gods were powerful ones. They'd already appeared in both our lives, even if we hadn't realized it. And I had no doubt they'd appear again.

⚓

During a break in the storm the next day, I crawled outside to clear the snow from our smoke hole. The drifts had grown as high as my chest. The sky was low and gray; Sila was not done with us yet.

Even once the weather cleared, we would make little progress across such ground without a sled. I waded through the snow toward the nearest stand of trees and began to haul on the nearest sapling.

"We have enough firewood already," Brandr called from where he huddled in the entrance tunnel, watching me.

"It's not for burning. It's for building. I'm making us a sled."

"And who's going to pull it? Or can you conjure horses from the air as you conjure geese?"

"The wolfdogs, of course."

"Why not?" he said with a laugh. "They say Freya rides in a chariot pulled by kittens."

I didn't know what he meant by a chariot—much less kittens—but for once I didn't ask. I was too busy sawing at the tree trunk with my slate knife. Soon we had two straight lengths of wood for runners. I had little experience shaping the stuff—we usually built with bone and antler—and Brandr knew how to carve only small figures and tools. We tried anyway. We didn't make much progress; when the wind picked up, Brandr shivered so badly he could barely hold the knife.

"How did you survive with that pitiful cloak in Leifsbudir last winter?" I asked, looking up from my work when I heard him drop the knife into the snow again.

"I barely left the longhouse. No sane Greenlander really does. We mostly stay indoors until spring." Picking up the sharp metal knife, he scraped angrily at the wood.

"Don't take out your frustration on my runner. We don't have any antler, so if we can't make the wood work, we don't have any other good options. Unless you want to lash together the bodies of frozen fish and glaze them with ice."

Brandr chuckled, then groaned. "I'm too cold to even laugh."

"Why would you laugh? It's not a joke."

"Frozen *fish*?"

"Ataata always said his own father used either that or whale jaws. I don't think you want to go out and hunt a whale, do you?"

"Hunt a whale?" he asked, his eyes wide.

I laughed at his shock. "Now I *am* teasing you. We can't very well bring down a whale without a boat."

"Your people hunt whales?" he asked again. "I saw the carcass at your camp, but I assumed it washed ashore."

"My own family doesn't hunt them," I admitted. "But some do." I regretted bringing it up. Issuk's face flashed before me, cruel in life, desperate in death.

Brandr looked at me as if I were a stranger. "Norsemen avoid whales whenever they can. Even a Viking longboat is no match for one. Dogs pulling sleds—especially dogs like yours—*that* I might believe. But hunting whales with nothing but skin boats and crude knives? That's absurd."

"You don't think that a people without your precious iron and steel could accomplish such a feat?"

"No, I don't," he insisted. "I've seen many things in my travels, but never that."

"For one so worldly, you're occasionally very stupid." I'd meant to tease him, but the cold made us both short-tempered, and I spat my words.

He leaned toward me like a sled dog itching for a fight. Then the deep crease between his brows relaxed, and he began to laugh.

"So, Omat of the fearsome whale hunters, tell me how you bring down a creature so mighty."

I felt myself relax in response. "We have a wide boat, an umiaq, and a harpoon with a toggle head," I began, picking up my tools and returning to work. I told him all the details of the chase, the kill. It felt good to be a storyteller again.

The Sun set as I finished the tale, sapping all trace of warmth from the air. Brandr began to slap his hands once more against his thighs and stamp his feet. Frost clogged his beard and whitened his eyebrows. Worse yet, as his sweat froze, ice glazed his entire tunic. Finally I put away my tools. "I'm going to make you a parka from one of the sleeping furs."

"There's no need," he protested through chattering teeth. "Really."

"Remember what I said about stupidity?"

He nodded, his cheeks reddening.

I turned to crawl inside the qarmaq.

"How do you know how to make clothing anyway? Our women do all our sewing."

I lied smoothly. "A hunter must know how to make his own clothes. It's not so hard."

After so long, I'd nearly forgotten to worry that he might learn the truth about my body. Now a chill sweat beaded the valley between my breasts, as if to remind me of my foolishness.

No matter my teasing, Brandr wasn't stupid. This was the first time he'd wondered at my womanly skills—but it wouldn't be the last.

CHAPTER
THIRTY-FOUR

↯

When night fell, and the storm began again in earnest, I started making Brandr's parka. I selected the only caribou pelt we had— the one I'd carried away as a sleeping fur from Issuk's camp. I'd have to use other furs for the arms and hood, but at least his torso would be warm.

As I worked, Brandr huddled close to the small fire inside our qarmaq, trying to get warm.

"I need to know how big to make it," I said, eyeing his looming frame. "There are no men as big as you among my people. Although"—I looked down at my torso—"they're not all as short as I."

"Thank the gods," he said with a smile. "If they were, I can't imagine how small your women must be. They'd be like little dwarves I might step on by accident."

I scowled to hide my rising discomfort. "Give me your shirt. I'll use it to get the size right."

"I just got warm!"

"Would you like your nice new parka to be so small you can't get into it?"

He grunted and pulled off his cloak and tunic, then yanked his sweat-soaked shirt over his head. In all our time together, I'd never seen his bare chest. Perhaps he'd just followed my example—I'd certainly never stripped in front of him. The braided tattoo around his wrist ran the entire length of his arm, twisting across the muscles of his bicep before ending in the head of a beast, its jaws open as if to taste the meat of his shoulder. The same curling orange hair that covered his arms and legs spread across his chest, then tapered into a thin trail to his navel, widening again into longer, soft waves just above the waistline of his pants.

He tossed his shirt across the qarmaq to me, though I was too distracted to catch it. The damp cloth struck me in the face, bringing with it his familiar scent. He laughed as I snatched it off my head. I thrust a sleeping fur in his direction, wanting him to cover himself completely.

He draped the pelt around his broad shoulders. We'd taken the hide from one of the wide-antlered animals in the forest—a *moose*, Brandr said. The same long-legged beast had provided all the sinew I would need for sewing.

He sighed, drawing the moose pelt close to his cheeks. "Will my new parka be as warm as this?"

I finally laughed as I lay his shirt over the caribou hide. Using his sharp knife, I cut the skin to a slightly larger size. How Puja would've loved to use such a tool! "I'm not that good at making clothes. My little sister, Puja, though, could make a parka so warm you could spend all day on an ice block near a fishing hole, and feel as if you were curled in a sunbeam on a summer's day."

"You have a sister?" Brandr asked. I'd never spoken much of my family, and I knew he was curious.

"She was the sister of my father."

"You mean your aunt."

"Yes, but as I am my father, then she is my sister."

"How are you your father?"

"He was also Omat."

"Oh. I'm Brandr Gunnarsson, because my father was Gunnar. And they named me Brandr after my dead uncle, hoping that by having his name, I'd have his bravery."

"Yes, like that, but not just the name. When I was a baby, my grandfather saw that I carried my father's soul—I *am* my father. Whose soul do you carry?"

"Only my own, I hope."

"That's impossible," I said, biting off a length of sinew. "Unless you're one of the undead, who have no soul?"

"I hope not!"

"As do I. It'd be a great waste of the meat I've been feeding you all these moons."

"The Christians think the soul is immortal, too. When the body dies, the soul goes to live with their Christ in a place they call *heaven*. But I think I prefer your idea of the afterlife: that our spirits play among the stars, and then they're reborn into someone else. The mystics in Greenland teach that if we die in battle, we go to Valhalla, the hall of the gods, to fight every day and die gloriously, just to be reborn the next morning and do it all over again."

I huffed as I threaded Uimaitok's bone needle and began sewing the pieces of hide together. "That sounds worst of all. To fight and die and fight and die. What kind of reward is that?"

He shook his head slowly, suddenly somber. "To be a warrior is the most glorious thing a Norseman can be. To be a Viking, traveling the world and conquering lands."

I looked up from my work. His eyes were distant in the firelight. "I thought you traded, not conquered."

"A bit of both," he said quietly. "The first time I left home, I was just a boy, very young, not yet ten. I went with some traders to Northway, and when a Viking crew needed a boy to tend to their horses, I decided to go with them rather than return to Greenland. We sailed to Englaland first, where there was a Viking settlement. The town wasn't so different from the villages in Northway, with women and children and farmers. But beyond the town lived people unlike any I'd ever seen. They were very short. When they went into battle, they painted their faces blue. Quite fearsome, I assure you, despite their height. Much like you."

"Though we don't need to paint our faces blue. It wouldn't scare the animals. More likely they'd laugh at us."

"Do you never war with other men?"

The old painted woman's memories—dead children, the growling of dogs—came unbidden. I shook my head and continued with my sewing, easing the needle through the thick hide, keeping my stitches small and tight so no air might seep through. "Not in my lifetime," I said carefully. "Tell me more of the blue men."

"Every few months, they attacked our town."

"What had you done to them?"

"I was a child. I had done nothing," he said sharply, suddenly busying himself with his sleeping fur.

I let the silence linger for a moment. "You don't need to talk about it."

Brandr laughed shortly. "And yet, with you, I know I will. Seems there's nothing I won't tell you, Omat."

My cheeks heated, as they often did when he said my name rather than calling me "kid." If he noticed, he made no mention.

"It's like the other world doesn't exist here," he continued. "Only you and I. There are no consequences to anything I say or do. No one to judge me for my past or expect anything from my future."

"I do expect something," I retorted. "I expect you to stop limping and learn how to hunt and sew so I don't have to be the only one keeping us warm and fed. I'm not going to serve you like a wife forever!" I blushed even more when I realized what I'd said.

Brandr threw back his head and guffawed so hard that Sweet One looked up and yipped. White Paw and Floppy Eared yowled in answer from the entrance tunnel.

"I'm not sure how it works among your people, but among the Norse, you'd make a poor wife indeed! Not to mention a very ugly one!"

He was right, of course. I had no tattoos, no woman's walk, no braided hair—nor did I want them. His words still stung.

"What?" He grinned. "Did I offend you? You're just as touchy as a woman sometimes." He quirked an eyebrow at me. "Perhaps you *would* make a decent wife."

I dropped the half-sewn parka as if urchin spines had sprung from the fur.

"I'm sorry," he said with exaggerated contrition. "Please, O great and valiant hunter, please don't stop making me that parka! I promise never, ever to imply that you resemble a woman in any way." He rose to his knees, the sleeping fur sliding away from his body. "And if I do, I promise to say you'd make an extremely beautiful one."

"I won't say the same about you," I managed. "Your nose is too big and your beard is too thick. You look like a dog. And not a beautiful wolfdog—an *ugly* dog."

"At least I *have* a beard." He was smiling still.

"I should throw you out into the cold right now."

"I'm afraid, O mighty and most brave of hunters, that despite your great skill, you still couldn't do that. I'm quite heavy, you know, and you're quite a little man."

I lunged across the qarmaq, latching my arms around his neck and pinning him to the ground in my best wrestling hold. He whooped in surprise, sputtering through his laughter. "You attack a lame man!"

"I'm throwing you out!" I tried to drag him across the qarmaq by his shoulders. But Brandr was right—he was quite heavy. Somehow, as we struggled, I wound up straddling his bare waist, pinning his arms to the ground with my face inches from his. His eyes shone as blue as a flame's heart. For an instant, he ceased to struggle and simply stared at me. A look of understanding flashed across his face.

I rolled off him as if burnt.

We sat in a silence as taut as an angakkuq's drum and just as loud.

"It's no challenge to fight an injured man," I said finally, trying to ignore the sudden pressure in my chest. "But even if you weren't injured, no Norseman could ever defeat an Inuk in a wrestling match."

I watched him sit up, his bare chest glinting with sweat. He made no response to my pitiful attempt at humor. In the space of a heartbeat, we'd moved beyond the teasing that had always bound us together while keeping us just far enough apart. He put his head in his hands, rubbing his face hard. "Omat." The word sounded heavy on his tongue. "You remind me so much of Galinn."

The look that had passed between us—one I'd taken for recognition of my woman's body—was only one of brotherly affection. I should've felt relieved. Instead, the strip of blue cloth binding my breasts had never felt so tight.

"Galinn always wanted to hear stories about my travels," Brandr went on, his voice catching. "Just like you."

Taking a deep breath, I took up my needle once again and asked, "Will you tell me more about the blue people?" I wanted to distract him from his sudden sorrow. I wanted to distract myself even more.

Brandr hoisted himself onto the sleeping bench and pulled the moose pelt around his shoulders again. "We took a few as thralls. They didn't look so different from other men once we washed off the paint."

"What's a thrall?" I interrupted.

"Someone you own."

"I don't understand."

"A bondman. Someone who has to do what you tell them, obey your orders. Don't you have them among your people?"

"Do you mean like a wife?"

At that he laughed. "No, no. Thralls are men or women. They wear a torque around their necks. A heavy metal ring that proves they're not freemen. They can't go anywhere or do anything unless their master orders it."

"Who'd agree to such a life?"

"They don't *agree* to it. They're bought or captured."

"Until when?"

"Until always. Unless their master chooses to free them."

I wondered if he was joking again. "Why doesn't the thrall just kill its master? Or run away?"

"I thought you wanted to hear about the blue men!" His smile returned. "Choose a story. I need to sleep. Either I can tell you about the Picts or about how thralls came to be."

"Tell me about thralls, if you're so weak that you can't stay awake to do both."

"All right." He took a deep breath. "Galinn says that once, long ago, Odin All-Father watched each man toiling on his own farm, or his own ship. Men wouldn't work together because each wanted to better his own family. And so no farm could be bigger than what one man could work, and no ship could be big enough to sail the oceans."

"Why wouldn't they all work together to better all the families?" I interrupted.

"That's not in man's nature."

"It's in an Inuk's nature."

"Well, we Norse are like all the other peoples I've met in my travels. Concerned above all for ourselves." I opened my mouth to retort, but he held up a hand in protest. "I know, I know, you think little of us. But this is just a story, after all, and not one I made up. Don't blame me." I grudgingly turned my attention back to the parka.

"So. Odin came down among the men. First he visited the fine wooden longhouse of a tall blond man and his wife, a woman of great beauty and bearing, with skin as pale as new milk and eyes as bright and blue as the noontime sea. And while the man slept, Odin took his wife to him, and nine months later she bore a son and named him Jarl. And from Jarl descends the race of kings, the firstborn sons of the god, who know his runic secrets and rule over all other men.

"Then Odin went to another house, this one the sturdy stone hut of a hardworking man, with an apple-cheeked wife with grass-green eyes who wove fine woolen cloth on her loom. And in the night, Odin slept with this wife, and she bore him another son, named Freeman, who in turn fathered Fighter, Farmer, House-holder, and Smith.

"Finally, when Odin had grown tired from his exploits, he visited one last house, a small hovel of turf. The man and his wife were dark and bent and ill-favored, and they served the god coarse black bread and watery broth. And when Odin took the woman to his bed, she bore him a third son, Thrall. A man as ugly as his mother. And from Thrall the race of bondmen was born. They toil on the farms of the Freemen and allow them to prosper, and in turn the Freemen pay tribute to the Jarls."

"Are all thralls short and dark?" I asked.

"No. Some are from Rus or Írland. Some are as red haired as I, or more blond than my own brother."

"I don't understand."

"It's just a story." He yawned. "Don't worry, it's not real."

"All stories are real."

"Of course they're not."

"Maybe not in the details, but they hold truth within them."

"How're you so sure?"

"I learned my tales from my elders, or from the spirits them-selves. They wouldn't tell a story that didn't hold truth—what would be the point?"

"You sound more like Galinn than ever. First you dream my past, now you're talking to the spirits?"

I shook my head. "No. They have no words for me any longer." I needed him to stop his questions. I didn't want to tell him about my time as an angakkuq—or how I'd lost such powers forever.

"No words." He sighed, cushioning his cheek on his arm and closing his eyes. "Sounds good." He yawned again.

The fire was dying, he was asleep, and I hadn't gotten very far on the parka—too much talking and too little working. Images of tall, pale-haired women with eyes like Brandr's danced in my head. I couldn't find them beautiful, but clearly Brandr did. I knew I'd dream tonight of jarls' wives and of thralls who looked like me, the most reviled among the Norse. *No wonder Brandr hasn't realized I have a woman's body*, I thought. *Surely no freeman such as he would look at a hideous thrall such as I.*

I looked down at the parka, the stitches as tight and neat as my unskilled hands could make them. The hem carefully flared so it would let in just enough air to dry his sweat. The shoulders wide enough for him to pull his arms inside on the coldest days. All my effort to keep him warm. Was I nothing more than a thrall to him? I'd played the role well enough, feeding and clothing him so he could live a life of ease off my labor. He lacked only a yellow-haired giantess to warm his bed.

I scowled at the parka and readied to rip it apart. Music stopped me.

Soft and sweet, rolling over me like the lapping waters of a summer lake.

Brandr took his lips from the whistle just long enough to give me a tired smile, then kept playing.

Long into the night, I matched my stitches to the rhythm of his song.

I awoke alone, with the parka still in my hands and my breath clouded with frost. The fire had died out while I slept. A real woman would never have tended it so poorly.

I crawled from the qarmaq, still holding the parka. Flurries crowded the sky like a flock of mad snow geese, first floating aimlessly, then darting against my cheeks in the sudden gusts of wind. Brandr had cleared the path to our half-finished sled. He bent over the runners in his blue cloak, the moose fur still draped over his shoulders for extra warmth.

Sweet One sat nearby, watching him like a young girl gazing at her promised husband. He scraped intently with the steel knife, straightening only when the wolfdog leapt up to greet me.

He grinned as I approached. "You've nearly missed the sunlight today. I've been working all day to make up for you."

I held up the parka in response.

Brandr dropped his tool and limped toward me eagerly. "It's beautiful!"

It wasn't really beautiful—any girl child would make one much better. The front and back were caribou, the arms an uneven patchwork of moose and squirrel. But for a cold man, a fur parka is glorious no matter how simply made.

He reached to grab it, but I pulled it back. "Aii! It's not done yet!"

"It looks perfect."

"Didn't you notice something missing?"

"All I know is it's warmer than this," he said, gesturing to his cloak.

"It doesn't have a hood yet."

"Oh."

"I couldn't make it without sizing your head." He bent toward me obligingly. I snorted. "Kneel down so I can do it properly. Not all of us are as tall as you."

He knelt immediately at my feet, bending first his good leg, then his bad, and looked up at me. The top of his head was nearly level with my chest.

"Go ahead," he said. The wolfdogs yipped and skittered around him, thinking he was ready to play. Sweet One nearly bowled him over before I could grab her ruff and tell her to stop. I shooed them off with a gesture. White Paw cocked her head at me as if to ask why Brandr's face was so close to parts better left untouched. I ignored her.

"You may hold it for a moment," I said, handing Brandr the parka. He placed the caribou fur to his cheek and thrust his hands into the dark folds. The crown of his head brushed against my waist. I took an instinctive step back. "Hold still."

He lifted his face and gave me a sly smile. "You like me down here, don't you?"

"I don't know what you're talking about."

"All that talk of thralls and masters. You like having me on my knees."

"Just be still." I placed my hands lightly atop his upturned head. The women in my camp did this—memorized the feel of a man's head so that his hood might fit snugly around his cheeks. The only man's face I'd ever touched like this was my grandfather's. His gray hair had been coarse and dry beneath my hands, his cheeks soft, the skin lying loose upon the bone. Brandr's hair was smooth and thick beneath my fingertips, the skin above his beard tight and rough. *An ugly dog*, I reminded myself.

With my thumbs, I traced the line of his jaw, stretching my forefingers to his ears to gauge the width of the hood opening, then pivoting my fingertips to his forehead to gauge its length. I could feel his eyelashes fluttering against my fingers. His lips, dry and cold, brushed the calloused skin between my thumb and palm.

"Good," I said finally, backing away and taking the parka from his hands.

As I left, he called to Sweet One. I knew if I turned back I'd see her presenting her strong back for him to lean upon as he rose.

I sat beside the fire and cut apart the sleeping fur that had kept me warm for so many moons: Black Mask's thick pelt. I wished I had wolverine to trim the edge, so the fur wouldn't ice over from Brandr's breath. But at least it was a hood.

I knew, even before I let him try it on, that it fit perfectly—tight along the cheeks, but loose enough around the back of his head to create a cushion of warmth.

I knew because I could still feel the shape of his face on my fingertips.

CHAPTER
THIRTY-FIVE

$\int$

O w!"

The string snapped against Brandr's wrist again. I was always too fast for him.

"Now you know to stay clear of the ice bear's jaws." I spread my thumbs, moving the mouth of my string figure.

"It doesn't really look like a bear."

"What do you mean?" I wiggled my pinkie fingers and the ears moved. Brandr laughed, and I warmed to see him happy.

Our sled was nearly complete, and I'd even fashioned harnesses and traces for the wolfdogs. At my direction, Brandr had whittled toggles and a fan hitch. Sweet One and White Paw had taken to pulling easily enough, far faster than any normal dogs would, though Floppy Eared had just sat on his haunches with his tongue lolling. Much nipping from his sisters finally got him moving. For now, they lay in the entrance tunnel, but when it came time to leave, my team would be ready.

But I no longer knew when that time would be. One storm had barely ended before another began.

Pushing aside the hanging bear pelt, Brandr stretched his long frame from one side of the sleeping bench to the other, as if desperate to break free of the qarmaq's walls. His head lay beside my hip. I unwound the string from my hands and shifted away, pretending I needed a drink from the pail of melted snow hanging above our fire.

"How long do you think we've been trapped in here?" he asked, his smile quickly fading back into a frown. The longer we spent inside, the quieter he became. I worried that he might crack into raving. Such things happened sometimes in winter.

"I don't know." I wiped the water from my lips and furrowed my brow in exaggerated contemplation. "Two hundred and fifty-seven days?"

That got him laughing again. He rolled onto his stomach and reached out to ruffle my hair. "I should never have taught you to count."

My people have no words beyond *twenty*, nor need for them. Anything more than the sum of our fingers and toes is just *many*. I had learned Brandr's Norse numbers more to pass the time than anything else.

"Six days, then," I offered, resisting the urge to smooth my short hair back behind my ears.

He sighed and sat up. "At least seven, kid." He dug around the sleeping furs for the new eyeshields I'd taught him to make, then started gouging the slits wider with the small knife.

"If you make them too big, they won't be much use against the sunlight once we're on the sled," I warned.

"Sunlight?" He snorted. "Feels like we'll never see that again."

As usual, I found waiting easier than he did. For all my desperation to reach Kiasik, I knew what I could control and what I could not. Brandr was like a restless child in constant need of distraction. But I could hardly blame him; the storm had lasted longer than most, as if Sila, usually so uninterested in the affairs of men, had trapped us together on purpose.

"She may be hard to see through the storm, but the Sun

definitely rose today," I assured him. "Otherwise I never would've shown you the bear game. Once the Moon of Great Darkness arrives, it's dangerous to play with string figures, lest the Sun get tangled in the sinew and fail to return."

Brandr had that familiar look that meant he didn't quite believe me.

I gestured to the faint trickle of gray light above the smoke hole. "She's setting now, but she stayed in the sky for longer than she should today. Malina must be stronger in the south. She doesn't hide from her brother as quickly."

"Malina?"

"You don't know the story of Sister Sun and Brother Moon?"

"I know the Norse tales of how Sol and Mani came to be. The Christians have another version. What's yours?" He rested his elbows on his knees and leaned forward, closing the distance between us.

Despite the chill, I sweated beneath his steady blue gaze—a gaze that felt warmer and bluer the longer the storm lasted.

I sought my own distraction in the story. It was a good tale, the first I'd ever performed as an angakkuq's apprentice, but I felt naked telling it without a drum in my hands.

I clasped my hands in my lap and began the story much as I always did: "This is a tale of the time before time."

White Paw crawled in from the tunnel and settled herself next to the fire as if she, too, were eager for a story.

"Taqqiq and Malina were brother and sister, both very beautiful, with full round faces and great shining eyes. Taqqiq joined the men of their camp in a special qaggiq to feast and tell tales." I added a little extra for Brandr's benefit. "The women and Malina did whatever it is that women do, probably mend clothes and gossip." My friend, who'd clumsily attempted to mend a tear in his shirt earlier, laughed. It seemed mockery of women amused men from any world.

I kept going, stretching out the story to fill the long night. But as I spoke of Malina waking in the dark, her lamp out, her iglu cold, I began to regret having chosen this tale to tell. With every word, I heard the whispered echo of my own humiliation. Never before had I spoken of that night when Issuk stole my body. Now the words tumbled out, Malina's story interwoven with my own.

"A stranger came into the girl's iglu. In the dark, Malina couldn't see his face, but she felt his hand—cold against her stomach as he fumbled with his trousers, and then...and then he was splitting her apart."

Without realizing it, I began to beat my clasped hands upon my leg as if it were an angakkuq's drum. Only with the dull, thudding rhythm could I bear to continue. "He pushed into her, ripping her flesh until she bled. She'd never known such pain. It did not end. It did not get easier. With every thrust he tore her anew, inside and out, for what felt like the whole of the long winter night."

My voice grew strained as the memory overtook me. I wanted to stop. But an angakkuq never refuses a tale.

"Finally, when she thought she might not survive until the dawn, he finished. He fell upon her like a stone. She lay there, suffocating beneath his weight. The pulse in his neck drummed against her cheek, and she wanted to turn her head and rip out that pulse with her teeth. Then, as suddenly as he'd appeared—he vanished."

"Did her brother avenge her?" Brandr asked softly.

"Taqqiq was still inside the qaggiq, and it's forbidden for a woman to enter the men's sacred space. So the girl went to sleep again the next night with her womb still sore, and again the strange man appeared in the dark, and again he took her. This time, he grabbed at her breasts with fingers like knives and bit them with his sharp teeth, pulling at her nipples until they bled. When he disappeared again, blood stained her from chest to thigh." I forced myself to lower my voice, to breathe, to keep the rhythm steady as I described how Malina had smeared her attacker's forehead with soot on the third night. "After he left, she lay in her pool of blood and sweat and tears. Her body burned with pain, and yet she smiled, for she knew she would finally have her revenge."

Of course, there had been no revenge for Malina. I told of how Taqqiq had been revealed as her attacker, and the siblings now continued their eternal chase as Sun and Moon. I, on the other hand, had taken my revenge—I watched Issuk bleed to death before my eyes. So why did I still feel so powerless? Maybe, like Malina, I'd always feel hunted.

"It is hard to run all the time," I went on, avoiding Brandr's eyes. "And Taqqiq never stops chasing Malina, for men do not give up easily. Sometimes she must rest. And so she hides from her brother each winter. And sometimes, it is said, the Moon catches the Sun in the sky, and she turns black and disappears. He rapes her once again."

I added an ending I hoped was true. "But even then, even after that, she always returns. Red with her blood, yes, but still strong enough to outlast him for another day. She never disappears forever. She will be back."

I unclasped my hands and took a deep breath. "Here ends this tale."

I'd never seen my friend look so uneasy. He rose from the sleeping bench and busied himself with tending the small fire, breaking the wood into smaller and smaller shreds of kindling. When he finally spoke, he wouldn't meet my eyes.

"You had a sister? Or a wife?"

I shook my head. "No wife. A sister who was my father's sister. Puja, like I told you."

He was silent for a long moment, staring at the flames. Then he spoke the words I dreaded.

"You couldn't tell the story like that if you hadn't seen it happen."

I wiped the moisture from my eyes before it could spill over and said lightly, "You're not the only one who knows how to tell

a good tale. Of course I never witnessed the Moon rape the Sun.
Even I'm not that powerful."

"That's not..." He stopped himself with a glance at my face.

"Besides," I continued, hoping to change the topic, "it's you
who have seen such things, not I."

"What do you mean?" Brandr's voice was low now, careful.

"All those villages you conquered, those shores you pillaged, did
you never rape a woman?" My dream of the screaming woman in
the stone hut came flooding back to me. I hadn't wanted to know its
ending, but now the question had been asked. I couldn't take it back.

Brandr shifted his weight and snapped another stick in his hands
before tossing it onto the flames. If he didn't stop soon, the blizzard
outside would bring a welcome respite from the heat. Yet I knew it
wasn't the fire that beaded his brow with sweat.

"The Vikings take women as they take gold or cloth or horses,"
he said warily.

"You didn't answer my question."

"Among your people, isn't it common practice? You're just a boy,
but you're old enough to take a woman. Did you never force one?"

"A wife should lie with her own husband if he asks. Men loan
their wives to other men, too, but if they're smart, they always ask
the women's consent."

"You didn't answer the question, either."

"No, Brandr. I never forced a woman. Never." Something in
my tone made him look at me sharply.

"Have you ever *lain* with a woman, Omat?"

I cleared my throat and picked up the length of string, twisting
it once more around my fingers, blindly forming the figure of a
raven. "No. Nor will I."

He narrowed his eyes. "You're not like other men. I sometimes
feel...Perhaps you're like Loki the Shapeshifter, who lies with
men and women?"

"Your trickster god? No, I'm no trickster."

He relaxed perceptibly. "A man who lets himself be taken by another man is cowardly. No Viking allows it willingly."

"Maybe they should. If they coupled with each other, they wouldn't rape women every time they anchor their boat."

"We don't... every time."

"But I know *you* have," I said finally, losing my patience.

"What?"

"I've seen it, Brandr. That vision I had in the painted woman's hut... it wasn't the only time I saw your past. I dream your memories night after night. A woman with light eyes and dark hair, not much older than I. A village perched on a cliff, houses made of stone and moss."

"Stop it."

"The other men held her down—"

"I said stop." His hands balled. I thought surely he would strike me.

"She was screaming, Brandr. She had no spear, no knife to defend herself with."

"I was just a boy," he whispered.

"Was that the only time, then?"

He bowed his head but did not speak.

"How many times, then? You have numbers for everything. Can you count that high? Or do you wish you were an ignorant skraeling so you could just say 'many' and have done with it?"

"That's what Vikings do," he growled. "If I hadn't, I would've been laughed off the boat. Taken for a weakling, or a shapeshifter... womanish. No one ever questioned the way we did things."

"The women you raped?" Before I knew what I did, I rose to my feet. "Did *we* not question it?"

His head snapped up. Only then did I realize what I'd said. Looking back, I think I picked the fight on purpose.

He focused on my face, my beardless jaw, my stocky form cloaked beneath my heavy parka. I closed my eyes, as if that would somehow hide me from his sight.

"Omat."

I clenched my jaw tight and crossed my arms across my chest. If I spoke, I'd cry. Womanish, indeed.

"Say that again."

I could only shake my head. I felt White Paw's nose nuzzle my elbow reassuringly—but hers was not the touch I wanted.

"Open your eyes."

I took a deep, shuddering breath and did as he asked. He stood across the fire from me now, the top of his head brushing the ceiling, his arms crossed in an echo of my own.

"What?" I demanded. White Paw swung her head from me to Brandr and back again, panting all the while. "Stop that," I snapped at her. She settled down at my feet obediently, still following us with her eyes. Sweet One padded in from the entrance tunnel, headed for Brandr. I stopped her with a curt hand signal.

The wolfdogs' antics had not distracted him. "You said you were a boy." His gaze remained steadily on mine, his chin lowered as he looked down at me.

"I never said that."

"That's true. You said you were a *man*, a great hunter full grown, if I remember correctly. An even greater lie."

"I never lied! I was born with a man's spirit. I've tried to explain that to you. My grandfather raised me as a—"

"Enough! You're a *woman*! The skraeling man I killed had a mustache. Your brother—if he was indeed your brother and that, too, wasn't a lie—had one, too. I assumed you were just too young. But now..." He reached across the fire and grabbed my chin in his hand, tilting my face toward his with bruising fingers. "I'm such an idiot," he spat, releasing me. "You reminded me so much of Galinn I was willing to believe any lie you told."

"I am both man and woman," I insisted weakly, but he wasn't listening anymore.

"You have a woman's breasts, no? That's why I've never seen you naked, even in the heat. Why I've never seen you take a piss since that first day." He groaned and sank back down to his knees. "I trusted you. Why did you lie?"

"How can you ask me that?" I nearly shouted the words. "After all you've done. *After all I've seen.*"

White Paw whimpered in the ensuing silence.

"That story," Brandr said finally. "That was you. With the Moon." With his head bent, I couldn't see his eyes.

I sat down before him, wanting to meet his gaze. I wouldn't run in fear. I wouldn't lie. I would tell him everything. "I'm no Sun Woman, but yes, I've been forced, and yes, the Moon and I have met before. He sent a man to take my body, and with my dignity he took my powers. I was a powerful seer, an angakkuq. I could speak with the spirits of the animals. Taqqiq took all that away from me."

He sighed deeply. "Galinn claimed to speak to the gods. I never understood him, either. Even when I know you're telling the truth, you speak in mysteries."

"*You're* the mystery, Norseman. You touch a wolfdog with so much tenderness. And I remember you with your brother. How you held him. But with those women..."

"The berserker rage comes on us. The red haze, Thor's gift." He seemed to be talking more to himself than to me. "I barely knew what I did."

I grabbed his chin and forced him to meet my eyes, just as he had done to me a moment before. "I know what it is to be a tool of the spirits. They hone us, use us, and throw us away. But we *always* know what we do." His bearded jaw flinched beneath my fingers, but he did not pull away.

I released him. I sat with my legs tucked beneath me as a woman would. Waiting.

His eyes traveled over my face, my neck, my hands, as if his shock had finally melted away and he saw me—truly saw me—for the first time.

Only then did I slowly draw my outer parka over my head and lay it aside. I pulled my arms inside my atigi and reached for the cloth binding my chest. The knot had grown stiff with sweat— only the thought of having to ask for help gave me enough strength to undo it. Still holding his gaze, I worked it open with trembling hands, then dropped the remnant of his blue cloak to the ground before slipping my arms back through the sleeves.

My breath came easier. My atigi hung differently, the curve of my breasts clearly visible against the thin caribou hide.

I had imagined this moment for a long time. Dreaded it. Longed for it. I had hoped he'd look at me with respect and perhaps— though I could barely admit it to myself—desire. I had feared he'd look at me with loathing and disgust instead.

His face remained stony, as if he couldn't allow himself any emotion at all. His eyes, however, burned. *Hunger*, I thought. But before I could unravel my own response—*No. Terror.*

Then his expression simply collapsed.

A dancer pulling off a carven mask to reveal the tortured human face beneath. He tried to duck his head again, to hide his shame.

"Look at me." Not a request. A command.

"I can't." His shoulders heaved like those of a man who has run beside a sled all day, never sitting, never resting, always slipping on the ice beneath his feet.

"You must."

We knelt facing each other, both still clothed, yet I felt that we sat naked, revealed. In opening myself to him, I'd somehow ripped him open at the same time. It scared me, but it scared him more.

I do not know how long the silence lasted. Long enough for his fear of keeping silent to finally outweigh his fear of speaking.

"To be berserk," he began, "is to be drunk without dizziness. To feel your skin swell and heat—as if lightning, not blood, crackles through your veins. It is a drive more fierce than hunger or thirst or sex." His voice grew thick. "But you're right. We know what we do. *I* knew what I did."

His entire body tensed, and I knew it took all his strength to meet the accusation in my eyes. "You asked how many. There were three." The words tumbled forth. "The first they forced upon me when I was little more than a child. The second time, I told myself she enjoyed it. The third—" The story halted suddenly, like a waterfall after the first hard freeze.

I would not speak. I would not make this easy for him.

"The third stared into my eyes the whole time. From the beginning until the end. She didn't scream or weep, just stared. And I knew I was doing something terrible, and she knew I knew. When I was done, I stepped away from her. The battle was raging outside her hut. Flames. Screams. But I held out my hand to help her stand." He shook his head slowly. "I thought...I don't know. I thought if I could save her, then maybe I wasn't a monster. She lunged for my dagger instead. Pulled it from its sheath, quick as a snake, and plunged it into her own breast." He clenched his fingers together. "Thor's gift—Thor's curse—drained away. I stood there for a long time, staring at the dead woman who stared back at me."

Brandr blinked back the tears that lined his lower lashes, and I knew he saw the woman's gaze in my own.

"I wondered if I should pull the dagger from her breast and thrust it in my own. I still wonder that, sometimes. It would've been better, in so many ways, if I had."

I knew what he wanted me to say. That I was glad he had lived to come into my life. That I would not have survived this journey without him. It was all true. But I said none of it.

"I closed her staring eyes. I left the dagger in her breast. And I vowed that I would never again accept Thor's gift. Whatever terrible choices I made would be fully my own—I would let no god's red haze ease my way. I went home. Back to Greenland. To my brother. If there was anything good left inside me, I knew that Galinn would find it."

"And did he?" I asked after a long silence.

He shook his head mutely, as if a single spoken word would shatter whatever meager defenses were left to him. He had never wept in front of me. He did not want to now.

I felt no pity. I *wanted* him to shatter. Only then could we, perhaps, begin to put the pieces back together again.

"You must tell me, Brandr." I needed to skin him like a whale until only bone and blood remained. "Tell me what happened to your brother."

"It is not a fit tale for a warrior."

"Do you think I care about that? Do you think I've behaved in every way befitting a hunter of my people? I use both ulu and man's knife. I break more aglirutiit than I obey. You and I are both beyond others' understanding."

"I dishonored my brother's memory. Is that what you want to hear?" he begged. "I fled Leifsbudir with little more than the clothes on my back. I knew I'd never make it back to Greenland—knew I'd die alone, starving, rotting from my wounds. And I didn't care. I didn't care that I'd never see Valhalla if I didn't die gloriously in battle. Besides, you were right—I don't want to fight and die and fight again. I just want to rest." His voice caught. I would not comfort him. I would not forgive. He went on, quieter now, wrapping his arms around his knees. "A thousand times I thought of leaving you. Sometimes I think I stayed with you as a punishment. Every day we travel, we draw closer and closer to Leifsbudir. I've been waking every morning terrified that today will be the day when we finally find them... or they find us. And then what would they do to me? What would *I* do? Run? Fight? Surrender? And worst of all"—he cradled his forehead in his palms—"what would I tell you?"

I did not understand. Even then, I didn't realize what I meant to him.

He took another hollow breath before he went on. "I thought Galinn could find whatever good was left in me. But he didn't. *You* did." His whole body tensed. "And now, when I tell you what happened, you will leave me."

"You have already told me the worst thing you could possibly tell me. I am still sitting here." I did not admit that I had almost left. When he told me of the woman with the dagger in her heart, I had imagined taking my wolfdogs and my new sled and leaving, storm or no. He would likely die without my help, and he would deserve it. Yet hadn't I killed Onerk with my sinew cord—playing with a man's life as thoughtlessly as the spirits might play with mine? Hadn't my own family slaughtered the dwarf men and stolen their women? My beloved grandfather had known the story— and hidden it from me.

"Good or bad—just tell me the truth, Brandr. Whatever the consequences."

His fingers twisted through his long orange hair, pulling it taut against his scalp. "I have buried the truth so deep I'm not sure I even know what it is anymore. I see it in my dreams every night, but each time it warps a little more, the nightmare grown at once more vivid and more obscure. How can I find the words for that?"

Silently I reached for my pack. From the very bottom, I drew out the small skin bag and the bark container I'd stolen from the painted woman's hut. He watched me take a long swallow of the stinging liquid.

I held out the bag to him. I knew what I was asking of him. It was one thing to tell me his story. Another to let me crawl inside his brain and see it for myself.

He took the bag from my fingers and drained the last of the liquid.

I tossed the dried flowers into the fire.

CHAPTER
THIRTY-SIX

ᛉ

I don't like the hollows beneath Galinn's cheeks. He eats enough, his wounds are healed, but the strife in our hall eats away at him.

"We should compromise with Freydis, before this comes to blows," my brother begs Finnbogi. I've rarely heard him so desperate. "Speak sense to her at the Althing tomorrow."

"Freydis Eriksdottir cannot be bargained with," the Icelander shoots back. "She says she wants to borrow our knarr for her own cargo. Steal it more likely. Just like she stole the good longhouse when we arrived and forced us to build out here in the woods. You saw how she raged when I told her she couldn't have my ship. She's a greedy *kunta* who wants to be as famous as her brother Leif."

"We know why she's truly angry," I say. "She told you not to bring any Christians on your crew."

Finnbogi snorts. "You try finding an entire crew in Iceland with no Christ worshipers! They spread like the plague. She either accepts my crew or she mans my oars."

"The *ambatts* don't row, and you brought them," Galinn says.

"The *ambatts* don't count," the Icelander retorts.

I glance to the corner of the hall, where the five thrall women sit beside a

lamp, combing each other's hair, sewing, preparing our next meager meal.
Even from here, I can see the small metal crosses Agata and Jeanne wear
around their necks.

"You should never have brought them," I tell the captain.

"Just because you don't sleep with them, doesn't mean we shouldn't."

"They speak about the Christ to everyone who'll listen," I insist.

Next to me, Galinn tenses. He doesn't hate the Christians as Freydis
does, but I know they make him uncomfortable.

"Already two more of your men have converted," I continue. "Freydis
thinks her Greenlanders will be next." I lean forward, whispering fiercely.
"Her own husband sleeps with Agata every chance he gets."

Finnbogi rises from the bench and braces his fists on his hips. "Next time
you lead an expedition to an uninhabited wilderness, Brandr Gunnarsson,
you can bring only men. Let them fuck each other or the sheep. See how
that works out for you."

"It wouldn't be sheep," I murmur as he strides away. It would be whatever women crossed our paths. I think of the last woman I took, at her staring eyes and bloody breast.

"Are you all right, Brother?" Galinn lays a hand on my arm.

I have never told him about the women I hurt. He thinks I am good and
kind for never taking one of the ambatts for myself. Let him keep thinking
that.

"No. I'm not all right. When Freydis came here to ask about borrowing
the Icelanders' knarr, did you see the way she looked around our hall? I've
seen that look before in the eyes of a Viking captain when he pulls up to
shore. He wonders how much resistance the village will give him when he
burns it to the ground and steals their gold and women for himself."

"Freydis may be greedy, but—"

"Freydis is a madwoman. Finnbogi is right: she cannot be bargained
with."

"She's one woman."

"One woman who rules her men like the strongest jarl. If there were still
shield-maidens, she'd lead the Greenlanders into battle herself. You saw her
with the red men, swinging her weaving sword as if it were a real blade. I

don't trust her, Galinn. And I don't trust this houseful of merchants and sailors, either. If Freydis and her men attack, the Icelanders will not be able to defend us."

"What are you saying?"

I stand but keep my voice low so the others might not hear. "I'm saying that we're already feuding with the red men. If another war begins between Icelanders and Greenlanders, then we will be caught in the middle. We are Greenlanders who sail with Icelanders! Who will we choose? Our neighbors or our crewmates?"

His face, already so pale from the long winter, blanches further. "So . . ."

"So we need to be ready to leave."

"Leave? I . . . I can't."

"We can take the rowboat," I begin, but Galinn cuts me off.

"No, you don't understand. My dreams . . ."

I have heard these dreams before. The same ones that brought us to Vinland in the first place. But I listen anyway.

"The goddess of love came to me again last night. She's more beautiful than you can imagine." He whispers, as if his wife, Geirlaug, were standing just beside him rather than far across the sea in Greenland. "Freya has long, shining hair the color of wheat sheaves, and she wears nothing but spring flowers girdling her waist. She looks scared. Her voice shakes when she speaks."

"You'd never left Greenland until six months ago, kid. What do you know of wheat?"

He doesn't smile, my serious brother. "My dreams roam farther than I do."

I sigh. "And what more did your dream goddess say?"

"The same thing she always says. That the end is near. For so long, the gods have prepared for the Ragnarok, the final, splendid battle with the Frost Giants. But now Odin has seen the future with his all-knowing eye and fears there will be no great battle after all—just a slow wasting away as the Christ approaches. A desert dweller who can raise the dead yet wields no weapon and lies with no woman. A god who let himself die, pinned to a cross like a spread-eagled man, rather than fight for his life. Now the

Christ comes for the Aesir, naked and bleeding yet somehow stronger than the mightiest god."

"So the Aesir would rather have the Ragnarok." I can't help the disdain in my voice. "A fight against their ancient enemies. Don't they ever get tired of blood?"

"They want to face death with swords in their hands, as warriors should." Galinn's eyes grow vague, as if he watches the great war unfold before him. My shepherd brother, who has never struck another man in anger, sounds nearly wistful as he describes the litany of bloodshed I've heard prophesied since my childhood. "Odin will battle the monster wolf, Fenrir. Thor will wrestle Jormungand, the sea serpent who circles the roots of the giant World Tree with its own tail in its mouth. Garm the hound fights Tyr the one-armed swordsman. One of Fenrir's brood, a wolf in troll's skin, will swallow the Sun... or perhaps the Moon. Gentle Frey will be attacked by Surtur, a fire fiend with sparking hair and a sword of flame." His eyes snap to mine, suddenly sharp. "Surtur looks like you, Brother."

"Is that what you think of me? An evil fire fiend?"

He shakes his head, as if to clear it. "No. I think you are the bravest, most generous man I know. One who would come all this way for his brother's dream. A dream you don't even believe in."

"I believe you're having dreams, Galinn. I just don't believe they mean what you think they do. Did the gods ever say they wanted you to come to Vinland?"

"No," he admits. "But Freya doesn't want to become a Christian saint, and Thor won't give up his war hammer to any virgin weakling. Greenland was the gods' last stronghold, but now the Aesir lose ground even there. I know they need a new home. Somewhere as far away from Rome as any man has ever traveled. Vinland is perfect. I must stay here until they arrive."

And so I do not argue with my brother. He is as stubborn in his own way as Freydis is in hers. I leave him there beside the fire, gazing at the flames as if he sees the future in their dance.

It's my turn to stand guard that night. When all are asleep, I steal a few rounds of flatbread and a sack of stockfish from our stores. I would *take my sword, too, but it hangs on the wall just behind the pallet I share with Galinn, and I dare not wake him yet. I stare at him from across the hall instead. The purple shadows beneath his closed eyes. The way he curls his shoulder to spare the scarred arrow wound at his collarbone. He has already suffered too much pain. I will not let him get hurt again.*

I slip from the turf hall, through the forest, and down to the shore, where the two knarrs lie anchored: Freydis's smaller Greenlandic boat and the larger Icelandic vessel she covets. I stow the supplies in the biggest rowboat, taking my time to lash them carefully, to find a pair of oars, a barrel of fresh water. It's a crazy plan to try to row all the way back to Greenland. One that can never work. But it's the only way I can think to protect my brother from these feuding fools. I pray that Galinn is right, that tomorrow's Althing will resolve the conflict. Such conferences often prevent bloodshed back home. But this is not home. This is a land where none of the old rules seem to apply. Where skraeling boats are faster than Norse ones, shepherds act like Vikings, and women can lead armies. I did not come all this way just to fight in another war. And I won't let Galinn, either, no matter what his gods tell him. If I have to tie him up and drag him into the boat, I will.

I head back through the woods. Then I hear the screams.

For a moment I cannot believe my ears. It cannot happen tonight. Before the Althing. Freydis wouldn't dare.

And I was supposed to stand guard.

I start running.

The Greenlanders, some of them men I've grown up with, stand in front of the Icelanders' house with their swords and axes drawn. I creep forward, dashing from tree to tree to stay out of view. On the ground in front of them lies a pile of dark shapes. Sheep carcasses? Maybe seals they found lying on the beach? In my panic to believe something other than what I know to be true, I even imagine they've come to share the spoils of some lucky midnight hunt.

I am right, in a way. A midnight slaughter of helpless beasts. A pile of men's bodies. Just bodies. No heads. I still don't understand what's before my eyes. Not really. Not until I hear Freydis's husband say, "Galinn Gunnarsson was no Christian. He was a Greenlander, like us. We should've spared him."

I hear nothing else. Only the rush of blood in my ears. My feet are rooted to the ground, my heart beating so fast I feel it might burst through my chest, leaving only my hollow carcass behind.

Then her voice cuts through. "Galinn was their friend, their crewman. He raised his brother's sword against us to defend them. Don't question me on this." She peers around the clearing. "Brandr must be somewhere. And when he returns, he'll seek justice for his brother. I want him dead. Be ready."

"Thorvard?" one of the Greenlanders calls to Freydis's husband. "We tied up the ambatts inside. What should we do with them?"

Thorvard answers quickly. "We should divide them among the men."

"No." Freydis's voice is calm. "They have plotted against us and against our gods. They die. All of them."

The men are silent. I can almost hear their ragged breaths. The Green-landers only play at being Vikings—this is too much. They might butcher a houseful of sleeping men, but they won't kill unarmed women, even Chris-tian ones. Freydis begins to scream at them, calling them cowards and worse, but they won't move. Even Ingharr Ketilsson, who slaughtered an entire family of fur-clad skraelings with his own sword, stands frozen in place.

Thorvard seizes his wife's arm, but Freydis twists from his grasp like an eel and grabs his hammer from him.

"If you don't do it, I will." Her cheeks burn so red they look black in the moonlight. I have never seen Thor's gift upon a woman's face before. It is monstrous. She is the fire fiend, not I, bringing the Ragnarok in her wake.

She marches into the house with the hammer raised high. The screams are terrible. But more terrible still is the growing silence as voice after voice cuts off. When Freydis finally emerges, her green dress is splattered with blood. I finally find the strength to move—but only enough to fall to my knees behind the tree and vomit. My face is pressed so low to the ground that I nearly smother in my own bile. I, who have seen so much blood, have never seen anything like this.

I watch as the men carry out the ambatts' bodies. The pile of corpses grows so tall it towers over the living. She orders her men to burn them all, without even the proper rites. And I just lie there, hidden in the woods.

Letting all of it happen. I am one man against twenty, but that shouldn't stop me. As a berserker, I would take them all on at once, even knowing such folly would mean certain death. I've vowed never again to seek Thor's gift, but now I reach for it. Beg for it. Instead I feel only a creeping coldness, as if all my limbs have turned to ice.

I lie there all night, wide awake, unmoving. The pyre finally burns out at dawn. It is one of those warm spring days that make you forget winter ever existed. The ground around me is sprinkled with tiny blue flowers that weren't there the day before. Galinn would've stopped to give thanks to the Aesir. To Frey, the god of growing things, and his sister, Freya, who wears spring buds in her hair. And to Thor, whose thunderstorms make both war and flowers bloom.

I hate them all.

Galinn came all this way to save his gods. But when he needed them to save him, *they ignored his pleas.*

I tear off the Thor's hammer from around my neck, the one Galinn made for me the first time I went viking, when he was just a child barely old enough to hold a knife. I bury it there in the dirt.

Two Greenlanders guard the Icelanders' longhouse against my return. One of them, Ulfar, has my sword sheathed at his hip.

I creep up behind him and press the point of my knife to his throat. His son Snorri raises his spear.

"If you don't drop it, I'll kill your father."

Snorri obeys.

With my free hand, I rip my sword from Ulfar's waist.

Dimly I hear the old man babbling in my ear. Begging for forgiveness for what happened to my brother. But all I can think about is that the blade is still clean. Galinn may have tried to defend the Icelanders, but he'd never even drawn blood. He'd wanted so much to be a Viking. Like me.

I don't pull back my hand to strike. I just press the knife into Ulfar's throat until the blood runs down my fingers and his body goes limp.

Snorri picks up his spear and lunges at me, screaming to wake his companions. I dodge and bat his spear away with my sword, but I'm using my left hand and we're both fighting with more rage than skill—he pierces my thigh. The pain clears my head: I slice the spear in half with my blade. One more swing and I'll take the boy's head.

I kick him in the gut instead, with force enough to burst his spleen.

He goes down, and I start running.

Blood courses down my leg.

Just get to the rowboat. Get to the rowboat.

Run, you fool. Run like the coward you are.

And don't look back.

CHAPTER
THIRTY-SEVEN

ᛉ

The first time I drank the red woman's potion, I awoke to Brandr's voice, begging me to come back to him.

This time, he had let me sleep. At some point in the night, he had carried me to the sleeping platform and tucked me beneath the furs.

Very slowly I sat up, my mind still whirling with memories of blood and flame.

Next to me hung the broad bear fur I'd strung between us. Brandr lay on the other side, fast asleep, one long arm extended to push the fur aside so he might watch over me through the long night.

Sweet One whimpered a quiet greeting from where she lay next to him, her chin resting on his hip. He twitched at the sound but didn't rouse.

I watched the even rise and fall of his chest. So different from his panting breaths as he fled Leifsbudir—breaths I could still feel burning my own throat. Some burdens could never be lifted, some crimes never forgiven, but in sharing his truth with me, some of Brandr's unseen wounds had finally healed. I had rarely seen his face so calm, his sleep so untroubled. I could not bear to wake him yet.

Trapped inside the qarmaq, we had traveled farther together than we ever had on our long trek south. Like angakkuit on a spirit quest, we had been ripped apart and made anew.

I had found the good in him, he said. Now I had rooted out the worst in him as well. But he was not the only one full of contradictions. Within us both, cowardice, despair, and violence warred with bravery, faith, and love. All we could do was keep fighting.

I reached up and unfastened the bear pelt from the ceiling. There should be no barriers between us now.

Then I noticed the silence.

Sila Itself seemed calmed by the peace between us, for the blizzard had finally ceased its roar.

I wanted to stay and watch Brandr wake. To see the new man he had become.

But if the storm had stopped, I had no time to waste. Our other journey must continue. White Paw and Floppy Eared, both curled beside the hearth, lifted their heads as I gathered my pouch of tools and pulled on my boots and outer parka. I motioned for them to stay. Brandr should not wake up alone.

I had to dig a little with my spear shaft to get out of the qarmaq, but I'd built the entrance in the lee of the wind so the drifts wouldn't trap us inside. The Sun nearly blinded me when I emerged, the bright rays reflecting off the snow in sharp stars of light. This time, however, I'd come prepared. I tied my new eyeshields tightly around my head.

I cleared the snow from the top of the sled and bent to chip the runners free of the frozen ground. Then I turned to the bay to check the clouds above the water. If the weather held, we would leave today.

I saw more than clear sky. Somehow, in making peace with Brandr, I had forged a truce with the spirits as well. Sanna had finally relented. The sea had given me a great gift: a narrow bark-covered boat, its prow stuck between two rocks and its stern floating free in the iceless ocean.

Cautiously I walked toward the shore, alert for approaching strangers. When no one appeared, I decided the boat had drifted free from the painted men's village up the coast. A paddle was lashed inside the hull—how could I resist it?

Had I not seen the seals, I would've fetched Brandr to come exclaim over my find, and our story would be a different one. But as I turned to the qarmaq, I noticed a dark mound on the snowy island in our bay. After avoiding my harpoon for so long, the seals offered themselves—more proof of Sanna's favor. Their meat would feed us on our journey; their pelts would make Brandr a much-needed pair of fur trousers to replace his useless cloth ones.

I resolved to catch a seal and return triumphant before he awoke. Stupid. Reckless. Yet after revealing my woman's body to him, I wanted desperately to prove my man's heart. *I can be both to him*, I decided. A vision came unbidden and unstoppable. Not a dream of the past but a hope for the future. I would drag the seal into camp. I would pound out the blubber and fill a shallow stone with the oil. Make a wick from a thick tuft of wolfdog hair. Then, by the warm, constant light of a proper lamp, I might finally dare to remove my atigi and, for the first time in years, choose to be naked in front of another person. And then...would he do the same? I had not forgotten the sight of his bare chest. My mind roved where my body dared not. Across the tattoo that circled his wrist. Over knots and around loops and through every twisting spiral. I wanted to trace them all. Up the long bone of his forearm. The swelling rise of his bicep. All the way to where the beast sank its fangs into the meat of his shoulder. I swallowed hard, imagining the taste of his skin.

The seals barked. The sound like laughter carrying across the water. *You haven't caught us yet. Stop dreaming like a woman, Omat, and come prove yourself a man.*

From the pouch slung across my chest, I retrieved a toggling harpoon head and fitted it into the foreshaft of my weapon. I stepped carefully into the birchbark boat, missing my kayak. I longed to paddle with my legs under the waterline, feeling the embrace of the sea around my lower body while my arms pushed and pulled like the waves themselves. Instead I splashed ineffectively with a one-bladed oar in the wobbly boat that was not quite kayak, not quite umiaq. The seals would hear me and be gone in a heartbeat, slipping off the rock and out of my reach.

But Sanna had indeed forgiven me—the animals remained on the island as I approached. I stopped paddling, taking note of waves and currents to keep the boat drifting silently toward the rock.

Despite all my precautions, one large bull seal lifted his head.

But he wasn't looking at me. I followed his wide black gaze to a flash of white on the horizon. *The jaw of a breaching whale,* I thought. But it didn't disappear beneath the waves. I sat, transfixed, as the white shape grew larger. As the monstrous wooden ship came into view.

Only then did I let myself understand—I had found the Vikings at last.

"*Kiasik,*" I breathed. I imagined him huddled defenseless among yellow-haired butchers. I imagined myself rushing to save him… but with what? My single harpoon? If they saw me here in the open water, the Norse would either kill me as thoughtlessly as they'd murdered Issuk's family or, at best, capture me as they had Kiasik. All this time, I'd thought I'd have time to plan a rescue. Now it was all happening too fast.

Jolted from my stupor, I paddled furiously for shore.

I glanced back toward the ship. I could make out the silhouettes of the Vikings now, could even see one standing in the prow, pointing at me. No matter how hard I paddled, the creaking of the ship grew louder, closer. My arms couldn't find an easy rhythm; the water churned and splashed around me as if bubbling with Sanna's laughter. My birchbark boat wasn't her gift—it was her trap.

I could just make out the low, snow-covered mound that marked our qarmaq. This far away, Brandr wouldn't hear a shouted warning.

Over the pounding of my heart and the splashing of my paddle, a Norseman's rough voice carried across the water. "If you let the skraeling get back to shore, he'll warn his people!"

Another man's voice. "Hand me my throwing spear. He won't get back."

I swung the boat with a swift stroke, realizing belatedly that I'd almost led the Vikings straight to Brandr. They would follow me to the qarmaq, where my friend slept beneath our furs, thinking himself safe. They would kill him. And I'd be to blame.

I balanced my paddle across my lap and hoisted my harpoon. I could take out one of them at most—but if they thought a band of fierce hunters defended these lands, they might decide to keep on sailing. Brandr would be safe.

But when I looked up at the bow of the ship, my courage drained away. The great monster on the prow loomed above me, so large and lifelike I felt its wide jaws might swallow me whole. Beside it stood a figure yet more terrible—Freydis Eriksdottir.

Nothing in my dreams had prepared me for her fierceness in life. Her orange hair whipped loose on the wind. Her nose slashed her face like a raven's beak, and her gray eyes bored into me even across the stretch of sea. A dark-green dress billowed around her wiry frame. She stood as tall as the massive, yellow-bearded man beside her—the murderer of Uimaitok, of Nua, of Kidla, of the baby boy I'd carried in my hood. Ingharr Ketilsson raised a long spear to his shoulder.

"Wait." Freydis placed her hand on his throwing arm. "Don't kill him yet. We don't want a war with these skraelings, too."

Ingharr nodded toward Freydis, and I thought for a moment they'd decided to let me go.

Then he flung his shaft. At the same instant, I threw my harpoon at his smirking face. Our weapons crossed in midair. He ducked away just in time, my harpoon flying over his shoulder and clattering to the deck. The Norseman's spear struck true—not into me, but into my boat. The long iron blade ripped easily through the thin bark. Water swirled around my feet as the boat slanted precipitously, bow-first, into the ocean.

My father and grandfather had both drowned. Now I would as well. I didn't know how to swim.

I scrambled backward, pulling my legs away from the gushing water, but there was nowhere to go. The cold hit me like a punch. Warmer surely than the northern ocean of my home, but still cold enough to kill. The sea poured in the tops of my boots and the waist of my trousers, weighing me down.

Before I squinted my eyes shut against the stinging salt, I saw long fronds of swirling black seaweed just below the surface, as thin and tangled as a woman's hair. *Sanna.* She had followed me all this way, waited for me all this time. The seaweed grabbed at me, twisting around my limbs. I struggled, lashing out, and opened my eyes in time to see a girl's thin face, glowing like an iceberg in the faint sunlight from above.

Sea Mother . . .

She seemed small, weak, perhaps unused to these southern waters. She reached out narrow arms, a gesture of both succor and menace. I heard her voice distinctly in my head. *Let go, little girl. Let go.*

Behind her, a mere shadow among shadows, I glimpsed a familiar profile: Issuk.

I had sent him to Sanna's lair. Now he rose up from the depths to seek his revenge.

I have my greatest nemesis to thank for my survival. I might have succumbed to Sanna's will—she was one of the great spirits, after all. She had the right to demand my death. But I would *never* give Issuk what he wanted.

I pulled Brandr's small, sharp knife from its sheath and slashed at the grasping seaweed, at Sanna herself, until I was free.

I pushed my way to the surface, gasping for breath, only to find myself in the chill shadow of the Viking ship. Beneath me, Sanna lay in wait, ready to drown me in her watery embrace. Would my fate be any better in the hands of the Vikings above?

My arms and legs swung in an instinctive effort to keep me afloat. I wouldn't survive much longer, but I had to warn Brandr. I opened my mouth to scream but could hardly make a sound for lack of air. I managed a weak shout in my own tongue, "Run! They're here! *Run!*"

A gray shadow slipped across the shore. White Paw had heard me. She raced toward the water, growling so fiercely that foam flew from her mouth.

"No!" I gasped. "Go back!"

I felt a rush of air against my head and glanced up—a long wooden oar swung toward me.

Then all was darkness.

BOOK FOUR

VIKING

*T*he infant girl lies silent within her cradle of snow, protected by a great white wolf. Soon her aunt will come to take her back into the embrace of her family. Watching from his stolen perch on Odin's silver throne, Loki smiles and turns away. For now, the child will be safe. The Trickster is patient.

But one girl alone is not enough, for Loki's plans are vast indeed. He looks to the East, toward those who worship Odin and Thor, Frey and Freya. Loki has found a home among these folk. They tell his tales of cunning and mischief with laughter and fear in their hearts. But even now, the fair-haired folk have begun to forget the gods of old. The Trickster must look far to find a land where Christ's cross has not replaced Thor's hammer.

There—there—at the farthest reaches of the known world. A vast island with shores as green as emeralds in summer and as icy as Jotunheim in winter. Perched on the slim stretches of habitable land, their backs to the glacier-strewn mountains and their faces toward the sea, a few hardy souls carve out their lives.

It is deepest winter now, and the folk leave their homes only to tend the sheep in their turf barns. Too weak to stand, the animals eat dried grass from their owners' hands and sip from pails of melted snow. Herdsmen have slaughtered the frailest animals before the winter even began—many more will lose their lives before it is over.

Loki watches a young girl with ember-bright hair coax a spindly ewe to eat a handful of hay.

"Come, sweet one, my babe. Come, eat," she murmurs, holding the sheep's head upon her small lap. "You've been my friend, little lamb. Don't you remember the springtime, when we ran together in the green meadows? Spring will come again—you need only live a little longer. When Father gave you to me, I knew you were the best gift any girl ever got. The best lamb in all of Greenland. I won't let you starve."

But the lamb will not eat. The girl strokes the soft wooly ears, the dry nose, the hollow cheeks.

"What can I do to make you better? Shall I pray to Frigg to make you healthy? Or Odin to make you wise? Or Thor to make you fierce?"

But still the sheep will not eat. Will not move. The child sighs deeply and strokes the soft brow one more time. She moves the sheep's head gently off her lap and rests it on the lip of a low leather pail. She fingers the hammer pendant at her throat. "Hear me, Thor. If you won't grant your gift to my lamb," she prays, "grant it to me. Make me fierce. Make me strong. Make me a weapon in your hand."

She takes the knife from her belt and slits the ewe's throat, making sure to catch every drop of the hot, nourishing blood. She does not cry.

From his high perch, Loki claps his hands and crows with delight. The Aesir's great hall is empty. No one hears his glee.

He looks down once more upon the icy island at another orange-haired child. The boy sits beside the fire in his turf house, carving designs onto a wooden sword. Around him, a family, warm and jolly even on this coldest of nights. The father, hair as bright as his son's, sips milk from a stone bowl.

"Ah, Brandr," he says, watching the boy's work, "what do you mean to do with that?"

"Practice. Until I can wield it like a true Viking."

The fair-haired mother laughs and bounces the babe at her breast. "You find a piece of driftwood—more precious than gold in a land without trees— and you make it a sword? Better a spoon, or a pail, or a shepherd's crook."

But the boy merely smiles and keeps carving the sword's hilt with spirals and dragons and beasts without name.

The baby ceases to suckle and cries softly. "Here," the mother says, handing the infant to her older son. "I'll tend the sheep if you'll tend your brother."

The boy doesn't complain but puts aside his carving and takes the babe in one arm. He pulls a small whistle from his pocket and begins a slow lullaby. The baby's cries subside. They sit together through the night, these brothers, blue eyes meeting blue, one whistling and one smiling.

Loki rubs his hands together. "They are all there. One to lead, one to dream, and one to swing the sword."

An approaching footstep rouses the Trickster from his reverie. He leaps from the forbidden throne and slips back into the shadows, donning his disguise as a slim goddess. But he grins still. He has seen enough. For all his love of chaos, Loki was born a Frost Giant—he is a patient god. He can bide his time until the children grow. Until the worlds collide, as he knows they must. Until then, the Christ will grow more powerful and Odin more frail. And Loki . . . Loki will merely smile. And laugh. And wait.

CHAPTER
THIRTY-EIGHT

⅃

The oar's blow didn't knock me unconscious for long, yet in those moments, I dreamed. Not of Brandr's past, this time, but of my own. Puja was there, and Ataata, but my parents as well, both Inuk and Wolf. I believed that when I woke—if I woke—I'd live in the body of a newborn babe, ready for a fresh start, safe within the embrace of my people.

Instead I woke in my own flesh—a body that, for once, I was happy to inhabit. There were too many things still to do in this life.

My wet clothes crackled with ice, and I shook uncontrollably despite the unfamiliar fur thrown across me. The pain from the rope around my wrists and ankles paled before the throbbing in my head. A slow trickle of blood crawled across my scalp to pool in the hollow of my ear.

I lay on the deck of the Vikings' wooden ship—a *knarr*, Brandr had called it. I could tell by the calm slap of water against the hull that it had stopped moving. A slender boy with a spear sat on a crate beside me, his hair as bushy and brown as the curled ruff of a musk ox. He nearly leapt off his seat when he noticed my eyes open.

"He's awake!"

A light tread. Freydis's stony eyes stared down at me. I expected her to raise her husband's bloody hammer and strike me down just as she had so many others. She frowned and looked out over the water as if sniffing the air. "Keep him alive."

A man's gruff voice from somewhere beyond her: "Why bother? Skraelings with furs like that murdered one of our men and almost killed Ingharr, have you forgotten?"

"Husband," she said with a sigh. "If he dies, he's worthless. Alive, he's a hostage in case his people attack. And if we need to land, he might show us the best hunting grounds."

The man moved into my sight. Balding, red-nosed, flabby about his waist and jowls. What hair he had left must once have been as yellow as Ingharr's, but now his beard was more gray than gold. I recognized him from Brandr's dreams as Thorvard Einarsson. He wore a war hammer across his back like the one his namesake, Thor, carried.

"Why do we need a skraeling to point the way?" he asked, sounding more like a petulant child than a grizzled old man. "If you'd let us go after that wolf, I could be wearing a fine pelt right now!"

"Have you ever seen a wolf run straight into the ocean?" she asked scornfully.

"No," he conceded.

"Animals in this land are not like those we know. You're too reckless with things you don't understand."

I felt a small knot of fear loosen in my gut when I realized White Paw had somehow survived, but my joy was short-lived. As Freydis turned to go, she said, "Ingharr—get the skraeling out of those wet clothes."

At that, I nearly cried out. I'd relinquished my secret to Brandr—I was not ready to hand it to these murderers. I bit back my outburst and tried to pretend I hadn't understood her. I couldn't reveal that I spoke Norse, not now. They'd know I learned it from another of their kind, and they might realize Brandr was nearby.

I struggled against my bindings, hoping to reach Brandr's knife. With a jolt, I realized it'd fallen from my hand when they knocked me unconscious. Now it lay on the ocean floor, deep in Sanna's lair. I would not see it again.

I was truly helpless.

Heavy footsteps shuddered the deck beneath me. I felt the chill of a long shadow cross my face and forced myself to turn toward the new threat.

Ingharr Ketilsson loomed above me. If he still suffered from the harpoon wound I'd given him beside Issuk's iglu, he showed no sign. As he bent over me, his plaited yellow beard swung over my nose, wafting a bitter scent like an abandoned fox den. No glimmer of recognition crossed his face. To him I was just another faceless skraeling. For that, at least, I was grateful. He leveled his knife a hairbreadth from my throat.

"Don't move now, skraeling, or I'll slit your neck along with your clothes."

I felt the chill from the knifepoint against my collarbone and heard my parka rip at the neck. My atigi next. I didn't raise my head to watch his progress—I couldn't bear to see the inevitable surprise on his face. Instead I looked straight up, to the vault of sky overhead. Everything else disappeared from view. Only Sila remained.

A few stray clouds moved across my vision, wisps of white like shed caribou fur. A thick stripe of black birds coursed between them, bending and shifting as one. *Once I flew on wings like yours. Let me fly again*, I begged. *Let me leave this earthly body, this rocking boat, this Viking stranger with his rough hands and his sharp blade.*

I felt myself grow lighter, almost dizzy and, for a moment, thought the spirits had answered my prayers. Then Ingharr's coarse laughter dragged me back to the earth, and I once more lay on damp wood. The cold air sliced across my naked breasts.

"No wonder this fish was so slippery in our nets!" he laughed, rocking back on his heels. "Come look!"

More faces peered down at me. The curly-headed boy, his mouth agape. Other Norsemen, young and old. Then Freydis herself, her green dress swirling at her ankles.

"Do you want to sink the ship?" she scolded. "Everyone back to your places. Don't stand and gawk. Have you never seen a woman before?"

"Not one in pants!" the boy exclaimed.

Ingharr laughed. "Nor one so ugly!"

My cheeks flushed hot.

A frail old woman with gray hair cropped short against her scalp leaned close to Freydis. "She's bright with fever, mistress." She lilted and hummed her words in a way the other Norse did not.

"Yes, Muirenn, cover her and keep her warm. Stand back, Ingharr."

And so the woman I most feared became my guardian. Together, Freydis and Muirenn, the old woman, pulled my ruined parka and atigi from my shoulders, then yanked off my trousers and wet boots. They wrapped me in scratchy wool blankets, covering my nakedness. On top of it all, they laid a heavy bear fur.

Slowly I grew warmer, but fear shook my body as violently as had the cold. Still, I couldn't sink into despair, not yet. My quest hadn't ended how I'd planned—but it had ended nonetheless. I would finally find Kiasik.

I peered furtively around the ship, searching desperately for my milk-brother. *What will I say when I find him?* I wondered belatedly. *What kind of fool would come all this way to rescue someone, only to wind up as helpless as the captive?*

Muirenn crouched beside me and offered a hunk of some strange white substance she called *cheese*. I hoped it tasted like blubber. It didn't. I almost gagged trying to force the crumbling, foul-smelling food down my throat.

Freydis stared at me for a moment with an appraising glance. "She looks like a dwarf."

"I wonder if all skraeling women are so short," Muirenn mused.

"We're not going to find out. Where there's a woman, there's sure to be a man, probably many. Probably a whole band of skraeling demons, ready to kill us. We sail north."

"The farther north we go, the harder the winter will be."

Freydis tossed her a scornful glance. "Yes, thrall, the winter will be harsh. But better to suffer through hunger than die at the end of a skraeling's spear."

"Surely Norsemen can protect us from mere skraelings!"

"For all your years, you still trust in the skills of men? Did they not fail me in the forests of Vinland? Cower like children from a band of skraeling men not half so fierce as this woman?" She laughed, a sound more bitter than joyful. "No, Muirenn, we go north."

She walked out of sight, but I heard her calling, "You there, come guard our prisoner. Make sure she doesn't kill herself in the night. We may find use for her."

Muirenn propped me upright. The curly-haired boy stood guard, his attempts to look threatening hampered by the dimples in his cheeks. He looked barely old enough for his first hunt.

Men bustled around the deck, grabbing oars and ropes. The ship creaked in protest, the hull swung northward, and we began to move. I strained against my bindings, hoping to catch a glimpse of my qarmaq. But the ropes were too tight and the sides of the ship too tall.

I wondered where White Paw had gone. Hopefully, she'd managed to warn Brandr. *You should take the wolfdogs and forget all about me and my foolish quest*, I begged him silently. *Stay far away, safe from your enemies, safe from reckless Inuit*. Yet I knew he wouldn't. Brandr would try to rescue me, just as I tried to save Kiasik. And his quest would end just as badly.

The wind pushed me forward faster than any man could walk. Faster even than a wolf could run. Brandr would never find me.

Only once before, that first night after the murder of Issuk's family, had I felt so alone. And then, at least, I'd had my weapons and my clothes. I *had* to find Kiasik. If I didn't—if all of this had been for nothing—Freydis was right to warn that I might take my own life. The scratch of wool on my unbound breasts reminded me that the Norsemen saw me as something even worse than a nameless skraeling. They saw me as a woman. With all their ambatts dead, how long before their disdain shifted to desire?

My eyes burned with unshed tears. The wind slipped over the side of the boat to find me where I crouched; the loose black strands of my hair swam before my eyes.

I will always remember that last glimpse of the shoreline— the screen of my hair, each strand grown huge in the Sun's glare, masked the thin sliver of treetops just visible over the edge of the ship.

The view slid away, and with it any hope for escape. Then I heard Ataata's voice in my mind and found a grim smile. *An Inuk can always make something from nothing.* Why pray for rescue? Why despair? A good hunter examines his surroundings, studies his prey, and never gives up. A good hunter survives.

The wooden ship was no monster, I reminded myself. Just a vessel built by men, not giants. Above me the narrow trunk of a huge, barkless tree soared above the ship, its top lost in the blinding glare of the sun. *A mast*, I remembered from Brandr's dreams. The boat stretched many times the length of the longest umiaq, with decks laid high at either end. In between, piles of logs and skins jammed an open hold. A few sickly-looking animals bleated among the cargo. Beside them huddled several too-thin thralls in shabby woolen rags.

As I watched, the crewmen, many with fur trimming their short cloaks and caps, struggled with the great white sail. It billowed and ruffled until they adjusted it to catch the wind. It snapped into a massive, taut square. The ship moved steadily now. From my spot on the stern, I could see the prow gently heaving as it cut through the swells far faster than any umiaq could manage. I had thought Sila sent the storm to bring Brandr and me together. Now Its breath ripped us apart.

I scanned the faces around me. No Kiasik. No familiar black hair, broad shoulders, flashing eyes. Only pale faces, mottled with sunburn. Hair of yellow and orange and brown escaping from wool caps and hoods. Eyes of gray and green and blue. The colors of Sanna's domain. The colors of ice. These Norse looked much like Brandr, but their cheeks were sharp with hunger and their gaze bleak with despair. They seemed a ragged bunch, scarred and broken from their journey to my lands. A young freeman had lost an arm—I remembered him from Brandr's past, lying on the ground clutching his wound while the red men stormed through Leifsbudir.

When the Norse looked at me, I saw only fear and hate.

I summoned the memory of the night before. Of Brandr's face, raw and open in the flickering firelight. Of the past we had just begun to heal, and the future we might build together. Had I left him behind forever—only to find that Kiasik was already dead? Then another grief: *When Brandr wakes, he will think I abandoned him.* He had feared that I'd leave if he told me what happened in Leifsbudir. I had just proven him right.

A moan escaped my lips.

Muirenn placed a chapped hand on my shoulder. "Hush. Get warm; get some sleep. There's nothing you can do about it now." Her voice was gentle. Pain shadowed her eyes. "When the Vikings come to take you, you best submit."

"She can't understand a word you say," my young guard scoffed.

"Neither do the sheep. But still we talk to them, eh?"

"What do you think Freydis Eriksdottir will do with her?" the boy asked, echoing my own thoughts.

"Claim her as a thrall, I expect."

"Some thrall she'd make. She doesn't even wear cloth. If her people are like the red skraelings in Vinland, they don't know how to weave or spin. What use would she be?"

Muirenn shrugged. "She could be taught."

He laughed. "If she's teachable! If she's even truly human!"

"Oh, she's human. Look at her eyes. She's listening to everything you say."

I glanced away at her words, then realized my mistake and looked quickly back at her, schooling my face to an expressionless mask.

The boy didn't notice anything amiss, but Muirenn looked at me carefully.

He prattled on. "She may be listening, but she doesn't understand. I hope you're right about her learning to do something, otherwise we've been wasting good cheese. Maybe if she's useless, they'll put her back onshore."

"Have you known the mistress to ever question one of her own decisions? No, she said the skraeling's too dangerous to return to her people. You saw that boat of hers, faster than any rowboat. The mistress doesn't want to risk a battle with a whole fleet of skraelings. If this one isn't useful, she won't be put ashore—she'll be thrown right overboard." Muirenn gave me a pointed gaze. A threat. Or perhaps a warning.

I kept my face blank despite my racing pulse.

From the far end of the boat, Freydis summoned the old woman. Muirenn creaked to her feet and moved unsteadily across the rocking deck. I was left alone with the curly-haired boy. Despite his youth, deep wrinkles scarred his forehead and shadows ringed his eyes. He slid his glance toward me with more curiosity than hostility. My ordeal in the water had exhausted me more than I realized, and so far the boy had caused me no harm. I let my eyelids droop. The bleating of animals, the creaking ship, the steady waves, all faded into a steady hum.

"Snorri!"

I jolted awake.

The boy answered back.

I knew that name. Snorri, son of Ulfar—the man who died with Brandr's knife in his throat the night he ran away from Leifsbudir. More than anyone else on this ship, Snorri wanted Brandr dead.

After that, I couldn't rest for fear that the boy somehow knew about my connection to his father's murderer and would kill me as I slept. A foolish thought, perhaps, but lying naked and bound beneath the blankets, I'd never felt more vulnerable. I watched the passing clouds and planned for my future. On the ship, I had no hope of escape; the cold water trapped me here as surely as the rope around my wrists. *If we go ashore*, I reckoned, *I might flee, but without weapons—not even an ulu or a snare—I won't survive the winter.* And if I escaped, I'd never know Kiasik's fate. He might still be hidden somewhere on the boat. I wouldn't leave without him.

By the time the Sun had set, I'd made my choice. To survive, I would make myself useful, just as Muirenn had warned I must. I would find the patience Ataata had always counseled. I would wait for sign of Kiasik. Eventually they'd untie me. And when they did, I could find a weapon, a tool, anything that might let me live when I finally returned to shore. As soon as the boat reached land, my milk-brother and I would run. And we wouldn't look back.

Ingharr Ketilsson's laughter carried across the deck. The same laugh I'd heard the moment before he'd dangled Issuk's son above the snow.

A baby's head crushed like an eggshell. A sword point through Kidla's throat, her own blood painting her parka red. Uimaitok's legs, twisted and still, in the entrance tunnel. Nua's body in a pool of gore . . . her head a few paces beyond. Wherever the Norse went, destruction followed. Another image flashed before me, the one conjured by Brandr's memories. *A pile of corpses mounded higher than the living. Red streaking*

Freydis's face. Galinn's blood. And the blood of ambatts. Of thrall women just like me.

No, I decided. When I found Kiasik, I wouldn't run. Not right away.

First Freydis Eriksdottir and Ingharr Ketilsson would die.

CHAPTER
THIRTY-NINE

ᛃ

To tell how fast we sailed, I needed only to look at Freydis Eriks-dottir's spindle whorl. When the round stone rocked swiftly, we crashed through waves. When it dragged and lulled, no breeze filled the sail, and we stood still. In the rough seas of winter, the lulls were few. We flew northward on cloth wings buoyed by the frigid wind.

I couldn't escape the ever-present spindles. And if I wanted to be worthwhile to the Norse, I had to learn how to use one. With my wrists tied, all I could do for now was watch. Freydis and Muirenn took armloads of sheep fur and brushed it into thick, fluffy ropes. They tied one end of the rope to a spindle—a short dowel weighted with a round leaden whorl. With an easy flick of the wrist, each woman rolled her spindle along her outer thigh, sending the whorl spinning faster than the eye could follow. The thick rope of fur twisted tight, transformed as if by magic into woolen thread finer than any length of sinew. Freydis's hands moved constantly—one holding up the fur at eye level and feeding it down into the spindle, the other running quickly along the thread to move the twist evenly up the rope. Then, before the spindle could start turning in the opposite direction, she rolled it once more along her thigh, starting the whole process over.

It seemed a tedious chore to me—only slightly better than chewing hides. Still, if I learned their women's skills, they might untie me. Even trust me. They'd already clothed me in a woman's long wool dress and cloak. They'd returned my sealskin boots to me, but in every other way, I dressed as a Norsewoman.

When the old thrall returned to feed me a few more bites of cheese at midday, I pointed eagerly to the round spindle whorl looped on her belt.

"See, Snorri!" Muirenn exclaimed. "She already wants to learn."

The curly-headed boy affected disinterest, but I didn't miss his fond smile as he watched the old woman scuttle off to ask permission to teach me to spin.

"Well, you'll have to learn now. The silly old woman will be disappointed if you don't."

Freydis strode across the deck, Muirenn smiling in her shadow.

"The old thrall says I should untie you."

I averted my gaze, attempting to look as passive and humble as possible.

"You're going to learn to spin, yes?" She cupped her hand under my chin and forced me to look into her eyes. They were dark gray in the middle, surrounded by a light halo like storm clouds backlit by the Sun. "Why would a woman who knows how to wield a spear want to learn how to spin?" She didn't think I understood— it was not to me she asked the question. Her face hardened. "Much is unknown."

Despite her skepticism, she hunkered down beside me and held up a small stone pendant carved with a strange symbol: it looked like a tree limb with two short branches. She moved to tie the cord around my neck but stopped when she saw my amulet pouch. Frowning, she reached to pull it off. I scrambled backward, clutching the small bag with my bound hands.

"You must wear a thrall's torque," my new mistress insisted. "You can't wear that thing, too." She reached again for my amulet, but I bared my teeth and growled like a wolf.

She slapped me hard across the face. I gasped more in surprise than pain.

"If I tell you to give it up, you must give it up," she continued, nearly growling herself. "Snorri, remove that thing from her."

The boy pulled the thong over my head and pried my hands from the pouch. All the while, Muirenn tutted softly. "Maybe it's sacred to her. Like a Thor's hammer?"

Freydis fingered an iron pendant around her own throat, shaped like a tiny ulu with an elongated handle, before dumping my amulets on her outstretched palm. My whole life lay on her white flesh like old bones discarded on the ice: the strange quartz blade, Kiasik's seal carving, Ataata's blackened bear claw, the tuft of Singarti's white fur, the penis-bone walrus and its mate—Brandr's wooden carving with its two perfect tusks. Freydis ran her thumb thoughtfully over the spiral whittled into the wooden walrus's back.

A gust of wind caught the tuft of wolf fur. I gasped and reached out as the ball of white flew from Freydis's hand, hung suspended for a moment in midair, and then floated over the side of the boat. The ocean wind tore it apart, each bright hair glinting for a moment before drifting out of sight. I dug my nails into my palms to stop myself from leaping at the stormy-eyed Norsewoman and ripping my other possessions from her grasp.

Freydis ignored my distress. Calmly she returned the other items to the pouch and tied it to the thin chain she wore draped across her chest between two large, oval brooches. A host of other small bags and strange metal tools hung from the chain. My history, my strength, my life—just one more ornament for her to flaunt.

In place of my amulet pouch, Snorri tied the strange new cord tight and high around my neck. Freydis placed one finger lightly on the stone bead. "You belong to me now, skraeling. This is the rune for my name, so everyone will know." She settled back on her heels and studied me for a moment. I breathed slowly, trying to will myself to look docile.

Finally she nodded at Muirenn. The old woman untied my hands.

I rubbed at the raw skin of my wrists for a moment. Then my mistress handed me a spindle. Thus began my first lesson.

It had never occurred to me that women's work could be so hard.

I'd learned to hunt and fish with Ataata—even learned to sew and cook with Uimaitok and Kidla. But nothing had prepared me for learning to spin.

An Inuit woman's tasks were more complicated than a Norse-woman's: the threefold looping of a waterproof stitch, the careful crimp of a boot sole, the perfect pressure of ulu on hide. I had never mastered the skills, but I had learned the basics, perhaps because I understood their importance. Spinning, on the other hand, seemed a useless exercise. Why work so hard to create woolen thread when fur and sinew were so much warmer than cloth? Still, I wanted to learn so I could prove my worth. Yet no matter how I tried, no matter how patiently Muirenn demonstrated her technique, I sim-ply couldn't keep the spindle going the right way. Before I could stop it, it would spin backward, unraveling whatever short length of thread I'd managed to create. Over and over the thread would break, and the spindle whorl would clatter to the deck. What little I spun was rough and lumpy.

At the end of our lesson, with my arms aching from holding up the thread, my fingers greasy and covered in blisters, I'd created no more than an arm's length of unusable thread. I feared Freydis might toss me overboard right then. Strangely, she merely smiled. "I suppose you hunt better than you spin. I saw you throw that spear. You almost struck Ingharr."

She rose to her feet and deftly started her own whorl spinning.

"Tomorrow we'll work more." She gestured toward my spindle, miming the action so I could understand. "Keep practicing."

She left to walk the ship, her spindle swaying before her while she checked on her small flock of sheep. Muirenn stayed beside me, one eye on my work and one on her own. Her gnarled fingers flew as she spun a thin, strong thread. Snorri sat stiffly nearby, leaning against the ship's side with his spear. He was no sailor; guard duty at least gave him a purpose. Occasionally he spoke with Bjarni, a blond, burly young bowman tasked with watching the shore for attack. Otherwise, Snorri usually kept to himself. When Freydis left, I noticed him reach tentatively for his throat. Muirenn noticed, too.

"Don't worry, my boy," she whispered. "The mistress can't know what you don't tell her."

Snorri blushed furiously. "I don't know what you're..."

"I'm too old for secrets, child."

"Do you think she..."

Muirenn chuckled softly and ran her fingers nonchalantly down her thread, checking its smoothness through touch rather than sight. "Don't worry. Freydis barely knows your name."

"You won't tell her, will you?"

"What purpose would that serve? I may be an old thrall, and you may be a young freeman, but we both know better than to make the mistress mad. You knew when you came aboard that your kind weren't welcome here, and you came anyway. You're a brave lad, or a foolish one. Be warned, Snorri Ulfarsson—Freydis Eriksdottir has eyes as sharp as an eagle's. What's around your neck should stay out of sight."

Intrigued and confused, I glanced back and forth between them, my spinning momentarily forgotten. Sure enough, the thread snarled wickedly around my dowel. My quick grunt of dismay attracted Muirenn's attention; she turned to help me, her conversation with the boy seemingly forgotten. But I saw Snorri clutch at some object beneath his shirt.

I watched him more closely after that. When he bent to retie my hands for the night, I glanced beneath the collar of his tunic. "Sorry, skraeling," he muttered, tying the ropes as loosely as he might to afford me some comfort.

He was soon asleep, but I lay awake, unable to forget the hidden pendant I'd seen around his neck: a small cross with four arms of equal length. From Brandr's descriptions, I recognized the carven figure of a man with arms outstretched upon the wood. The Christ.

I tried to sleep, matching my breathing to Snorri's, but my mind spun like the whorl, faster and faster until my fears for the future became a tangled nest, then lurched in the opposite direction, unfurling into the past—then knotting once more. I plucked at my blankets with my bound hands, trying in vain to wrap the coverings more tightly around me. I longed for White Paw's warm flank against my back. As I finally drifted in and out of a restless sleep, I was plagued with vague nightmares of drowning and death— usually my own, sometimes Kiasik's. Brandr appeared only as a dim figure on the periphery, unable to help me, unable to hear my burbling screams.

Right before I awoke in the weak dawn light, a thin, black-haired man staggered through my dream. He walked across empty, pale sand that glared as bright as snow in a relentless summer Sun. A wreath of thorns drew trickles of blood across his brown forehead.

An instant later, I saw him pinned to a cross of wood. He hung there, his life leaking out through the bloody holes in his hands and his side. Yet all the while, he smiled softly.

As if he knew something that his tormentors did not.

CHAPTER FORTY

$\downarrow$

As the days passed, I succeeded in transforming myself into something resembling a Norsewoman. But inside, I resented the ever-present spindles that branded me a woman as surely as my ulu had. My manhood, so carefully cherished through my long sojourn with Brandr, was stripped away once more.

Still, my plan was working. Snorri and Muirenn still kept a watchful eye on me when I walked along the ship's deck, but they no longer bound my hands when I slept. I listened as I walked; I peered into every corner of the ship. No sign of Kiasik. But I'd heard the men speak of a second boat—the larger knarr stolen from Finnbogi the Icelander. Somewhere behind us, it followed our course north. I had to believe my milk-brother was on board. It was all that kept me going.

As I watched the sea behind us, searching for the missing knarr, I kept an eye on the distant shore as well, searching for signs of my past—and my future. The others thought it an unrelieved coast of dark trees. Markland. But to me every landmark emerged heavy with memory. My past unspooled before me: the long days walking across the earth alone, then with my pups—then with my Viking.

From the ocean, the land looked different than it had from onshore, but certain landmarks were unmistakable: the shape of the mountains, the curve of a bay, the shadow cast by a steep-sided island. We saw no sign of the red men's camp where I'd first shared Brandr's dreams—it was too far inland—but after only a few days, the forests dissolved, and we passed the place where my friend had first arrived with a brown bear fast on his heels.

Soon after, the familiar whale's carcass, now stripped of every morsel of meat by scavenging birds and foxes, appeared onshore. Its snow-covered ribs marked the site of the massacre; its long, sharp jaw pointed toward me like an accusing finger as I sailed past on the wooden ship, traveling amid enemies.

What had taken me so many agonizing moons to traverse on foot now passed by in a matter of days. Soon we would be in the place the Norse called Helluland—Land of Flat Stones. Home.

We left the coast behind and entered the strait. What had been melting drift ice and wide leads when I crossed with Issuk was now open ocean, broken only by floating patches of grease ice. But as we neared land, mush ice formed along the shore. The next morning, wide disks of ice floated around the boat, man-size flower petals strewn on the sea. As a child, I'd thought one could leap from disk to disk, like a giant bestriding tiny ice islands. Now, as I watched the knarr's hull plow through the white circles, I knew the great sea would soon freeze solid around us. There were no sleds or dogs on board to cross the ice. *These Norse are as arrogant as Issuk*, I thought. *Either the ice will rip holes in their boat and we will drown, or it will trap us until spring and we will starve.*

Ingharr ordered the sail taken down and sent the thralls to man the oars. The knarr moved more slowly after that, carefully wending its way through the open water while the freemen pushed aside the pans with long poles.

The farther north we rowed, the more I felt Taqqiq's eye upon me. Malina walked along the mountaintops and across the waves only briefly each day before sinking once again. And as she weakened, her brother's lust to catch her only increased. Every day, he remained overhead a little longer, ruling the sky at night and lurking in Malina's wake for much of the day. I felt his stare like an icy chill as he watched for his chance to finally destroy me.

Like me, Freydis often seemed haunted. She, too, kept watch on the shoreline, either from fear or from longing. As the air grew colder, her mood darkened. The thralls got the brunt of her ire as they stumbled about the treacherously rocking ship, trying to obey her orders. I could tell she resented her lack of control over this floating household. Sweaty sailors constantly got in her way, and the pitching of the ship could snarl even her spinning. Yet at times, when she stood at the prow with her red hair whipping around her face, she seemed almost peaceful. Some spark of her famous father's Viking spirit burned bright in this woman.

Freemen such as Ingharr stayed out of her way, busying themselves with the tasks of sailing and navigating. Those who were useless on board, such as Freydis's lumbering husband, Thorvard, or one-armed Magnor, stayed seated on the sea chests, repairing weapons if they were hardworking, or telling stories if they were not. A good number of them had little strength for either task—thralls and freemen alike were often sick with the motion of the boat. When the wind calmed, the whole place stank of vomit.

I scoffed at their weakness; the motion of the waves comforted me like the lapping of a mother's womb. But I had other problems. The strange milk foods I'd grudgingly accepted played havoc with my bowels. I didn't understand how these Vikings ate such large chunks of hardened cheese and drank bowl upon bowl of sour, watery *skyr*. Were they babes at the breast to guzzle milk so greedily? When I ate more than a few bites, my innards clenched and roiled all night. Eventually the cramps plagued me so much that just the sight of sheep, to say nothing of the smell of milk, made me ill.

Finally, one morning when Muirenn came to me with my portion of skyr, I placed a hand on my stomach and groaned, shaking my head. Freydis arrived later to check on my progress. "Muirenn says you won't eat. I didn't spend my time teaching you to be useful so that you could starve yourself to death." She turned to the old thrall. "Try some meat."

My mouth watered at the words, and when Muirenn offered me a sliver of dried mutton I gobbled it down and grinned. It was no caribou meat, and it would've been better raw, but it was still the best thing I'd eaten in days.

Snorri was livid. "And if I decide I'd prefer a nice morsel of meat to a bowl of old skyr and a flake of stockfish, do I just have to ask nicely?"

The old woman ignored him and patted my head. "I've never seen the girl smile so broad. Isn't that worth a little meat?"

Snorri merely rolled his eyes.

Muirenn looked to her mistress. "Maybe we'll be landing soon, and there'll be fresh meat for all."

Freydis looked up at the sky. Her voice was distant, as if she spoke to the clouds or the winds or the spirits themselves. "The air gets colder. The Sun sinks faster every day."

"The ice will only get worse the farther north we go," Muirenn noted, echoing my own concerns. "We'll be trapped until the spring."

"Trapped?" Snorri asked.

Freydis's attention snapped toward him. "The gods keep open a path for us. We will make it home." As always, Erik the Red's daughter sounded completely confident. Snorri and Muirenn looked far less assured.

On Freydis's orders, Ingharr steered the boat ever northward, just out of reach of the landfast ice quickly forming along the rocky coast. Though their home in Greenland lay straight across the sea from the northern tip of Markland, they had to follow the coast in order to navigate, which meant traveling past Helluland before they could head east. We rowed without stopping to collect fresh water, cook food over a fire on the shore, or sleep on solid ground. Only once did we pause—to welcome the second knarr, which finally appeared on the southern horizon.

Heart racing, I hurried to the rail as the larger boat pulled close. A small crew of Greenlanders worked the oars. A grizzled man with a missing eye stood with his hands on the steering oar. I remembered him vaguely from Brandr's memories: Olfun. The one who'd so admired Ingharr's skill at spread-eagling the painted man.

I looked past him to the cargo hold between the decks, desperate for a glimpse of Kiasik's black hair, his sparkling eyes. But I saw only plunder: towering piles of tree trunks and great mounds of pelts.

My knees weakened. Only my grip on the rail kept me from sinking to the deck. *Kiasik is dead.* I thought the words but could not bring myself to say them aloud. The Norse wouldn't have known to lay his body on the earth, where the birds could take his soul to the sky. They would've thrown him overboard. *Do you live now as Sanna's captive beneath the waves?* I wondered. *Or did Sila take pity on you and lift you into the stars?* I squeezed my eyes shut, sending a silent prayer to all the spirits who haunted me. *Do not punish Kiasik for my failings. Let his soul be born anew. Let him return to the family that loves him.*

When I opened my eyes again, I saw only the massive piles of furs, each mound as big as an iglu. I had always believed that the spirits of the hunted animals would return to earth somewhere else, just as an Inuk's did. But I'd never seen such slaughter. Bear, wolf, caribou, fox. Enough to feed many families from one Great Darkness to the next. *The Norse break every rule. Their very presence rips through the aglirutiit that bind our world together.* I felt suddenly sure that even the spirits could not overcome such wanton destruction. The animals would not return. And neither would Kiasik.

From that day on, I lived only for revenge. The new knarr fell behind again, moving slowly through the spreading ice with its heavy cargo and undermanned oars. I could rarely make out more than a bright speck on the horizon. Freydis didn't wait for it. She pushed the men as if the spirits themselves goaded her on. I could've told her it was hopeless.

My prediction came true—more swiftly than I'd even imagined. The ice appeared not with its usual slow crawl, but with a sudden, vicious lunge. I woke shaking beneath a frost-rimed blanket. The sailors looked like old men, their once-bright hair limned in white. The ship sat unnaturally still. I rose to my knees and peered over the side.

The cold had arrived so quickly that the waves themselves had frozen; a great swell of clear ice streaked with seaweed lay off the bow. To the east, a vast expanse of white stretched as far as the eye could see, trapping the knarr in place. To the south, the Icelanders' ship sat motionless on the horizon. To the west, a snowcapped mountain rose above the shore.

I caught my breath, blinking in astonishment. I knew the shape of that mountain. Even from far out at sea, I recognized its silhouette—large and square like the head of a whale, a tall spur of rock rising from its flank like a fluke, then tapering down to disappear in a deep valley to the south. I'd grown up in its shadow. I'd journeyed through its valleys on wolf's paws and soared above its peak on raven's wings.

I clutched the blanket closer to my shoulders, chilled now by more than just the bitter dawn air.

My visions of revenge were forgotten. Once more I heard Nua's screams and Kidla's pleas. I saw Ingharr's foot crash upon the baby boy's head. And threaded through the memories of the past—a vision of the future. One I couldn't banish no matter how hard I tried: Ingharr Ketilsson running toward a domed qarmaq with yellow hair flying and sword raised high.

And Puja standing helpless and trembling before him.

CHAPTER
FORTY-ONE

⚡

"Come!" Ingharr shouted to the gaping sailors. "Looks like we're not getting home after all. So unless you want to stay on this boat all winter, we need to set up camp. Throw down the ladder and get going."

My only thought was of escape. Even with the whale mountain in sight, my family's camp still lay several days' travel away. I'd need a weapon and food for the journey, but as soon as I could gather supplies, I'd run. I'd make my way to Puja and the others and lead them far from shore. We wouldn't return until the ice melted and the Norse left.

Though clearly unnerved, the men followed Ingharr's orders. Bjarni, the brawny freeman who never went anywhere without his bow, swung over the rail to test the ice. Finding it solid, he whistled in awe. "I've never seen a cold snap come up so fast."

Magnor leaned his one arm on the rail to peer over. "We're like flies in amber." Only I was close enough to hear him murmur, "And just as dead."

Across the ice, the crew of the Icelandic knarr left most of their precious cargo on board, but they unearthed a large, strange sled from the ship's hold, piled high with supplies. The Norsemen called it a *wagon*. It rolled off the ship on circular disks that spun like stone whorls—quite impressive until these *wheels* slid uselessly across the ice. It took three men to keep the wagon going in the right direction.

Among the bustle, I was momentarily forgotten. I headed toward the food supply, thinking to steal some dried stockfish for my escape, but Muirenn stopped me. "You can help me across the ice," she said, linking her arm through mine. Despite her fragility, she dug her fingers into my forearm like a bird's talons. "Why don't you carry my pack?" She pushed the large bundle of blankets and clothing toward me with a sweet smile, but her eyes gleamed knowingly. "My old bones can barely shoulder the load anymore."

Grudgingly, I hefted her heavy bundle. I would've rather carried meat, but I trusted that once ashore, I could steal a knife or a spear. With a strip of cloth stolen from Muirenn's pack, I could at least fashion a snare. *I will not starve. I will not slow. I will make it home.*

The morning sunlight created a thin sheen of melt on the ice. Muirenn clung to me, fighting to stay upright. Around us, men stumbled to the ground regularly, their boots slipping out from under them. Freydis clutched a cloak of white bear fur across her breast, her chin high even as she staggered and slid. No one dared say aloud what we were all thinking: she'd been wrong about reaching Greenland that winter. Whatever gods had opened the ice before had now turned their backs on her.

Eyeing her mistress, Muirenn sighed. "She's regretting having left Leifsbudir, mark my words. Now we'll have to build a whole new winter camp and be trapped here until the summer thaw when we might've stayed cozy right where we were." From the barely restrained muttering around us, Muirenn wasn't the only one missing the warm longhouse they'd left behind.

Before long, we reached the beach. The Norse scrambled gratefully up the snow-covered slopes. Many of the thralls simply sank down, oblivious to the cold seeping through their garments.

"There's no time to rest," Freydis called angrily. "We must find a place to camp before it grows dark." For the first time since my capture, she wore a wimple that tied tight beneath her chin; without her flying red hair, she looked diminished, like a lamp wick turned to cold ash. I wondered how much longer her men would listen to her foolish ideas.

As Malina rolled across the sky, we came to a sheltered spot among the foothills. After a short consultation with Ingharr and her husband, Freydis signaled a stop. Standing with her hands on her hips, her cloak thrown back to show off her fine chains and brooches, she spoke to her men.

"We Greenlanders will live no longer in Leifsbudir. This is *Freydisbudir.*"

I could sense their displeasure with her arrogance, but they obeyed when she ordered half of them to erect cloth tents as temporary dwellings and the rest to start building the sod longhouse that would shelter them for the winter.

While the freemen and thralls got to work, supervised by Olfun, the one-eyed man I'd seen at the Icelanders' steering oar, Muirenn led me to a low rise overlooking the campsite. She handed me a basket of wool and a spindle and admonished me to stay put. By this time, I could acknowledge my understanding of a few words, much like a puppy, and *stay* was one of them. But as she moved away, I had no intention of obeying.

I forced myself to breathe, to wait until Muirenn was out of sight.

Consumed by thoughts of escape, I almost didn't hear the man striding toward me up the hill. Ingharr had avoided me since our first too-intimate encounter, but now he tromped up the slope to my overlook, his face pink with anger. "Skraeling! Who told you to sit up here like a queen while the rest of us work? Come! Up!"

I tried to look confused, but he saw right through me.

"I know you know what *come* means." He reached down and grabbed my wrist to drag me to my feet. Last time he'd handled me, my hands and ankles were bound. No longer.

I stood up just as he pulled and let his own momentum drag him backward. I slipped easily from his grasp as he fell awkwardly on his side—the same side I'd once wounded with Patik's harpoon. I looked at the dull gray sword belted at his waist. With such a weapon, I could hunt, I could make an iglu, I could survive the trip to my family's camp.

And I could kill the murderer before me.

I lunged for its hilt, but Ingharr lurched away, clutching at the old injury in his side. He swatted at me as he might at a gnat. I ducked his blow and skipped to the side, hoping to circle around and tackle him to the ground.

I tripped on the hem of my long dress and fell to my knees instead.

Ingharr grabbed my waist, hauling me off the ground. He swung me over his shoulder feetfirst. I hammered my fist into his stomach, but before I could land a second blow, he snatched my arm with his free hand and pinned it behind my back until it almost ripped from its socket. He galloped down the hill, every pounding step sending waves of pain down my wrenched arm.

For a moment, I saw only the snow-covered rocks beneath his booted feet. Then I was sailing through the air, flung to the ground like a caribou carcass. I tried to break my fall, but my numb arm crumpled, and I skidded on the slick ground, ice burning my cheek.

"Here's your skraeling, Freydis. I told you before to get rid of her. She tripped me. Struck me. Looked ready to kill me." He drew the iron blade I'd tried so hard to steal. "Let me kill her. One less mouth to feed this winter."

I dared a glance up at Freydis. She'd protected me before—maybe she would again. But as I looked at her stony gray eyes, Brandr's memory flashed before me. Freydis had murdered the Icelanders' women with her own hands and without hesitation. The moment I got in her way, she'd do the same to me.

"Stupid girl," she spat. "You may not understand much of our tongue, but I thought you weren't quite so foolish." She made a sound of disgust deep in her throat. "Do what you want, Ingharr."

The yellow-haired man leveled the tip of his sword at my throat.

Muirenn threw herself at Freydis's feet. "The girl didn't understand, I'm sure! She doesn't know a thrall's place, but she can be taught. She picked up the spinning quick enough. Please, give her one more chance. I'll take responsibility."

"You already had responsibility, old woman, and you've already failed."

Ingharr drew back his sword. One blow. That was all it would take to sever my neck.

A gentle breeze fluttered against my cheek. *Sila*, I thought, suddenly aware of Its presence. *You alone have not abandoned me.*

The breeze blew some of the anger from Freydis's face. "Hold, Ingharr," she said. "No food for three days. To teach her obedience. But, Muirenn, if she ever attacks one of us again, she will die. And *you* will be severely punished. I'm tired of dealing with disobedient thralls."

Ingharr lowered his sword with a grunt. "And what of my recompense? I've been injured by your property."

Freydis bristled. "Recompense?"

Ingharr would not be cowed. "In Greenland, I could take you to the Althing. I demand payment."

Freydis tossed her head. "First put away your sword, Ketilsson. Do you think to threaten me?"

The baleful look in his eye spoke volumes. I waited for Freydis to back down. For her to relinquish her power to this man who thought himself more suited to rule. Instead, she simply narrowed her eyes and said, "Need I remind you that *I* am the leader of this expedition? That *I* paid for this ship and secured the other? That *I* fought off the skraeling band that attacked Leifsbudir while you were playing in the woods?"

Ingharr's lip curled in a snarl—but he sheathed his sword.

Freydis gave him a curt nod, their bloodless battle over. A clever leader does more than punish those who rebel; she rewards those who obey. "I've taught the thrall to spin," she said, gesturing toward me, "but she's clumsy and slow. I have little need of her. As a sign of my goodwill, I give her to you as your ambatt." Muirenn uttered a stifled cry, but Freydis cut her off. "I'll hear no sound from you, old woman. I've spared the skraeling's life."

"That's a poor gift indeed, Freydis Eriksdottir," Ingharr grumbled. "She's too ugly for me to bed." He looked at the redheaded woman with one brow raised. "I'd rather a true Norsewoman."

Freydis stared at the man as if he were meat gone bad. "For too long, you've prowled the ship like a hound after a bitch in heat. Take what I offer. I'll give you nothing else."

Muirenn looked at me, shaking her head sadly. I read the message in her gaze: *I know you understand. You know what awaits you. And for that I'm sorry.*

As Ingharr hauled me away, the old woman held my eyes, a silent line of comfort passing between us. The tall Norseman's fingers bit into my upper arm as he dragged me toward the center of the camp. "First you work. Then later—we'll see if you're worth bedding."

Young Snorri stood near the gang of poorly clad, skinny men digging fruitlessly at the frozen earth with iron tools. Their torques, some of metal, some as crude as the rope and stone around my own neck, branded them thralls. They'd scraped away the top layer of thick snow—but the earth beneath was hard as stone. What were they doing? I knew Brandr's people usually made their homes of turf blocks, but surely even a Norseman knew he couldn't dig up the ground in winter. They were wasting their time.

"Help the thralls dig," Ingharr ordered, shoving me toward the workers. "If we don't get some houses up soon we'll all freeze. Here, Snorri, give her a pick."

The curly-headed boy passed me an iron tool with a long

wooden handle. Ingharr motioned that I should copy the other slaves. "Go on. Dig so you—"

He stopped midthought, the blood draining from his face as he looked me up and down. I stood with my feet planted, the sharp tool clenched tight in my fists, glaring at him. For the first time since I'd been with the Norse, I held a weapon. I had little hope of escape—not with so many of my captors surrounding me—but at that moment I was willing to kill Ingharr and take my chances. And he knew it.

He moved a hand slowly to his sword hilt. The iron pick felt unwieldy in my arms, its heavy head pulling toward the earth. I longed for a well-balanced spear. Or the sharp steel knife I'd lost in the waves the day of my capture.

Ingharr took a step back, his eyes never leaving mine, his hand still resting on his sword. The caution slowly drained from his expression. He smiled thinly, his gaze narrowing like that of a fox about to pounce.

He raised his voice so all the surrounding thralls would hear. "This woman has already disobeyed me once today. For that, she has lost her meals. Now she threatens me. She'd rather fight than work. Well, who said I wasn't a generous master? Go on, skraeling! Fight me, if that's what you want."

"She doesn't know what you're saying," Snorri interjected anxiously. "She doesn't speak Norse."

"Perhaps not, but she understands. Look at the fight in her eye." With a keening scrape of metal, Ingharr drew his sword from its scabbard and took a step toward me. "Come on, kunta."

"Ingharr—" Snorri began hesitantly.

"Stay out of this, Ulfarsson."

I raised the pick higher to defend myself, hoping his blade wouldn't sever the wooden handle with one blow.

"*Omat?*"

I started at the sound of my name.

One of the thralls, scrawny and stooped, stood before me, his face hidden beneath a thin hood. He must have come on the Icelanders' knarr, because I hadn't seen him before; I would've recognized the motley assortment of colored patches on his ragged cloak. He pushed back his hood.

"Kiasik..."

Ingharr reached forward and grabbed the pick from my unresisting hands. "So these two skraelings know each other!" He laughed, the sound conjuring memories of slaughter. "Now I know a better punishment for her."

He strode quickly to my milk-brother and struck him across the face with the flat of his sword.

Kiasik crashed to the ground, not even trying to brace his fall. He lay with eyes closed, blood seeping from his torn cheek, an eerie echo of how I'd last seen him on the day the giants sailed out of the mist.

Ingharr raised his sword again. I threw myself across Kiasik's limp form.

"Don't touch him!"

Too late, I realized I'd shouted in Norse.

CHAPTER FORTY-TWO

♪

Been playing us for fools, huh?" Ingharr grunted. "I told you, Snorri, she knows more than you think."

"I guess she picked it up on the boat."

I rose to my feet. My small frame was a poor shield for Kiasik's prone form, but I would defend him with my fingernails alone if need be.

Ingharr shifted his grip on his sword, ready to strike if I made another move. "How much do you understand?" he growled.

With all my energy divided between him and Kiasik, I only dimly sensed the gathering crowd of thralls and freemen. Dark-green cloth fluttered in the corner of my vision; Freydis was here.

"I understand everything, Ingharr," I said coolly. "And if you strike my brother again, I will kill you."

Snarling, he lunged toward me.

"Wait!" Freydis thrust her way through the crowd as Ingharr stumbled to a halt. Unarmed, she stood fearlessly between us. "Tell me, skraeling! How do you speak our language?"

I looked the taller woman straight in the eye. I would not cower.

I, too, had been a leader of men. "I am a great seer among my people. Our gods taught me your tongue."

Ingharr was not impressed. "All the more reason to let me kill her, Freydis. If what she says is true, she's dangerous."

The Norsewoman dismissed him with a flick of one long-fingered hand. Her eyes pierced mine. "How do I know you're telling the truth?"

I shook my head, the gesture reminding me of Brandr. I must keep him safe. "You don't. But how else would I know Norse? You really think I could pick it up from living with you for so short a time? Even an Inuk is not that smart."

A murmur of astonishment rippled through the crowd. Freydis merely smiled. She looked as if she might even laugh. "Which gods have taught you so well?"

"Ones not unlike your own. Gods of ice and fire. Thunder and wave. More powerful than any Christ."

Freydis's eyes flashed. "What do you know of the Christ?"

"There are Christians among your own people." I heard a hiss of breath behind me, but I couldn't worry about Snorri now. "My gods warned me about them." I raised my voice, wanting all the gathered freemen to hear. "The Christ approaches these very shores." For the first time, I saw fear enter Freydis's eyes. "Don't worry." I smiled tightly. "My land is too cold for a desert man. He won't survive long."

Hands on hips, Freydis returned my grim smile. "Come, skraeling. Bring your...brother, is it?...to my tent. We must speak more of this."

Ingharr placed his hand on her arm as she turned to go. He spoke with barely concealed rage. "Have you forgotten you said I could use her as my ambatt?"

She laid her own slim fingers on his meaty ones and looked up at him with soft eyes. So—Freydis ruled her men with more tools than one. "Be patient."

I bent to help Kiasik. Too rushed to examine him closely, I couldn't tell the extent of his injuries, only that he seemed to have shrunken like a hide left too long in the sun. "It's me," I whispered in our tongue. "Please wake up."

His eyes fluttered open, and he tried to push himself upright. His elbows wobbled and bent; he collapsed again. I slipped my shoulder beneath his arm, but still he listed to one side, dragging me down. To my surprise, Muirenn appeared, hoisting him up with unlikely strength. Together we hobbled after Freydis with our limp burden, leaving the other Norse dumbfounded in our wake.

Inside the cloth tent, Freydis gestured toward her own low pallet. "Put him there." Only one other item furnished the space: a tall wooden frame strung with hanging threads, each kept taut by a dangling rock. Woven cloth in stripes of yellow and white stretched across the threads. A loom.

Carefully I laid Kiasik down on the pallet and wiped the blood from his head. The new injury was minor compared to the old. A deep, still-angry scar ran from his temple to his jaw, snaking through a field of newer swellings that distorted his mouth. Livid bruises mottled his skeletal face, each a different shade of purple. Such injuries, at least, would heal in time. The searing heat of his flesh worried me more. The patches of skin that showed through the layer of filth were corpse gray. The swollen pouches beneath his eyes were nearly black, the skin of his lips cracked and torn. Kiasik was dying.

I reached instinctively for his amulet pouch, thinking to summon his protecting spirits—but he wore only a thrall's torque around his neck.

"What have you done to him?" I demanded.

Freydis shrugged. "Ingharr captured him. What he does to his thrall is his business."

"Yet you just protected us from him."

"So far."

I turned away at the implicit threat, unwilling to let this woman distract me from my brother's pain. Freydis and I would have our test of wills. Of that I had no doubt. For now, there were more important things to attend to.

"Omat?" Kiasik crawled his fingers up my arm.

"Yes…yes, it's me," I said hoarsely in my own tongue.

"How? I don't understand…"

"I came for you. Did you think I'd let them take you without a fight?"

I thought I'd be embarrassed to have failed so utterly in his rescue, but relief overcame my shame. He wasn't dead yet. There was still hope. And we were together once more.

In all our winters together, I'd never seen Kiasik weep. Not once. Not when Ipaq died or Ataata. Not even as a child, when Puja scolded him or he fell on the rocks or he almost got gored by the caribou bull. But now his tears sliced tracks through the grime. "I—I don't deserve that from you."

"We will always save each other," I insisted. "You told me that, remember?" I felt myself once more his younger brother, always loving him, regardless of his faults. I wanted nothing more than to clasp him in my arms, yet I couldn't show such emotion in front of the Norsewomen watching us from across the tent. I took his hand in my own, channeling all my love and strength through our pressed palms.

Kiasik wiped the tears from his face, smearing blood and dirt into his mustache. "What happened to the others? Issuk—"

"All dead."

He paused for a moment. I didn't want him to ask, but I knew he would. "Kidla, too?"

"Yes."

He didn't cry again. He merely blinked up at the ceiling, his face turned to stone.

"How did you find me?" he asked finally.

"A friend showed me the way."

"And you speak their language."

"The same friend taught me."

"The Wolf Spirit? You can call upon him again?" he asked hopefully. "Will he help us escape?"

"No," I conceded. "But these Norse don't know that. I told them I'm an angakkuq, full of mysterious power."

His brow furrowed. "You tried this once before, Little Brother. With Issuk. It didn't work then."

Little Brother. That lessened the sting of his criticism.

"Trust me." I squeezed his hand. Despite the chill inside the tent, his grip was as hot as sun-warmed stone.

Freydis spoke over my shoulder. "What are you saying to him?"

"That I'll make sure he's not beaten again."

"Then you lie. Ingharr sent him to the other knarr as a rower. He told Olfun to beat him if he didn't work hard enough. If Ingharr chooses to have his thrall beaten, he may. If I tell you to serve as his ambatt, you will."

"Then why am I here with you and not in Ingharr's bed?" I retorted.

She raised a pale eyebrow at my audacity. "You say you're a seer."

"Yes."

"You speak to the gods. To your own gods." She paused for a moment, eyeing me carefully. "Could you speak to ours?"

I must tread very cautiously here, I thought. Kiasik was right; the last time I tried and failed to speak to the spirits, I was forced from my home. *If I disappoint Freydis, my fate will be far worse . . . and I may get Kiasik killed as well.*

"I've never spoken to your gods, so I don't know," I admitted. "But I could try. What would you ask of them?"

Freydis moved to the tall loom, her back straight. She reached for the shuttle and passed it through the threads as she spoke—but not before I saw the sudden tremor in her hands. Freydis, always so controlled, was scared. I could use that to my advantage.

"If you speak of what I'm about to tell you," she began, her voice clipped, "I will kill your brother. Ingharr's thrall or not, I shall kill him myself."

I looked to Muirenn.

Freydis followed my glance. "The old woman knows. She nursed me as a babe. She can be trusted. I cannot trust you. But know that if you speak to the others, neither of you will survive the night."

I nodded solemnly, my hand damp in Kiasik's feverish grip.

He propped himself on an elbow. "What did she say?"

"I'll explain later," I cautioned. "My brother doesn't know your tongue," I continued in Norse. "You may speak freely."

Freydis picked up a long piece of ivory shaped like a sword. It looked good in her hand, as if she were born to be a warrior, not a weaver. She knocked the threads upward, tightening the weave before picking up the shuttle once more. The constant action of the loom calmed her trembling, just as an angakkuq's drum might do for me.

"I dreamed of Vinland before I ever saw it," she began. "Many years ago, a ship blew off course and spotted a forested shore. When the crew brought word back home, my brother Leif dared make the voyage to seek out this new land. He returned two years ago, speaking of fields of golden grain, rich purple grapes, forests of towering pine—things never seen in Greenland. You must understand that we are a family of voyagers. My father, Erik, left Iceland and discovered Greenland. Leif has traveled beyond the boundaries of the known world. Many of my kinsmen are merchants, sailing to Englaland and Northway and beyond, returning with tales of lands far and wide. Yet *I* had never left Greenland."

She thrust the threads upward with her sword again, as if to push away the words. "The dreams started coming that first night after Leif's return. I saw golden fields and thick forests—or at least, what I imagined those things must look like. Visions from the gods, I thought. Why else would they haunt me night after night? In my sleep, I walked on the Vinland shore, the sun hot on my neck. Then I'd wake in my freezing longhouse, still sweating from my dream. I convinced my husband to allow me to organize this voyage. I gathered men and women and thralls so I might reap the rich Vinland harvests and bring them back for the glory and wealth of Greenland."

And for your own, I thought. *I know what sort of men and women you gathered—I know what happened to them*. Still, I held my peace.

"Leif had lied, of course. I wasn't surprised—men can't be trusted. Vinland has forests, but no grapes. Still, the wood and furs alone will make me rich. I should've been content—I even thought I might settle there forever, shipping our goods across the ocean and living luxuriously on the profits. But then the red skraelings came."

Her knuckles whitened on the shuttle. "At first I tried to trade with them, but my foolish men killed two of them in a quarrel. That was the beginning of our troubles. A blood feud. I cursed my men's stupidity, but then Thor appeared in my dreams. He said he *wanted* me to fight. The Aesir wanted Vinland for themselves, and no red men would stand in their way. No Christians, either. I did as he asked. I fought off the skraelings; then I cleansed our ranks of Christians."

She makes murder sound as easy as scraping fat from a hide, I thought, remembering the tall pile of corpses in Brandr's tale.

"I thought that would be enough..." Freydis faltered for the first time, the shuttle striking the edge of the frame and slipping from her fingers, the thread unspooling. She bent to retrieve it, deftly rewinding the wool, using the excuse to pause for a few long breaths, as if summoning her courage for the rest of the tale.

"My dreams returned," she continued finally. Her fingers moved slowly now, wandering across the threads as her mind wandered through the past. "This time, blood drifted through the Vinland forests like snow. I ran, chased by slavering wolves. Frost Giants stormed through the trees, and the ground itself rose up to destroy me. One of my own men, a Greenland Viking whom I'd come to trust, led an army of skraelings against me, crying out curses upon the Aesir. And all around, my men died. Every night, without respite, the same nightmare. A new sign from the gods. I knew that to stay in Vinland would be death."

"Who was this Viking who fought against you in your dreams?" I asked, a sudden dread raising the hair on my arms.

Freydis shook her head angrily, as if to banish the memory. "He no longer matters. He ran away like a coward. He couldn't have survived alone in the wilderness." She spoke as if to convince herself. "He must be dead by now."

I swallowed. Brandr wasn't merely the hapless victim of Freydis's rage; he was the enemy that strode through her nightmares—and he didn't even know it.

She continued her tale. "Winter approached—I knew we should wait until spring to travel. But I had to obey the gods' warning and go back to Greenland. The men didn't believe my tales of skraeling armies and Frost Giants. They thought me mad—perhaps they still do. But my dreams were clear, and they kept coming. Night after sleepless night. So we set off, and when the sea stayed open for us, even as winter descended, I knew I'd made the right choice. But now the ocean freezes around us and stops our journey entirely."

She paused and looked up from her loom to stare at me with stormy eyes. I tried to look solemn and wise, when in truth I had no idea what she wanted from me. When she spoke again, her voice trembled. "Was I wrong? Did the Aesir want me to stay in Vinland? I've always been a faithful follower of Thor...and yet I have no answers." She clasped the hammer pendant around her neck. "Tell me what the gods intend." She did not beg as an Inuk might entreat an angakkuq. Freydis Eriksdottir never begged. She commanded.

Even if I'd still possessed my magic, I couldn't help her. What did I know of Odin and Thor besides the stories Brandr had told me? Still, she'd given me a sort of power—one I wouldn't fail to wield.

"I will speak with your gods," I said. "But only if you will let me care for my brother." Give something, ask for something else.

I'd learned such bargaining tactics from her. "And you will make sure Ingharr doesn't hurt either of us again."

Freydis's chin bobbed in the smallest gesture of acquiescence. It was all the promise I would get from her.

I let my eyes flutter closed. After a long moment, I began to shudder and shake, as if possessed by my helping spirit. *I am a fool and a fake*, I knew. *Ataata would be ashamed.* But if it meant saving Kiasik, I would do whatever it took.

My eyes flew open; my hands stretched toward Freydis. "I have heard the words of Thor," I intoned, deepening my voice. "He looked at me with eyes as brilliant as lightning, a voice as loud as thunder, a beard as bright as sunlight. He sings his praise for you, his favorite child, whom he has graced with hair like his own."

To my surprise, the tall woman left her loom and knelt beside me. We were closer than we'd ever been. Her sharp nose reminded me of Brandr's, but never had his gaze pierced like steel. "You see the god clearly. You have magic, indeed," she said. "Tell me, what should I do?"

What more can any mortal say of the gods than that we cannot always understand their ways? But I wouldn't pass up the chance to protect not just my brother, but my entire family. I would ensure the Norse never threatened us again.

I summoned all my knowledge of the Aesir and the Jotuns. "Thor says beware Loki the Trickster!" I cried, my eyes glazed. "When the gods seem contrary and their signs confused, Loki the Jotun must be at work! You have done all Thor has asked, and now he wants you home. He opened the sea for you, but now *Loki* freezes it with his Frost Giant magic. It is he who would trap you here, powerless against his wiles."

Freydis looked at me like a hooked fish, eyes wide and unblinking.

"Thor says you must not give up hope. He will protect you." I lowered my voice and spoke in an urgent whisper. "But *only* if you stay in this camp. You must never stray inland, nor walk northward along the shore. *That* is where Loki presides, and Thor will be of no help to you. As soon as the ice melts—leave. This is Loki's world—not yours." My eyes closed once more. My arms fell limp.

Freydis nodded. "So I was right." She clutched her hammer pendant once more, as if to assure herself of Thor's protection. "We will follow the gods' will, and stay in this camp only as long as we must." For a heartbeat, she bowed her head to me. That was as close as she would come to gratitude. She stood and wrapped a fur cloak around her shoulders.

"I've done what you asked," I ventured. "Now my brother and I would return to our people. Let us leave this place."

Freydis's mouth twisted. "Oh no, little seer. I promised to help you—not release you. You're more useful than I thought." She picked up her thread and spindle, then stared down at me one last time. "And remember, if you want to *keep* my protection, not a word about this to anyone. My men must never know I sought a skraeling's advice." She strode from the tent.

I sank back on the pallet beside Kiasik, my lies more exhausting than any trek through ice and snow. Puja and the others, at least, would be safe for now. But Kiasik and I were still at Freydis's mercy. And Brandr...?

Muirenn chuckled from her spot in the corner of the tent, where she crouched beside a basket of wool. I'd nearly forgotten she was there. "You're smarter even than you know," she said.

I grunted. I didn't feel particularly smart. Only tired.

The thrall clambered to her feet with a groan, patted my brother's hollow cheek, and flashed me a crooked smile. "The mistress reeled in a slippery fish when she pulled you from the sea."

More than a fish, I thought, watching the old woman go. *A shark.*

CHAPTER
FORTY-THREE

ᛓ

With Muirenn gone, Kiasik and I were finally alone in Freydis's tent.

He seized my hand in his. "When are we getting out of here?" His words were strong but his voice rasping and weak.

Right away, I longed to say. But that would be a lie. "As soon as we can."

"Did you see the mountain?" he begged. "We're near the Land of the Great Whale."

"Our camp is still many days away, and you—"

"But if the mountain is close enough to see," Kiasik interrupted, "then our family's close enough to reach. We can go home."

"We would have to move swiftly," I cautioned. "You're so weak—"

"Not so weak I can't run."

He'd always been brave, my milk-brother. Too brave. He could barely walk, and a journey would surely finish the work the Norse had already begun. I placed my free hand on his, noting a new kink in his longest finger. In breaking his bones and tearing his skin, Ingharr and his men had opened a path for evil spirits to enter

Kiasik's body. It would take a real angakkuq to chase them away again.

"Freydis said she'd protect us," I assured him. "And I've made sure our family will be safe for now." I explained the lie I'd told the Norsewoman; she would keep her men from wandering far.

"That won't stop Ingharr from killing us whenever he feels like it," Kiasik insisted. "You don't know him like I do. We run. We run now."

Every instinct cried out for me to agree. *Perhaps he's stronger than he looks*, I reasoned. *And if his strength fails, I could use his cloak as a sled and drag him home.*

A wracking cough tore from his throat. He curled around the pain in his chest. When the fit passed, his lips were speckled with blood.

"You can't travel," I said firmly. "Not like this." I held up a hand before he could protest. "No. We wait until you're healed. Freydis will look after us. She'll make sure you get some decent food, and I'll take care of you. Then, as soon as you can walk without collapsing, we leave. I promise."

Muirenn bustled back inside before Kiasik could say anything more. "You have to leave the tent, my dears."

"Freydis said—"

"Sorry, but she and her husband need the pallet for a spell." Muirenn blinked one eye at me, conveying some inscrutable message.

With Kiasik leaning heavily on my shoulder, we stumbled from the tent. Freydis watched me coldly; Thorvard Einarsson had eyes only for his wife. His cheeks were flushed, his needs clear from the bulge in his trousers. Muirenn held the flap open for them. Before she let it fall, I saw Thorvard grab his wife around the waist, his thick hands pulling at her green gown. Freydis stiffened as he placed his mouth on hers, his lips moving ravenously.

"Why—why is he doing that?" I asked Muirenn.

"Oh, you *are* a young one! Never seen a man bed his wife?"

"No, I mean…biting her. On her mouth," I whispered, wondering why Muirenn wasn't as shocked as I.

The old woman looked confused for a moment. "You mean, when he kissed her?"

"Kissed?"

She burst into laughter. "Never seen anyone kiss before? Well, what a strange girl you are! I'd kiss you myself to show you how, but it's not the same coming from an old woman. You need some strong young man to do it for you." She blinked one eye again and scuttled off to help the other thralls unload Freydis's possessions.

I helped Kiasik hobble behind a low hillock and lowered him gently to the ground. He leaned against the snow, too tired to worry about the cold. I huddled beside him, wrapping my arms around him and wishing for a good fur parka. As his eyes drifted shut, I touched my own lips tentatively. Ice bears clacked their jaws together before mating. I'd always thought it a violent act—the male was often already bloody from fighting off his competition. Yet when I thought of Brandr's jaw beneath my fingers that last night in our qarmaq—

Ingharr's braying voice yanked me from my memory. "So Freydis is done with you."

I'd hoped to rest out of sight for a moment; now I feared what Ingharr would do without the others watching. Kiasik dug his fingers into my arm. He had told me to run.

Ingharr's hand strayed toward the handle of his sword. "Thorvard is in there enjoying himself. Now it's my turn, ambatt."

"Freydis protects us."

"Freydis *gave* you to me."

I would never understand these Norse and their talk of ownership. If Ingharr truly claimed me, then perhaps, for all my clever lies, Freydis couldn't help me even if she wanted to. But men were men. I knew one thing that could dampen his lust: fear.

"I speak with the Aesir," I warned him, rising to my feet. "*They* will avenge any wrong you do me."

"Then why do you wear a thrall's torque?" His lip curled. "You're just another kunta to me."

My milk-brother might not have known the words, but he understood the tone. He jerked forward unsteadily, as if he would rise to defend me. Ingharr didn't bother drawing his sword. He simply slammed his boot beneath Kiasik's chin. Black hair flying, Kiasik's head whipped backward, his torso following. He fell hard, eyes closed.

Before I could go to my brother, Ingharr charged, grabbing me with both hands. He spun me to the ground, pinning me beneath his weight, and fumbled for the hem of my dress.

I drove my fists into his shoulders, his back.

His roving hand found my bare thigh.

I screamed my defiance in my own tongue. *"Nuqqarit!"* Stop. The same word had ripped from my throat moons before, when I'd watched Ingharr crush Kidla's son beneath his boot.

"Nuqqarit!" I shouted again, baring my teeth in a snarl.

His face froze above mine, his mouth dropping open in sudden recognition.

I slammed my knee into his groin.

He curled like a snail. I crab-walked out of his reach and scrambled to my feet.

"Not just another kunta after all," he gasped. Something like a laugh croaked between his words. "I remember you now... The skraeling with the harpoon beside the silly little snow hut." He lurched to one knee. Then, bracing himself against the ground, to his feet. One hand drifted to his lower ribs. "I have you to thank for this scar."

His sword rasped from its scabbard.

I did not flinch. Never again would I allow a man to touch me as Issuk had. I'd fling my own breast upon his sword if I had to—but I'd much rather turn the blade on him instead.

His lust had drained away, replaced not by fear, but by rage. "I owe you a wound, I think." He leveled his blade at me. "Shall it be here?" He moved his sword point toward my waist. Then lower. "Or here?"

"You wouldn't dare touch me, Ingharr Ketilsson," I said slowly, my eyes never leaving his. "Didn't you hear? I am more powerful than you can possibly imagine." I raised my arms straight above my head, as if I would call down the Sun herself to punish this man before me.

"Oh, I doubt that, skraeling. I saw you trembling when I ripped the clothes from your body. You cower like any woman."

"Then how can I speak Norse?"

He shrugged. Then he swung, so suddenly I barely had time to twist away. The blade cut through the air—a gust of cold raked my cheek in its wake.

"And how can I read your mind?" I shouted, desperate now. I thrust my finger toward him. "You think *you* should be the leader of this doomed journey. In Vinland you said, 'Thorvard Einarsson is a mewling coward. Freydis Eriksdottir is a greedy fool.' I was not there, and yet I know these things!"

Ingharr's eyes grew huge. "Shut your mouth!"

I stood my ground. "If you strike me or my brother again, I'll tell everyone of your disloyalty. Freydis will believe me."

"Then I'll have to kill you before you say another word."

"You still don't believe in my power, Norseman? You couldn't harm me even if you tried." I glared at him, summoning the strength I'd learned from Ataata, from Singarti. Had I been a wolf, my hair would've stood on end, my tail flattened like a spear. Freydis thought I was the wise one. Instead, I'd learned from her. A woman didn't need a weapon to control a man.

Doubt crossed Ingharr's face. He no longer knew if attacking me was worth the risk. He took a tentative step backward, his sword lowering. I'd won. He would leave me and Kiasik alone, at least for a while. Kiasik would heal. We would steal supplies. We would escape.

I should not have goaded him with my gloating. If I had hidden my feelings of triumph, my story would be a different one.

But I have always been proud.

I smirked at his surrender.

Ingharr's cheeks flared red. He lifted his sword overhead.

I raised my arms above my face. A useless shield against edged iron.

"Ingharr Ketilsson!" Snorri panted, running toward us. "Ketilsson!"

"Off with you, boy," Ingharr growled.

Snorri continued, undaunted. "Freydis sent me to give you this." He held out a narrow twisted armband made not of iron or steel, but of solid sunlight. Beast heads capped each end of the braided crescent. The same creatures that rode upon the knarrs' prows. I knew their name now: *dragons*.

Ingharr lowered his sword and took the proffered gift. "This was Finnbogi's armband," he said, turning it to catch the light.

"Until Thorvard took it and gave it to Freydis. And now she gives it to you." Snorri cast me a worried glance. "In payment for your injury."

"She said the thrall would serve as my ambatt. *That* was my payment." Ingharr's fist tightened around the gold circlet.

"Now she offers gold instead. A fair trade for two useless thralls."

"*Two?*"

Snorri swallowed. "She wants to buy the sick one from you. He's near death. Why would you want another mouth to feed?"

"Why would *she?*"

Snorri glanced in the direction of Freydis's tent, as if afraid of being overheard. "Perhaps she feels remorse for killing the ambatts," he whispered. "Perhaps she's tired of blood."

"Freydis will never be tired of blood." Ingharr's pale gaze fixed on me, his suspicions clear. I let a small smile play across my lips. *Let him think I'm powerful enough to bewitch Freydis, to convince her to part with her treasure to save my life*. The Norseman pulled at his braided beard in obvious discomfort, then gave a snort of disgust. "Freydis makes a bargain. Freydis breaks a bargain. The woman is sly as a fox and just as slippery." Still, he pushed the armband up his forearm. It was too narrow for his bicep—Finnbogi must have been a slimmer man.

He looked at me one last time, his gaze still hungry. But if Freydis was a fox—I was a wolf. I stared back, unbowed. *I have ripped the throat from my prey with my bare teeth. I will not hesitate to do the same to you.*

As if he'd heard my silent vow, Ingharr turned away.

I hurried to Kiasik's side. He was still unconscious, but his breath came evenly. He still had a chance. Snorri came to help me lift him. "Thank you," I said to the boy. "For everything."

He gave me a shy smile. "Thank Muirenn. She's the one who gave me the armband."

"Without asking Freydis?"

"Freydis was with her husband, and Muirenn said her mistress would understand." He looked suddenly uncomfortable. "She said Freydis had promised to protect you, and that was one vow she had to keep, even if it meant breaking faith with Ingharr. She said you're"—he swallowed hard—"more powerful than he is. Is that true?"

No, I wanted to say. *If I were truly powerful, I would chase the evil spirits from Kiasik's body, seize him in my raven's beak, and fly him home to where we both belong. Instead I stand here amid strangers, with my brother dying in my arms.* But I said nothing. Just smiled my small smile and let Snorri believe what he would.

CHAPTER
FORTY-FOUR

ᛗ

For a full turning of the Moon, Ingharr tracked me through camp like a hunter sniffing for prey. But he never pounced.

Freydis did not punish Muirenn for giving away the gold armband, though her eyes narrowed every time she saw it upon Ingharr's forearm. As if to make sure I was worth the price she'd paid for me, Freydis kept me close, twisting prophecies from me as surely as she pulled thread from wool. I didn't care. I would make up tales all night long if it meant giving Kiasik a chance to heal.

Ingharr and the others found seals upon the ice. They brought the dark-red slabs of flesh to Freydisbudir, and Muirenn always managed to slice off a raw hunk for me to feed to my brother. The rest they destroyed over fires just as Brandr had always done. The thralls could never dig deep enough in the frozen earth to make a decent turf dwelling. They were forced to build their longhouse from the Vinland trees they'd hoped to sell back in their own land. I could have taught them to build igluit from snow and save their precious wood—but I didn't want them to get too comfortable.

Every day, the Sun rose more weakly, dragging herself above the horizon only briefly before collapsing once more. But for once, I welcomed her absence. "When the Great Darkness finally comes," I told Kiasik, "we'll make our escape."

He always agreed, though I saw the fear in his eyes. He could walk now, but not without panting after a few steps. And though the fresh meat and my careful tending had finally chased some of the pallor from his cheeks, his bloody coughing had only worsened. When I fed the slivers of seal meat to him, I sent a prayer to Ringed Seal, thanking her for the gift and asking that she heal the hunter who had once worn her amulet. But I was no angakkuq any longer; the spirits wouldn't listen to my pleas.

"I feel like something inside is ripping apart," he croaked. "I want to come with you, but I—" A cough tore from his throat. "Please, Omat," he begged when he could speak again. "Go without me. You've waited long enough. I'm not going to get better."

I should have listened to Kiasik.

Instead I refused to give up hope. I watched the sky. I watched my brother. And I hoarded what extra meat and dried fish I could, along with a rope and a patchy seal hide. The Norse guarded their knives too carefully, but I managed to snatch a small throwing ax from one-armed Magnor while he slept. It would have to be enough.

A dawn arrived without the Sun. Only a single narrow beam of pink pierced the dusky sky. Still, Kiasik could not travel.

I waited a little longer.

The Norse around me grew restless and afraid. The nights were long in their own land, but never did the Sun refuse to rise at all. There were at least thirty Greenlanders and thralls crowded into the longhouse—not to mention twenty sheep—and the tension grew as thick as the stench.

Freydis never spoke of her own worries, but the thread upon her loom snarled beneath unsteady fingers.

"The Sun will return," I assured her.

"I know." She sounded defensive. "I've heard tales of this darkness. In the far reaches of Northway, they say it happens every year."

"But hearing about it is different from seeing it yourself."

Freydis didn't reply. She only turned back to her loom, bending close to see the threads in the flickering light of the central fire. Her husband, Thorvard, threw another precious Vinland log into the flames. The Norse had long since run out of the peat they preferred to burn, and their seal oil lamps were too small to warm such large dwellings.

I put down the ragged spool of thread I'd been spinning and moved to join my milk-brother where he crouched before the fire. "I saw the heralding stars during the false dawn," I whispered to him. "If we wait any longer, the Sun will rise again; the days will lengthen, and they'll be able to hunt us down in the light. If we're going to leave—"

"I'm ready," he whispered back.

I knew he was lying. I could see the way he clasped his bent hands to hide their trembling. But he had always been brave. And we had no choice.

"Then as soon as they're all asleep, we leave. Tonight."

Muirenn sat at the opposite end of the chamber, pounding the oil from a square of seal blubber. She couldn't have heard me, yet her head jerked up when I spoke. She turned quickly to Freydis. "This is the last of the seal, mistress. We should ask Ingharr to hunt again."

A breath later, Ingharr himself pushed past the flap of seal hide over the entrance, as if summoned by Muirenn's words. He strode across the longhouse with a gust of cold air following in his wake. "I'm going onto the ice for seals."

Freydis didn't look up. "It's too dark."

Ingharr crossed his meaty arms over his chest. "We can't wait for the Sun. The Moon is bright enough to hunt by. We've already eaten all the seal meat I brought back two days ago. We're down to our last wheel of cheese. Soon we'll finish the stockfish. Would you have us starve?"

"He's right," Thorvard ventured. I'd seen how Freydis's husband always took the largest portions for himself. If the Norse were out of food, he was largely to blame.

Freydis cast Thorvard an angry glance. "If he can't see where he's going, he won't be able to stay close to the shore."

Ingharr's brows lowered. "Why do you care so much about where I hunt?"

"The gods sent me a message. They warned us not to venture inland. I told you that."

"The gods have said nothing to me." Whatever patience Ingharr had for the woman had long grown thin. He turned to go.

Muirenn leaned toward her mistress and whispered something in her ear.

"Wait!" Freydis stood and hurried toward me. "Take my thrall. She's from a land like this. She can guide you to the best hunting grounds, even in the dark." She grabbed my elbow, her fingers biting into my flesh in a silent reminder that I must keep her secret. No one could know that *I* had warned her to stay close to shore.

I looked to Muirenn. The old woman had helped us once again. It'd be far easier to escape from a small band of hunters on the sea ice than from an entire camp of Norsemen onshore. "Yes," I agreed quickly. "And Kiasik is well enough to come. He's a great hunter among my people and will bring back many seals."

I translated for Kiasik, who rose to his feet, making a surprisingly convincing effort to appear strong. Hope surged through me. Once we were upon the ice together, no Norsemen could stop us.

Ingharr's laugh was a harsh bark. "I'm no fool, Freydis. If you let these two out together, they'll be gone the moment I turn around." He fingered his braided beard. "But I'll take the woman."

Freydis pushed me toward him, and Ingharr seized my shoulders. His next words were to me alone. "She and I have work yet to do."

I forced myself to meet his eyes. *I'll go with you*, I thought. *And I'll make sure you don't make it back alive.*

As if reading my thoughts, Ingharr grabbed me by my thrall's torque, twisting the cord against my throat until I could scarcely breathe. Freydis said nothing to stop him.

"If you escape from me," Ingharr warned, "I'll return and kill your brother." He raised his voice, addressing every freeman in the longhouse. "Hear me now. If I don't come back from this hunt, know that this thrall woman is to blame. Swear upon Odin's eye to kill her skraeling brother in recompense." The men nodded briefly before returning to their tasks, as if murdering my brother were just another chore for them to perform.

"Do you understand?" Ingharr hissed in my face. "His life is in your hands."

He dropped me and strode away.

"Omat," Kiasik asked. "What did he say?"

"I go to hunt with him. You stay behind. If I try to escape, they'll kill you."

"That shouldn't stop you from running," he said solemnly. "You don't need to save me. No woman would risk herself like this."

"Since when was I like any other woman?" I demanded. "Did I not hunt beside you our whole lives? Would a woman have traveled so far to save you? Would she?"

For once, he didn't argue.

"You've seen Freydis, the woman who leads these men." I didn't say more. My meaning was clear. *If Freydis exists, why can't I?*

"Then use all your skill," he begged me. "Find prey quickly and come back to me. We can still run tonight."

I could only pray he was right.

Sanna moved unseen beneath the sea ice. I could feel her presence trailing my footsteps through the liquid ocean far below, my old nemesis following me with renewed vigor. With every step I took, she scattered her children farther from our hunting party.

Sea Mother, I begged silently. *Forgo your vengeance, just for a moment. Send a seal to Ingharr's spear. He won't go back until he's wetted his blade with blood, and I can't wait much longer to run.*

I led the men steadily south on our fruitless hunt, away from the Land of the Great Whale. We walked through a world of black sky and glowing blue snow, Taqqiq's bright eye our only light. For days now, he'd coursed overhead in a high, undulating circle, dipping briefly toward the horizon only to rise again.

Strong Bjarni, with his keen eyesight and wooden bow, had joined us on the hunt. Old Olfun, who seemed to know something of hunting despite his missing eye, trailed after us. Freydis had ordered Snorri to come, too. He stayed close beside me, his slim form my only protection from Ingharr; I could feel the yellow-haired man's gaze burning into my back, daring me to run.

Snorri guarded me only on Freydis's orders, I knew. But the boy's concern for me seemed genuine, and he spoke with sur-prising deference, awed by my confidence on the ice. He'd lent me a flimsy, blunt-edged wooden staff. I tested the ice in front of me, careful of the darker patches where the ocean depths showed through. Snorri stepped carefully in my footsteps.

"How do you know where to go?" he asked breathlessly.

"We go south. That's where the wind will blow the ice apart, opening leads where the animals come up to breathe." *If Sanna hasn't chased them away already.*

"But which way is south? How can you tell when the Moon's so bright you can barely see the stars?"

I felt almost like an angakkuq again, teaching others about the world. With the tip of my staff, I pointed briefly at a ridge of blown snow. "You see how the snow ripples lie? The wind blows from the sea, pushing the snow into a line as clear as a finger pointing to the east." I gestured ahead of us. "So that's south."

Snorri nodded, clearly impressed. I stifled a snort. These Norse thought they knew so much.

"Woman!" Ingharr's voice rang across the ice. "I see no seals!"

"Nor will you, if you speak so loud!" I called back. Snorri choked down a chuckle. The other men shifted uneasily. "Seals have keen hearing. You're scaring them off."

Ingharr stomped toward me. *Please,* I thought, *let the fool fall through the ice.* But Ingharr clearly had a spirit guide of his own. Despite his heedless stride, the ice remained firm.

He grabbed the torque around my throat again. "You forget you're a thrall," he hissed. "I have been hunting all my life. If I say there are no seals, there are no seals." I kept my staff in one hand, barely able to restrain myself from slamming it against his skull.

He released me with a shove. I slipped backward. "You should be careful," he growled for my ears alone. "Many accidents happen on the ice."

I cannot die here, I thought, pushing myself upright. *Not with home in sight.*

A faint blue fog rose in the distance. Frost smoke from an open lead meeting colder air.

"There—" I pointed. "If there are seals, they'll be there."

—— ◆◆◆ ——

We stood upon the ice edge until my wool-covered arms grew numb from cold. Still no seals appeared. Olfun shifted his feet impatiently. Ingharr slapped his arms and legs with his mittened hands to stay warm. I wanted to strike him for his foolishness. The sound only further ensured no seals would come.

Finally, as Taqqiq hovered just above the mountains, Olfun dared speak.

"Ingharr, we must go back." He rubbed the frost from the seamed scar that puckered his eye socket. "There's no game here, and Freydis warned us—"

Ingharr held up a hand for silence and pointed a single thick finger toward the horizon. There, barely visible in the moonlit dark, a silhouette thrust from the water in a distant lead, growing larger. Getting closer.

"A whale," Snorri whispered, awestruck.

"A herd of seals," Ingharr offered confidently.

Olfun squinted his one gray eye and said nothing.

Bjarni, the most keen-sighted among us, slowly raised his bow. "No...not either of those, I don't think."

I didn't need Bjarni to tell me what approached. *A man. In a boat.* Cold flooded my veins. I'd thought us far enough from my family that we wouldn't stumble upon Tapsi or Ququk on their hunt. I was wrong.

"Turn around!" I screamed in my own tongue. *"It's not safe!"*

Ingharr clapped a hand over my mouth, stifling my warning. His angry curses nearly drowned out the faint cry floating toward us over the ice.

I knew that voice. Not Tapsi. Not Ququk.

Brandr.

CHAPTER
FORTY-FIVE

⚡

Brandr's boat drifted into view—a misshapen raft that had once been a sled.

A paddle waved toward me from the distant lead like a desperately flailing arm. Fast as a hare, I twisted from Ingharr's grasp and bolted along the ice edge toward Brandr. Holding my skirts above my knees with one hand and my staff with the other, I ran so hard I feared I'd crash through the frozen sea. But for once, the Sea Mother withheld her ire. I could hear Ingharr and the others running after me; only surprise had kept me out of their reach so far.

The open channel before us was as wide as four spear lengths, but to reach the raft in the distant lead, I'd need to cross it. Nearly impossible for a leaping man, but not for Bjarni's arrows. Brandr would fall before he even understood the danger.

I paused only long enough to take a few steps backward and get a running start. My sealskin boots gripped the rough ice, my arms pumped like a raven's wings—and I jumped.

All those long summer games of agility and strength served me well. The toes of my boots struck the far edge of the ice; I flailed and stretched and strained. Then I tumbled forward, safe on the other side of the channel.

Behind me, Ingharr and the others shouted curses, unwilling to make such a leap.

I kept running. "Turn around!" I shouted toward Brandr.

My cries only made him paddle harder.

Suddenly a long pale horn split the water beside his raft, rising from the depths like a spear wielded by Sanna herself. For a moment, I was sure the Sea Mother meant to rip through Brandr's raft.

Then another horn appeared, and another.

With a whistled wail, three narwhals lifted their round, glistening heads above the surface. Rather than attack the raft, they guided it, pushing it swiftly through the water with the points of their spiraled horns.

I could see Brandr's face now beneath his dog-fur hood. The familiar sharp plane of his nose, the thin cheeks. His blue eyes glinted like black stones in the moonlight. I skidded to a halt, my toes brushing the steaming edge of the lead, where ice and water met.

"Hurry, before they make it across," Brandr looked past me toward Ingharr and his men. "Get on!"

"No! I can't leave. You have to—"

"Get on the raft, Omat!"

With a final stroke of his oar, the raft struck the ice. Brandr stretched a hand toward me, his eyes pleading, confused, betrayed.

"Please, Brandr. They'll kill Kiasik if I leave now," I begged through sudden tears, clutching my arms around my chest to prevent myself from reaching for him. Brandr's hand slowly dropped away from mine, his gaze darting between my tear-streaked face and the Norsemen on the other shore.

The narwhal tusks shot from the water as the small whales surfaced once more. Then, rather than splashing back into the ocean, they behaved as no normal whales would, launching themselves onto the ice before me. One white, one dark, one mottled gray.

I started back, terrified. The ice groaned beneath their weight.

The whales rolled onto their sides, their long, twisted horns flailing like the lances of untested hunters. Then, in a flash, I understood.

Whales who had once been wolves.

Wolves who would cross an ocean to find me.

The gray narwhal humped awkwardly across the ice, tusk bobbing. "No!" I shouted at White Paw in my own tongue. She was no aarluk, no fierce fanged whale who might fight off her attackers. Narwhals are peaceful, their tusks for show, not battle. "You can't help me like this!" I reached to push her back into the sea.

Strong hands grabbed me by the shoulders and hauled me away. I struggled, kicking backward.

"Stop!" Brandr shouted in my ear. I hadn't seen him leave the raft, but now his arms circled my chest, squeezing tight. "We've got to get out of here!"

Too late. An arrow sailed toward us. Brandr ducked just in time, the motion sending us both toppling to the ice.

"Careful, Bjarni!" I heard Olfun warn. "That's no skraeling— he's speaking Norse!"

"Beware, Norseman!" Ingharr shouted, squinting through the dark. "Leave the thrall to us!"

The narwhals shimmied forward, forming an arc around us.

Ingharr let out a whoop of surprise when he saw them. "You've led us to rich hunting after all, woman!" he called. "Three narwhal tusks will fetch more gold than a man can spend in a lifetime." He finally dared to take his own running leap across the channel. He almost didn't make it. Almost.

The narwhals whistled in protest as Ingharr sprinted toward us. Their horns, each as long as a full-grown man, pointed toward the approaching Norseman in warning.

But a whale on land was no more threat than a wolf in the waves.

"No!" I cried, crawling free of Brandr and rising to my knees.

I held out my hands, palms up in surrender. "Take me back, just don't hurt them."

Brandr scrabbled to his feet. "What are you *doing*?"

"You can't save me without killing Kiasik!" I screamed at him. "Stop fighting and *go*!"

"Not without you." A Viking in an Inuk's hood, he drew his sword and leveled it at Ingharr.

The hunter froze in place. "Who *are* you, Norseman?"

I heard the creak of Bjarni's bowstring as he shifted his aim from me to Brandr. The faint snap of a loosed arrow.

With a torrent of angry clicks and squeals, the dark narwhal who had once been Sweet One slid across the ice and into the path of the oncoming shaft. It sliced through her tail, pinning her to the ground. I bent to grab the arrow in both hands and yank it free, then threw my whole weight against the injured narwhal, shoving her into the open water. "Get them to safety," I begged White Paw. If I couldn't save Brandr, I could at least save my pack.

She swung her heavy head toward me. Her long, spiraled horn scraped uselessly against the ice, and her yellow-rimmed eye, more wolf than whale, burned into mine.

Another arrow, clearly aimed at me, clattered beside Floppy Eared's flank. White Paw whistled once, then slammed her tusk into her sibling's flank until he slid across the ice. They both splashed into the open lead.

Olfun and the others had made a bridge of sorts across the channel by lashing their spears together. Bjarni ran across it, nocking another arrow to his bow as he came and aiming for the departing whales. I grabbed my staff and charged him. He was stronger than I, broader; I could never defeat him in a wrestling match. But I didn't need to. I swung my staff wide, catching the tip on Bjarni's bowstring and sending the arrow sailing harmlessly overhead. I couldn't kill him without ensuring Kiasik's death, but I jabbed my staff at his stomach; the young freeman took a swift step to the side, reaching for the ax at his belt to fend me off—and plunging through a dark patch just beside his left heel.

He slammed his arms against the rim of stronger ice, holding his torso out of the slushy water while Olfun rushed across the make-shift bridge and hauled him free.

Brandr had already lunged for Ingharr, his hood flying back-ward as his sword flashed in the moonlight. The yellow-haired Norseman skidded away, barely avoiding the blow.

"Brandr Gunnarsson," Ingharr hissed. "You're supposed to be dead." He dropped his hunting spear and slid his own sword free. Beside Brandr's gleaming blade, Ingharr's looked as flat and unre-markable as an Inuk's slate knife. He blocked Brandr's next slash, but the hardened steel bit into the softer iron—and stuck there.

In the space of a single breath, I saw the future as clearly as if I were an angakkuq again: Brandr would free his blade, strike again, shatter Ingharr's sword. Then he would slice the head from Ing-harr's body as easily as he'd once done to Patik.

And Kiasik would die.

Yet if Brandr stopped fighting now, *he* would lose his head.

I stood frozen, unable to choose between my milk-brother and my Viking.

Snorri made the decision for me.

The boy who'd once protected me now surged forward like a winter gale, knocking me from my feet.

My cheek burned against the ice as he knelt on my back. I stopped struggling when he pressed his knife against my bobbing throat.

Brandr jerked his sword free of Ingharr's and spun toward Snorri.

"One more step, Gunnarsson," the boy snarled, his voice made old and rough by rage, "and our blood debt is paid. This woman dies for your sins."

I tried to choke out a warning, to tell my friend that if he sur-rendered now, the Norse would only kill him later. Snorri cut through skin. Hot blood trickled across my neck like tears.

Brandr stood as stony and silent as an inuksuk. Only his eyes spoke of his torment.

His gaze fixed on mine, full of regret, full of fear. He knelt upon the ice, bending first his good leg, then his bad. Slowly, as if fighting against a rushing current, he laid his sword on the ground before him and surrendered to his fate.

CHAPTER
FORTY-SIX

ᛁ

Only scant torchlight seeped around the edges of the crude door that imprisoned us in the knarr's storage hold. I wanted to bend the light to my will and cast it on Brandr's face so I might read his expression. His silence weighed on me more heavily than the iron chains around my hands.

I made a grim attempt at levity. "At least this time they didn't cut off my clothes."

"They shouldn't do that to a woman." His voice was solemn.

I snorted. "But when you thought I was a man, then it would've been fine?"

"That's not what I meant."

"I'm still the same."

"No," he said with a forcefulness that surprised me. "You're not. Neither of us is."

Despite Snorri's pleas, Ingharr hadn't killed us on the ice. Remembering the way he'd savored the red men's spread-eagling, I decided he preferred executions with a little more spectacle. While Olfun tended to shivering Bjarni, and Snorri paced with ill-concealed rage, Ingharr bound our hands with rope. He dragged us like recalcitrant dogs back to Freydisbudir.

A great commotion had greeted our return. I saw little but hatred in the Greenlanders' eyes as Ulfar's murderer walked by. They would welcome Brandr's death.

Kiasik had stood among them in his patched cloak. Blinking as if snow-blind, he swiveled his gaze from me to the tall, flame-haired stranger who walked protectively at my side.

But even Kiasik's shock paled next to Freydis's. At the sight of Brandr, she raised her hands to her mouth as if to stifle a scream. Then loathing twisted her features. She finally understood: I was no seer sent by her gods—only an accomplice of her great enemy.

"Where Brandr Gunnarsson comes, an army follows!" she snarled, a finger jutting toward us.

Even Ingharr looked stunned by her pronouncement.

"Wife," Thorvard began. "He came alone. Why—"

"Quiet," Freydis snapped, all pretense of wifely patience gone. "Lock Gunnarsson and the skraeling woman in the hold of my knarr. Put her brother in the other. Then back on board, all of you. "

"But the longhouse—" protested Olfun.

"Is not safe with an army on the move," interrupted Freydis. "Now, hurry! And bring the flock. I won't lose our sheep to this treachery."

The Norsemen dragged us to Freydis's boat and thrust us in the hold beneath the foredeck that had once held the milking ewes and their lambs. They wrapped cold iron chains around our wrists and ankles. A tattooed freeman stood guard outside the make-shift cell. Shouting seeped through the deck above as the Norse-men argued our fate, their words muffled by the nearer bleating of the sheep milling outside our cell. I wondered if Freydis's men finally believed her dreams of Frost Giants coming to kill them. Or that Brandr had truly planned to lead an army of skraelings against their camp. *It doesn't matter what they believe of dreams and prophecies*, I realized. *They know Brandr killed Ulfar. That alone will seal his fate.* Snorri's voice—high-pitched with youthful outrage—cut through the noise. He wanted vengeance for his father. Blood for blood.

In the darkness of the ship's hold, I tried to block out the sound of our doom.

After so long apart, Brandr and I could finally resume the conversation we'd begun so many days before. But our newfound intimacy had vanished, replaced by a reticence we hadn't felt since our first meeting. With no secrets to cloak me, I felt unsure how to speak to him. I had imagined pulling off my atigi, running my hands along his skin. But now...

"You thought I'd left you," I said. A statement, not a question.

"I awoke and you were gone. White Paw and Floppy, too. And for a moment...yes. I thought you'd seen what happened with Galinn, seen me for a coward—and you'd run. But then I saw you'd taken down the bear pelt. And I knew. Even before Sweet One dragged me outside by the cuff of my parka, and I spotted the knarr on the horizon, sailing north. I knew. You had seen it all. And you'd decided to stay."

When I thought of how he'd turned our sled into a boat to chase after me, I felt like new ice above a rising tide, swaying with emotions I couldn't control.

"You're cold," said Brandr.

"Me? I'm used to the cold!"

"I can hear your teeth chattering. I'd give you my parka if I could get it off," he apologized, the chains clinking as he raised his bound hands.

"I don't need it," I insisted, my teeth still knocking.

"Omat." The warmth of his voice only increased my trembling.

He didn't reach to touch me, yet I could imagine the muscles straining against his parka as he clenched and unclenched his bound hands.

Finally I couldn't stand it anymore. For so many moons, I'd

feared to touch him. And I knew that after learning about the horrors in my past—and acknowledging the horrors in his own—he wouldn't reach for me first.

I eased closer and lay down, resting my head on his lap. I didn't speak, just lay there shaking. After a long moment, his calloused fingers brushed the hair from my cheek. The iron chains around his wrists hovered above me. When he finally spoke, it was with an unusual hesitancy.

"Did I ever tell you of Frey and the giantess?"

I shook my head. It seemed a strange time for storytelling. Then again, we had always spoken best through tales.

He took a deep breath and began. "Frey, the god of growing things, once owned a magic sword. Dwarven forged. Odin All-Father warned him to keep it close, for it would be needed to fight Surtur, the fire fiend in the Ragnarok."

Brandr settled into his usual easy cadence, reciting this tale as he had so many others. I could almost imagine myself back in our warm qarmaq with the wolfdogs curled nearby. "But one day, Frey glimpsed a beautiful giantess emerging from her father's home. He vowed he'd give anything to make her his wife. A stranger appeared—as they so often do in tales such as these—and offered to get the giantess for Frey. The stranger asked only one thing in return: the magic sword. And Frey, whose heart has always been stronger than his head, let the stranger have it. The giantess's name was Gerda, and she was a fearless shield-maiden—but even in all her battle rage, she could not withstand that magic sword. They say that when the stranger brought her before gentle Frey, all her wrath disappeared, and she fell in love with the golden god."

Brandr twisted his fingers gently through my hair. "Frey went to thank the stranger for retrieving his beloved. The man removed his disguise—and there stood Loki. The Shapeshifter. They say Frey has a sword no longer, and the other gods mock him for falling for Loki's tricks. Why sacrifice such a weapon for a giantess? Gerda isn't fair and slender like the goddesses of the Aesir. But

Frey doesn't mind. He thinks she's the most beautiful woman he's ever seen." He paused just long enough to trace a finger across my heated cheek. "Besides"—a smile warmed his voice—"he doesn't need a sword any longer. He has *her* to protect him."

I thought you didn't believe in tales, I wanted to say. *You shouldn't believe in that one. If you think I'm strong enough to protect you, you're wrong.*

We sat in silence for a moment longer. Against the top of my head, I could feel the rhythmic pulse of his breath. My eyes fluttered closed as he traced my lashes, my lips, the smooth curve of my jaw.

"I guess you'll never grow a mustache," he mused, breaking the sudden tension.

I found a thread of laughter for him and felt rather than heard his chuckling response.

He fell silent when an angry shout pierced the walls of the hold.

"You know what they're doing up there," he said, his tone somber again. "They've gathered in council to decide if we live or die."

I sat up, wishing once more that I could see his face.

"Are you afraid to die?" I asked.

"You know the answer to that. I wasn't. Until I met you." I could feel the warmth of his gaze even with his eyes in shadow. "I've only just found you. I'm not ready to let you go."

An iron bolt clanked, and the rough door jerked open.

Freydis stood silhouetted in the light of the guard's torch. She'd removed her wimple, and her hair gleamed like fresh-shed blood in the firelight.

"The Althing has decided," she said. "For the murder of Ulfar, you, Brandr Gunnarsson, will be put to death on the morrow. The gods demand it. You escaped their justice once before—you will not do so again."

Brandr's shoulders straightened. "You killed a houseful of women with your own hands. It's *you* who should be tried."

"I only did as the gods demanded." Color flooded her pale

cheeks. "I know you, Gunnarsson. I know your plans." She turned her flashing eyes on me. "But *you*. As strange as you are, I thought I understood you. A woman who fights like a man—I thought you and I had something in common. Now I find you with this traitor—this demon who would lead an army to destroy me and mine. You bring him here to kill us all. You thought to trick me into leaving your land, but now I see the truth. You lied to me, skraeling. Loki doesn't freeze the ice to trap me; *Thor* does it to reward me. He *wants* me to stay. He sent me dreams of battle not so I would flee Vinland, but so I would ready myself for the fight to come." She tossed her head like a proud caribou bull displaying its antlers. "The men do not believe me. They think I rave about a phantom only. But I know better. We will defend the ships from whatever demons you send against us. And I will *not* leave when the ice thaws. I'll send the other knarr back to sell our timber and pelts. It will return with swords and horses and men. Your brother will stay as my thrall; he'll tell me the ways of your kind. Then any skraelings who think to fight us will die upon our blades. From Helluland to Markland to Vinland—*all* will be Freydis-budir." Her voice rose, as if buoyed by her visions of conquest and triumph. She looked at me as if at a beetle to be smashed beneath her heel.

"I don't know how Brandr Gunnarsson came into your life," she went on, "but you'll regret he ever did. Tomorrow, at the sky's first lightening, he will be spread-eagled upon a cross of wood. You, skraeling demon, will be right next to him, watching him die. And when the blood has left his body and he hangs there, a harmless husk of a man, then you, too, will be killed."

Brandr strained against his iron chains. "Have you gone mad, Eriksdottir? Drunk on Vinland wine? There is no army! And Omat has never harmed you. Neither have I."

Freydis paced closer to him, laying one white hand upon his bearded jaw and turning his face to the torchlight. "Not yet. But the gods tell me you're a danger. Ulfar was only a prelude to the destruction you want to rain down upon us all. And this skraeling will help you do it. So I will kill you both—just as I killed poor Galinn. He bleated when Ingharr's sword carved out his gut, you know, as weak and mild as the sheep he herded."

Nostrils flaring, Brandr snapped his teeth as if to bite off her fingers. Freydis stepped calmly out of his reach.

"Tomorrow you will die, Brandr Gunnarsson. And finally, you will cease to haunt my dreams. I'm looking forward to a good night's sleep."

The guard bolted the door behind her, throwing the hold once more into darkness.

My shaking resumed.

Brandr sank back against the curve of the boat's hull. I could see it before me even now: Just as they'd done to the red men, the Norse would lash him to a cross, slit open his back, pull out his lungs, and spread them wide. They would pump like the flapping of an eagle's wings.

He reached his bound hands to me, his fingers barely visible in the dark. I crawled closer; he clutched me awkwardly against him. In the racing of his heart, I knew his easy confidence was shattered. This was no flimsy bark hut for us to break through. No wolfdogs would come to our rescue. We both knew we would die. And not just us.

"My family," I groaned. "You heard Freydis. She'll stay. She'll destroy my people. If I hadn't tried to trick her, she would've fled to Greenland when the ice melted and never looked back."

"Perhaps," he acknowledged, "but other Norse would hear of Vinland's riches, and they'd make the journey. The future is already spun, or so my brother would say. Freydis or not—the Norse will come."

I knew he spoke to relieve me of my guilt. He only made it worse. "I've killed my family. And you with them." My voice shook more with anger than with grief. "Why did you come for me?" I demanded. "You, at least, might have survived."

"I don't regret it," he whispered against my hair. "The only thing I regret is all those months with you, never knowing what was right before my eyes."

An exclamation, half laugh and half sob, burst from my lips. Freydis and Kiasik, Vikings and skraelings—it was all too much. I was no angakkuq. No leader. No hero. Tomorrow we would die. For now, I'd make the most of the time I had left.

I took his hands and raised them to my face.

His fingertips rested gently on my cheeks, my neck. "I've been thinking about nothing but you all the way up the coast. Of all I'd told you—and all I had left to say. Nights in the boat, the narwhals breaching around me, no real hope of finding you, much less rescuing you. Knowing I faced almost certain death. I dreamed only of this."

He pressed his lips upon my eyelids. He tasted my new-sprung tears, my skin, the corner of my mouth. I'd wondered about this Viking custom, this kiss. I wondered no more.

His lips closed over mine, his beard rough upon my chin. I opened my mouth willingly to his, breathing the scent of his skin, tasting his tongue. I pressed my own bound hands against his chest, wishing I could split apart our chains and put my arms around him—

Then his hands suddenly dropped from my face. He broke our kiss, breathing heavily. His nose rested upon my cheek in an unconscious imitation of an Inuk's caress. I turned my face into his, feeling the roughness of his skin, the smooth bone of his straight Viking nose.

In a voice hoarse with desire, he echoed my thoughts from a moment before. "I want to get out of these chains. I want to hold you. And I do not want you to be afraid."

"Afraid? It's too late for that. I am afraid of spread-eagling. Afraid my family will be killed. Afraid for Kiasik and for you and for the fate of us all. But afraid of *you*? Of your touch?" I took a deep breath and gripped his hands in my own. "No, Brandr. I am not afraid of you."

I heard the relieved smile in his voice. "I should've known

better. What does the fearsome hunter Omat, whose skills in a fight, against man or bear, I could never doubt, have to fear from a lowly Norseman, and a chained one at that? I might've been blind for the past months, but I wasn't deaf. I heard many times about how an Inuk would never lose a fight against a Viking, and I believed you. You've nothing to fear from me, unless you've been lying to me all this time about more than just your sex."

Even now, with the whole world against us, we laughed together. He kissed me through his laughter, light feathery brushes against my mouth, the tip of my nose, my chin, his aim unerring despite the dark. My hands had found his jaw, angling his mouth to mine, when the door flew open behind us. We split apart just as the light from a torch spilled across the cell.

"Hey!" cried Snorri. "Have you two lost your minds? Gunnarsson, you murderer—I forbid you to laugh. Nor you, skraeling, who I fed and protected, only to have you spit my kindness in my face. You two have no right to happiness." His voice cracked, but his fury was a man's, not a boy's. "Not with my father's blood on your hands." His voice fell to a fierce whisper. "You should ask Jesus to offer you salvation. That's your only hope now."

Neither of us looked at Snorri. We barely heard him. All my attention was on Brandr, and all of his on me.

In that one stolen moment of firelight, I could see him clearly. It felt like seeing him for the first time. Tomorrow, surrounded by our enemies, I knew my friend's face would be closed to me. He wouldn't show weakness, any more than I would. But in this brief moment, he was mine. I'd thought I knew his face better even than my family's—yet I'd never seen him like this. His eyes burned hot and clear. His cheeks were flushed; his beard sparked gold and orange in the torchlight. In the deep crease between his brows, in the emotion playing along his lips, I saw the conflict of joy and despair that echoed in my own heart.

Snorri slammed the door behind him, thrusting us back into darkness more complete than before.

"I think, finally, I might die happy," Brandr murmured.

"No," I protested, my voice catching. "No. I have finally seen you."

He made a sound more growl than sigh, and I could hear the creak of chains as he strained at his fetters. "Where are you?" he begged. "I can't feel you."

I struggled toward his voice. His searching hand found mine. He pulled me toward him, and I awkwardly slipped beneath the circle of his arms so that my cheek might press once more against his chest.

He sighed deeply and lay back against the curved bottom of the boat. My head rested on the pillow of muscle above his heart. His fingers made slow circles just along the base of my spine. His chains cut into the small of my back, but I felt no pain.

A tight, thrumming pleasure flushed my skin with heat.

For once, I was glad of my woman's body.

CHAPTER FORTY-SEVEN

Still clasped in Brandr's arms, I kept my eyes glued to the border of the door, watching for the light of the false dawn that would herald our deaths.

I tried to tune my ears to Brandr's heartbeats alone.

The iron bolt clanked open.

"It's too soon," I whispered. "The sky is still dark."

He only held me tighter in response.

The door swung slowly ajar, revealing not our executioners but the hunched figure of Muirenn holding a small oil lamp. The thrall stepped inside and moved to close the door behind her.

"Careful, woman," the tattooed guard warned her, stepping into view. "Freydis says they're more dangerous than they look. In that, at least, I believe her."

"This one wouldn't hurt me," she chided impatiently. "Go on now, shut the door before their little wisp of heat escapes and you freeze them to death before tomorrow."

The door closed firmly behind her. She placed her lamp on the floor. I smiled to see the dish she carried in her other hand. If it was up to Muirenn, we wouldn't die hungry. She offered me a piece of dried stockfish, then presented Brandr with a hunk of strong cheese.

He took an enormous bite and closed his eyes. "I've missed this. A dying man's last wish fulfilled." If I hadn't known better, I would've accused Brandr of flirting with the old woman.

She patted him on the head. "It's good to see you, my boy."

"Muirenn used to stay with me and Galinn sometimes after our mother died," he explained to me, swallowing the last of the cheese. "I tormented her ceaselessly, but somehow she's forgiven me."

"Ach, don't believe him. He was always a good child. The only cruel thing he ever did was run off to go viking and leave me behind."

Brandr smiled—then yawned.

"You've had a hard day," she soothed. "Don't fight it. Go to sleep, my boy."

And to my surprise, he did. He curled into a loose ball—and slept.

Dumbfounded, I turned back to Muirenn.

Except Muirenn was gone.

In her place stood an impossibly tall man who glowed with an inner light that put the lamp to shame.

"Ia'a!" I threw my body in front of Brandr's.

"Quiet now, you don't want to wake him, do you?" the strange man scolded in a voice that was musical, multilayered—like a man's and a woman's and a bird's all at once. "The poor thing needs his rest. And you and I need some time to talk." His narrow lips quirked, mirrored by one raised dark brow. Intricate braids wound through his long black hair. Though he was beardless, a long mustache plaited with gold thread fell past his pointed chin.

His features seemed not Norse, not Inuit, but some combination of both. His narrow eyes sparked in the darkness like snow crystals in sunlight; I couldn't bear to look at them. His lithe figure was almost feminine; flowing silver robes clothed his arms and legs, their delicacy belied by a bronze breastplate embossed with a man's muscles.

With every smooth motion of his limbs, the silver robes glittered, casting points of light around the dark hold of the ship. The man himself seemed to shift and blur with the motion.

"What did you do with Muirenn?" I managed.

The stranger laughed delightedly. "*Do* with her? I *am* her. I've been her on and off for years now! Which was excessively dull for a long time, by the way. Ever since she got so old and wrinkled." He leaned against the wall of the hold, completely at ease. "I've often thought it's about time to be some pretty young thing for a while, but Muirenn knows all the right people, you see. It's not easy to get close to Freydis Eriksdottir without her great protector Thor noticing. So"—he sighed dramatically—"here I am, old and frail and humble. At least for now. I am a shapeshifter, you know." He blinked at me, his eyes suddenly spinning with rainbows.

"Loki?"

"Very good, Omat! Your lover taught you well."

My shock quickly turned to suspicion. I'd met the spirits before: Taqqiq had stolen my power; Sanna haunted my steps. What torment did this new god have planned for me?

"I thought the Aesir chained you up beneath a venomous serpent after you killed innocent Baldur."

He brushed aside my concerns with a graceful wave of his hand. "*Some* of us cannot be held by chains, my dear." He cast a pointed glance at the iron links around my wrists.

"What do you want of me?"

"Oh, not much." He shrugged, grinning again. "Don't worry, I'm not going to hurt you—or your friend. I merely desire guidance."

"Guidance?" I choked. "From me?"

"Well, an introduction, if you will."

"I don't understand."

Again the loud sigh. "I'm a Jotun."

"A—a Frost Giant?"

"Right!" He brightened. "And I've come home."

"To here?"

"Precisely. To Jotunheim."

"You're mistaken. I lied to Freydis. There are no Frost Giants here."

"Of course there are. You just call them Wolf and Bear and Raven. Sanna and Sila. Malina and Taqqiq. And now that Freydis has finally arrived, I am here to join them!"

He spoke in riddles, and I was tired of being the spirits' plaything. I wanted answers. I wanted to know if he would hurt me—or help me. Nothing else mattered.

"You couldn't come before?" I asked with thinly disguised impatience. "Aren't you a god?"

Loki's face darkened, his humor vanishing in an instant. "If we gods could do whatever we liked, do you really think *you'd* even *exist*?" He pushed off the wall and came to stand above me. "Why would we bother? Why not just live atop our World Tree in a constant state of bliss, loving and fighting and feasting? No, no. We *need* you, as much as I'm loath to admit it. You created us from dreams and prayers and hopes and fears, and we in turn grant you sustenance for both spirit and flesh. Now that the Norse have come to your shores, *I* have, too—borne here by the power of their faith as surely as they are borne by the wind in their sails. We create them. They create us. A great circle." His gesture took in the cell, the ship, the whole of the world. "We all need each other. And right now," he continued, catching my eye in his rainbow gaze, "I need *you* in particular." Smirking at my bound hands, he added, "And, if I'm not mistaken, you need *me*."

"Desperately," I admitted, allowing myself the first spark of hope.

"Why do you think I'm here?" Loki twisted his long, braided mustache around a slender finger. "You've been missing something, haven't you? The other Jotuns took it from you." He released his mustache and placed a hot finger on my cheek. "Well, I'm giving it back."

With Loki's touch, a glimmer of power coursed through my

flesh. For a brief moment, I could almost see the glow move from his skin to mine.

"My magic...," I said softly, my eyes trapped in Loki's sparkling gaze. I reached out with my mind, flexing senses stiff with disuse, seeking some way to test my newfound strength.

I found Brandr, still sleeping under Loki's spell. I reached deep inside him. I had never done this to another person, and yet I found no barriers, nothing, just his spirit calling to my own. Deep within his soul, a single image burned and danced like the Sun's ghost on closed eyelids: a young Inuk, lit only by torchlight. My round cheeks flushed and dotted with birthmarks, my hair brushing the tops of my ears, my lips swollen from his kisses. All these things anyone might have seen. But I saw myself not as anyone would have, but as Brandr had—and I was beautiful. I was strong. For all the fear in his breast, he clung to the knowledge of all we had been to each other—and all we still could be. He had hope.

I could've stayed in that moment forever, but Loki's touch pulled me back.

The god stroked my cheek—not as a threat, as the Moon Man once had, but with a grandfather's affection. Loki had been man and woman. He moved between spirit and flesh. He could understand what it was to have that ability taken from you.

"Why have you helped me?" I begged.

"Because we want the same thing. To protect this land from invaders."

I sucked in a breath. I had found an ally indeed. "Go on."

"You will take me to Sanna. She will send her icebergs to rip through the ships' hulls. The knarrs will founder and sink. All the Norse will drown and Jotunheim will once again be the realm of my people and yours."

I wanted to agree. I wanted to link hands with Loki and help him defeat our enemies. But his plan had a fatal flaw.

"I can't go to Sanna. She'll kill me."

He shrugged. "Perhaps, but that's a risk you must take. I left this land in another age—I no longer speak the Jotuns' tongue. *You* must summon her."

"The spirits have turned from me. Why would they listen now?"

"The spirits of the animals have never abandoned you. Who sent your wolfdogs? Who made them whales?"

"*Narwhals.* One who truly wanted to protect me would have sent the fierce, fanged whales instead."

Loki clicked his tongue. "I suspect your Wolf Spirit would've happily done just that. But your wolfdogs chose which sort of whales to become. Think, my dear. Narwhals never leave the north, not even in winter. They stay close to protect their own family, not to massacre the families of others. And though usually only their males have tusks, sometimes a rare female is born with one as well." He lifted a brow. "Sounds like someone I know."

I scowled at him to hide my weakening resolve. "But Sanna?" I protested. "She bears me an old grudge for stealing my father's spirit from her."

"That's exactly why she'll come when you call her. She wants nothing more than to have you in her clutches."

"Exactly. If she catches me, I'm dead."

"There's no rift between you that cannot be healed. You two have more in common than you think."

"Perhaps...," I conceded, an idea blossoming in my mind.

"So, Inuk. You're the only mortal who can speak both the Inuk's tongue and the Norseman's—who can see the world of both flesh and spirit. You will help? Or should I take back your powers and leave you here to die at first light?" He smiled still, but I wasn't fooled. He wanted this. Needed it.

"No, no. I'll do whatever it takes to save my people. I'll go to Sanna. Just help us escape first."

"I'm afraid I can't just magic you both out of here, my dear. I have to be quiet. Subtle. Odin is a farseeing god. He heard Galinn's plan—a new land, safe from the Christ. Though Galinn, poor child, was too mild and meek to see it through. Odin and Thor sent Freydis Eriksdottir to claim it for them instead. To fight off skrae-lings and Christians alike. They must wonder why she changed her mind and fled Vinland." Loki sighed. "So far, Odin thinks me still imprisoned, so it cannot be me sending her such confusing dreams. But if he realizes I've escaped, he'll send Thor and Tyr to seek me out. And trust my words—you do *not* want to battle the might of the Aesir. So you see why I can't just go around displaying my godly powers to every Greenland shepherd."

"That's why you put Brandr to sleep?"

"It's easier this way, you must admit. To him, our tales are just tales—he doesn't really believe in the spirit world, much less the Aesir. And so he wouldn't be able to see me. I'd appear to him still only as old Muirenn."

"I don't care what Brandr sees or doesn't. You must promise that if I go to Sanna and do as you ask, you'll come back—as an old woman, or a young god, or a *goose* for all I care—and help me and Brandr *and* Kiasik escape."

Loki threw back his head and laughed. I took that for agreement.

The door creaked open.

"Muirenn?"

Snorri squinted into the cell. A harmless old woman looked back at him. For a moment, I wondered if my conversation with the god had all been a delirious vision.

Brandr stirred and cracked open his eyes.

"You've been here long enough, old woman," Snorri said with a frown. "What could you have to say to them?"

"You don't understand." Muirenn lifted the empty dish of cheese. "Ever since the Vikings stole me away from my peo-ple in Írland, and I left my own suckling babe dead behind me, I've had to find what friends I can." Snorri turned pale. "And now"—Muirenn's tone remained light, but her eyes narrowed with pain—"now they take from me once again. Stealing away the boy I once cared for as my own son." She patted Brandr's head once more before turning to Snorri. "Shame be upon your people. Wherever you go, you shed blood—and we shed tears."

"Let's go, thrall," the boy said gruffly. "Enough from you."

"You will be judged. Odin's ravens know all." Her eyes caught mine. "The *ravens*," she repeated, "know all."

"Did I fall asleep?" Brandr asked as the door closed once more. He rubbed his face, looking bewildered.

I barely heard him, my mind still slotting together the pieces of Loki's plan. *It won't work*, I realized, remembering what Brandr had said about the Greenlanders' lust for grain and timber. *Killing Freydis and her men won't be enough—I need to kill the Norsemen's dreams of Vinland as well.*

"They're going to spread-eagle us, right?" I asked quickly. "Didn't the Christ man also die upon a cross?"

"So they say...," Brandr replied. "With a crown of thorns upon his head and a spear in his side."

"And do the Christians not call him a god? And say that he lived again?"

"Yes."

"Then we, too, shall become gods. We, too, shall defeat death."

"Omat, what—"

"You must trust me. I have to go now, or it'll be too late."

"Go? We're still tied up!"

"My body will stay here, but my spirit will leave. Don't worry!" I went on, before he could interrupt. "I told you I was a seer. An angakkuq."

Brandr moved toward me as if he would grab my shoulders.

"Stay back!" I whispered fiercely. He winced as if struck. "You can't touch me while I'm in a trance. If you wake my body before my spirit returns, I'll be wrenched from the other world—I may never make it back to this one."

"*This* is your plan?"

"You saw my wolfdogs turn to whales, and still you don't believe there's more to this world than what you see?"

"*What?* I didn't see that," he insisted. "I started north with the wolfdogs pulling the sled, but when we got to the strait, there was too much open water to cross. So I ripped it apart and made a raft. When I launched it, I had to leave the wolfdogs behind. That first night on the water, three narwhals showed up, circling me, pushing me with their horns. And"—he paused, as if realizing he was proving my point—"they never left." He groaned. "Perhaps there is magic there. I don't know—perhaps you learned the animals' tongue as you learned mine and summoned the narwhals to help me. But I can't believe your *spirit* can leave this cell."

"Yet whether you believe or not, you must trust me, my dear one," I urged, the endearment slipping unbidden from my lips. "You must stay here and be patient."

"Where am I going to go?" he asked, some spark of his old humor returning. "Just make sure you're back before first light." He didn't need to remind me what horrors the false dawn held. "You will return to me," he added softly. More a decree than a question.

"As the Sun follows the heralding stars," I vowed. This was one promise I meant to keep.

CHAPTER
FORTY-EIGHT

ᛉ

The Norse had bound my wrists and feet for me, unwittingly readying me for my journey.

I twisted the chains together, bending low so my nose pressed against my knees. My whispered trance song hummed against my lips.

I could feel Brandr's presence beside me, but I forced myself to block out his warmth, his smell. To spread my awareness into the other world that had denied me for so long.

The moment I began, I knew it would work. Power built within me, a tingling warmth that dotted my forehead with sweat even in the frozen confines of our cell. The song died on my lips but continued unabated in my mind, as if Sila Itself had taken up the chant.

I was an angakkuq once more. Iron chains meant nothing now.

Exhaling loudly, I pushed away my human shell as a whale tosses water from its blowhole. With no vent in our cell for me to fly through on a raven's wings, I inhaled the spirit of a lemming.

My hands contracted; my fingernails grew into long winter claws. My cheeks itched from sprouted whiskers. Fur and fat warmed me as my flimsy woolen dress never could.

Through beady eyes, I looked up at my mortal body in all its enormity. It hunched against the hull, spiritless and still. Brandr sat motionless an arm's length away. While he strained to see me in the dark, my lemming sight could make out every familiar contour of his face. He clutched his arms about his knees, and only his shoulders moved with the rapid rise and fall of his breath. I wished I could do something to reassure him, but without angakkuq powers of his own, he couldn't even see my spirit lemming. I knew he would sit that way until I returned.

I scurried on silent spirit paws across the wooden floor and through the crack beneath the door. The tattooed guard stood whetting a small iron knife. Snorri crouched beside him, his face gray and drawn in the moonlight. He rolled a spear between his palms, his eyes fixed on its spinning point as if imagining drilling it through Brandr's heart.

Humans couldn't see me in my spirit form, but animals had keener sight. I scampered across the hold, dodging the hooves of panicked sheep, up and over the side of the boat and down onto the frozen sea. I listened for the whispered hush of owl wings with my tiny ears. If my lemming body died on a spirit journey, I'd never awake from my trance—and then I'd be no help to anyone.

Out of sight of the knarrs, I released the lemming's soul with one breath and assumed the raven's with the next. The bird spirit felt clean and sharp in my nostrils, like winter air after the first snow.

My tiny paws grew longer. For a moment, I almost tripped over impossibly long front toes until they spread into the webbing of a bird's wings. Black feathers cloaked my flesh.

I was aloft.

Only the stars greeted me. To my relief, a raft of clouds shielded me from the Moon's glaring eye. Sanna might be persuaded to listen to my pleas—Taqqiq never would. If I entered his domain, he would only strip me of my magic once again.

With a rush of wind and wing, another bird swooped to join

me. Its rainbow eye glinted in the darkness. *Loki.* I had not been deaf to Muirenn's message. I had known I'd find him cloaked in raven feathers like my own. A cunning bird for a cunning god.

He began a slow, circling descent to a jagged dark lead in the ice. I followed, my bird's heart pattering as swiftly as raindrops beating the ground.

I breathed out slowly through my beak and inhaled my own spirit with the sharp sea air. Human once again, I stood dressed only in a cape of black feathers, the ice burning against my bare feet. The Trickster settled onto the ground, pacing for a moment on his bird legs. I blinked; when I looked again, Loki stood before me in his silver robes and bronze breastplate. He scanned the ice impatiently. "Where is she?"

"Now that I'm in Sanna's realm, she won't take long to hunt me down."

"Good. Then we'll go back and get your lover and your cousin. Sanna will drown the Greenlanders. Then you can go home."

Home. Puja and Ujaguk tending the oil lamps. Millik picking crow-berries. Tapsi and Saartok smiling at each other. If my plan failed, all of that would disappear. I'd seen what Vikings did to helpless villages. "Muirenn spoke of being taken from her home," I ventured.

Loki nodded. "Yes, she was born in Írland, an island far from the Vikings. They came to her village, killed her babe, and took her as a thrall. Then, when she learned to worship the Aesir as her own, she prayed to me to release her from her misery." He smiled at the memory. "Few turn to the Trickster, you know. They prefer brutal Thor, or wise Odin, or even weak Frey. And women pray to Frigg the Mother or Freya the Beautiful. But Muirenn prayed to *me*—an outsider among the Aesir just as she was an outsider among the Norse. I answered her prayers."

"You helped her escape?"

"No. I let her finally die." He sounded proud. "Her body became mine."

"What the Norse did to Muirenn's land...they'll do to mine."

"Not if we kill them first."

"No. That's not enough. The Vikings dream of conquest. Brandr warned me: even if this expedition never returns to Greenland, other Norse will remember Leif's tales. Like Freydis, they'll dream of grapes and grain too tempting to resist."

Loki narrowed his eyes. "What's your plan, Inuk?"

I was suddenly sure of the path I must choose. "We don't want all the Norse to die. We need at least some of them to *live*. Don't sink their ships—just set them free. We need them to go back to Greenland with dreams not of furs and forests, but of demons and giants. Nightmares so terrible that no Viking will ever venture this way again."

Muirenn's crooked smile crept across his face—or perhaps she'd borne Loki's smile all this time. "Ah, child. You always take the weight of the world on your shoulders."

"This can work, Loki. We'll need help, but we can do it."

He laughed. "Then summon Sanna! Let us begin!"

I hadn't expected him to agree so readily. "Wait—we must be careful. She won't help unless we give her something she desperately wants."

Loki raised one perfect eyebrow. "You're about to tell me what that is."

I looked around the ice, wary of listening spirits, and bent close to whisper my plan.

When I finished, Loki's eyes glowed brighter, and he clapped his hands in childish delight. "A trick worthy of the Trickster. Yes, yes, bring her up!"

"Quiet!" I hissed. "Like the seal, she hears the hunter before he approaches. We must not scare her off."

I cast an uneasy glance at the dark sea. When I turned back to Loki, he'd already obeyed my instructions: the Shapeshifter had transformed once more.

I caught my breath and looked away, unable to bear the gaze of the new man standing before me. I didn't realize I was crying until

I felt the sting of frozen tears upon my cheek. I wouldn't look at him again until I had to.

Drawing a deep breath, I began the chant in the secret tongue:

Sea Mother, Great Woman down there!
Come, come, Spirit of the Deep,
One of your earth dwellers
Calls upon you.
Come, Spirit of the Deep!

My voice sounded small amid the vast emptiness of the frozen sea, the silence broken only by the faint plash of water along the edges of the lead. "Forgive me if I have angered you in the past," I begged. "Come up from the ocean. Return to the air."

Loki grumbled when the ocean remained still and empty. "Perhaps I chose wrong. You're not as powerful as I—"

We both spun toward the sound of a plosive inhalation—the noise a whale makes when surfacing. I resisted the temptation to run away, to hide. I could only hope that Sanna would let me speak before she snatched me from the ice and dragged me down to her watery lair.

A girl huddled a few paces away, where before there had been only frozen ocean. Younger than I. A long cloak of seal fur puddled about her feet. Her black hair streamed across the ice until the ends disappeared into the open lead as if rooting her to the ocean floor. She looked up through the blowing strands of her hair and blinked, blinded by weak starlight. Her nostrils dilated as she drew in great hollow breaths, remembering once again the taste of air, and when she spoke it was in the language of the sea—whistles and moans, clicks and barks, like the creatures she ruled over. Yet I understood every word.

In my mind, her voice sounded like that of a child just waking, whispery and hesitant, almost petulant. "Why do you call me from my warm sea berth? It's cold up here." She rubbed her eyes with fingerless palms.

I planted my feet firmly. "I am Omat, child of Omat."

She blinked once. Twice. Then she began to laugh, the sound like rippling bubbles. "I have felt you above the ice for days, but I hardly recognized you in those foolish clothes!" She rose on spindly white legs and tottered to the edge of the open water. "Come, consort," she called down into the slice of ocean. "Look at the gift the Moon has given to us!"

"The Moon did not send me," I insisted. "I have come of my own free will. And as a sign of my good faith, I have brought you a gift." I gestured for Loki to come forward. Sanna blinked once more, screwing up her delicate face as she peered toward him.

The man reached out a hand to her. She drew a sharp breath. "*Omat . . .*"

Only then did I allow myself to gaze upon the Shapeshifter's new form.

He stood only a little taller than I. That was my first surprise. I'd always imagined my father a tall man. But this Omat was far broader than I, and muscles thickened his outstretched arm. He wore the parka my mother had made for him, dark caribou fur with patches of speckled feathers at the shoulders. His thick hair, chopped low across his forehead, just brushed his dense, indrawn eyebrows. All this I could accept. What I found hard to grasp was that my father was younger than I.

Sanna placed her mutilated, fingerless hand in his. "A fine gift, indeed." My father's eyes whirled in rainbow colors. Sanna stepped closer, her gaze trapped in his—and then stopped short.

Her head jerked backward as a hand emerged from the black water, clutching at her long hair.

I thought surely she'd be pulled into the sea, but despite her frail appearance, the Sea Mother stood firm while a large man used her hair to haul himself from the deep.

His name hissed through my teeth. "*Issuk.*"

His flesh was corpse pale; his black eyes now glowed faintly red. He stood naked before me, brows drawn low, arms tensed and ready to strike. "Omat the little girl *and* Omat the little man." His dark lips did not smile. "Has the Moon finally caught you both?"

I glanced up at the forbidding white orb that crept from its cloak of clouds to set Issuk's pale skin aglow. "We should forget old grudges, old prophecies devoid of sense," I said, though I wanted more than anything to kill him all over again. "I would ask your help, not your enmity. A new people have come to our land. They already murdered your wives, your children. Two of their great wooden boats now wait at our shore—but more will come. And when they do"—I turned to the Sea Mother—"seal and caribou, spirit and Inuk...all will fall beneath their iron blades."

Sanna shrank back, drawing her dark sealskin cloak tight about her slim shoulders. "Evil child with an evil spirit! The Moon Man warned me that you would be the end of our world. You have flouted the aglirutiit! You have brought these strangers!"

"No! Taqqiq would have you blame me. But he divides us only to protect his own power. You need not fear me." I took a bold step closer to her. "My grandfather taught me your story. He told me how the bird-man came with glowing eyes and lured you away from your family. Did he not rape you? As the Moon raped the Sun? I, too, have been abandoned by my family, left in the power of a man without mercy. I, too, have found power in my solitude." From the corner of my eye I saw Issuk tense, but I forged ahead. Sanna was listening now—really listening—for the first time. "Like you, I am woman and more than woman. I have felt a woman's pain, but I have hunted like a man. Who else has lived both lives? That scares Taqqiq, don't you see? But you need not be afraid of me, Sea Mother. I seek to stand with you. You can summon the animals of the deep. They will fight beside us like avenging spirits, so fierce the Norse will never want to return. Then, this very night, you will break the ice that holds them fast, and they will flee. They will not come back."

Loki might not have understood our words, but he seemed to follow the gist of our conversation. He bent to whisper in my ear,

"Tell her to lift you to the Moon. She cannot break the ice without his tides to help."

I ignored the god's demand. "Issuk is Taqqiq's grandson," I said to Sanna instead. "Send *him* to the Moon to ask his help in our quest."

Sanna glanced fearfully at Issuk. "If he leaves, I will be so lonely."

"How can you be alone with the seals and whales to comfort you?" I asked quickly. "You who rule the vast ocean deep, who grant life and succor to all earth dwellers—you have the love of us all. You are never alone."

A faint smile fluttered across her lips. She stood a little straighter.

"Besides," I continued, "I have brought you my father, whom once you loved. Remember how you held him close to your breast so he might warm your heart amid the frozen sea? Issuk owes his loyalty to the Moon, but *Omat* will be yours entirely."

Sanna took a step toward Loki-in-Omat. She raised one thin arm; her sealskin cloak slipped down her shoulder, revealing one small, high breast topped with a dark nipple. Not unlike my own.

Loki grabbed Sanna's hand before she could back away. He raised her palm to his lips and kissed it. She frowned at first, confused by the gesture, and I silently cursed the god for not knowing our customs, but then, to my surprise, Sanna smiled. And then she blushed.

"Issuk, go to your grandfather," she commanded. "Tell the Moon his tides are needed."

"Don't trust this woman," Issuk growled. "She seeks her revenge—"

"Quiet!" Sanna roared. The ice shifted and groaned in response. "You are my *consort*, not my master. You will do as I demand."

"The Moon will not like it—" Issuk began.

Sanna reached swiftly into the open water and twisted her arms into the dripping ropes of black seaweed. With a strength that belied her slender limbs and fingerless hands, she dragged the fronds onto the ice. Then, like Freydis with her thread, Sanna worked her magic on the kelp, slinging it swiftly around Issuk's throat.

"I told you to be quiet," she said, calmer now, as Issuk pulled desperately at the choking fronds, his breath coming in ragged gasps. She let him suffer a little longer. "Will you go now? Or must I put the seaweed down your throat instead of just around it?" Issuk choked an assent, eyes wide and watering. "Good." Sanna pulled one end of the seaweed with a quick yank—it slid easily from his body and back into the water.

Issuk bent double, gasping. He glared at me, at Sanna, at the man who had taken his place. He turned his eyes skyward, eyes that now blazed as red as fresh-flowing blood.

In an instant, his nose elongated to grotesque proportions, his arms grew dark feathers, and his strong legs wizened to scaly bird feet. In a rush of wind, he was gone. Above us only his red eyes remained, burning like stars amid the black. Then they, too, disappeared.

"I thought I had killed him," I said softly. "Yet still he shadows my path."

Sanna merely smiled. "That which is dead can always come back. Men live in many worlds at once. So do gods. Surely you understand that now."

I looked at her more closely. Her form remained unchanged, and yet her eyes were older, her face grave and filled with ancient power. The shivering, petulant girl had vanished with Issuk. In her place stood the Great Woman.

"You, Omat," she said, speaking to my father. "Go below—I will meet you there when I return, and we will once more warm each other in the deep."

She raised her arms to him, her gesture unmistakable. Loki-in-Omat shot me a wide-eyed glance. He had no desire to be dragged beneath the ice by a needy goddess. Yet if he revealed his true form, surely Sanna would refuse to help us.

"I beg your patience, Sea Mother," I said, thinking quickly. "But I need my father for a little longer."

Sanna frowned. "You gave him to me."

"He must stay in the world above until the Norse are gone. But then he will return to you." Sanna's scowl only deepened. "He told me that life among the stars was cold compared to life at your side," I added. "He dreams only of holding you again."

The words came easily to me, an echo of Brandr's confession right before he kissed me for the first time: *I dreamed only of this.* It felt wrong to use them now as a lie, but they melted Sanna's heart as easily as they had mine.

The Sea Mother's face softened. Loki dared to step forward and press another kiss upon the back of her pitiful hand.

"I have waited for you a long time, Omat," she said wistfully. "Perhaps I can wait a little longer." She turned to me. "So, what else do you need of me, daughter?"

No one had ever called me daughter before. I had been son, grandson, brother. Now a new name, one I was surprised to find myself liking. "You must call the animal spirits to you. Together we will bring Freydis's nightmare to life upon the frozen sea."

Sanna raised her eyebrows in acquiescence. "It will be done."

"But hurry. We must be at the ships before Malina's rays touch the sky. I have a promise to keep." I'd already been gone too long. Brandr would be nearly mad with worry.

But Sanna reached out to stop me. "Your promise is not mine, daughter. I cannot bring the animals with such speed." She glanced up at the arching stars. "Let the Sun reach once more for the horizon. Let the false dawn come and go. Then, when the night sky is once more bright with the spirits of your ancestors—then the animals will arrive."

"No! That's too late!"

Sanna's glance darkened. "They must be summoned from the three corners of our land, from sea and sky and earth. Such a task is not easy."

"Please, Great Woman," I begged, all my newfound hope slipping away. "I must have help before then. Please."

She held up a fingerless palm to silence me and tilted her head as if listening to a far-off call. Her sudden, whistling cry split the night. Loki and I clapped our hands to our ears.

"You need not be alone," she said, her voice soft once again. "There are those who would join you now."

Far out in the lead, three long yellow tusks waved above the water. My pack.

"Go," Sanna urged, "I will see you at the sky's next darkening." She turned without another word and stepped off the ice, her body disappearing soundlessly into the black.

"And you, Loki," I said, turning to the god. "You will not fail me?"

He slanted a grin at me, the expression sitting uneasily on my father's features, and transformed into a raven with a snap of light. I took that for agreement.

The bird rose skyward on sharp black wings, melting into the stars.

I was no god, to shift so effortlessly from shape to shape. In this one night, I had already gone from Inuk to lemming to raven and back. Ataata had warned against shifting too frequently lest I grow too weary to regain my human form. But as the narwhals approached, I had no choice. At the sky's first lightening, the Norse would kill Brandr. And my mortal form would die on the cross alongside him. I took a deep breath and willed myself a wolf.

Nothing happened.

Great Sanna, I prayed silently. *Help me now.*

A scream, part raven's caw, part wolf's howl, part woman's cry, tore from my throat as my body split apart. First one long wolf leg, then another, thrust through my skin.

The narwhals breached once, tall plumes of spray spouting behind their long horns, then sprang from the water to land on wide-splayed wolf paws beside me. I struggled upright, long claws gripping the ice. We stood together for a moment, four wolves, panting and shaking our new skins.

Then White Paw, Floppy Eared, and Sweet One padded over to me, their tails lowered submissively, ears back. They sniffed my jaws, my belly, under my tail. I'd never truly smelled my pack before, not with a wolf's nose. White Paw exuded strength, confidence, health. Deep inside, I felt drawn to her. I imagined running across the tundra, following the banner of her gray tail. Floppy Eared smelled less dominant, but healthy and strong. I could scent injury in Sweet One; a patch of dried blood marked her tail, where Bjarni's arrow had pinned her whale form to the ice, but she was eager to hunt.

Their tails wagged furiously; their mouths lolled open. Floppy Eared stretched out his front paws and crouched in an offer to play. White Paw pressed her flank against mine. We spoke the same language now, a tongue of gestures and motion, odors and sounds.

We are glad to see you, Mother, said White Paw. *We have missed you.*

It is good to be with you again, I replied, licking her jaw, somehow not surprised that I had always been Mother to my pack, not Father. *How did you find me?*

Great Singarti showed us the way.

Floppy Eared yipped in excitement. *He made us whales so we could follow you on the water. Then wolves again so we can follow you on land.*

Sweet One tucked her tail between her legs. *Where is your mate?*

My mate? Brandr. *He is in danger. Captive among a strange pack. And my brother is there, too. We must help them both.*

Floppy Eared cavorted around us. *Yes! Let us go! I am tired of being a sea creature. Glad to be on four legs again! Let us run and play! Let us fight and bite!*

White Paw panted her agreement. A howl rose in my gut, working its way up until I felt compelled to sit on my haunches, throw back my head, and let it fly.

The others joined in, eyes closed, howling in long, sonorous waves that danced from one pitch to the other, our voices overlapping like the strands of a woman's careful braid.

My throat raw but my weakness forgotten, I led my pack across the ice toward the knarrs. As we ran, I told them of my plan. *It will be just like bringing down a moose*, I assured them. *But we must hurry! They must not see us coming. If they do, they will shoot at us with their arrows before we can rescue anyone.*

We slunk, bellies against the ice, toward the Greenlanders' ship, approaching in the moonshadow. With my wolf nose, I could smell Ingharr, as rank as a fox and full of gloating joy. Kiasik's scent floated from the Icelanders' knarr, where Freydis had ordered him held. Hopeless, injured, sick.

I could smell Brandr, too. He was terrified. Sweet One whimpered softly.

The heralding stars were twin points of light hovering just above the glowing horizon. Tomorrow, perhaps, Malina would rise in truth.

For now, only a false dawn lit the sky. The Sun's rays limned the clouds in blood.

First light.

CHAPTER
FORTY-NINE

⌇

Floppy Eared and White Paw dashed to the stern of the boat; Sweet One and I ran to the prow, our wide paws silent and sure on the ice. I crouched below the tall knarr, invisible to all but the dragon figurehead.

Beside me, the sharp scent of fear rose from Sweet One's flanks. I almost yipped for joy when White Paw and Floppy Eared began to howl near the stern to attract the Norsemen's attention.

From above us, footsteps and shouting on the deck. The ship's shadow sharpened on the ice as the torchlight moved toward the commotion at the stern.

Freydis's voice rang above the clamor: "Ingharr, get your sword. Bjarni, your bow! Someone kill those wolves!" I sent a silent prayer to Singarti to protect his children. We would have to work quickly.

I padded from the shadows, ears pricked forward. The curved ship's rail loomed above me, higher than a tall man's head, but I leapt over it in one smooth movement and landed silently aboard. With Sweet One close behind me, I prowled the empty foredeck.

Only the faintest rays of sunlight lit our way—all the sailors, with their torches, had rushed to the stern at Freydis's command.

Two tall wooden crosses stood like barren trees at the prow of the ship. My empty human body, thankfully still unconscious despite being moved, lay in a crumpled heap at the foot of one, my wrists still locked in iron chains.

From the other cross hung Brandr.

They'd removed his fur parka and wool shirt and tied him chest-first to the beam so they could more easily pull the lungs from his back. He faced the ship, not the sea, his neck twisted painfully against the top of the cross. Ropes bound each wrist to the beam, his arms stretched so tight the muscles of his chest seemed close to splitting. Another rope bound him cruelly across the waist, slicing into the bare flesh of his stomach.

The tattooed guard stood beside the cross, armed with a short iron knife. At his waist hung a dark iron key. A few thralls sat nearby, peering toward the ruckus at the stern. They were oblivious to our presence—the sheep were not. At the smell of wolf, the panicked animals bleated manically and tried to clamber from the hold, futilely scraping their hooves against the hull.

Sweet One and I bounded forward before the thralls noticed us. She bowled into the guard's legs; I struck his shoulders with my front paws. He screamed in shock and surprise and fell to his knees. The thralls spun toward the sound.

I'm invisible, I remembered as Brandr's eyes roved right past me and latched onto Sweet One instead. *I'm a spirit wolf, not a wolf in flesh.*

Yet spirit or no, I could kill.

I ripped the guard's throat from his neck. Warm blood gushed into my mouth. My long wolf tongue wanted to lap at the rich red feast. My Inuk mind wanted to scream. This did not taste like the fresh blood of the seal, the caribou, the whale. This was man's blood, and I should not be drinking it.

I shook my head, specks of red flying from my snout, and let the man's corpse rest. With my jaws, I ripped the iron key from his belt. The cold metal stuck to my tongue. As I made my way to my hunched human form, Sweet One rushed to keep the now-terrified thralls out of my way.

I turned wolf eyes on Brandr. He stared at Sweet One in turn. Bewildered, hopeful, scared. I inhaled his familiar scent one last time, then forced the air from my lungs, dispelling the wolf soul.

I expected to awaken in my human form. Instead I was nowhere. Nothing. Not wolf, not Inuk.

Trapped and rootless, my exhausted spirit hovered above the ship, watching while Sweet One corralled the herd of screaming thralls and White Paw and Floppy Eared dashed among the flying arrows of the Norsemen.

No! I screamed silently, my voice resounding only in the oblivion between worlds. *Not now!* I'd made it this far. I needed only one more transformation...

"Omat!" Brandr shouted. "Come back to me! You promised."

His plea struck me like a harpoon, lodging beneath my ribs, and his words dragged me toward myself as surely as a line reeled in around a hunter's hands.

Gasping for breath, I awoke. My eyes fluttered open. My surroundings spun for a moment, then resolved into a flat, indistinct world perceived through a human's inferior senses.

"Omat!" Brandr's cry sharpened my mind.

I grabbed the iron key lying before me on the deck and managed to unlock my chains. Clutching at the wooden cross for support, I struggled to my feet.

With the dead guard's iron knife, I sliced through Brandr's ropes. Then he was loose, his body falling off the cross and into my arms.

Sweet One feinted toward the sheep and thralls one more time, driving them like a caribou herd into a tight mass that clogged the entire width of the ship. None of the armed men in the stern would reach us.

Hope surged through me. I called my wolfdog to my side as Brandr and I stumbled toward the ship's rail. Sweet One spun and dashed ahead, leading the way.

But I should've known it would take more than a crowd of panicked thralls to stop Ingharr Ketilsson. He pushed through some, trampled others, and managed to reach the rail before my wolfdog. He stood before her, his own teeth bared in a simulacrum of her snarl. His face swelled with Thor's berserker madness.

He raised his nicked iron sword above Sweet One. Without thinking, I howled a warning and hurled my stolen knife. Ingharr ducked just in time; my blade sliced through the flesh of his ear, a hairbreadth from his skull.

That was all the opening Brandr needed.

My friend drove his shoulder into Ingharr's knees—the two men crashed to the deck in a tangle of limbs.

Ingharr's sword flew from his grasp, nearly shearing Sweet One's nose. It struck point-first into the deck, vibrating just within my reach. Still dizzy from my recent return to humanity, I wrenched it from the wood. Heaving the massive weapon with two hands, I staggered forward. I dared not swing the sword into Ingharr's neck, not with Brandr's body twined with his. The yellow-haired man stuck out a leg to brace himself against the deck—I brought the sword crashing into his thigh. He bellowed, foam flying from his lips.

Brandr wriggled free, but nothing could stop Ingharr's berserker rage. He grabbed Brandr's ankle to stop his escape and slammed a fist into his bad leg. My friend grunted in pain, sweat popping on his brow despite the cold.

I heaved the sword again, ready to bring it down on Ingharr's flushed neck.

A high-pitched scream tore through the night, freezing me in place. A slight figure flew through the crowd of sheep and thralls, a spear held in both hands.

Snorri.

For an instant, my eyes met the boy's, but he didn't recognize me. I was only an obstacle on the way to Brandr.

I didn't think, didn't pause, simply hurled the sword as I would a harpoon. The blade's weight dragged it from the air. It clattered beside Snorri's feet and skidded across the deck and into the open hold. The boy didn't even slow.

I threw myself in front of him, twisting sideways to avoid his spear point, and grabbed the weapon's shaft. Snorri's momentum slammed us both against the side of the ship.

"*Omat!*" roared Brandr, still grappling with Ingharr. "Be careful!"

I tried to twist the spear from Snorri's grasp, but he wrenched it from my hands and struck me across the face with the shaft. I fell back for a moment, and he turned on his father's killer, growling with wordless rage.

"*No!*" I flung myself at Snorri's back, calling up all I'd learned in the winter wrestling matches. This time I had the upper hand. Snorri's strength was no match for my own. I pinned his arms to his sides—he bucked and twisted in my grasp, trying in vain to throw me off. I slid my hands to the shaft, holding Snorri between my arms as Ataata had once held me when he taught me to hunt. Pitting my strength against his, I dragged the spear past his chest, up to his throat, and pulled.

Snorri kicked backward, his heels digging through the soft hide of my boots, but I would not release him. My cheek pressed against his sweating neck as I held him in this awkward lovers' embrace, feeling the life drain from his body as I choked the air from his throat with the spear.

"I don't want to kill you, Snorri," I spoke in his ear. "I know what it is to hate someone who's taken away those you love. But killing me or Brandr won't bring back your father. And killing you won't bring back mine." I tightened the shaft against his neck. "Your god teaches you that, doesn't he?" I remembered the Christ from my dreams, hanging limp from his bloody cross, his eyes soft. "He did not fight what he could not change, and when he met his end, he dreamed of love—not hate."

I felt some of the fight leave Snorri's body. Tears leaked from his eyes. I relaxed the pressure again, allowing him a ragged gasp.

I went on, more gently. "Christ wants there to be peace between us. You saved me from Ingharr, now let me save you from yourself. I will let you go. But you have to leave here, do you understand?" My final words were a growl against his cheek. "You can't go after Brandr. If you do"—I gave the spear a final warning yank against his bobbing throat—"your life is forfeit."

"I won't," he choked, sounding once more like the skinny boy he was. "I—I don't want to die."

"Nor do I, Snorri." I lifted the spear clear of his neck and pushed him roughly away. "Now go."

The boy stumbled toward the rail and fell to his knees. He pressed his palms together and raised his face toward the sky. I left him there, praying to his strange god, and turned back to the battle behind me.

Brandr sat astride Ingharr, his hands circling the other man's throat. The muscles of his bare chest and arms swelled, and I wondered if my friend had finally allowed the berserker rage to take control again. But no, his gaze was his own. Ingharr's own acceptance of Thor's gift was all too apparent; he still hadn't given up, bucking beneath Brandr like a boat in a storm.

Around us, chaos reigned. Freydis's voice rose above the clamor, desperately ordering her men to bring down the three wolfdogs that now prowled the deck. Blood slicked the boards. My pack had been busy. But even they couldn't hold off a whole boat of Vikings forever.

First save Brandr. Then Kiasik. Then we flee, I decided, hurrying toward the struggling men with Snorri's spear at the ready.

Brandr saw me coming. "No," he grunted, his knuckles white around Ingharr's neck. "I want to kill this one myself."

With both hands, I rammed the spear through Ingharr's stomach. "No time for vengeance." I yanked the shaft clear of Ingharr's intestines and whistled shrilly to my wolfdogs. "We have to find Kiasik."

CHAPTER FIFTY

ᛋ

The drop from ship to sea was longer in my Norse skirts than it had been in my wolf guise, but I landed safely enough. With Brandr beside me, I sprinted toward the Icelanders' knarr, hoping Loki had fulfilled his side of the bargain. My wolfdogs soon outpaced us, bounding ahead across the frozen, moonlit sea.

Freydis's screams of rage chased us across the ice.

Around us, arrows clattered like hail. Bjarni wasn't the only Norseman with a bow—just the one with the best aim. The wolfdogs' bodies twisted lithely as they dodged the shafts. As a human, even with my magic restored, my senses were not so keen. I trusted my luck—and ran.

The Icelanders' ship rose before us. Only Olfun and one-armed Magnor stood on the deck, and neither had a bow. Still, they weren't about to lower a rope to help us aboard, and I no longer had a wolf's ability to leap to the deck.

Thankfully, I didn't have to.

"This way!" a quavering voice called from the shadows beneath the ship's hull.

"Muirenn!" Brandr cried. There, nearly hidden behind the

carven figurehead, the old woman stood on the ice with a large, awkward bundle on her back. Beside her waited Kiasik, standing taller than he had since I first found him among the Norse.

"*Skraeling!*" shouted Olfun as we rushed beneath the hull and out of his sight. "*Traitor!*"

"Where are you going?" screamed Magnor. "Come here and fight!"

"Where's her brother?" I heard Olfun ask as I embraced Kiasik.

"I tied him up on the foredeck."

"Well, he's not here now! No, wait—there they are!"

"Bjarni!" Magnor called over the ice toward the bowman on the other knarr. "Do you see them?"

An arrow thrummed toward us, sinking deep into the sea ice near Kiasik's feet. He took a quick step backward; I grabbed him before he could slip on the ice. "Watch out!"

"I'm fine," he said. "You don't need to worry about me anymore."

I looked at him more closely. His breath came evenly; his eyes gleamed. "How did—"

"The old woman," he said, jerking his chin toward Muirenn. "She must be an angakkuq, because she laid her hands on my chest and the pain stopped."

"*Now* you heal him?" I hissed at the woman. "After all this time?"

"Can we discuss this later?" she asked calmly. "When there aren't a dozen men trying to kill us?"

I grunted but led the way. As we left the shelter of the boat, I sent Snorri's spear sailing toward the broad bowman on the Greenlanders' ship. This was a weapon of wood, not unlike the ones I'd wielded my whole life. My aim was true. The blade sank into Bjarni's shoulder.

Magnor roared his displeasure, but with one arm, he couldn't climb over the ship's rail and wield his sword at the same time. Olfun hurled his own spear at Brandr, but it skidded harmlessly across the ice.

Freydis continued to shout at her men. Her husband took up Bjarni's bow, but his arrows all flew either too wide or too short. The other freemen on Freydis's boat were sailors and shepherds, not fighters. Despite her increasingly furious demands, they dared not come after us. Not after seeing what I'd done to Ingharr.

"Now we run," I urged my companions.

"Good," said Muirenn. "Freydis said she'd punish *me* if you attacked another Norseman. I think at this point she'd probably string me up as bear bait and laugh all the while."

Brandr took her by the elbow. No berserker, only a man concerned for an old friend. "Well, then, you're going to have to move faster."

"Don't worry about me, my boy," Muirenn chuckled, shambling along beneath her awkward pack.

"Here, give it to me," I said, grabbing her burden. I didn't trust Muirenn, whether possessed by a god or no, to move quickly.

Kiasik swiped Olfun's spear from the ground and sprinted ahead, his recklessness restored. I dashed after him, gasping under the surprising weight of Muirenn's pack and silently begging Sanna to hold the ice firm beneath our feet.

White Paw ran before me with Floppy Eared and Sweet One on our flanks. We headed for the coast, not slowing even when we reached solid ground. Back past the longhouse we sprinted, then north along the edge of a deep fjord that pierced the land like an accusatory finger, jutting toward the whale mountain. There, on the fjord's edge, with the frozen sea on one side and the steep mountains on the other, we finally rested.

Kiasik crouched on the snowy ground, breathing heavily. He leaned his weight on the stolen Norse spear but looked ready to keep going at any moment. Brandr collapsed beside him without a word. The sweat on his bare chest glittered with frost; his skin quickly paled from pink to blue.

Muirenn took her pack from me and hauled out Brandr's parka and his sword.

"By Thor's beard, you're a clever old woman." He hefted his weapon in one hand. The swirls in the metal danced like the wavering lights of the aqsarniit.

Brandr drew the parka over his shivering body. Sweet One curled beside him, laying her large head in his lap and staring up with adoring brown eyes. Brandr buried his hands in her fur and rested his head upon hers. "However you got here, girl," he murmured to her, "I'm glad you did."

Floppy Eared showed no signs of fatigue; he dashed from Kiasik to me to Muirenn to Brandr, sniffing each of us in turn, nearly bowling over Inuk, god, and Viking alike with his enthusiasm. White Paw ignored her brother's antics and laid her huge gray head against my hand. Only then did I notice the small sealskin bag in her jaws.

"Where did you...?" I clutched the familiar amulet pouch to my breast. "Thank you, my friend." I couldn't imagine how, in the heat of the battle, she'd ripped the amulet from Freydis's gown, but I suppose a wolf who could transform into a whale was capable of all manner of magic. I placed my cheek upon her snout in a gesture I knew she'd understand. She merely licked my nose, wagged her tail once, and then stood with ears swiveling, scanning for danger.

I unknotted the cord from my neck and slipped off the rune-carved stone. I looked at the mark that had branded me a thrall—the strange branching symbol Freydis claimed as her own—then flung the stone away. In its place I secured my amulet pouch, slipping its familiar weight beneath the neck of my dress.

Kiasik rose to his feet. With a violent gesture, he tore his own torque loose and threw it to the ground. Then, without preamble, he began to walk north.

I grabbed his arm. "Where're you going?"

"Home."

"You can't."

"What do you mean? Where are *you* going?" he asked, dumbfounded.

I swallowed. The plan hadn't sounded outrageous until I said it out loud.

"Back to the boats."

"What?"

"It's not enough to escape from them and move our family farther west," I explained. "We must make sure the Norse leave tonight, before they can come after us—and that they never return."

"And how will they leave with the sea frozen around them?" he demanded.

"We'll break the ice. I have my magic back. The spirits once again guide my steps."

"You've gone mad, Little Brother. I'm finally healed and we're finally free. You would throw all that away?"

"Don't you understand? Freydis told me she wants *all* our land. We could never run far enough to escape them forever. The Norse killed Muirenn's family. They killed Issuk's. They will kill ours just the same."

I turned to Brandr and switched to Norse, trying to explain. "Freydis dreamed that you led an army against her—an army of skraelings, like Kiasik and me. I want to bring that nightmare to life. Only then will she believe that her gods don't want her here." Translating for Kiasik, I added: "We all have a role to play."

"Not me. I'm no angakkuq, or have you forgotten?" retorted my brother, his voice sharp with old jealousy.

"I don't need an angakkuq. I need my friend, healed and whole, ready to stand beside me. Great hunters protecting our family. *Together.* Just like you always said we would."

I thought my words would sway him. Instead, he set his lips in a stubborn line. "Our family is close. We should run as far as we can, as fast as we can."

My own expression hardened in echo of his. "You don't think of the future! You never have." Ignoring his wounded expression, I whirled to Brandr and Muirenn. "What about you? Will you follow me in this?"

"I'm an old woman," Muirenn said with a crooked smile. "But I never wish to be a thrall again. I'll go along with your crazy plan, child."

Brandr took my hand in his own. "I'll follow where you lead," he said quietly. "You need only ask."

I looked down at our entwined fingers. All I wanted was to have him by my side. For a moment, uncertainty shivered through me. Could I really lead this man back into danger after saving his life? And Kiasik, too? I turned my eyes to the whale mountain, to my family's home. Unable to resist, I imagined Brandr safe beside me, his face warm in the glow of a good seal oil lamp. It wouldn't be hard to take my family far from here—there were other hunting grounds, other valleys and mountains and rivers. Let the Norse have what land they would.

Perhaps Kiasik was right.

Then I felt the weight of my pouch around my neck. I pulled my hand from Brandr's grasp and felt the contours of my amulets through the worn sealskin. A quartz blade to remind me that one people can replace another. A black bear claw to remind me of the animal spirits who had watched over me from the moment of my birth. I looked to the wolfdogs, who sat patiently guarding me as they always had. A gift from Singarti.

White Paw's yellow eyes caught mine and held. *The spirits of my world have not abandoned me*, I knew. *I cannot abandon them.*

"The Moon Man once told me that I would be the destroyer of my world," I said slowly. "I never believed him before. But he was right. You heard Freydis—because of me, she wants to stay here. She wants to destroy my people. If we don't act now, Brandr, your people will enslave mine. They will steal and rape as they always have. Maybe not for many moons, for many winters, maybe even many generations. But eventually, your people and mine will collide." I looked from Brandr to Kiasik, repeating my words in our tongue. "Let us end it now. Let us fight tonight so we might meet tomorrow a free people."

Brandr nodded. He would fight by my side now as he had every day since we faced a brown bear on the summer tundra. He raised his familiar sword in salute. Already false dawn had given way once again to false sunset, and the last red beams ran along his blade like bloodied water.

Kiasik was not so easily swayed. "You're blind," he grunted. "Even if the strangers leave and never come back, we won't be free of them." His nostrils flared. "I see how you look at that man." He jerked his chin toward Brandr, who looked up, startled. "*He'll* still be here."

"Brandr's different," I insisted coldly. "He'd rather stay with us than with his own people."

Kiasik's brows lowered. "He's your husband now, is that it? Aii! All your talk of being a man, a hunter, and yet the first strange giant who shows you any attention, you throw yourself at him! Issuk wasn't good enough for you, but you would lie with this man? He means more to you than I do?"

I struck him, hard.

A livid red mark blossomed on his cheek. He gaped at me. I clenched my fist, regretting the blow. This was not how Ataata had raised me. Had I become like Issuk, like Ingharr, that I would strike a man who was no threat to me? A man whose face already bore the scars of so much injury? I knew that Kiasik spoke more from thoughtless jealousy than from anything else, but for once I couldn't find the will to excuse him. After all I'd done, he still didn't believe in me. His long war between love and envy was finally over. And envy had won.

"I have loved you as my sister's son," I said, my voice shaking. "As my elder brother, as my cousin, as my friend. I have traveled across land and sea for you. I have rescued you from your enemies." I knew I should leave it there. This was not the time or place for such a battle, yet my composure had fled. I spat the words at him. "Brandr would never abandon me as you did. You left me to Issuk. You pitied me—but you didn't have the courage to *fight* for me. And you still don't."

Kiasik looked more stunned than when I'd struck him. He opened his mouth to respond; I silenced him with a curt gesture. "Go!"

"Please, Little Brother—"

He would have said more, I knew. Would have kept begging me to flee to safety. But I could not hear it. I cut him off.

"You aren't listening," I growled. "I do not need you to save me anymore. I do not *want* you to save me. I want you to *trust* me. And if you cannot do that—then I want you gone."

He took a step back from me, his proud shoulders drooping.

"Go back to Puja and Ququk!" I thrust an arm to the north, pointing the way. "Back to Tapsi and Saartok! But do not forget to warn them that an enemy is close. They will need to start running. And they can *never* stop."

I turned away to hide my angry tears. The wolfdogs stood at my back, hackles raised.

After a moment of pained silence, I heard the crunch of retreating footsteps in the snow.

When the wolfdogs finally lay down at my feet, I knew Kiasik was out of sight. I sank beside them, leaning into their warmth.

"And now?" Muirenn asked mildly. I'd almost forgotten about the old woman. She slanted a smile at me, and I knew Loki laughed at the dramas of mortals.

I glanced once at the hovering Moon. "Now we wait. We rest. We don't need Kiasik. We will have other allies."

━━◆◆◆◆━━

As the sky darkened from violet to black, Brandr finally succumbed to sleep, his head on Muirenn's lap. She hummed a lilting tune through lips quirked with Loki's smile.

White Paw rose suddenly to her feet, ears swinging forward, her nose pointing toward the mountains. I squinted into blackness, worried. Sanna would come from the sea, not the shore.

A large white form materialized from the darkness, glowing in the moonlight. It stalked toward us on silent feet. *Taqqiq? Come to hunt me down at last? Or to fight by my side, finally my ally?*

I reached to shake Brandr awake, but Muirenn shook her head. "Let him rest," she said softly. "He can't see it anyway."

The wolfdogs approached the figure cautiously, tails between their legs, completely submissive. This was no Moon Man. Now I could see the four long legs, the pointed snout, the proud tail held aloft. Yellow eyes glowing like firelight. My protector had returned.

"Singarti."

As if summoned by the name, one by one the stars appeared above me. The spirits of my family lit their lamps to guide our way. Ataata watched once more from the heavens.

I stood to greet the Wolf, feeling stronger than I ever had. The combined power of all my ancestors stood with me. Sanna would walk by my side. Even Taqqiq would light our way and lend his strength.

With their help, I could chase the Norse from our shores forever.

Far into the night, my army grew. Qangatauq the Raven came next, black wings so wide they blotted out the stars. With a sharp caw, he landed on the ice beside Singarti. Where Wolf traveled, Raven followed. Then another great animal appeared, twice as tall as the tallest Inuk, as wide as an umiaq, as white as the snow: Uqsuralik.

"Aii," I gasped.

Never before had the great Bear revealed himself to me. Like Singarti, he loomed larger than any animal of the flesh. His black eye sought mine, and in his gaze I saw the wisdom and strength of my grandfather. On his right forepaw, only four black claws scraped the surface of the snow.

Between his feet scurried a dark shadow: Lemming. Bounding among them, a flash of white: Hare. Dancing over the ground, sniffing eagerly with her black nose: Fox. Slinking forward with heavy tail and wicked claws: Wolverine. With a clatter of hooves on ice, thick antlers scraping the sky: Caribou. Plodding slowly toward me, curved horns lowered and shaggy coat rippling in the wind: Musk Ox. Flying on wings of white and black and brown: Owl, Falcon, Ptarmigan. All the winter animals of land and air.

I turned to look over the sea ice, where the rest of my allies struggled toward me. Massive dark forms with ice crystals hanging heavy and pendulous from their whiskers: Bearded Seal and Walrus. If I listened very closely, I could hear the wet sighs of Black Whale and White Whale, the curious clicking of Narwhal, and the keening whistle of Fanged Whale—the aarluk—all swimming through the distant leads.

Through it all, Loki-in-Muirenn stroked Brandr's hair steadily with one gnarled hand. The Viking slept on beneath her spell.

The most powerful of my new allies finally appeared. She arrived behind a guard of dappled seals, hobbling on legs weak from disuse and clutching a cloak of fur around her slim, pale shoulders. The Sea Mother.

She stepped to the very border between sea ice and earth. Her bare toe hovered above the land for a moment, then withdrew as if burnt.

Flopping across the ice, a familiar ivory-handled blade clutched in her whiskered jaws, came Ringed Seal. She dropped the steel knife at my feet with a barking cry, swung her ponderous body, and galumphed back toward her mistress. It seems things lost at sea could always be recovered.

Sanna looked up through her waterfall of black hair and blinked twice.

"Well, daughter?" she asked, the hint of a smile on her lips. "What now?"

CHAPTER FIFTY-ONE

᛭

Your bears and wolves will strike fear in the heart of Freydis Eriksdottir," Muirenn said, "but I'm not so sure about the rest of them." She cast a doubtful eye on Lemming and Hare. "She expects Frost Giants to storm the ships, not rodents."

"You said the animal spirits were *all* Frost Giants, like you."

Muirenn nodded. "But Freydis doesn't know that. To her, Giants are...well...*giant*."

"Fine, then." A plan swiftly took shape in my mind. "I'll make us some giants."

"Out of what?"

"Out of nothing, of course. As my grandfather taught me to."

I called to Uqsuralik. The great Ice Bear with his graceful, swaying walk came to my side, lowering his head so it hung level with my own. I placed one hand tentatively on his wide, white cheek. "Great Uqsuralik, protector of my grandfather, help me now."

He bowed his head to me. I clambered up his neck and onto his broad back. My legs didn't reach around his chest, so I sat as I would on a sled, one leg tucked beneath me, hands fisted into his fur. "Watch Brandr," I called down to Muirenn. "Keep him safe until I return."

The spirit animal began to run. I bounced to his stride, my tailbone slamming painfully into the sharp ridge of his spine. I called out to barnacled Black Whale and gleaming Fanged Whale. In answer, they blew a wet burst of air as we passed by the lead in which they swam. As we hurtled across the ice, they followed through the water. We stopped not far from the knarrs, their wooden outlines barely visible in the darkness.

At my instruction, the Whales lifted great stones from the sea-floor. Ice Bear pushed them into place. Five inuksuit rose between the ships and the shore. Three times the height of a man they stood, taller than any figures my people had ever built to scare a caribou herd. Their bare stone faces glared across the frozen sea, daring the Norse to approach.

If man and beast were not enough to terrorize Freydis Eriksdottir, then Frost Giants would be.

— ◼◆◼ —

The Moon alone ruled the sky when I returned to the shore to lead my allies against the Norse ships.

Never had such a strange procession crossed the ice.

As we traveled, the great spirit animals called to their flocks and herds and packs. Soon we walked among a swelling mass of other animals, large and small.

Proud Caribou trotted among a herd of smaller caribou, guiding them toward the ships with his antlers bobbing. Horned Musk Ox moved across the ice amid a swirling curtain of trailing fur. Swift Falcon added her piercing scream to those of her flock. Ptarmigan sheltered a throng of smaller birds beneath wide wings of winter white. Even Lemming scurried within a teeming mass of her smaller, frantic children.

Through it all, Sanna watched calmly. At an open lead, she

slipped into the water with the seals and walruses so they might work from beneath the ice.

Floppy Eared could not be contained. He feinted at Hare and Ptarmigan, crouched before Ice Bear and offered to play, leapt in the air to taunt Raven. Singarti watched complacently as he padded along beside Caribou, their ancient enmity forgotten for one night.

Brandr walked beside me, his eyes wide in wonder at the assembled beasts. He could not see the great spirits, but the animals of flesh were shocking enough. He kept a hand on Sweet One's back, seeking reassurance in her familiar presence.

"Remember," I said to him, "we seek to break the ice and send the Greenlanders off with their tails between their legs. You need only *appear* fierce to convince Freydis. She's already dreamed you're coming after her, so it won't take much. You don't need to risk your life."

He nodded and took a practice swing with his gleaming sword. I felt a creeping unease about his role in this.

A slow lightening of the sky, from black to blue, began in the east. The Moon and stars still gazed upon us, but the Sun hid just beneath the horizon, waiting for her ascendance.

We came within sight of the knarrs. The men onboard waited at the rail, an undifferentiated mass of silhouettes. Only Freydis stood out, her orange hair a fire among coals.

I looked to Muirenn, who nodded at me with Loki's easy confidence. I glanced at the sky and prayed that Issuk had succeeded in securing Taqqiq's help.

"Now!"

The screams of raptors and the sharp caws of ravens filled the air. A black-and-white swarm, barely visible in the still-dark sky, hurtled toward the Norse archers, heedless of the arrows fletched with the feathers of their kin.

The Greenlanders ducked, shielding their faces from talon

and beak. They tripped and tumbled over the lemmings that had climbed the knarr's side and swarmed across the deck like ants.

Bears stood on their hind legs and crashed forward with their massive paws to break the ice, just as they did to open a seal's den. But tonight, bear and seal worked together. Seals scraped at the underside of the sea ice with their teeth as the bears pounded from above. Caribou and musk oxen ran in wide circles around the knarrs in a stamping, bugling, lowing herd, weakening the ice with their sharp hooves.

Brandr and I rushed forward with the wolfdogs leading the way, slavering and snarling as if Valkyries rode upon their backs.

And then, the moment I'd been waiting for. A shout. A new cry of alarm. Bjarni, his shoulder bandaged, stood beside the dragon prow, his good arm pointing past me toward the distant shore.

The brightening sky had brought the inuksuit into view. From here they looked like giants indeed, summoned from the earth itself to guard my people. The flocks of birds rose into the air like a black mist, angling away from the ships as if they, too, feared the stone giants' approach.

I heard Freydis's cry, urging her men not to flee. "Stay and fight! This is the battle foretold! Do not fear this skraeling magic!"

But my skraeling magic had just begun.

The Moon dragged dark, towering clouds across the sky, wrapping darkness around him like a seal fur cape. He hid his face. He hid the stars. Thunder drummed, echoing off the mountains, an angakkuq's song gone mad. Lightning lit the ice with a sharp blue glow.

The wolfdogs crouched, tails between their legs, shaking. And I felt a surge of fear—this was more than I'd expected.

"It does not storm like this in winter!" Brandr shouted to me over the din. "What's going on?"

Muirenn stood with the ease of a much younger woman and looked beyond the knarrs, to the vastness of the frozen sea. A lopsided smile spread across her face, making her look half-crazed.

A new peal of thunder thrummed through my bones—not from the sky, this time, but from the sea. At the bases of the knarrs, the ice swelled and rolled, thrusting up great icebergs as it went. *Sanna*, I thought at first. But then I realized such power could only be Taqqiq's.

"The Moon brings his tide!" I exulted. "He frees the ships!"

But my joy turned quickly to horror as the buckling wave increased in speed and rolled inexorably toward us. The knarrs would float—but we would drown.

"What's happening?" I begged Muirenn. "Taqqiq's supposed to help us!"

The old woman's eyes grew suddenly distant, as if she listened through the thunder, through the roar of the ice, to a voice very far away. A tear rolled down her lined cheek. She looked at me, her gaze full of pity and regret.

"He comes to kill you, child."

I shook my head numbly, unable to speak. I could barely believe that even now, when I had asked for his forgiveness and nearly chased the invaders from our shores, Taqqiq could not forget his hatred. The old fear seized me. I had seen his eyes. I had felt his touch. Now, once more, I had put myself within his power.

Muirenn shouted above the groaning ice and clashing thunder. "He'll kill us all if you don't stop him, Omat! A sacrifice must be made!"

Brandr grabbed the old woman by the shoulders and shook her. "A sacrifice? What are you saying? What do you know of Omat and her gods? This has nothing to do with her! We must turn back!"

"We won't make it to land!" Muirenn insisted, just as the rolling tide flung us high into the air. We crashed back onto the bucking ice, struggling for a handhold.

Small cracks spread around us, as fast and jagged as the lightning bolts that now split the sky.

The stone inuksuit swayed and shook as if possessed with spirits of their own. "Go to Taqqiq!" Muirenn screamed once more over the thunder. "Fly! Or we'll all die. You needn't be a raven—I'll give you the strength to go in your human form!"

Brandr hauled himself across the shifting ice toward me. "She's gone mad, Omat! We're getting out of here together."

"No—she's right! I can't run any longer. I must go to the Moon."

"What?"

"Trust me!"

White Paw dashed forward, her claws skittering on the shifting ice. She butted me with her head, worrying the sleeve of my dress with her teeth as if to hold me down.

"Stay back!" I growled, grabbing her by the scruff of her neck. "You, too," I barked as Floppy Eared and Sweet One made their way toward me. "Stay! Look after Brandr." I didn't bother to admonish the wolfdogs to look after themselves. Wolves who could transform into whales would not fear the bucking ice. "Be strong, Brandr. And listen to Muirenn—she's wiser than you know."

Brandr seized my arm in an iron grip. "You're not leaving me." He was no wolfdog to be commanded. I knew then that he wouldn't let me go unless I lied.

"Not forever," I assured him. "My human body will be right here in a trance. You've seen me do it before. I just need to talk to the Moon."

He laughed caustically. "Oh, is that all?"

"You wouldn't understand."

"Muirenn said *sacrifice*." He tightened his grip. "I heard her."

"It's not what you think."

"Promise you'll be back."

"Of course. Since when have I been wrong?"

"I know, I know. Your people bring down whales." There was no laughter in his voice, only bitterness. "You killed a bear three times your size. Geese fall from the sky in fear when you approach. How much harder could this be?"

I forced a twisted smile. "So let me go, my friend."

"Omat!" Muirenn interrupted. "The ice won't hold much longer!"

I couldn't tear my gaze from the red-haired Viking at my side. "Brandr..."

"I know..." He pressed a desperate kiss on my lips. "If anyone can survive this," he whispered, "it's you."

CHAPTER
FIFTY-TWO

⚡

I did not bind my body for this journey. There was no time.

I lay on the swelling ice and screamed my chant at the stars.

As Loki-in-Muirenn had promised, I needed no raven wings to reach the sky. The god's power bore my spirit aloft in the shape of my own body. The wind burned my human flesh as it never had my raven's feathers. I closed my eyes to slits against the stinging cold. Frost glazed my hair into tiny knives, slicing my cheeks as I flew upward.

I was not alone. Singarti, white coat gleaming as brightly as the Moon himself, climbed through the heavens with the stars as his stepping-stones, leaping from one to the next. I followed, jumping the vast distances of oblivion as if skipping over narrow creek beds.

Together we conquered the sky and strode across the vast, frozen plain on the face of the Moon, an icy world colder than the deepest winter on earth. Before us rose Taqqiq's iglu. Blue light shone through its wide ice window, interrupted by the agitated pacing of a dark shadow within.

Singarti's nose twitched, and his ears thrust backward. I understood well enough.

My enemy awaited, and I must go on alone.

I bowed my head to the great Wolf. "Thank you for bringing me this far."

He licked my cheek, a final goodbye, then turned and bounded off into the distance.

I was alone once more. Steps away from the end of everything.

It won't be so bad, I thought. *I will see Ataata and Ipaq. I will finally meet my mother and grandmother. And on winter nights, I will play the kicking game among the stars.*

All of it was a slim recompense for the loss of Brandr's smile.

I crawled into the Moon's vast iglu.

"Omat." My name rushed through his lips like a winter storm. He was much as I remembered him. Paler even than a Norseman, bald, his naked body etched with muscle. The soot mark on his forehead wrinkled as he raised his hairless brows in shock. Deep shadows ringed his eyes.

"I come as a sacrifice."

My voice did not quaver, but his did, thrumming with barely concealed excitement. "The Inuk I have hunted for so long. I did not expect to see you in my realm again."

"Do whatever you want to me, but leave the others alone. This fight has always been ours."

He moved a step closer; the cold wafting off his body raised the hair on my arms. "Whatever I want?" The Moon placed an icy fingertip on my chin and tilted my face toward his. "I have wanted many things. When you first slipped from your mother's bloody womb, I wanted you dead in your snowy cradle. Then Singarti saved you, and I realized you might be more help than hindrance to my cause. You have played your part well. I have no need of you any longer, but now that you are here...I might keep you alive. Keep you with me to warm my flesh when my sister is out of reach."

"Make up your mind, Taqqiq," I said through gritted teeth. "Take me or destroy me, as you will." I did not tell him the truth:

that I would die either way. I would kill myself before I let him lie with me. "The ice is broken; the Norse ships are free to leave. Now stop the tides before you kill us all."

"Stop the tides? Oh no, little angakkuq-that-was. Your body is not payment enough for that."

"What do you mean?" I asked, growing impatient with his riddles. "Loki said you wanted me. I had to sacrifice myself."

"He lied."

I slashed my hand through the air, refusing to believe, but the Moon pressed on. "Your death is the least of my concerns. I have more important things to destroy. You have gathered all the gods, old and new, Inuit and Norse, together in one place."

"What Norse gods? Only Loki's down there."

"Who do you think brings the thunder? Not I. Not Sila, who cares so little for the workings of the world. That's *Thor's* work. Summoned by the prayers of his faithful."

Freydis. I remembered the hammer pendant at her throat. Loki said the Greenlanders brought him here on the wings of their prayers. I had not counted on their bringing the other gods as well. Dread tightened my throat. *I have left my friends alone to face the might of the Aesir—they must be warned.*

Taqqiq huffed. "Where are you going, little girl? You think to return to earth—how? You have no strength left for raven's wings. Loki helped you get here, but he will not help you go back. He wants you out of the way. You forgot he is the Trickster, and *this* is his greatest trick."

"I don't understand." The words sounded weak, pitiful. But I had no others.

"He seeks to fight his final battle with all the spirits of our world arrayed around him. Sanna, Singarti, Uqsuralik—and you and your Brandr, too—all have fallen prey to him. But not I." The Moon Man thrust back his shoulders. "I have tricked the Trickster. My tides will drown them all before the fight has even begun."

"No...no...," I stuttered. "That can't be true."

"I always said you would destroy the world—"

"I seek to save it!"

"Yet you've brought it all to an end. Sanna and the animals would not gather at my command—only at your request. Now they will *all* perish. Not just the Norsemen. Not just your lover and your dogs. But Sanna and Singarti and Uqsuralik, too, and every strange new god who has dared to enter my realm. With them gone, only my sister and I will reign." He laughed. "And my sister—she only runs, always runs."

I staggered backward as if struck. Had I done this? Had I led them all to their end? I'd known Taqqiq had no love for the other spirits, but I hadn't thought he would dare destroy them all.

"I will not let you kill them."

"No? What will you do? What can a mortal do against a great spirit?"

"It is you who know little," I answered darkly, remembering what Loki had told me of the endless circle between gods and men. "We create you through our tales, our prayers, our belief. Without us, you are nothing."

"And you will convince all Inuit to cease their worship of me?" he asked contemptuously. "I have nothing to fear from you."

I pulled Brandr's knife from my belt. "Yet if what you say is true, gods will die tonight. If *they* are not immortal, then neither are you."

"And with what will you slay me?" he scoffed. "With that knife? Do you think *steel* can bring down the Moon? Do not forget what power I hold over you."

"You can make me bleed. Yes, I know. Well, I am no longer scared of my own blood. I am no longer scared of being a woman—it doesn't make me any less a man. I am both. I am neither. I am only myself."

The Moon Man's white face allowed no flush, but he drew his hairless brows low over his eyes. His lips curled back from perfect teeth in a snarl. "I command the tides. I could pull that orange-haired mate of yours into the sea."

"Brandr will live a little longer yet. Long enough for me to stop you."

His eyes flashed with red. Issuk's, I remembered, had done the same. In that moment, I finally understood Taqqiq's place in the world. "They say a bird-man with glowing eyes stole Sanna from her family. Issuk became that bird when Sanna sent him here, to tell you of our need. But he's more than your grandson. He's a part of you. Over and over, you steal our bodies for yourself. You rape your sister. Sanna. *Me.* Each a woman of power, brought low beneath a man's touch." I brandished my small knife.

"So now you think to kill me," Taqqiq said, smirking, "and take your revenge?"

"Not just *my* revenge. I come for Sanna. And for Malina. And for all Inuit women."

"I have nothing to fear from you."

I smiled faintly. He was nearly right. "But you do from your sister."

"Malina? My sister has been running from me throughout all time!"

"The Sun shines brighter than you ever will. You wax and wane while she stays constant. She has been hiding, but today she returns. And this time, she will have no reason to run. *Can you hear me, Malina?*" I cried suddenly, willing my voice to travel through the iglu walls, through the void of space to the Sun's ears. "Listen, great Sun—the Norse call you Sol, and your brother they call Mani. They know of you both, yet they have no stories of rape and flight."

"Quiet, girl," Taqqiq hissed.

"Hear me, Malina! You have a choice! You can change your story, as I have!"

Taqqiq grabbed my arm with frozen fingers and dragged me closer. With his other hand, he reached for my throat.

"Enough, angakkuq!" he growled, his eyes suddenly afraid.

No, I was no threat alone, but with Malina's help, I might have a chance.

Once more, I stood in the Moon's embrace, my life in his hands. But this time, I was armed with a new story. Brandr had told me mere mistletoe had killed immortal Baldur. It's a reminder that you cannot save the innocent, he'd said. But I heard a different meaning: with enough cunning, even the weak and small can kill an invincible god.

Taqqiq's fingers closed around my neck; his hooded eyes glowed dimly red. I did not struggle or scream. I let my body go limp. My vision darkened as the breath fled my body.

"Enough," Taqqiq said again, an icy whisper against my cheek.

Then the Moon's eyes widened. A trickle of red ran from the corner of his white lips. A blinding shaft of yellow sunlight pierced the window and struck sparks from the hilt of my knife—the knife I now twisted deeper beneath his rib cage.

"Yes, enough," I gasped as his fingers fell from my throat.

The Moon crumpled to the ground, clutching the welling wound in his gut. Around me the white world swayed and dimmed as I fought to suck air into my lungs, my throat still burning from Taqqiq's grasp.

"You cannot kill me," he sputtered, his face contorted with rage.

"No. But now *she* can."

The sunlight grew stronger, falling upon Taqqiq's upturned face. The iglu melted around us in the sudden heat. There, striding across the white plain, a figure clothed in brilliant light. I turned away from her blinding glare, but not before I glimpsed a round, young face with gleaming brown skin, wreathed in white braids twined with bright yellow poppies. Blood, crimson and scarlet and ochre, stained her misshapen chest. Malina. Sun Woman.

The Moon covered his face with his hands and screamed as his sister approached, faster now, lifting the apron of her shining parka so she could run. The stench of burning flesh filled my nostrils. Black soot spread across the backs of Taqqiq's hands as the Sun's rays scorched his skin. He screeched with pain and thrust his hands against the ice at his feet.

I pressed my hands to my ears to block his agonized screams, but they only grew louder as the sunlight struck his forehead like a spearpoint, scorching the old soot mark from so long ago.

Once more Malina had branded her attacker.

"Run, Brother, run!" roared the Sun—so close now I had to close my eyes to slits. And yet her heat didn't burn my flesh, but only bathed me in gentle warmth. I felt like a babe snug in its mother's hood.

Taqqiq scrambled to his feet, gasping, "Sister, Sister—"

"*I said RUN!*"

And run he did.

With Malina on his heels.

CHAPTER
FIFTY-THREE

↯

I had no strength left to revel in my victory.

I staggered across the quickly melting world, my vision blinded by the glare of sunlight on ice. I had not intended to survive this journey; I had not thought of how to get home. Taqqiq had spoken true about one thing: I had no strength left to transform.

I stumbled to the edge of the icy plain, hoping to catch one final glimpse of my friends below. Instead, I saw only black clouds, roiling like soup in a pot. Malina's light streamed overhead, warming my shoulders, but it did not yet strike the earth.

Please, Sila, I prayed to the Air. *I must see.*

As if in response, a hole opened in the clouds. I watched Brandr struggle to his feet, Sweet One by his side. The sea ice lay still and calm, no longer rocked by the tides. He would survive.

I wanted to cry out to him, to beg his forgiveness. *I cannot keep my promise. I will not return.*

A bolt of lightning shot through the sky, throwing his features into sharp relief. He stared up at the Moon. He couldn't see me, I knew, and yet tears filled his eyes as if he heard my words. Thunder rolled across the sky. Another cracking spear of lightning. Brandr's face jerked toward the knarrs—I followed his gaze. The Norsemen aboard no longer looked scared. Instead their jaws hung slack, their eyes glazed, as if the lightning had burned their souls from their bodies.

Again the drumming of thunder, like the footsteps of giants racing across the sky.

I watched the faces of the Greenlanders, stark and pale in the lightning's glare. I watched as their features snapped apart and then back into place, forming something beautiful and terrifying and altogether new. The Norse were men no longer.

They were gods.

One by one, the Aesir leapt easily over the side of the knarrs and advanced on my friends.

Where once stood Freydis's husband, Thorvard Einarsson, now strode red-bearded Thor. He swung his war hammer across the sky, striking lightning bolts from the stars to light their path. Other freemen now followed in his wake, each one transformed into a god I recognized from Brandr's tales: Magnor became Tyr, the god of war, his sword held high in his one remaining hand; keen-eyed Bjarni, the wound in his shoulder somehow healed, transformed into Heimdall the Watcher, carrying a huge, curved horn beside his bow. Another freeman, slight and pale, became Freya, waist girdled with vines and flower-studded hair streaming across her shoulders. The metamorphosis rippled outward, striking one man after another. Old Olfun was next, his body growing tall, his hair long, but his eye still missing. Two ravens curled from the sky to land on his shoulders. Odin. All-Father.

A new figure jumped from the Greenlanders' boat. One I'd never thought to see again.

Ingharr. He stumbled at first, clutching at the bloody wound I'd drilled through his stomach. But even as I watched, his skin knit closed, his back straightened. Barley sheaves twined their way through his long yellow hair. The viciousness of his gaze faded away, replaced by a gentle warmth. Frey. The god of growing things, who'd once given away his sword for the love of a giantess.

The thralls who stayed on board the ship observed the procession with interest, but not shock. *They can't see the gods before them*, I realized. *Like Brandr, they aren't true believers.* Only Freydis watched wide-eyed and pale, her hands clutching at her hair. She saw. She would be the witness.

The transformation struck her next, painting her green skirts with swirls of silver and gold, darkening her orange hair to gleaming bronze. Her thin figure rounded; she grew even taller. But her features remained sharp and imperious, and her eyes were the same steely gray. Frigg—wife of Odin, proud foster mother of Thor and grieving mother of Baldur—did not subsume Freydis as the Aesir had done to the other Greenlanders; she simply cloaked the woman in new glory.

Frigg-and-Freydis watched the carnage unfold with none of the other Aesir's fierce joy or bloodlust. Her voice was little more than a whisper, yet Sila's breath carried her words to my ears as if she stood beside me on the Moon's edge:

"Ragnarok."

I knew this prophecy. The Fate of the Gods. The final battle between Aesir and Jotuns.

Taqqiq was right: Loki had lied. Muirenn's kind smiles were simply the Trickster's ploy. He'd used me to bring Brandr and Sanna and all her animals to fight in a war far greater than the one Freydis had imagined. A war I barely understood. One that would bring nothing but carnage to my world. What use were wolves against gods?

To the west, the hordes of Jotunheim gathered beside their long-forgotten brother, Loki. Ice Bear and Raven, Walrus and Hare, Ringed Seal and Whale, all assembled behind the Shapeshifter in his silver-clothed glory, black hair twisting in the wind.

Loki raised a hand to my inuksuit.

The stone Frost Giants lifted their massive legs from the earth and turned their blank faces to and fro, seeking their enemies among the Aesir.

My wolfdogs crouched for the kill. They didn't follow Loki's orders, but mine. I had told them to defend Brandr—they would follow my wishes to the death.

My flame-haired friend stood beside them, holding his sword. He didn't notice the stone Giants, much less the silver-robed Jotun.

"Run!" I screamed down at him in vain. "This is not our battle! You can't win!" But Brandr was as powerless in Loki's trap as I had been. He couldn't hear my pleas. Couldn't see the truth of the enemies before him. He thought he fought the Greenlanders who had murdered his brother. He had run from them before. This time he would fight.

I took a deep breath, trying to will myself a raven so I might fly to my friends. But not even the faintest glimmering of power coursed through my flesh. I had gone from lemming to bird to wolf to woman, all in one day. I laughed bitterly. Loki had left me stranded here, powerless, on purpose.

I watched as Odin strode across the ice toward Brandr. White Paw leapt in front of him. She threw back her head and howled. Her fur stood on end, her body swelled, her teeth lengthened. She was more than my wolfdog now; she was Fenrir, too: Loki's monstrous wolf-son, fated to fight the All-Father in the battle to end all battles.

Powerless in the face of prophecy, White Paw bounded toward Odin, her jaws wide. Wolf and god rolled across the ice, spear and fang flashing in the lightning.

At the same time, Sweet One and Floppy Eared lunged forward to defend Brandr from his next attacker—one-armed Tyr. Suddenly my two wolfdogs merged in my vision, becoming a single, slavering dog of shifting black and white. Garm, the hound of Hel, grabbed at Tyr's leg with its immense jaws, worrying the flesh until the god's blood ran through its teeth to stain the ice below.

The ice cracked and strained as the creatures of the deep rose to join the fray. A great slab thrust from the sea with a sound like thunder. Fanged Whale burst forth to grab red-bearded Thor in its toothy maw. Sanna rode upon the beast's back, her thin legs straddling its vast head, her long black hair streaming like seaweed across her shoulders. She was at once the Sea Mother and a hideous Norse ogress, riding a beast whose fangs lengthened like swords and whose tail grew sinuous and scaled—Jormungand, the sea serpent that encircled the world.

I sank down onto the ice, the battle far below blurring with my tears. The crash of sword and shield, the howling of wolves, the screaming of man and beast, warred with the thunder.

If I couldn't help, then I did not want to see.

There on the edge of the Moon, I buried my face in my hands and waited for the spirits to do with me what they would.

It didn't take long.

An unseen force yanked on my boots, dragging me toward the edge. I slammed my palms against the ice, wishing for a wolf's claws or raven's talons to hold me in place. I screamed and scrambled, but still I skidded closer to the lip of the Moon.

Brandr must be pulling on my human body, I realized, *trying to wake me from my trance while my soul is still here in the spirit world.*

"Stop!" I shouted. If I awoke now, I'd be soulless, undead. But he couldn't hear—and I couldn't fight back. My mind spun as my two braided worlds suddenly ripped apart. My legs now dangled over the edge, my feet swaying above the infinite expanse of empty sky. I flipped onto my stomach and dug my pitiful human fingers into the slick surface of the Moon. My nails ripped free. The force on earth kept pulling. Torso dangling, shoulders straining, only my fingers left to clutch at the ice. No breath left to scream.

I plummeted off the Moon—and into oblivion.

BOOK FIVE

RAGNAROK

The tale of the Ragnarok has its ending. The skalds spread the story far and wide through the realm of the Norse. As they tell it, the legend grows and shifts, until it little resembles what really happened that night upon the frozen sea. Only those with the eyes to witness know how much it has been changed. Only two women, one small and dark, one tall and fair, can see the truth.

The Fate of the Gods unfolds.

CHAPTER
FIFTY-FOUR

ϟ

I fell for what felt like an age.

Ripped from one world into the next, I plummeted earthward, powerless to help myself. The stars whirred by, streaks of white and blue and pink. The air rushed cold across my face, freezing my tears against my cheeks and eyelashes. I could no longer blink. Could barely breathe. My thin Norse clothes ripped from my flesh. I fell in tatters.

I looked upward, toward Taqqiq's looming eye. No longer white, it hung like a drop of blood in the dawning sky. Slowly, so slowly, a round black shadow eclipsed the reddened orb, covering him from my sight and me from his.

Malina had finally caught her brother.

As the Moon's light dimmed, the stars grew brighter. One by one, they shot across the sky, falling from their assigned places like snow in a blizzard.

I had no breath to scream.

Ataata, I thought, *is this what you saw for me? Have I made you proud? Am I not a great hunter, to have brought down the Moon?* The victory meant nothing. I had saved no one.

Ohhhhh-mat. Ohhhh-maaaaat.

At first the voice sounded like Brandr's, welling up from the earth to embrace me at the moment of my death. Then the voice echoed overhead—from the falling stars themselves.

Omat!

Omat!

A chorus of voices, calling my name. I recognized my grandfather's. I recognized my father's. The woman's voice I did not know, but it seared me like hot oil, and fresh tears froze against my eyes. My mother. Only once before had I heard her voice, in the moment of my birth. Now, at my death, she called to me again.

I floated on their cries like a kayak on salt water. My fall slowed, stopped. I hovered in midair. Only when I felt the tug on my shredded dress did I realize that the voices had summoned help. Owls, ravens, falcons flapped around me in a swirling cloud. They grabbed my ragged clothes and bruised flesh in their beaks and talons, their wingtips scraping my cheeks.

Slowly, slowly, they lowered me to the earth, their sharp talons drawing blood until my spirit form rested safe in my worldly body once more.

I felt ice against my back. My head rested on a pillow of frozen wave.

The voices of my ancestors faded. The cloud of birds lifted like morning mist and disappeared into the sky. I dragged a hand upward to melt the ice from my eyelashes and cheeks, blinking as my eyes unfroze.

Something pawed weakly against my arm. I turned slowly toward the disturbance that had ripped me from my trance and almost cost me my life. I blinked as the blurry shape slowly resolved before my eyes. Not Brandr, I saw now. A wolf. White Paw? Sweet One? I could barely tell. Her coat was black with blood. Where her mouth should have been, only a gaping hole of ragged flesh remained, half her jaw hanging loose and broken. I reached out

one tentative hand. Air whistled through her mangled mouth—
the closest she could come to a whimper.

"No, White Paw. No," I gasped, gathering the wolfdog's head
in my arms. "What have they done to you?"

A god had torn her apart. But not before she had fulfilled her
task. Odin, I saw now, lay sprawled across the ice not far away, his
throat torn out by a wolf's teeth, his one eye glazed. The Far-Seer
would never see again.

I wiped the blood from my friend's eyes so she might see my
face—and so I might watch her gaze slowly dim as the spirit fled
her body.

I clutched her to my breast, this animal I'd once carried in my
hood, now grown so large that I could barely lift her ruined head
in my arms, so large that she could destroy the All-Father himself,
so large I'd thought her invincible.

I opened my mouth to howl my grief. I wanted to mourn her
as she would have mourned me. But no sound came out. Only a
weak, choking breath, thick with tears. Heedless of the blood, I
pressed my cheek against hers and lowered her head to the ground.
Inuit have no words for final parting, and for once I felt the lack.

"*Farthu vel,*" I whispered in Norse to my friend. *Farewell*.

She had fought for me—for those I loved. It was up to me to
save them now. I pushed myself to standing, swaying with exhaustion and grief, and stumbled toward the crash and roar of the battle
before me.

"Brandr!" I screamed. "Where are you?"

Nearby, Loki fought with Heimdall, the great Watcher of the
Aesir. To my eyes they were gods indeed, larger than life, clothed
in silver with weapons of gold. Yet as they wrestled each other, I
saw another reality layered upon the first. Flashes of the bodies they
inhabited: Muirenn's hunched form in her ragged woolen dress,
and strong, stout Bjarni. Beneath the glorious conflict of gods lay
the ludicrous scrabbling of an old woman and a young man.

Loki caught my eye and stumbled for a moment, shocked to see me alive. Heimdall lunged at him; Loki snaked his arm around the burly god's neck and squeezed tight before turning back to me. "Welcome to the battle you're too late to stop!" the Trickster crowed. "You're more clever than I thought, little Inuk."

"Why?" I demanded. "I stopped Taqqiq from destroying everything—and now you're doing it instead!"

"I'm simply ridding your land of the Norsemen, just as you—"

"Stop your lies! I can see the gods before me and the men within them."

"Omat the Inuk thinks she sees the truth, yes? Well, the truth is that this battle has been foreseen since Odin fashioned the world from Ymir's skull." Heimdall struggled and roared in his arms, but Loki just squeezed tighter and saved his rage for me. "Now leave, Inuk! You have no place here!"

"Not until I find Brandr."

"Freydis to dream. You to lead. Brandr to swing the sword. Your lover is mine."

"For *what*?" I demanded. "You think you can defeat the Aesir?"

Heimdall smashed his elbow into Loki's face. Blood splattered the Trickster's braided mustache as he leaned close to the other god's ear. "I can defeat you *all*," he hissed. "All that time Odin spent preparing for the Ragnarok, he never realized we would fight here, in Jotunheim. On *my* ground. *That* is why I will win."

"We took you in," Heimdall gasped. "Odin treated you like his own son."

"And then he bound me beneath a serpent's dripping venom. After I gave Baldur a swift death, Odin gave me eternal suffering. And *this* is his reward."

I had seen enough of vengeance.

I left the wrestling gods behind and threaded my way through the chaos, searching for my friend. *I thought to create Freydis's nightmare tonight—but a different horror has come unasked for and swallowed me whole. This is what comes of playing with stories.*

The inuksuit strode across the ice, towering Frost Giants given life by the Shapeshifter himself. Huge wolves darted between their feet—wolves, I knew, that had once been sheep. On their backs rode Valkyries in glinting breastplates, their swords spraying chips from the Giants' stone legs. Singarti and his pack joined the fray, teeth bared as they leapt upon their enemies. The ice swirled with fur and stone, blood and steel. All the prophesied destruction had come true. *One of Fenrir's brood, a wolf in troll's skin, will swallow the Moon.* So I had heard Galinn explain in Brandr's memories. That was me, a wolf's child in the flesh of a mortal who had taken down Taqqiq himself. Yet even when falling wingless through the air, I had not felt so helpless.

I could barely tell friend from foe as I ran. The Aesir had brought wolves, just as I had. Odin's raven companions looked no different from those who flew in my own dreams. And always, the vision spun from one reality to another—a wolfdog become hound, a woman become ogre, a whale become serpent and whale once more.

Finally I spied Brandr amid the maelstrom. His red hair gleamed in the crackling lightning, and he held an unfamiliar golden sword that flashed like a sunbeam. As bright as flame, he danced around Frey, the god of growing things. The yellow-haired god held Ingharr's iron weapon, dull and nicked. No match for Brandr's shining blade. For an instant, Frey's form shivered and shifted in my vision. I saw Ingharr's body within, battered and bloodstained, but moving easily despite the many wounds Brandr and I had inflicted on him. The Aesir were powerful indeed to heal their worshiper so. Magic sword or no, this was a battle Brandr couldn't win.

Brandr's cries of rage rang above the clash of sword and shield and thunderclap, demanding justice for the death of his brother.

"No!" I screamed, rushing forward. "That's not Ingharr!"

Brandr turned at the sound of my voice. I expected Frey to lunge forward and strike my friend unaware. But the gentle god merely sighed and leaned upon his battered sword.

"Omat?" Brandr blinked. Unlike with the other Norsemen turned gods, my Viking's mind was still his own—though with his vision clouded by the swirl of magic around him, he barely recognized me. "You came back?" His relief soon surrendered to ferocity. "Get back!"

"It's not Ingharr you fight, but *Frey*! Don't you see? You're Surtur, the fire fiend, just as Galinn dreamed." I clung to Brandr's sword arm. "Where did you get this blade?"

"It's my sword. Muirenn gave it to me, remember?" He shook his head as if to clear it. "She stole it back when we escaped."

"Stole it indeed. *Loki* took it from Frey, don't you remember the story you told me? This isn't your sword—it's the one Frey traded for the love of a giantess."

He turned the weapon over in his hands. Branching symbols snaked along the golden blade. Its yellow pommel stone glowed like trapped sunlight. Yet Brandr merely scowled, unseeing. "It's the same steel sword I've had for years."

Just then, a woman's scream cut through the battle's roar.

Uqsuralik, his coat covered in blood, had pounded a hole through the ice with his forepaws. A young woman lay upon the frozen sea, sliding forward into the watery deep. A young woman with blue flowers in her golden hair.

"Sister!" Frey cried, all his composure fled. The goddess of love slid inexorably toward the water, scrabbling in vain. Her hair streamed behind her, shedding its flowers. Before Frey could move to save her, she was gone. He slumped down, his battered blade falling from his grasp.

"Get up, Ingharr!" Brandr lifted his sword high. "Stand and fight! This isn't done yet."

He was right. The carnage was far from over.

I watched in horror, spinning slowly in place like a bewildered child, almost able to hear the story taking shape within my brain— not the story as the Norse would tell it, but the one I knew to be true:

No Aesir will survive the Ragnarok, and no Jotuns, either. In battle after battle, no one emerges victorious.

One-armed Tyr slashes at Garm with his sharp sword, opening the white hound's throat and severing the black hound's head from her body. But before he dies, the white hound's jaws tear the god's heart from his chest. Together they crash to the ground, their lives slipping out in the pulse of blood upon the ice.

The white dog's long tongue, which lolled so often from smiling jaws, now freezes to the frozen sea. His wagging tail lies still as he curls beside the black dog's motionless form. Her warm brown eyes scan the plain one last time, looking for her mother's mate—then grow dim.

Loki the Betrayer laughs and laughs, feinting and twisting from Heimdall's grasp, but finally his laughter turns to gurgles, to chokes, to silence as the two gods stand with their hands circling each other's throats, each sinking to his death, hushed for eternity. The three towering Frost Giants fall still, their mighty limbs turning from flesh back to stone.

Held tight in Jormungand's bloody maw, Thor raises his hammer and crushes the beast's skull. A last bloody plume of spray shoots from its head, then falls upon the ground in shards of ringing ice. Upon its back, the ogress named Sanna weeps with fingerless hands upraised, until Thor's hammer crashes against her bare breast.

The ice shudders as the serpent-whale slides back into the chasm from which it erupted. Sanna, limp and still, tumbles from its back and disappears beneath the waves.

Thor looks around, dazed and bloody from the whale's jaws, then takes nine paces toward the smaller of the ships, where his mother, Frigg, watches in horror through the steely eyes of his most faithful follower.

But no woman's love can save him now.

Thor's knees buckle and he crashes to the ground. With his death, the lightning ceases.

The last roll of thunder echoes off the mountains and falls silent.

Thor's iron fingers slacken and his hammer falls free, cracking the ice in its path, rolling faster and faster until it reaches the ships.

The battle draws to an end as it began—with the bending and buckling of ice.

To the east, I watched the Icelanders' large knarr rock and pitch in the sudden rush of water as the ice, already weakened by the blows of the animals and the tides of Taqqiq, finally gave way beneath Thor's hammer. This part of my plan would work—a few Norsemen would escape to tell the tale of carnage. But even as I watched, an iceberg slid forward, crashing into the boat's side and opening a wide, splintering hole. The overloaded knarr tipped to the waterline, the last of the long Vinland logs rolling across the deck like thunder, then plummeting beneath the waves.

Soon the sea had swallowed it all.

Frigg-and-Freydis stood in the prow of the other knarr, face twisted in terror. A circle of ice still held the Greenlandic ship in place.

Brandr had eyes only for the yellow-haired man bowed in front of him. He raised his brilliant sword.

"Stop!" I begged. Even if Brandr's weapon *could* kill the gentle god, he would forever regret it. "This is Frey!"

"I see Ingharr before me. A murderer." He lunged.

I flung myself between them. Everything slowed, the whole world confined to our tiny patch of ice, the last dying gasp of a battle to end the world.

Brandr twisted aside with a curse, just managing to angle his blade away from me. But then—a hum beside my ear, a gust of breath as Frey swung Ingharr's sword at my back.

A grunt. A loud crack of breaking wood.

I spun to face the god—but a familiar broad back stood in my way.

Kiasik.

My brother raised the severed haft of his stolen spear.

Frey, his tears now dry, his face suffused with rage at his sister's death, lifted his sword one more time. I reached forward to defend my brother with my bare hands, but Kiasik thrust me aside.

As one, they came together—Ingharr's battered iron blade passing through my brother's woolen rags and into his heart, while Kiasik's splintered spear shaft bounced against the god's flesh like shell striking stone.

Kiasik stumbled forward, and I threw my arms around him, cradling his trembling body there on the ice. Over my head, another blade hummed, this one so bright I felt the warmth of sunlight on my cheek as it passed by. Frey's own magic sword passed beneath its former owner's ribs and emerged, bright with fresh blood, on the other side. Brandr leapt over me to slam the wounded god into the ground.

Now I saw Frey as Brandr had. The spirit gone from his body, the slack-mouthed corpse beside me was only Ingharr Ketilsson. Barley sheaves no longer twined through his long yellow hair. He wore his carven metal helm instead. Through clothes torn by blade and claw, I could see the puckered scars that disfigured his body, each wound suffered at my hands. One on his side, made by my harpoon head when he'd killed Kidla. A long seam across his thigh from the sword wound. A deep indentation in his stomach from my spear, like a second navel that tied him to death instead of birth. Other wounds marked his body, large and small, all healed with thick white flesh. Ingharr should've died long ago—only the gods could've kept him alive. Now he was just another tool, used up and discarded.

Like me. Like my brother.

Kiasik's blood poured onto my hands as I tried to stanch the flow from his wound. "Why?" I begged. "Why did you come back?"

"It was my turn," he gasped, blood burbling at the corners of his mouth. "To save you, whether you wanted me to or not."

"Foolish, foolish Sister's Son," I moaned, rocking him in my arms. Soon his shaking ceased. His eyes glazed, and I knew he looked not at me, but at the sky above.

I wanted to weep, to scream. I had come so far, fought so hard, to get him home, and he had died within sight of the whale mountain. The weight of that knowledge crushed my chest, stifling my sobs. I could barely breathe.

I pulled his old seal totem from my amulet pouch and curled his fingers around the carved bone as I watched the spirit leave his body on a last whistling exhalation.

"You will play the kicking game among the stars," I managed, "with Kidla at your side, and Ataata always watching."

The first warm beams of the risen Sun bathed Kiasik's still face. But I could take no joy in Malina's return.

Brandr sank down beside me, wrapping a long arm around my shoulders. His head rested against mine. He knew what it meant to lose a brother.

We sat like that for a long moment, barely able to comprehend the slaughter around us.

Thorvard Einarsson fallen beside his battered war hammer. One-eyed Olfun with his throat ripped out. White Paw with her torn jaw and glazed eyes. Sweet One and Floppy Eared, their bodies curled together in a tangle of bloody limbs. Uqsuralik, his hide pierced with many blades, lay beside the sprawled forms of Bjarni and Muirenn. An aarluk's fanged corpse bobbed in a patch of open water, its blowhole crusted with blood. Sheep and wolves and birds and Norsemen, their bodies already stiffening with frost, lay among the scattered boulders that had once formed Giants. One form larger than the others. A mound of white fur, streaked with frozen blood. Singarti.

So many men. So many animals. So many gods.

The world was empty indeed. The Aesir had fallen, as Loki had desired—but so too had his kinsmen—my own gods. Not at Taqqiq's hands after all—but dead nonetheless.

Nearly all the mortal men who had ventured to my land had also lost their lives upon its shores. Most of those who still stood with Freydis aboard the Greenlanders' knarr were thralls. Men captured from distant lands where the Aesir held no power. Like

Brandr, they did not believe. They couldn't see the true battle that surrounded them. They witnessed only a bloody skirmish between Norsemen and beasts.

But Freydis saw. She saw it all.

She balanced atop the ship's rail, one hand grasping a line, the other outstretched toward the carnage. Frigg was gone, and Freydis's own red hair danced like tongues of fire about her tear-streaked face. The wind twisted her green skirts around her legs. Eyes wild, she began to chant a new tale—one destined to be retold for a thousand years:

> It is an ax age, a sword age,
> A wind age, a wolf age,
> Before the world falls;
> Men shall never spare each other.
> The Sun shines from the swords of the battle-gods,
> Mountains are sundered, and ogresses sink,
> The dead throng the road to Hel, and the sky is riven.

Brandr no longer looked confused.

Grasping his sword firmly once more—no magic blade now, but merely his familiar steel—he set off across the ice toward his old enemy.

"Wait!" I cried. But he was deaf to my pleas. I lay Kiasik's limp form on the ice and ran after him. "Let her go!"

"Don't try to stop me."

I dashed ahead of him. Seizing Thorvard Einarsson's fallen hammer, I began to pound at the weakened ice edge, opening a new, spreading lead toward the trapped knarr.

"What are you doing?" Brandr roared. He sprinted past me, leaping over the lead and onto the circle of ice. Too late. The knarr rocked now in open water.

Freydis Eriksdottir wiped the tears from her face and turned to her few remaining Norse sailors. Once more she was the woman I knew. "Raise the sail! While the sea is open. Hurry!"

Brandr landed on a floating ice pan barely the length of a man's stride. He dropped his sword into the water as he tried to balance, swinging his arms like a new-fledged bird.

"Get down!" I screamed. "Lie down, spread your weight!"

He tumbled onto his stomach. I crawled toward the ice lip, careful to stretch my limbs wide, as an ice bear would, and reached out a hand for him. Beside us, the Greenlanders' ship had already sailed through the open lead, Freydis's urgent orders growing ever fainter.

Brandr looked at me with such hate I almost drew back my hand in fear. "Why did you do it?" he asked, his voice rough with despair, his cheek pressed against the ice.

"Freydis had to go back. Someone had to tell the story of how the Norse were defeated by strangers and skraelings. So no Greenlander, no Viking, will ever come again."

"She ordered Galinn's murder."

"She ordered the murder of the man I love, too," I retorted, stretching my hand toward him. "This is not easy for me, either."

His face softened at my words. He took my hand in his, and very slowly, carefully, I pulled until the floating pan knocked against the solid ice. He struggled forward—I dragged him free with a final burst of strength as the pan beneath him finally flipped over.

We lay in each other's arms, staring up at the ever-lightening sky.

Malina climbed higher.

Blackness turned to purple. Pink. Blue.

But our trials weren't over. The lead I had opened in the ice soon met with the larger cracks opened by Thor's fall. The entire ice shelf was collapsing. If we stayed much longer, we would drown, and this time it would not be Taqqiq's doing. Brandr and I struggled to our feet.

We ran through devastation. Past the still forms of those I'd hated and those I'd loved. Those I'd worshiped and those I'd feared.

I looked back only once. The great crack widened, the ocean surged through. The bodies of the fallen, gods and wolfdogs, Inuk and inuksuk alike, slipped into the sea.

CHAPTER
FIFTY-FIVE

$\wedge$

Back on land, we huddled inside the crude iglu I'd managed to build with my small knife and bare hands before the sunlight disappeared once more.

With no lamp and no window, our iglu was as dark as a cave. Slowly our breath and bodies warmed the interior. We rubbed at our hands and cheeks. We melted snow in our palms so we might lick a little moisture to soothe our parched tongues.

I could not stop trembling. Now that we were safe, the full horror of my actions rushed upon me in a smothering wave.

"Taqqiq was right," I whispered. "Kiasik dead. Singarti dead. I *am* the destroyer. I thought that if I sacrificed myself, you'd be safe from the Moon Man, but I hadn't counted on Loki. I hadn't counted on the Aesir."

"What are you saying, Omat?" Brandr begged. He smoothed the hair from my brow as if I were feverish.

And so I told him all of it. Muirenn's possession by Loki. My conversation with Sanna. My visit to the Moon. The death not only of so many animals, so many Norse, but of all the spirits and gods, too.

He did not question me this time. He had seen too much to doubt that all my wildest tales were true. "Then I really killed…"

"Frey," I sighed.

"How did he—"

I explained what Loki had told me of gods possessing those who pray to them. "But now the prayers don't matter," I groaned. "Now they're all gone."

All except Malina, whose presence offered me little solace. She hunted Taqqiq across the sky, but she would be little help to those of us below.

"If what you say is true," Brandr said slowly, "why mourn their loss?" He rose to his feet and poked a vent hole in the roof. Some of our heat escaped, but at least we could see each other in the starlight. He stood looking down at me. "I already gave up on the gods long ago. We'll survive without their help. The Moon still hangs in the sky. The Sun will still rise, the animals still roam the tundra, the tides still ebb and flow."

"Yes, but there's no spirit in it, Brandr. When Loki gave me back my magic, I could sense the spirits around me once more, could feel the power in the wind, hear the voices of the sea. Now all is silence. I'm powerless again."

"But you're not hunted. No one stalks your path. No spirits to please, no gods to fear. No Aesir, no Christ, no Norse to conquer your land. You've lost your brother and your magic. You will grieve. But you're *free*, Omat. Free for the first time." He sounded so sure that I almost began to believe him. He slid his arms around me, and the warmth of his embrace finally penetrated my fear, my self-loathing. For all that I had lost, I had gained something, too. Brandr was right. I had a future. With him.

Then we heard the crying.

I crawled from the iglu, peering into the darkness.

"Kiasik?" I shouted, knowing he was dead and yet daring to hope.

"Help!"

I stumbled toward the voice—then stopped in my tracks when I realized it spoke in Norse.

"Help!" Again that cry, ragged and hoarse.

A figure plunged through the darkness and into my arms, babbling through his tears.

"It was so dark! Then the lightning and the sea ice—I looked again—the ships were gone! And I couldn't see, so I followed the snow ridges like she said and—"

"Shhh..." I held him awkwardly. "Shhh. You're safe, Snorri."

Brandr sat, tense and angry, on one side of the small iglu. Snorri shivered on the other, his legs drawn up against his chest so his feet might not touch his enemy's. I had little patience left for their hatred.

"How did you survive, Snorri?" I asked, my own grief tempered by my need to care for the shivering boy.

"Freydis—she was so angry after you escaped." His story came out in fits and starts through his numb lips. "She was bent over Ingharr, praying to Frey to heal him, and shouting at the men to go after you. Then she saw me holding my cross and realized I was a Christian. And she went mad—slapped me and kicked me, like I was a dog. Threw me off the boat. I just stood there on the ice. Where was I supposed to go? I stayed in the knarr's shadow for a while—thought she'd change her mind. I fell asleep—on the ice—woke up when the thunder started. I could see the ships, could see Olfun and Thorvard and even wounded Ingharr jumping overboard and heading toward shore. I called out to Bjarni, thinking he'd help me, but he left, too, walking like a deaf man toward the strange piles of stones.

"The ice started cracking. I was caught on an iceberg, floating adrift. The waves came up and the knarr was sailing away in the open water and I was sure the iceberg would carry me off to sea. I prayed. To God and to Jesus." The boy pulled the cross from beneath his shirt. "And He saved me, as He has saved us all through His death on the cross. The iceberg drifted to shore in the darkness, and I got off and followed the snow ridges north and then you found me."

"Your god didn't save you," Brandr interjected with an anger I didn't fully understand. "*We* did. If we hadn't heard you crying, you'd be frozen to death by now."

Snorri's face darkened. "*You* had nothing to do with it, Gunnarsson. The skraeling found me. If you'd come to me, I would've told you to shove your compassion up your arse where it belongs."

"Then you'd be dead for sure," I snapped. "Enough of this, you fools. Has there not been enough fighting today?"

The men settled into an uneasy silence.

"Snorri, let me see your hands."

Even in the dim light I could see the ice-white skin of his fingertips. I scraped a fistful of snow from the ground and began to work it into his flesh.

"Ow!"

"That's the life coming back. It's good that it hurts. If it didn't, you'd lose them."

Snorri gritted his teeth and nodded. "Thank you," he finally whispered.

"Why're you bothering?" Brandr asked me, his voice tight.

"What do you mean?"

"You're saving his hands. For what? Do you think there's a future for him here?"

"He saved me from Ingharr once. I promised him that if he didn't try to kill you, I'd let him live."

"So now you think he'll stay with us, is that it? You'll take him back to your people? We'll all be one smiling family?"

"I don't want to go with you," Snorri protested. "I just want to go home."

"Home?" Brandr barked. "Didn't you see the boat leave, boy? They took off without you. No one missed you. No one noticed you were gone."

"Muirenn will notice."

"Muirenn!" Brandr laughed. "Indeed...except she's dead."

"Christ help me." Snorri squeezed his eyes shut and began to pray under his breath. I didn't catch all his words, for he spoke quickly and low—these were words he'd said many times before. "The Lord is my shepherd, I shall not want..."

A look of distaste crossed Brandr's face. For all that he no longer worshiped the Aesir himself, he still disdained this god of sheep. "You see now why the boy can't stay?"

I finally understood his anger. "The gods exist only where there are people to worship them," I murmured. "If Snorri stays here..." I sucked in a breath. "What are these Christians really like?" I had to know. Perhaps their god could live among us without destroying everything I held dear.

"The tentacles from Rome spread out across all the world like those of a hungry squid." Brandr curled his lip. "Ravenous. Insatiable."

Snorri wasn't even listening; his frozen hands still clutched in my own, he rocked in place, murmuring his prayer.

"On Írland," Brandr went on, "it started as just one priest, they say, and within a generation, all the island had forgotten their old gods of Moon and Sun and turned to the Christ. I have yet to travel anywhere where he has not taken hold. Even in Greenland, Snorri is far from the only Christian. Erik the Red's own wife built a stone church, and already all their thralls and half the freemen pray with her. Trust me, if Snorri had not been afraid for his life, he would've preached his faith to every man on board. Their desert god tells them to spread the word, and they won't stop until the entire world bows before him."

"Is this true?" I shook Snorri's slowly warming hands, dragging his attention back to me. "You want everyone to share your god?"

He sniffled before he answered. "It's our duty to spread the gospel. You can only go to heaven if you accept Christ, and mine is a loving faith. We only want what's best."

"My own gods are dead—my people will turn to yours instead,"

"Once the Christ has a toehold here we will never shake him loose," I said with a groan.

"And what's so wrong with that?"

I peered into the boy's pinched face. "Do you believe the animals have a spirit?"

Snorri shook his head.

"Do you believe that all my ancestors watch me, protect me—that they live still in the stars?"

"Not exactly..."

"That they live again in the bodies of the newly born? I carry my father's spirit inside me. Does your faith understand that?"

"No. They—well—all your ancestors didn't know Christ. They'd be in hell."

Brandr laughed shortly, a sound more of disgust than of humor. "Galinn came to Vinland to save his gods from people like you, and yet he gave his life trying to defend the Christians in Leifsbudir. That's more than *you* did for them. Now he is gone and you are here." He turned to me. "I can't let my brother's death have been in vain."

I am the destroyer of my world. I could deny it no longer. We could never survive if we traded our multitude of spirits for one god of deserts and death. Just as I was man and woman, just as the fanged aarluk was wolf and whale, my people could not be contained in a single god.

I dropped Snorri's hands.

Brandr's voice was hard. "You should've let him die, and his Christ with him."

Snorri's gaze swung from Brandr to me. He slunk back against the iglu wall like a trapped animal, tucking his fingers beneath his own armpits for warmth.

"There has been so much death," I said. "So much blood. Snorri survived—perhaps his god saved him, perhaps one of mine, or one of yours. But he lived."

"I just—I just want to go home."

"You have a choice, Omat," Brandr said darkly. "Either we kill him now, or we let him live. But if he lives, he cannot stay here. You said yourself—he'll bring his god to your shores."

"I could make a boat, maybe," Snorri interjected. "Could try to sail home."

"You'd never make it," Brandr snorted. "On your own? It would take a real Viking to make it all the way to Greenland without help. *You* certainly can't."

"So—I die here at your hands—or I die at sea by my own? Are those my choices?"

Huddled there in his cloak, the boy looked younger than ever. A deep shiver coursed through me.

"Rest now, Snorri. It's not a choice any of us can make right now."

He tried to keep his eyes open a little longer, but exhaustion soon overcame his fear.

We sat there, watching him sleep, for a long while. Sometimes his jaw would clench and his brow furrow. Beneath thin eyelids, his gaze twitched back and forth, scanning the dream world for his enemies. For Brandr.

I looked to my friend. His face had softened.

"You couldn't really kill him," I said finally. "You're not Freydis."

"Nor am I my gentle brother. I would rather Snorri die than watch you lose everything you've fought so hard to save."

"You gave up the berserker rage for a reason, Brandr. You don't kill children anymore. And I will not do it, either."

With a low moan, he dropped his head into his hands. His fingers threaded through his orange hair as if he'd pull it out.

"Why do you really want him gone?" I asked.

"He's a fatherless boy . . . because of me." His voice was calm, but his shoulders trembled. I put a hand on his arm; he pulled me into his grasp and buried his face in my neck to hide from the world.

"I thought I could find forgiveness in your arms. I thought all my debts were paid. But not for this—not for killing Snorri's father."

I could only hold him, too afraid of what I might say to dare speak.

"You know what I'll have to do . . ." He pressed his cheek against mine. "If we can't kill him, and we can't let him stay here, then . . ." His tears ran down my cheeks, where they mingled with my own. "*That's* why I hate him."

I could not protest. After all that I'd destroyed, it seemed only right that I should sacrifice the one thing I had left. Now Brandr would leave me, too, and I could not ask him to stay.

"You have to take him home," I whispered. "You could build a boat and help him sail it." He nodded, silent. "Follow the islands back the way you came. And when you returned to Greenland, he would be safe, and you would have paid recompense for the death of his father. That's how your Althing works, yes? Debts must be paid." Again he nodded. I knew he didn't trust himself to speak. "And you would keep the Christ from our shores. For that, we would be grateful." I straightened so I might look in his eyes. "I will sing such songs of you . . . My family will never forget what you've done."

I tried to smile, to hearten him, but my lips shuddered of their own accord, and I found myself close to tears instead. "Besides, you wouldn't have been happy traveling from one patch of ice to the next—you who've seen deserts and geysers and volcanoes. You told me once you didn't want to settle down with a wife and a homestead, remember? Just imagine, after you take Snorri home, you can go anywhere you want." The Greenlanders wouldn't welcome Brandr back, not after the tales Freydis would tell of his role in the Ragnarok, but I had no doubt he'd find a way to survive. He always had.

I kept talking, trying to convince us both that this was the right decision. "Perhaps you can go back to Rome, with its sweet grapes, and—"

"Omat," Brandr interrupted. "Do you really think I would ever want to leave you?" A mixture of fear and disbelief hardened his brow.

I took a few shallow breaths before I managed a "No."

"If I go"—he traced the constellation of marks on my cheeks— "I go because it's the only way."

"You will stay until summer," I said when I could trust my voice once more. "The ice broke last night beneath Taqqiq's tides and Thor's hammer, but it's still deep winter. It will freeze again. You'll have to wait many moons before the ocean is open enough to sail."

Silently I counted. One—the Moon of the Sun's Rising. Two— the Moon for Bleaching Skins. Three—Seal Birthing Moon. Four—the Moon When Rivers Flow. Five—the Moon When Animals Give Birth. Six—Egg Gathering Moon.

Six moons before one small boat could pass safely east. Six moons—I had known Brandr hardly that long, and yet the last six moons seemed a lifetime.

The next six would seem as fleeting as breath.

CHAPTER FIFTY-SIX

↯

Without my wolfdogs to lead the way, the journey to our winter camp seemed longer than ever before.

I missed their prancing and playing, missed the wagging tails and lolling tongues. I had sacrificed them to protect my world, but now there was little left to protect. True, animals still roamed the tundra. Hare and lemming darted from our path. A falcon soared overhead. But these were animals of flesh alone: animals to warm our bodies with meat and fur and feathers, but with no guiding spirit to warm our hearts.

Long before I reached our camp, I learned of my family through their footprints. Tapsi had big feet; his prints were easy to recognize. And the shuffling step beside the indentations of a harpoon point must be Ququk, grown older and more frail. Millik's gait was short, her prints shallow. Saartok's footsteps, too, were easy to spot, although she must have gained weight rather than lost it, for her prints were deeper than they should have been. Finally I found the one set of tracks I most wanted to see.

I knelt in the snow, heedless of the cold seeping through my makeshift woolen trousers, and traced the outline of each familiar boot with my finger. I knew this step.

Puja lived.

A day later, I spotted the familiar humps of qarmait on the horizon. I began to run, ignoring the protests of Brandr and Snorri, both too slow to keep up with me.

The camp's dogs howled; grief clutched at my heart. How I missed my wolfdogs! But joy quickly replaced mourning as a familiar figure crawled from the nearest tunnel and stood with one hand raised against the glare, peering out suspiciously.

"Anaana!"

The woman I called Mother stumbled toward me across the snow. She opened her arms wide and clutched me to her. I could feel Puja's ribs even through her parka. I buried my face in her shoulder, inhaling the familiar smell of her—soot and sweat and seal.

She stroked my hair with her fur mitten and whispered against my cheek. "You're home now. You will not leave again." Unspoken, but understood: an apology. She would never again watch me dragged away.

Finally she pulled back to ask, "Kiasik?"

"I tried. So hard." I finally released the tears I had not yet shed for him. "We were almost home."

Puja pulled her hood low, hiding her face in mourning. The others gathered around, all the familiar faces, thinner than before but no less dear: Tapsi and Saartok, Ququk and Ujaguk, Niquvana and Millik. They joined in Puja's lamentation, a long, low cry of grief followed by silence.

And then—an unexpected gurgle. Saartok turned to show me the tiny face peeking from her hood.

"Alianait!" I exclaimed, brushing away my tears.

"He was born a moon past," Saartok said proudly. "Tapsi has been hunting to keep us fed."

She smiled at her husband, who blushed in response and stroked his son's downy hair. So my cousin had not lost his gentleness, only his fear. With Kiasik and me gone, it seemed Tapsi had finally become a man.

"Our son has not yet been named," he told me. "We were waiting for an angakkuq..."

"Kiasik," I said firmly. "He is Kiasik."

The baby gurgled with delight and pounded his fists against his mother's shoulder. I knew I had chosen rightly. Already the child showed his namesake's spirit. Puja smiled faintly through her tears. Her son lived again.

"You've brought us tidings of both grief and joy, Older Brother," she said.

"And more than that," Ququk interjected, his voice filled with alarm as he pointed out across the snow.

Brandr and Snorri approached.

"Ia'a..." Tapsi stepped protectively in front of his wife and child. "Have you brought giants in your trail?"

"No, it's all right," I said quickly. "They're friends."

My family stood tense and afraid as the Norsemen joined us.

Snorri shifted from foot to foot, prepared to flee in case these new skraelings decided to attack. Brandr's face split into a wide grin, and he moved closer to me.

"This man is Brandr," I explained.

My friend cocked his head at the sound of his name.

"He is..." How could I describe him to my family? How would they understand?

Brandr knew enough of our tongue to understand my struggle. His smile only broadened. "How do you say *husband*?" he asked in Norse.

I swallowed. *"Uik."* For so long, I'd dreaded the word. I had fought too long for my man's spirit to give it up easily now—even for Brandr.

"Ui...gijaa...nga," Brandr said firmly, his meaning clear despite his halting Inuit speech. *I am Omat's husband.*

Shouts of amazement, confusion, pleasure, and disbelief echoed around us. I waited for him to step in front of me as Tapsi had done for Saartok, or to put an arm around me, claiming me as his own. I wasn't sure what I would do if he did, but I cast him a warning glare. I did not intend to spend my days tending the lamp or sewing his boots or—

He took a small step backward, his eyes never leaving mine. He stood just behind my shoulder like a hunting companion ready to help reel in a seal from the hidden deep.

I remembered the song he'd played for Sweet One that first morning he awoke in my tent. Listening, I'd felt like a longspur flying over a valley of bright flowers. Now his gaze alone could lift my wings. And for all I worried about where my flight would take me, I could not bring myself to come back to earth.

——◆——

Long into the night, I told the story of my journey. Some of it seemed unimaginable, even to me—perhaps because I had lived with Brandr so long. But my people never questioned the reality of other worlds. They gasped, to be sure, but they believed every word.

Little Kiasik lay fast asleep against Saartok's breast, and even the adults grew weary in the warmth of the crowded qarmaq by the time the story was over. One by one, they left for their own homes, until only the Norsemen and Puja remained. Then, to my surprise, my milk-mother stood and spoke to Snorri.

I translated. "She wants you to visit the other families with her."

Snorri opened his mouth to protest, then shot Brandr a quick look and changed his mind.

"You don't need to leave," I insisted weakly.

Puja scowled at me—the familiar expression only made me smile.

She and Snorri crawled from the qarmaq.

With only the howl of the wind outside to disturb the silence, Brandr and I were finally alone. We stared at each other for a long moment.

"I don't know what kind of husband you'll be," I finally blurted out. "You won't even be here for more than a few more moons—"

"Do you need me to stay and hunt for you?"

I snorted.

"Exactly. I'm not an Inuit husband to keep you fed. Nor am I a Norse husband, who would bring you jewels and thralls and fight for your honor. You don't need anyone to do those things. You've been hunting for me, protecting me, fighting for me, since we first met."

"True. So what kind of husband are you, then?"

"I am your mate, Omat," he said simply, taking my hand in his.

He kissed me then, long and slow. There was no guard at the door to disturb us, no sunrise to bring our doom, only a very long night ahead. We knew each other's stories now, knew to be gentle, knew how to banish memory with kisses. His lips moved along my jaw, my neck, my collarbone.

"Take off these useless rags," I groaned finally. "I'd rather be naked than ever wear them again."

Brandr laughed, his grin bright in the lamplight. I remembered our first night together; he'd grimaced with pain as I dressed his wounds. I grabbed his face between my hands, my voice catching with desperation. "I would have you always laughing."

"And so would I." He smiled down at me, kissing the tip of my nose. His lightness was infectious. Together we pulled the remnants of the wool dress from my shoulders and the fur parka from his. For a moment, sitting in only my makeshift trousers with my breasts bare, I was shy again.

I picked up his discarded parka, resisting the urge to cover myself with it. "We'll ask Puja to make you a better one."

"I would wear none but one made by your hands."

"You may call me wife, but I never plan to sew again!"

"So you *are* my wife, then!"

"Can I be a wife if I'm not a woman?" I asked, suddenly serious. "Or," I conceded, "not *only* a woman?"

His solemn gaze matched my own. "I told you once I didn't want to settle down with a wife. Now I know I never wanted *only* a wife. I wanted a wife and a partner and a friend. Spirit upon spirit curled one within the other like the spirals of a shell. Isn't that what you told me once?"

He brushed the hair from my forehead and took my lips once more in his. I dropped the parka. His hand moved to cradle my naked breast. I felt all my spirals uncurl beneath his touch. I moaned, deep in my throat, and his lips grew more urgent; he bent to take my nipple in his mouth.

"Aii!"

Then, as he settled into his task, I moaned a soft "Alianait" of pleasure and buried my fingers in his orange hair.

He turned bright eyes toward me. "Are you so happy you've forgotten how to speak Norse?"

"Norse doesn't have quite the right words."

He traced one finger over the curve of my breast. "Alianait..." He drew out the exclamation like a caress. My nipple hardened beneath his touch. "Yes...that is the right word."

Perhaps it was hearing my people's words on his lips. Perhaps it was simply the drive of my own desire. Perhaps it was the light in his eyes. I was ready. Together we pushed the trousers from our hips and clambered onto the sleeping platform. He pulled me on top of him, and I moved instinctively, seeking release, my hands digging into his shoulders, my feet pressed against his legs.

"My—my thigh."

"Sorry! I forgot—"

"No, no, come back. Don't move! Well, I mean move, just how you were, just put your hands—"

"Here?"

"Ow!"

"Here?"

"Yes. There, there, perfect."

"And how about here?"

"There's good, too."

"Here?" I guided him inside me, slowly, achingly slowly.

"Alianait..."

CHAPTER
FIFTY-SEVEN

ᛇ

I always knew he would leave. That didn't make our parting any easier.

In our last moons together, we hunted side by side, filling my family's scanty meat caches. We slept side by side as well. No longer alone most nights, for that is not our way, but that didn't stop us from enjoying each other beneath the sleeping furs. I was still a man to my people, but a woman now as well. Finally I lived in both spheres, enjoyed both lives. A woman in Brandr's arms, a man upon the open ice.

Puja made me a new parka, and despite Brandr's protests, she made one for him as well, although he insisted on keeping the dog-fur hood from his old one.

"For luck."

"Sew a ruff for it," I said to Puja. "He can't complain about that, and he'll need it on the open sea."

That was one of the few times I spoke of his leaving. But the signs of it were everywhere. The Vinland logs from the Norsemen's knarrs washed upon our shores, but no corpses followed suit. All trace of gods and giants had disappeared. Brandr and Snorri wasted no time constructing a small boat. They were no shipwrights, but Brandr had been a sailor once, and seemed more at ease in the boat than he ever had on our hunting trips.

Side by side they worked, and slowly their hatred softened and melted like the ice around them. Snorri was grateful for Brandr's help, and I think perhaps Brandr saw something in the younger man that reminded him of Galinn.

Saartok and Millik helped sew a patched sail of scraped seal hides, and Ququk crafted strong walrus-skin ropes. The old man didn't fully trust this strange wooden boat, continually insisting that only a crazy fool would build so heavy a ship, but Brandr merely laughed, clapped him on the shoulder, and continued hammering together the long slats of wood.

Niquvana and Ujaguk, the oldest women in our camp, sewed a parka and trousers for Snorri as well. Puja fashioned containers from bladders and hides to hold food and water for the journey.

When the ice finally melted from the sea, everything was ready.

Brandr and Snorri, with Tapsi and me helping, pushed the boat over the rocky shore and out into the open water. Ququk harrumphed, but had to admit that yes, it did float.

Oblivious to the frigid water, Brandr waded out and hauled himself over the side. He stood proudly, hands on hips, his smile gleaming in the summer sun.

Onshore, I turned away.

Puja walked beside me, back to our camp. "You could go with him."

I stopped in my tracks. I looked at the woman who had been the only mother I'd ever known. I didn't need to say anything more. She understood. I'd never leave my people. Not even for my mate.

The Norsemen left later that day.

With all our camp gathered onshore to see them off, Brandr came to embrace me one last time. I kept him at arm's length.

"It's easier if you just go." If I broke down and cried, if I clung to him, if I begged him to stay, there was the slimmest chance that he might not leave. And he had to leave. For Snorri. For my way of life. I knew that if I succeeded in protecting my heart, I'd fail to protect my people.

"It is *not* easier," he insisted, reaching out a hand to me. "This will *never* be easy."

"Please, Brandr."

I let him take my hand in his. That's all I could allow. But before I could stop him, he pressed his lips against my palm. My fingertips brushed his orange beard for the last time.

"Tapvauvutit," he whispered. *Here you are*. An Inuk's words of parting.

"Farthu vel," I said in response, knowing he was wrong. I would never be with him again.

When he drew away, a chill wind reminded me of summer's fleeting beauty.

I did not watch their boat disappear over the horizon. Ququk did, I think, marveling at the way the sail moved the craft so smoothly across the water. But I left. I grabbed my bow and arrows and walked inland, toward the caribou herds. No wolfdogs ran down my prey for me. No brother teased when my arrow missed the caribou. No friend told me tales to fill the silence at night. No spirit guided my steps or calmed the weather.

I was alone once more.

―――◄◆►―――

By the time I returned to camp several days later, I brought two pieces of news. One, the caribou herd had moved northward and we should follow it. Two, I was with child.

My woman's blood had always been as unpredictable as every-thing else in my life. On my long sojourn, it had sometimes come with every moon, sometimes not for two or three in a row. But when I woke every morning on my solo caribou hunt and vomited outside my tent, even I, with my limited knowledge of a woman's world, knew the signs.

On our summer migration, I found myself looking at the world with different eyes. I searched the ground for the tracks and scat of the caribou, yes, but I also watched for black lichen and field moss and willow scrub. Puja didn't need to be asked, she simply took to walking beside me, pointing out which plants could make a warming tea or form a lamp wick that would burn smokeless and strong—or wipe up an infant's mess.

Once I might have chafed at walking next to her—now I relished it. She had much to teach. Much I'd never taken the time before to learn. If we hadn't been scanning the ground together, I never would've noticed the *qiviut*—great furry clumps of brown musk ox fur—hanging off the branches of the low-lying bushes. The massive beasts must have passed this way during the spring, shedding their thick undercoats. Most qiviut was quickly snatched by birds to line their nests. But somehow these clumps had waited here for many moons.

A rustling drew my attention to a nearby hillock. A raven, tall and proud, strode across the moss, her black beak twitching toward us, then away, one bright eye meeting mine. She took to the sky in a scraping of feathers and disappeared in lazy circles into the sunlight, loosing a single croaking call as she went.

Puja sneaked her hand into mine. She knew I watched the bird's flight with envy.

I squeezed her hand in return, and whispered my gratitude to the raven. She'd been guarding the qiviut for me all summer.

Together Puja and I gathered the ragged sheets of fur from the branches, marveling at the thick softness.

Later I sat in our tent with the pile of wool on my lap. Snorri's hair had once reminded me of the curling undercoat of a musk ox. Now that I had the qiviut in front of me, though, I thought only of Freydis. A woman whose life was ruled by wool. I'd always seen her constant spinning and weaving as a burden. But now, as I pictured her standing before her loom with her ivory sword, I thought about the women's magic I'd discovered so many moons ago on the whale hunt. I'd killed a man through the mere tying and unty-ing of cord. How much more power lay in weaving string together than in breaking it apart?

It took me nearly until the end of the Moon When Birds Fly South to carve a workable spindle. By the Moon When Winter Begins, I'd spun only half of the qiviut into thread. As I twisted the fibers together, I felt a strange power building within me. Not that of an angakkuq, not quite. Perhaps it was only the strength of my child. Had every mother felt the stirrings of such power?

Puja and Ujaguk and Niquvana stared at my new thread, at first skeptical, then fascinated. They begged for spindles of their own. Ququk and Tapsi agreed to carve them from the antlers of the cari-bou we'd killed. Soon the women walked with their spindle whorls swaying before them, like spiders birthing their silk. None of us had Muirenn or Freydis's skill, but together we collected a thick spool of qiviut thread by the Moon of Great Darkness. Rougher, thicker, less fine than the Norsewomen's—but stronger, lighter, and warmer.

I both hated and loved the child growing inside me. I hated how protective Puja had become, treating me like some fragile girl. I hated that I could hardly lower myself into a kayak, much less paddle long enough to hunt down a seal along the ever-widening ice edge. But when the baby moved inside me, when I felt the contours of its feet pressing against my palm, I couldn't help but smile.

Unable to hunt any longer, I began to fashion a loom. It took me three frustrating moons to complete. I never did figure out how to make a working shuttle; I resorted to passing the qiviut threads under and over each other by hand. To tighten the weave, I used a blunted snow knife in place of an ivory sword—a tool for building, not bloodshed.

I'd woven a scant finger's length of cloth when the first pangs began.

My family built a birthing iglu for me on the outskirts of our camp. Puja stayed by my side as she had stayed by my mother's. Taqqiq had told me that every passage was one of blood. Birth and death, we are torn apart and re-created.

I was ripped open once more, but this time my tears were those of joy, not rage.

CHAPTER
FIFTY-EIGHT

᛭

With my baby swaddled in seal furs by my side, I sat before my loom. For a day and a night, I did nothing but nurse my child and stare at the small stretch of cloth.

With my eyes open, I dreamed. But they were not my dreams. They were Galinn's, and the old painted woman's, and even the All-Father's. I dreamed of one people destroyed by another, leaving nothing but ruins and shards of clear quartz. I dreamed of a land where all the spirits would live in peace. I dreamed of an ending, where Odin's ravens flew with my own and Inuit wolfdogs lived in a Norse god's prophecy.

Then I dreamed of a beginning.

I took up the thread again. My cloth, if it could even be called cloth, was ragged and patchy, all loose threads and snarled edges. Still I wove, my task lit by sunlight and seal oil. My fingers flying over my loom, I began to sing my story to my child.

I started with my own tale—the melting of girl into boy, of man into woman and back. And back again. Of a journey to a land of towering trees and back once more to flat stone. Of a man with eyes the color of ice and hair the color of flame and a smile to warm the coldest night. Of brothers lost and found and lost again. And always, always, the spirits watching from above and below, from my own land and from across the sea, until finally the gods themselves melt away, never to return again.

My child's eyes wandered unfocused across my face, across my fingers—not yet able to see, to understand. But able to hear. And, one day, to remember.

As I sang, I wove together the strands of my story. I wove together my own past with that of my father and my grandfather and my mother. I wove Issuk's family into the warp and my own into the weft. I twined the strength of Freydis with the innocence of Snorri, the laughter of Brandr with the courage of Kiasik. Singarti's grace. Uqsuralik's power. Loki's cunning. Frey's gentleness.

I wove together the gods I'd led to destruction, those who couldn't see that my land was big enough for them all. The Aesir saw my land as theirs to conquer. Loki saw it as his to defend. I, too, had wanted the Norsemen gone. Yet did my child not share the spirit of the Viking I loved? Odin walked with a raven on each shoulder—he could have found a home here with the animal spirits. Instead he had come to fight. To the Norse, battle was a way of life. They couldn't live in a land without subduing it. And, as much as I hated to admit it, my own people were little different. I had not forgotten the old painted woman and her memories of slavering dogs. My ancestors had driven the first iglu builders from this land. One people replacing another in an unending cycle. A cycle I wanted to finally break.

When I finished my tale, I cut the cloth from the loom with Brandr's sharp knife. I ran my fingers over the rough brown weave, each stitch and snarl loosing a flood of memories. My story made tangible. Never to be forgotten. The threads knotted and gaped—weft and warp joining as uneasily as Inuk and Norseman. But the cloth held together. With this I had woven my shattered world back together. With this I would wrap my child.

I swaddled my baby in the ragged qiviut blanket and crawled from the qarmaq. Together we stared up at the Moon. I no longer feared Taqqiq—he turned his face away from us and stared over his shoulder at the sister who chased him instead. My future lay only in the world at my feet and the new life in my arms.

Or so I thought.

— ⚏ —

Seal Birthing Moon found us back in our igluit on the landfast ice. Every morning, Tapsi and Ququk left by dogsled to hunt on the frozen sea, while I stayed behind to nurse my child. But come summer, when the ocean rippled beneath the never-setting Sun, I would be a man again, teaching my people how to hunt the whale as Issuk had done.

I made my own aglirutiit now.

I stared off across the frozen sea. In the moonlight, loose snow blew across the ice in long, undulating ripples like watery waves, as if summer had come a few moons early. I let myself dream that the sea ice had melted—that somehow Brandr had made it all the way to Greenland, seen Snorri safely home, and returned to me. A foolish hope, I knew.

Still, when I heard the heavy footsteps behind me, I nearly jumped. When I heard the Norse-accented voice call my name, I nearly cried.

When I turned around, a tall, red-bearded man stood before me.

"Thor..."

"Omat."

"I thought..."

The god smiled, his teeth very white in the moonlight. "You thought we were dead?" He laughed, a low, thunderous rumbling. From the dim light behind him, other figures emerged. Odin and Frigg, Frey and Freya, and a host of others... All the great gods of the Norse assembled before my iglu. Their clothes no longer sparkled with gold and silver, their weapons no longer glinted with iron and steel—only driftwood and slate and bone.

I pulled the qiviut blanket tight to shield my child.

"Don't hide her," Freya urged. When she spoke, the wreath of yellow poppies and pink saxifrage in her hair bobbed and waved. "She's why we're here."

Gentle Frey stepped away from his beautiful sister to peer at the baby in my arms. I could barely meet his gaze, yet this god whom Brandr had struck down seemed to bear me no malice. "We thought the Fate of the Gods would be our end," he murmured. "Eternal death without rebirth. Darkness without light."

"Among my people, the heralding stars always return," I explained hesitantly. "Dawn follows darkness. The Sun rises again. Each end, even the Ragnarok, is also a beginning."

I could hardly believe it, but my women's magic had worked. When the spirits had died in battle, I'd lost my powers as an angakkuq. But I'd tapped into something far older and deeper. That which I had destroyed I now restored.

"We do not live as we did before," Frigg said, her voice grim but resigned. "We are Norse gods no longer."

"Inuit. Norse. Both are people of dwarfs and giants and ravens and wolves," I replied. "We will give you sanctuary here among the ice."

"We may have been reborn in Jotunheim," Odin said, "but we will move south. It would be nice to live among the trees once more."

The wind picked up, as if Sila wished to hasten them on their way.

The snow rose from the ice in a swirling curtain. One by one, towering figures emerged from the whiteness. Striding. Prancing. Soaring.

Wolf, Raven, Bear, Caribou.

I fell to my knees before Singarti. "You haven't abandoned me,"

I managed, choking back tears. I held up my child for my guardian spirit to sniff.

You cannot kill a spirit so easily. Singarti's voice spoke into my mind. *We move. We change. We do not die.*

To my surprise, Thor seemed to hear the Wolf. "Not unless there is no one left to worship us."

Odin nodded. "That is the only way to kill a god."

You told the tale to your child. Singarti's nose painted a stripe of wet on my daughter's cheek. *In her we are reborn.*

"She is Norse and Inuk both," Frey added. "She allows us to stay. From now on, when your people pray to Raven or Wolf, we, too, will listen. And when they call upon Sanna, Loki will hear them as well."

"Loki?" I hadn't dared ask about him, but his familiar slanting grin was nowhere to be seen among the crowd of Aesir.

Beautiful Freya sighed. "That sad little sea girl was so lonely. And Loki had promised to be her companion, after all." A knowing smile flickered across her lips. "It was the least I could do, after what we did to her."

"Sanna?" I asked, dumbfounded. "And Loki?"

"You wove us all back into existence with your tale," Frigg explained. "The Trickster, too. Sanna seemed to think he was her old lover and demanded he go with her beneath the waves. He could not refuse."

I smiled grimly, imagining Loki beneath Sanna's unrelenting gaze, forced to soothe and service her for eternity.

"It is for the best." Odin's one eye was stern. "He will not trick us again."

"So...," I ventured, "if Sanna and all the spirits of the animals are still alive..." Hope tightened my breath. "My wolfdogs? Are they here, too?"

"They are not immortal," Frey said gently. "Not like us."

"So they are gone, then..."

"Not entirely. Their wolf forms were destroyed, but they were beings of great power, sent by Singarti himself to guard you. You may see them again."

I turned back to the frozen sea, searching for the glint of narwhal horn thrusting through the ice. I wished I still had an angakkuq's eyes.

"And my magic?" I ventured.

Singarti whimpered and licked my hand. His ears lay flat and his tail tucked. That alone answered my question, but Frey continued, smiling sadly. "My child, never again will you journey to the spirit world. You have brought us back to a place of peace, and for this we owe you much. But you did, after all, help Loki raise an army against us. And you overthrew your own Moon—sent him scampering across the sky with his tail between his legs. You reminded us all of the dangers of letting mortals play with such power. We cannot take such a risk again. Our worlds are better off apart."

"Still, we thank you," interjected Frigg. She stepped close, and I let her move the blanket away from my daughter's face. The goddess placed one long finger on my baby's cheek, and for a moment the eyes of infant and goddess met. "You and your babe have saved us. Even now, the Christ approaches our last strongholds. A god without women or sex." She shuddered.

"Or fighting and feasting," added Thor. "A desert god with no understanding of the ice, the animals, the sea."

Odin gestured to the south. "We will walk to Vinland. To live among the forests and meadows of a new world, just as Galinn wished." He leaned on a long, slate-pointed spear. "Even now, Freydis Eriksdottir tells her people of the Ragnarok—of the great battle fought on your shores. The skalds will sing of it for an age. To them, this land is doomed—the burial ground of the gods. No Norseman will ever dare sail past here again, not even to reach Vinland." His voice was heavy with sorrow. Regret. Saving the Aesir meant losing the people who'd worshiped them for so long. It could not have been an easy choice. "If the Norse stay away," he went on, "the Christ will as well. We will be safe."

"And we have met our end with our weapons in our hands." Thor puffed out his broad chest. "Rather than wilting away through the neglect of an ungrateful people."

"That was Loki's doing," I couldn't help mentioning. "He brought the battle that let you die a glorious death."

Frigg nodded. "The Trickster sought to destroy us. He helped create us anew instead."

Singarti padded toward the gods who had once been the Aesir. Caribou stamped his hoof.

Freya pressed her lips briefly upon my daughter's brow before rejoining the others. Spirit and god stood arrayed before me—tall and beautiful, proud and strong. I knew this was the last time I would see them.

I held up my daughter so she, too, could witness this great assembly of the gods she'd helped to save.

I expected them to turn and disappear into the snow. But before they left, Odin turned his single gray eye on me. "One more thing, Inuk. For bringing us back, for weaving us together, for bearing the child who will protect our future—we owe you. What would you have of us? Whatever is in our power to grant you, we will."

I took a step backward from his piercing stare and turned to look at the other gods. In each of their faces, I saw a silent question. Would I ask for my child to grow strong and live long? wondered Frigg. Would I ask for wisdom and farsightedness? wondered Odin. Would I ask that my wolf pack run at my side once more? wondered Singarti. Would I ask for Brandr returned safe to my arms? wondered Freya.

But I have always been proud.

I would make my way in this world without their aid.

That didn't mean I wouldn't ask something for my people. "Do not go south. Stay here, with us. Always."

Odin's eye widened. Thor grumbled his disbelief. Singarti whimpered.

I stayed firm. "The Norse will not come back—but others may. Brandr told me of many worlds across the ocean. Great villages of stone, where men drink the spoiled juice of grapes. Desert lands of searing sand. Islands of trees and blue-painted men. I saw the pelts the Norse piled on board their ships—so many that even the greatest caribou herds might never recover. If these other strangers come to my shores, they will slaughter seal and whale, fox and bear, with equal abandon. Without animals, there is no Singarti, no Uqsuralik."

Thor scowled. "And what would you have us do about that?"

I looked to Singarti, silently asking his permission before I said more. He stared back for a long moment before opening his mouth in a wolfish smile of agreement.

"If you stay," I said to Odin, "you can weave your strength with ours. Your own people may forget the spirits of ice and snow, or wolf and raven, but mine will not. We are stronger together."

"You ask for much," Odin said.

"I have given you much," I returned, refusing to quail before him.

Odin's gray eye glazed suddenly. He looked beyond me, beyond the tundra, all the way to the future. "We will do as you ask, child."

Thor rumbled. Freya gasped. But none dared defy the All-Father.

"We will stay," he continued, his face still slack in the trance's power. "We will work with Sanna and Singarti and all the others to help defend you. And this time, we will be more vigilant. We will divert the ships from your shores, we will keep the sea frozen, we will hide you among the icebergs. For five hundred years, we will keep the strangers from your land."

"And then?" I dared ask.

"For five hundred years more, you will remember the Aesir, though you may call us by different names. You will remember Singarti and Uqsuralik. And the strangers that come will not stay long. The land will remain yours. After that..." He shrugged, his eye sharp once more. "Well, after that, I can promise you nothing. You will have to guard the wolves and the whales yourself."

Odin turned abruptly away. Singarti lifted his tail in a final salute, then bounded ahead of the Aesir. The Wolf led the gods west, toward the mountains and valleys of my home. Before they'd taken more than a dozen steps, the gods disappeared into the whirling snow. All but Frey and Freya, who stood just within sight, their golden hair like bursts of sun amid the clouds.

A sharp caw drew my gaze to the sky. Qangatauq the Raven shouting a last farewell. He tilted his wings and circled lower, close enough for me to catch a rainbow glint in his black eye.

Loki, I remembered, always escaped his chains.

Qangatauq, or Loki, or some being that was now both at once, cawed again in joyous bird laughter before he winged away into the white.

As I turned back to my iglu, I noticed a splash of color in the icy world at my feet. A patch of yellow flowers that hadn't been there a moment before. Flowers that shouldn't bloom until the Moon When Animals Give Birth.

Poppies.

Some lay loose on the snow. As if they'd fallen from a woman's hair.

Some sprang forth from the earth, their narrow green shoots thrusting through the snow, their bright petals fluttering in the stiff wind.

I looked up, toward Frey and Freya. The god of growing things and the goddess of love.

But they, too, were gone.

CHAPTER
FIFTY-NINE

ϟ

One should never underestimate the gods.

I had not asked for it. Could barely dream it. But Freya and Frey sent him back to me nonetheless.

My daughter could already walk. She had learned to call me *Ataata* when I taught her to hunt, and *Anaana* when I removed her tiny boots and warmed her feet in my hands.

I let Puja teach her how to sew.

She and Little Kiasik were not the only children in our camp anymore. When she was just out of my hood, five long sleds appeared on the horizon. Hunters bringing food and laughter and families, rather than fear. Other Inuit would come soon, they promised, when they heard of our rich hunting grounds. Now a dozen tents crowded our summer camp.

Life, as Ataata always said, attracts life.

In the warm summer days of Caribou Shedding Moon, I sat my daughter between my legs and we paddled my kayak along the shore, looking for seabirds and seals. As we went, I told her of the great spirits of our world—both old and new—that watched over us still. But I told her, too, that the world was ours to live in, ours to enjoy. I knew her father would have wanted her to know that.

The water was calm, the Sun high. We grew drowsy on our journey, lulled by the gentle rocking motion of Sanna's breast.

"Look, Ataata!" she said, pointing to shore.

"Sharp eyes! It's a wolf!" But not just any wolf.

A Wolf with a coat so white it hurt my eyes. A Wolf as tall as a man. One I'd never expected to see again. He pricked up his ears and lowered his tail. I remembered enough of his tongue to understand his meaning: *Listen*.

Note by note, a song danced across the waves from far out at sea—from a place no songbird should fly.

With a deft stroke of my paddle, I turned the kayak eastward.

A speck of white, as bright as Singarti's flank, glistened on the water. As it approached, it took the form of a small square sail flying proudly before a wooden boat just large enough to carry one man.

I did not wait for it to come to me. With my daughter's warm body pressed against mine and her laughter twining with the whistled melody, I went to meet it.

He must have seen me coming, for the song stopped, and the white sail soon fluttered loose. An anchor splashed overboard, and the boat came to a rocking halt just as my kayak pulled alongside.

Brandr's smile gleamed down at me, then faded quickly when he saw the little girl in my lap. My daughter grinned guilelessly up at him, ready for adventure, unafraid of any stranger.

I lifted her free of the kayak and held her up to him. Before he could protest, she was in his arms. With her small face close to his, he couldn't fail to recognize her straight nose or the gentle curl of her black hair.

"What's your name?" he asked the child huskily. She didn't understand him, of course, not when he spoke in Norse. She merely grabbed on to his orange beard and laughed delightedly at this strange new plaything.

"Her name is Nona, for she carries my mother's spirit in her breast. But I call her Aktut. It means 'knife.' "

"A sharp name for one so soft."

"You gave me this," I said, holding aloft the small sharp blade I always wore at my waist, "and you gave me her. Two things I didn't know I needed until I had them."

"Aren't you going to come on board?" he asked finally, reaching out his hand to me.

My fingertips brushed his. A promise.

"And miss the joy of racing you to shore?"

I paddled as hard as I ever had. The sun glinted off the sea swells, bringing tears to my already brimming eyes. My smile stretched as wide as my daughter's as I heard the luff of the sail behind me and knew that Brandr followed behind, Aktut safe in his arms.

Here ends this tale.

GLOSSARY

∫

Inuktitut Words

A note on spelling: For most nouns, I have used modern Inuktitut spellings of the South Qikiqtaaluk dialect. Some character names, such as Omat and Saartok, use older spellings.

A'aa: an exclamation of pain
Aarluk: killer whale
Agliruti (pl. aglirutiit): taboo
Aii: an exclamation of surprise
Anaana: mother
Angakkuq (pl. angakkuit): shaman
Aqsarniit: the Northern Lights
Alianait: an exclamation of pleasure
Ataata: father
Atigi: a man's garment, worn alone in summer or beneath a parka in winter, with the fur facing inside
Hnnnn: an expression of assent
Ia'a: an exclamation of fear
Iglu (pl. igluit): igloo, a temporary house made from snow blocks
Ilisuilttuq: Stupid One, literally "one who does not learn"
Inuk (pl. Inuit): a real human
Inuksuk (pl. inuksuit): large stones piled to resemble the figure of a standing man
Kayak: a slim, closed one-man boat (from the Inuktitut *qajaq*)
Maktak: edible skin of the bowhead whale

Nuqqarit: Stop!

Qaggiq: large ceremonial iglu built for special gatherings

Qarmaq (pl. qarmait): a permanent, semisubterranean house made from whale bones and skins, insulated with sod

Qiviut: wool shed from the undercoat of the musk ox

Tapvauvutit: goodbye, literally "here you are"

Uiluaqtaq: in Alaskan legend, a woman who lives without men and hunts for herself

Ulu: a crescent-shaped knife used by women

Umiaq: a large, open boat used for whale hunting or for group transportation

Great Spirits of the Inuit

Malina: the Sun Woman, sister to Taqqiq (Modern Inuit generally name the Sun Woman *Siqiniq*. In the eighteenth century, however, some West Greenland Inuit used *Malina*, from the root meaning "following.")

Qangatauq: the Raven Spirit, "One Who Hops"

Sanna: Sea Mother, Great Woman who guards the animals beneath the sea

Sila: Air, Weather, and Sky

Singarti: the Wolf Spirit, "One Who Pierces"

Taqqiq: the Moon Man, brother to Malina

Uqsuralik: the Ice Bear (Polar Bear) Spirit, "The Fatty One"

Inuit Calendar

January/February: Moon of the Sun's Rising
February/March: Moon for Bleaching Skins
March/April: Seal Birthing Moon/Whaling Moon
April/May: Moon When Rivers Flow
May/June: Moon When Animals Give Birth
June/July: Egg Gathering Moon
July/August: Caribou Shedding Moon
August/September: Moon When Birds Fly South
September/October: Antler Peeling Moon
October/November: Moon When Winter Begins
November/December: Moon of the Setting Sun
December/January: Moon of Great Darkness

Old Norse Words and Places

Althing: council of freemen
Ambatt: concubine
Englaland: "Angles' Land," present-day southeast Scotland
Freydisbudir: "Freydis's Booths" or "Freydis's Houses"
Helluland: "Land of Flat Stones," present-day Baffin Island in Nunavut
Írland: present-day Ireland
Jotunheim: mythological realm of the Frost Giants
Knarr: deep-bottomed merchant ship
Kunta: vagina
Leifsbudir: "Leif's Booths" or "Leif's Houses"
Markland: "Land of Forests," present-day Labrador
Northway: present-day Norway
Ragnarok: the "Fate of the Gods," the final battle prophesied between the Aesir and the Jotuns
Rus: present-day Russia
Skald: poet, bard, or storyteller
Skít: shit
Skraeling: barbarian, wretch (used in the sagas to describe the indigenous peoples of North America)
Skyr: a yogurt drink
Thrall: slave
Valhalla: Odin's hall, where those who die bravely in battle enjoy endless feasting
Vinland: "Land of Wine," present-day Newfoundland

Norse Gods and Monsters

A note on spelling: For simplicity, I have used Anglicized spellings rather than the more accurate (and less familiar) Old Norse transliterations. For example, Freya rather than Freja and Baldur rather than Baldr.

Aesir: the ruling family of Norse gods, including Odin, Thor, Frigg, and others

Baldur: bright god of life and beauty, son of Odin and Frigg, killed through Loki's trickery

Fenrir: a monstrous wolf, child of Loki

Frey: god of growing things, Freya's brother

Freya: goddess of love and beauty, Frey's sister

Frigg: goddess of magic and destiny, Odin's wife, Baldur's mother, and Thor's foster mother

Garm: the hound of Hel

Heimdall: the Watcher of the Gods who carries a horn to warn of the Ragnarok's approach

Hel: goddess of death, daughter of Loki

Hod: blind brother of Baldur

Jormungand: the serpent or sea beast that encircles the world

Jotun: a Frost Giant, mortal enemy of the Aesir

Loki: trickster, shapeshifter, who was born a Jotun but lives with the Aesir

Odin: the one-eyed All-Father and leader of the Aesir; god of war, kingship, and farsightedness, armed with a spear and often accompanied by two ravens; husband to Frigg, father of Thor and Baldur

Surtur: a flame fiend who will fight beside the Jotuns in the Ragnarok

Thor: red-bearded thunder god; son of Odin and the Earth, raised by Frigg; a god of battle who carries a war hammer

Tyr: one-handed god of war; son of Odin and swordsman of the Aesir

Valkyries: Odin's wolf-riding handmaidens, who choose which of the slain will go to Valhalla

Ymir: a giant defeated by Odin at the beginning of the world; the Aesir formed the world from his blood and bones

A NOTE ON THE HISTORY OF THE NORSE AND INUIT IN NORTH AMERICA

Omat's family belongs to the first expansion of Inuit ancestors—called Thule (TOO-lee) by anthropologists—from Siberia to Alaska and then to Nunavut in the eastern Canadian Arctic sometime between 800 and 1200 AD. With dogsleds and skin boats, the Thule may have accomplished this spectacular journey—several thousand miles through some of the least hospitable environments on earth—in only a few years, rather than many generations. Scholars speculate that they undertook the migration to follow bowhead whales, whose travel through the Arctic Sea was made possible only by the lack of sea ice during several hundred years of climate change known as the Medieval Warm Period.

Arriving in the eastern Arctic, the Thule found the land already inhabited by a people known in later Inuit legends as Tuniit and in anthropological literature as Dorset. Some myths portray the Tuniit as exceptionally large but gentle people. Other stories describe them as dwarfs, likely due to the tiny, delicate tools found in the ruins of their rectangular stone-and-turf dwellings. In either case, the Tuniit are depicted as extraordinarily strong. The Dorset did not use bows or dogsleds—they may not have even owned domesticated dogs. Thus, within a relatively short time, the Thule displaced the Dorset, perhaps by force, perhaps by simply outcompeting them in the warming climate. The Dorset disappeared, but the innovations they taught the Thule, including the building of snow houses and the use of inuksuit, lived on.

Around the same time that the Thule headed east, Norse explorers began their own epic migration in the opposite direction. Erik the Red left Iceland and discovered Greenland in approximately 982 AD, establishing several permanent settlements of shepherds, cowherds, and hunters. Soon afterward his son Leif heard reports of a new land to the west and led the first European expedition to North America. As recorded in *The Saga of the Greenlanders*, after sailing past Baffin Island and Labrador, Leif landed on the northern tip of Newfoundland, naming the new land Vinland and building a longhouse at Leifsbudir. Following clues in the sagas, Icelandic archeologists discovered the remains of the settlement in 1960. Today a reconstructed longhouse stands on the site at L'Anse aux Meadows, Newfoundland.

Several years after Leif's journey, his sister, Freydis, launched an expedition of her own, accompanied by a second ship owned by two Icelandic brothers, Helgi and Finnbogi. Discord soon arose, instigated by Freydis's insistence on taking Leif's longhouse for herself and, later, her demand that the brothers give her their larger knarr. Eventually Freydis coerced her husband, Thorvard, into slaughtering the Icelanders while they slept. Then, for unexplained reasons, Freydis herself seized an ax and murdered the five women they had brought with them. There is no mention of religious strife playing a role in this massacre, but my depiction of Freydis's motives reflects the history of the period. By 1000 AD, Christianity had spread throughout most of Scandinavia. Greenland, due to its relative isolation, was the last stronghold of those who worshiped the Aesir.

The Saga of Erik the Red adds more detail to Freydis's story. It relates that a band of skraelings, or "wretches," attacked her settlement. Freydis took up a sword, struck it against her bare breast, and chased them off single-handedly. I have chosen to portray this as a conflict with Newfoundland's Beothuk Indians, who provided the inspiration for the "painted men" Omat and Brandr encounter. The saga also includes an obscure passage about a scouting expedition northward to Markland (Labrador), during which some of Frey-dis's men encounter five skraelings—a bearded man, two women, and two children—living in a hole in the ground and dressed in white, fringed garments. The Norse steal the children and take them back to Vinland. From this brief incident comes the story of Kiasik's capture and Omat's journey to rescue him.

I hope I will be forgiven for taking some dramatic license by portraying the conflict as one of Norse versus Thule, when in fact the Dorset/Tuniit were likely also present on Baffin Island and in Labrador at the time. The displacement of the Tuniit would have taken far longer than I have implied in *The Wolf in the Whale*. However, their stories are long forgotten, while the rich mytholo-gies of the Norse and Inuit are simply too compelling for an author to resist.

The encounters portrayed in *The Wolf in the Whale* were far from the last meetings between Inuit and Norse, although Baffin Island did indeed remain free of permanent European settlement. In the next few hundred years, as the climate cooled once again, the Thule expanded eastward, to Greenland. If Leif Erickson is the European credited with "discovering" North America, then the Thule should surely be credited as the first Americans to "discover" Europeans. For several centuries, the two groups both lived in Greenland, although we have little knowledge of their interactions.

By the fifteenth century, the Norse, who had scraped out an exis-tence on the island's coasts for five hundred years, fell prey to a com-bination of climate change and a crash in the price of walrus ivory, their main export. They abandoned their settlements, leaving behind the stone foundations of churches and barns, still visible today.

Unlike the import-dependent Norse, the Thule never aban-doned Greenland. Their descendants, modern Inuit, have built a civilization that stretches from there to Alaska. Despite climate change, European whaling, and cultural repression, Inuit have endured—they have *thrived*—for a thousand years. I have no doubt they will do so for a thousand more.

A NOTE ON SOURCES
AND RESEARCH

⚡

The Wolf in the Whale is not an Inuit story. It is a fictional creation by a non-Inuit writer profoundly inspired by Inuit history, culture, and myth. Given my status as an outsider and our incomplete knowledge of the distant past, I have no doubt made mistakes. I am a novelist, not an anthropologist. A Qallunaat, not an Inuk. With those limitations in mind, I hope this story is received as it is intended: as an attempt to honor the Inuit past, not to claim it.

Although Inuit groups from Alaska to Greenland each have their own unique stories, dialects, and practices, I have borrowed from the traditions of several different regions in creating Omat's belief system and behavior. Since I envision her family as one of the first to migrate across North America from Alaska to eastern Canada, I assume their cultural practices would not be identical to any single modern group's. Thus I have mixed several different traditions to create my own fictional community: the gender conventions of some central Arctic Inuit; the Alaskan aarluk myth; Greenlandic incest taboos against first-cousin marriage; hunting techniques from Alaska's Iñupiat and Nunavut's Uqqurmiut and Nuvumiut; and myths, shamanic practices, and astronomical lore recorded in the community of Igloolik. I hope I will be forgiven for taking such license.

My first exposure to the concept of an Inuit "third sex" came from the work of anthropologist Bernard Saladin d'Anglure, an expert in Inuit shamanism and cosmology who has spent over forty years working with the Inuit community in Canada. His descriptions of the Inuit belief in rebirth through a "name-soul"—and the gender switching and occasional cross-dressing that can accompany the practice—provided the original inspiration for Omat's character. Saladin d'Anglure's own understanding emerged from interviews with Inuit elders in Igloolik, notably Iqallijuq, a woman born with her grandfather's name-soul who was raised as a boy until menstruation, when she was forced into a woman's role.

The Inuit myths retold throughout *The Wolf in the Whale* are based on those remembered by Inuit elders and recorded by anthropologists over the course of the twentieth century. This book would not have been possible without their stories. My retelling of the Sun and the Moon tale was inspired by an adaptation in Tom Lowenstein's *Ancient Land, Sacred Whale: The Inuit Hunt and Its Rituals*, which in turn was based on the words of Asatchaq Jimmie Killigivuk from Point Hope, Alaska, recorded in 1975. Lowenstein's book also provided information on whale-hunting techniques and taboos. The story of the Sea Mother (known by countless names, including Sanna, Sedna, Niviaqsiaq, Talilajuq, and Nuliajuk) comes from the revered Igloolik angakkuq Aua, as recorded by anthropologist Knud Rasmussen in the early 1920s. Rasmussen's seminal work, *Across Arctic America: Narrative of the Fifth Thule Expedition* (New York: G. P. Putnam's Sons, 1927), also includes Aua's descriptions of spirit journeys, trance states, and many other practices, all of which played a role in the creation of *The Wolf in the Whale*. Ataata's descriptions of his spirit journey to meet Uqsuralik in chapter 1 and his song for the return of the Sun in chapter 4 both quote Aua directly, with permission from the shaman's great-grandson Solomon Awa. Omat's words to summon Sanna were inspired by those of Horqarnaq, an angakkuq from Kugluktuk, also interviewed by Rasmussen.

My descriptions of the heralding stars, Northern Lights beliefs, snowdrift navigation, the Inuit calendar, and the rituals around the return of the sun come primarily from John MacDonald's *The Arctic Sky: Inuit Astronomy, Star Lore, and Legend*, which in turn draws on knowledge transcribed in 1990 and 1991 from Igloolik elders

Paul and Maria Quttiutuqu, Mark Ijjangiaq, Noah Piugaattuk, Niviattian Aqatsiaq, Pauli Kunuk, and others.

Inuit still hunt caribou, seals, whales, and walruses in Alaska and Canada. Sealing in particular has come under severe criticism in recent decades, leading to a complete ban on the importation of seal products into the United States and severe restrictions on imports into the European Union, despite the facts that seals are not endangered and Inuit hunters use all parts of the animal. I encourage you to watch the excellent documentary *Angry Inuk*, which articulates the Inuit perspective on this debate. My own understanding of traditional Inuit hunting practices comes from my discussions with Alex Flaherty, Solomon Awa, and Loasie Anilniliak and from Richard K. Nelson's *Hunters of the Northern Ice* and *Shadow of the Hunter*, which offer detailed descriptions of daily life among the Iñupiat of Wainwright, Alaska. The knowledge Nelson recorded in the 1960s came from Waldo Bodfish and other members of the Wainwright community. *Sinews of Survival: The Living Legacy of Inuit Clothing* by Betty Kobayshi Issenman affords an unparalleled examination of skin sewing and preparation.

Before I ever traveled to the Arctic myself, I was able to gain a profound appreciation for the mystery and majesty of its landscape and wildlife through two incomparable books: Katherine Scherman's *Spring on an Arctic Island* and Barry Lopez's *Arctic Dreams*.

For anyone interested in seeing what Omat's world might have looked like, watch Zacharias Kunuk, Norman Cohn, and Paul Apak Angilirq's cinematic masterpiece, *Atanarjuat: The Fast Runner*. Its punching-game scene inspired Omat and Issuk's confrontation in *The Wolf in the Whale*. Shot entirely in Nunavut, this impeccably researched film affords an invaluable window into Inuit life centuries ago.

The Norse myths have been told and retold by various authors for nine hundred years. However, most versions are based primarily on the same two medieval Icelandic sources: Snorri Sturluson's

Prose Edda and the anonymous *Poetic Edda*. Both were written down long after the Christianization of Scandinavia. Freydis's description of the Ragnarok is adapted from Henry Adams Bellows's 1923 translation of the *Poetic Edda*.

The Lofotr Viking Museum and Oslo's Viking Ship Museum, both in Norway, provided invaluable insights into the life of the medieval Norse. The beautifully curated Lofotr museum, in particular, is well worth a trip north of the Arctic Circle. At its annual Viking Festival, I managed to eat in a longhouse, sail on a longboat, and learn the rudiments of Norse spinning, all while gazing at one of the most awe-inspiring landscapes in the world.

My own journey to Nunavut, the Canadian territory that includes Baffin Island, allowed me to experience Omat's homeland for myself. There I was honored to meet the residents of Iqaluit and Pangnirtung, whose firsthand knowledge of Inuit life and language made essential contributions to this narrative, and who are personally thanked in the acknowledgments. With the wind chill at forty below, my teeth aching from cold, and the taste of raw narwhal skin still on my tongue, I began to get a tiny feel for what my heroine's life might have been like.

For photos of my research journeys to Norway and Nunavut, visit jordannamaxbrodsky.com. They are two of the most spectacular places on earth, so perhaps it is unsurprising that they gave birth to two of the planet's most spectacular cultures. I have tried, in this book, to do justice to them both.

ACKNOWLEDGMENTS

Everywhere I traveled in Nunavut, I encountered people whose generosity and humor made the stark landscape feel as warm as a well-made fur parka. Ooleepeeka Arnaqaq at Pangnirtung's Angmarlik Centre enthusiastically explained the museum's excellent collection. Neil Christopher, cofounder of Inhabit Media and author of *The Hidden: A Compendium of Arctic Giants, Dwarves, Gnomes, Trolls, Faeries and Other Strange Beings from Inuit Oral History* and several other beautiful books, shared his own passion for Inuit myth. The staff at the Pirurvik Centre were always willing hosts, no matter how many times I showed up at their door: Myna Ishulutak and Liz Fowler shared their knowledge, laughter, and raw caribou meat, while Peter Evvik, surely the most patient man in Iqaluit, showed me how to cut sealskin and answered every question I could throw his way.

My trip to Nunavut would never have happened without the patience of Allison Silvaggio. My thanks to her for putting me in contact with Alex Flaherty's Polar Outfitting in Iqaluit. Alex, himself an accomplished Inuit hunter, answered my questions, showed me around town, led me to the Nunavut Research Institute, and introduced me to Nancy and Loasie Anilniliak in Pangnirtung. The Anilniliak family opened their home to me, allowed me to try on their magnificent fur parkas and boots, demonstrated how to light a traditional oil lamp, and feasted me with char, seal, caribou, and narwhal skin. Alex also connected me with Jovin Simik—dogsled musher extraordinaire—and with Solomon Awa, who drove me onto the sea ice and showed me how to build an iglu. An expert like Solomon can build one in twenty minutes. With my stunning incompetence and lack of physical strength to slow him down, it took several hours. I would have happily let it take several more; in between deftly shaping the snow blocks, Solomon told me of the shaman Aua (his great-grandfather) and of his own experiences hunting a bowhead whale.

Angela Michielsen, an Iqaluit local, gifted me with her expertise and insights after reading the manuscript. She also pointed me toward Hagar Idlout-Sudlovenick, who in turn connected me to Leena Evic at the Pirurvik Centre, who put me in touch with the incomparable Aaju Peter and arranged for me to sit in on the center's Intro to Inuktitut class, taught by Myna Ishulutak and Chris Douglas.

My deepest gratitude to Bernard Saladin d'Anglure, whose scholarship inspired this book, for generously offering his feedback on my manuscript, teaching me the shamanic names for the great spirits, and sharing his phenomenal new work, *Inuit Stories of Being and Rebirth: Gender, Shamanism, and the Third Sex*. I must also offer my sincere thanks to Aaju Peter, Inuit activist, lawyer, teacher, and designer. She honored me by reading the manuscript and patiently answering my questions, all the while inspiring me with her fierce intelligence, tremendous charisma, and exceptional style.

Despite the input of so many experts, no doubt mistakes remain. For those, I alone am responsible.

The Wolf in the Whale has been a work in progress for over a decade, beginning with chapters written for Jennifer Belle's novel-writing class at the New School. My thanks to her and the other members of the workshop who provided feedback in those early days. More recently, Louis Chartres generously read the manuscript and provided insights on Arctic living. Bobby Webster sent me to Dan Starkey, who provided Old Norse translations, and to Andrew Okpeaha MacLean, who kindly spoke with me about Inuit storytelling and identity.

As always, a cohort of beloved friends lent their brilliance to the editing process. A single paragraph cannot encompass my immense gratitude for both their contributions to the manuscript and their impact on my life. Dustin Thomason not only gave me the courage to write the book in the first place but also made vital suggestions on an early draft. He made my career as a novelist possible. Jaclyn Huberman, Emily Shooltz, and Jim Augustine also shared their critiques, love, and support. Tegan Tigani and Helen Shaw both read multiple drafts, their exceptional insights matched only by their unfailing enthusiasm. Christopher Mills, my beloved brother-in-law, contributed hours of painstaking research on everything from Arctic astronomy to umiaq construction. Kathy Seaman once again donated her proofreading expertise. Jennifer Joel, my friend and agent, shepherded this manuscript from beginning to end with both compassion and wisdom.

Anne Clarke, my editor at Redhook, is brilliant, patient, hardworking, and kind. I count myself blessed to have her on my team. Sarah Guan and Joseph Lee at Hachette Book Group and Nicolas Vivas Nikonorow at ICM Partners also shared their thoughts on the book. My sincere thanks to them and to the rest of the Hachette crew, including Ellen Wright, Tim Holman, Tommy Harron, and Lisa Marie Pompilio, who have taken such good care of me.

My husband, Jason Mills, is the real reason this book exists. He gave me the tools to write it, he offered feedback on countless drafts, and his limitless faith convinced me that someday it would get published. He has been beside me every step of the way, from brainstorming in our cramped apartment on West Eighty-Eighth Street to singing me down the mountains of Norway to keeping me warm in the vastness of Nunavut's frozen sea. If I ever get stuck in an iglu in a raging blizzard, I know whom I want curled beneath the sleeping furs with me.

Finally, I will never repay the debt I owe my parents, Lewis and Cathy Brodsky, who drove a little girl from suburban Virginia all the way to the wilds of maritime Canada. There, amid fern-cloaked forests and mysterious tide pools, I first began to dream of encounters among Vikings, Native Americans, and Inuit. Thirty years later, using the passion for nature, history, and storytelling that they instilled within me, I can finally share that dream with everyone else.

extras

www.orbitbooks.net

about the author

Jordanna Max Brodsky is the author of the Olympus Bound trilogy, about Greek gods living and dying in modern Manhattan. She holds a degree in history and literature from Harvard University. Her research has taken her from the temples of Artemis in Turkey to the frozen tundra of Nunavut in subarctic Canada. The rest of the time, she lives in New York City with her husband.

Find out more about Jordanna Max Brodsky and other Orbit authors by registering for the free monthly newsletter at www.orbitbooks.net.

about the author

if you enjoyed

THE WOLF IN THE WHALE

look out for

THE SISTERS OF THE WINTER WOOD

by

Rena Rossner

Every family has a secret . . . and every secret tells a story.

In a remote village surrounded by forests on the border of Moldova and Ukraine, sisters Liba and Laya have been raised on the honeyed scent of their Mami's babka and the low rumble of their Tati's prayers. But when a troupe of mysterious men arrives, Laya falls under their spell — despite their mother's warning to be wary of strangers. And this is not the only danger lurking in the woods.

As dark forces close in on their small village, Liba and Laya discover a family secret passed down through generations. Faced with a magical heritage they never knew existed, the sisters realise the old fairy tales are true . . . and could save them all.

1

Liba

If you want to know the history of a town, read the gravestones in its cemetery. That's what my Tati always says. Instead of praying in the synagogue like all the other men of our town, my father goes to the cemetery to pray. I like to go there with him every morning.

The oldest gravestone in our cemetery dates back to 1666. It's the grave I like to visit most. The names on the stone have long since been eroded by time. It is said in our *shtetl* that it marks the final resting place of a bride and a groom who died together on their wedding day. We don't know anything else about them, but we know that they were buried, arms embracing, in one grave. I like to put a stone on their grave when I go there, to make sure their souls stay down where they belong, and when I do, I say a prayer that I too will someday find a love like that.

That grave is the reason we know that there were Jews in Dubossary as far back as 1666. Mami always said that this town was founded in love and that's why my parents chose to live here. I think it means something else—that our town was founded in tragedy. The death of those young lovers has been a pall hanging over Dubossary since its inception. Death lives here. Death will always live here.

2

Laya

I see Liba going
to the cemetery with Tati.
I don't know
what she sees
in all those cold stones.
But I watch,
and wonder,
why he never takes me.

When we were little,
Liba and I went to
the Talmud Torah.
For Liba, the black letters
were like something
only she could decipher.
I never understood
what she searched for,
in those black
scratches of ink.
I would watch

the window,
study the forest
and the sky.

When we walked home,
Liba would watch the boys
come out of the *cheder*
down the road.
I know that when she looked
at Dovid, Lazer and Nachman,
she wondered
what was taught
behind the walls
the girls were not
allowed to enter.

After her Bat Mitzvah,
Tati taught her Torah.
He tried to teach me too,
when my turn came,
but all I felt was
distraction,
disinterest.
Chanoch l'naar al pi darko,
Tati would say,
teach every child
in his own way,
and sigh,
and get up
and open the door.
Gey, gezinte heit—
I accept that you're different, go.

And while I was grateful,
I always wondered
why he gave up
without a fight.

3

Liba

As I follow the large steps my father's boots make in the snow, I revel in the solitude. This is why I cherish our morning walks. They give me time to talk to Tati, but also time to think. "In silence you can hear God," Tati says to me as we walk. But I don't hear God in the silence—I hear myself. I come here to get away from the noises of the town and the chatter of the townsfolk. It's where I can be fully me.

"What does God sound like?" I ask him. When I walk with Tati, I feel like I'm supposed to think about important things, like prayer and faith.

"Sometimes the voice of God is referred to as a *bat kol*," he says.

I translate the Hebrew out loud: "The daughter of a voice? That doesn't make any sense."

He chuckles. "Some say that *bat kol* means an echo, but others say it means a hum or a reverberation, something you sense in the air that's caused by the motion of the universe—part of the human voice, but also part of every other sound in the world, even the sounds that our ears can't hear. It means that sometimes even the smallest voice can have a big opinion." He grins, and I know that he means me, his daughter; that my opinion matters. I wish it were true. Not everybody in our town sees things the way my father does. Most women and girls do not study Torah; they don't learn or ask questions like I do. For the most part, our voices don't matter. I know I'm lucky that Tati is my father.

Although I love Tati's stories and his answers, I wonder why a small voice is a daughter's voice. Sometimes I wish my voice could be loud—like a roar. But that is not a modest way to think. The older I get, the more immodest my thoughts become.

I feel my cheeks flush as my mind wanders to all the things I shouldn't be thinking about—what it would feel like to hold the hand of a man, what it might feel like to kiss someone, what it's like when you finally find the man you're meant to marry and you get to be alone together, in bed ... I swallow and shake my head to clear my thoughts.

If I shared the fact that this is all I think about lately, Mami and Tati would say it means it's time for me to get married. But I'm not sure I want to get married yet. I want to marry for love, not convenience. These thoughts feel like sacrilege. I know that I will marry a man my father chooses. That's the way it's done in our town and among Tati's people. Mami and Tati married for love, and it has not been an easy path for them.

I take a deep breath and shake my head from all my thoughts. This morning, everything looks clean from the snow that fell last night and I imagine the icy frost coating the insides of my lungs and mind, making my thoughts white and pure. I love being outside in our forest more than anything at times like these, because the white feels like it hides all our flaws.

Perhaps that's why I often see Tati in the dark forest that surrounds our home praying to God or—as he would say—the *Ribbono Shel Oylam*, the Master of the Universe, by himself, eyes shut, arms outstretched to the sky. Maybe he comes out here to feel new again too.

Tati comes from the town of Kupel, a few days' walk from here. He came here and joined a small group of Chassidim in the town—the followers of the late Reb Mendele, who was a disciple of the great and holy Ba'al Shem Tov. There is a small *shtiebl* where the men pray, in what used to be the home of Urka the Coachman. It is said that the Ba'al Shem Tov himself used to sit under the tree in Urka's courtyard. The Chassidim here accepted my father with open arms, but nobody accepted my mother.

Sometimes I wonder if Reb Mendele and the Ba'al Shem Tov (*zichrono livracha*) were still with us, would the community treat Mami differently? Would they see how hard she tries to be a good Jew, and how wrong the other Jews in town are for not treating her with love and respect. It makes me angry how quickly rumors spread, that Mami's kitchen isn't kosher (it is!) just because she doesn't cover her hair like the other married Jewish women in our town.

That's why Tati built our home, sturdy and warm like he is, outside our town in the forest. It's what Mami wanted: not to be under constant scrutiny, and to have plenty of room to plant fruit trees and make honey and keep chickens and goats. We have a small barn with a cow and a goat, and a bee glade out back and an orchard that leads all the way down to the river. Tati works in town as a builder and a laborer in the fields. But he is also a scholar, worthy of the title Rebbe, though none of the men in town call him that.

Sometimes I think my father knows more than the other Chassidim in our town, even more than Rabbi Borowitz who leads our tiny *kehilla*, and the bare bones prayer *minyan* of ten men that Tati sometimes helps complete. There are many things my father likes to keep secret, like his morning dips in the Dniester River that I never see, but know about, his prayer at the graveside of Reb Mendele, and our library. Our walls are covered in holy books—his *sforim*, and I often fall asleep to the sound of him reading from the Talmud, the Midrash, and the many mystical books of the Chassidim. The stories he reads sound like fairy tales to me, about magical places like Babel and Jerusalem.

In these places, there are scholarly men. Father would be respected there, a king among men. And there are learned boys of marriageable age—the kind of boys Tati would like me to marry someday. In my daydreams, they line up at the door, waiting to get a glimpse of me—the learned, pious daughter of the Rebbe. And my Tati would only pick the wisest and kindest for me.

I shake my head. In my heart of hearts, that's not really what I want. When Laya and I sleep in our loft, I look out the skylight above our heads and pretend that someone will someday find his way to our cabin, climb up onto the roof, and look in from above. He will see me and fall instantly in love.

Because lately I feel like time is running out. The older I get, the harder it will be to find someone. And when I think about that, I wonder why Tati insists that Laya and I wait until we are at least eighteen.

I would ask Mami, but she isn't a scholar like Tati, and she doesn't like to talk about these things. She worries about what people say and how they see us. It makes her angry, but she wrings dough instead of her hands. Tati says her hands are baker's hands, that she makes magic with dough. Mami can make something out of nothing. She makes cheese and gathers honey; she mixes bits of bark and roots and leaves for tea. She bakes the tastiest *challahs* and cakes, *rugelach* and *mandelbrot*, but it's her *babka* she's famous for. She sells her baked goods in town.

When she's not in the kitchen, Mami likes to go out through the skylight above our bed and onto the little deck on our roof to soak up the sun. Laya likes to sit up there with her. From the roof, you can see down to the village and the forest all around. I wonder if it's not just the sun that Mami seeks up there. While Tati's head is always in a book, Mami's eyes are always looking at the sky. Laya says she dreams of somewhere other than here. Somewhere far away, like America.

4

Laya

I always thought
that if I worshipped God,
dressed modestly,
and walked in His path,
that nothing bad
would happen
to my family.
We would find
our path to Zion,
our own piece of heaven
on the banks
of the Dniester River.

But now that I'm fifteen
I see what a life
of pious devotion
has brought Mami,
who converted
to our faith—
disapproval.
The life we lead
out here is a life apart.

I wish I could go to Onyshkivtsi.
Mami always tells me stories
about her town
and Saint Anna of the Swans
who lived there.

Saint Anna
didn't walk with God—
she knew she wasn't made
for perfection;
she never tried
to fit a pattern
that didn't fit her.
She didn't waste her time
trying to smooth herself
into something
she wasn't.
She was powerful
because she forged
her own path.

The Christians
in Onyshkivtsi
built a shrine
to honor her.
The shrine marks a spring
whose temperature
is forty-three degrees
all year,
rain or shine.
Even in the snow.

It is said
that it was once home
to hundreds of swans.
Righteous Anna used to
feed and care for them.
But Mami says the swans
don't go there anymore.

There is rot
in the old growth—
the Kodari forest
senses these things.
I sense things too.
The rot in our community.
Sometimes it's not enough
to be good,
if you treat others
with disdain.
Sometimes there's nothing
you can do
but fly away,
like Anna did.

5

Liba

When we get back from our morning walk, Mami is in the kitchen making breakfast and starting the doughs for the day. Tati shakes the snow off his boots as he walks in. "*Gut morgen*," he says gruffly as he pecks a kiss on Mami's cheek. She pins her white-gold hair up and says, "*Dubroho ranku*. Liba, close the door quickly—you're letting all the cold in."

I let the hood of my coat drop down. "Where's Laya?"

"Getting some eggs from the coop," Mami sings. She and Laya love mornings, not like me, but I'd wake up early every morning if it meant I got time alone with Tati.

I shrug my coat off and hang it on a hook by the door as Mami pours tea at the table. "*Nu?* Come in, warm up," she says to me.

I shake the chill off and start braiding my hair, which is the color of river rocks. Long and thick. I can't pin it up at all. "Your hair is beautiful like moonstone, *dochka*," Mami says. "Leave it down."

"More like oil on fur," I say, because it's sleek and shiny and I never feel like I can tame it. It will never be white and light like hers and Laya's.

"Do you want me to braid it for you?" Mami asks.

I shake my head.

"Come here, my *zaftig* one," Tati says. "Your hair is fine; leave it be."

I cringe: I don't like it when he calls me plump, even though it's a term of endearment, and anyway, I know what comes next. Laya walks in and he says, "Oh, the *shayna meidel* has decided to join us." The pretty one. I concentrate on braiding my hair.

Laya grins. "*Gut morgen*. How was your walk?" She looks at me.

I shrug my shoulders and finish braiding my hair, then sit at the table and lift a cup of tea to my mouth. "*Baruch atah Adonai eloheinu melech haolam, shehakol nih'ye bidvaro—Blessed are you, Lord our God, king of the universe, by whose word all things came to be.*" I make sure to say every word of the blessing with meaning.

"*Oymen!*" Tati says with a smile.

Instead of trying to be something I will never be, I do everything I can to be a good Jew.

6

Laya

When I was outside
gathering eggs,
I searched the sky,
hoping to see something—
anything.
One night I heard
feathers rustling
and turned around
and looked up—
a swan had landed
on our rooftop.
It was watching me.
I didn't breathe
the whole time
it was there.
Until it spread
its wings
and took off
into the sky.

Every night I pray
that it will happen again
because if I ever see
another swan,
I won't hold my breath—
I will open the window
and go outside.

That's why I rake my gaze
over every flake of bark
and every teardrop leaf,
hoping. I see that
every finger-branch
is reaching for something.
I am reaching too.
Up up up.

At night I feel
the weight
of the house
upon my chest.
It's warm
and safe inside,
but the wooden planks
above my head
are nothing like
the dark boughs
of the forest.
Sometimes I wish
I could sleep outside.
The Kodari is
the only place
I feel truly at home.

But this morning
I'm restless
and that usually means
something is about to change.
That's what the forest
teaches you—
change can come
in the blink of an eye—
the fall of one spark
can mean total destruction.

There is a fever
that burns in me.
It prickles every pore.
I'm not happy with
the simple life we lead.
A life ruled
by prayer and holy days,
times for dusk and dawn,
the sacred and the profane.
A life of devotion,
Tati would say.
The glory
of a king's daughter
is within.

But I long for what is
just outside my window.
Far beyond
the reaches of the Dniester,
and the boundaries
of our small *shtetl*.

It hurts,
this thing I feel,
how unsettled
I've become.
I want to fit
in this home,
in this town.
To be the daughter
that Tati wants me to be.
To be more
like Liba.
Prayer comes
so easily to her.

Mami understands
what I feel
but I also think
it scares her.
She is always sending me
outside, and I'm grateful
but I also wonder
why she doesn't
teach me how to bake,
or how to pray.
It's almost like she knows
that one day
I will leave her.

Sometimes I wish
she'd teach me
how to stay.

I close my eyes
and take deep breaths.
It helps me
resist the urge
to scratch my back.
I want to crawl out
of this skin I wear
when these thoughts come
and threaten to overwhelm
the little peace I have,
staring at the sky,
praying in my own way
for something else.

Something is definitely
inside me.
It is not glory,
or devotion.
It is something
that wants to burst free.